SANDPAPER
FOR THE
SOUL

A TALE OF TWO SISTERS

LORNA HOWARTH

For Clair and Rani

READERS' PRAISE:
SANDPAPER FOR THE SOUL

An exceptional novel with heart and purpose, beautifully
structured and with protagonists I really cared about.
Jane Turnbull, Literary Agent

It cracked me open in the subtlest of ways and set me down gently
in another emotional landscape, allowing me to become truly alive
to the magic and tragedy of life. This book is a precious gift.
Sophie Poklewski Koziell, literary consultant, writer and editor

I have just finished *Sandpaper for the Soul* and it was terrific. I have
been reading it all day, unable to stop. It's such a good story but I
was not ready for the ending. That was shocking.
William Blyghton, author The Suffolk Trilogy

I cried, twice! This story is intimate and powerful; a deftly woven
narrative that maintains pace through the passage of years, with a
true plot twist at the end. It is life-affirming in so many ways.
Pauline Smith, author of Tales of the Torridge

The story drew me in from the first to the very last page. I cannot
believe I read an entire novel in a weekend!
I don't remember EVER doing that.
Kathy J. Sotak, author, 2-minutelift.com

Okay, so I'm upset now. My whole cleaning and packing schedule
is messed up because I can't put your book down.
Please tell me it gets boring at some point?
Teri Martin, Interfaith Minister

Word magician and wise woman, Lorna Howarth has created another inspiring narrative with this new book.
Jemma Jackson, Founder, Venus Rose Club

I finished reading your book on the train to London with tears pouring down my face. It was absolutely gripping, however it should come with a warning: May cause emotional outbursts – not to be read in public!
Maya Mitchell, Tango Dancer

The unexpected crashing-in to the story of a large scale, real life event that we all know of so well left me absolutely reeling. It's a reminder that no matter how hard we work to structure our lives for a comfortable future, it can all get snatched away regardless. It's a timely message: to live for the moment.
Jacqueline Barnett, Marketing & Design Pro

PANACEA
BOOKS THAT REIMAGINE
THE WORLD

Published by Panacea Books, 2023
www.lornahowarth.com

ISBN: 978-18382866-2-0

With thanks to Beth Lewis for the interior design
and to Ana Marinović for the cover design.

Author's Notes

Though much of this novel is based on true life events, names and places have been changed for the purpose of anonymity, and certain aspects are purely fictitious.

With loving gratitude to my beta-readers and gentle critics, Kathy Sotak, Pauline Smith, Teri Martin, Betty Howarth, Mavis Battersby, Lynn Batten and Robin Swan. Especial thanks to Sophie Poklewski Koziell for her editorial guidance and enthusiasm for this story, and for her commitment to help it reach a wider readership.

Contents

Monsoon Tears

Cardboard boxes can be put to many good uses, but as makeshift mattresses, they leave a lot to be desired. For one thing, they absorb the damp, which seeps through each layer creating a sodden mat with little comfort for the weary. Rain shifted her weight to avoid whatever it was on the earthen floor of her home that was piercing through the soggy cardboard and making her thigh sore.

She recalled a story she had once read during those precious few years when life was carefree, a time when she was able to dive into imaginary worlds through the well-thumbed and slightly crumbling books in the library of her school. *Now, what was that story called?* Rain pondered, *Oh yes, 'The Princess and the Pea'. How the Princess would detest my horrible bed. She'd feel every stone and piece of grit on this floor as if it were a boulder.*

Rain had loved her time at school, which had been founded in 1907 by an enlightened English tea plantation owner. Mr Brown believed that all children, girls and boys alike, deserved a good education and fortunately for Rain, had stocked the school's library with 'classics'.

That night, it was not just the discomfort of her bed

that was keeping Rain awake; it was not just her stomach grumbling and growling from lack of food that made her feel light-headed and nauseous. Though she was hungry, she had offered her brother Anuja the last roti saying she didn't want it. He knew that she did and tore it in half to share with her, but Rain was worried that he looked so thin, and she insisted he ate it all. Instead, she drank a large glass of water, hoping that somehow it would make her feel full. No, it was far more than being hungry and uncomfortable. She felt exhausted and overwhelmed, as if at any moment she might collapse and be consumed by ants. And nobody would notice, not even Anuja.

Tonight sleep evaded her, as it did most nights, and so she lay staring at the corrugated tin roof watching the shadows as they danced across it, cast by the flickering votive candle she had left burning on the small altar in the corner of the room. She'd found it under Anuja's bed, dusty and half-burned, and as they'd not had a candle on the altar for what seemed like forever, she lit it and prayed for Jesus to forgive her sins. Momentarily, she was reminded of happier times, though now it seemed the shadows had transformed from dancing figures into prowling beasts, ready to pounce. On her. She looked away.

The altar – although that was a rather grand word for a small wooden shelf – was dedicated to St Bernadette, patron saint of the poor and the ill. Her father had made it, then placed a small painted statue of the beloved saint upon it, assuring them that now Bernadette would surely help their family. But her mother had insisted on adding a brass statue of Lord Ganesha the Hindu elephant God, saying, "It is he who is the remover of all hardship and obstacles. It is he who will help us."

This made Rain's father cross, an emotion he rarely expressed, at least not within the family home.

"St Bernadette cannot help us with an elephant in the room," he had barked. "Now she will not come."

And he was right. She did not.

It amazed Rain that she could hear Anuja breathing despite the thunderous monsoon rain pelting the metal roof above. His breath was regular and settled; at least he was asleep. She listened to the constant drip-drip-drip as heavy, elongated droplets of water fell into the buckets she'd placed under each rusting hole in the tin roof. The monotony of the dripping grated on her nerves. She had to fight the urge to get up and kick the buckets over. That was exactly what Anuja had done two mornings in a row, when his alarm clock had awoken him and bleary-eyed and reluctant, he'd inched out of his warm bed and immediately tripped over a brimming bucket. The water had quickly seeped into the floor and was what had made her own bed damp.

It was one of the last things her father, had said to her. "I promise I'll buy some tarpaulin from the market next week, Rain. Then I'll be able to fix the roof."

Bapu always kept his promises, but not this time.

Rain sighed deeply and turned over. How had it come to this? And although she knew exactly how it had come to this – for she had mulled over the course of events in her mind for weeks on end, she could still hardly believe it, and the question continued to rattle around in her brain like a mantra. *How had it come to this? How had it come to this?*

A tear slipped from the corner of her eye and then another, and because the rain was so loud and Anuja was asleep, she let the tears come. Deep sobs welled in her chest and caught in her throat, her shoulders convulsed with sorrow and tears found a way into her ears and then soaked into her long hair, sticking it to her neck. She was drowning in the monsoon, drowning in her own tears and she didn't care if she ever came up for air.

"Rainy? Rain… don't cry."

"It's okay. Shhhh, shhhh – go back to sleep Nuji."

After a while, he said, "It'll be alright Lakmini, you'll see. Everything will be alright."

The candle spat and flickered and then went out, and in the darkness, Rain reached toward the metal frame of his bed, found her brother's hand and squeezed it tightly. He only called her Lakmini rather than her childhood nickname of 'Rain' when he was being serious, when he was trying to be the man about the house. Her mother had chosen to call her Lakmini, but Rain was the name she'd been given by her father because she'd been born during an unseasonably heavy rainstorm that had caused terrible flooding in town and was still a talking point.

"I know it will, sweet one. We will get through this together. Be quiet now and go back to sleep. Let us see what the morning brings."

She listened in the darkness as her brother's breathing settled back to sleep, but sleep continued to elude her as it had done for many weeks. Dark rings encircled her tired eyes, already bruised and sore from her tears. How could she possibly sleep knowing it was all her fault?

"Go to the church Rain and light a candle for us. Pray to St. Christopher for our safe journey. Once I get your mother to Colombo, all will be well. We will see the specialist and he will make her better."

"And will you see a specialist too, Bapu?" She knew he was not well, had seen him steadily lose weight and strength. She thought perhaps it was because Bapu was spending so much time and energy caring for his wife, who'd been ill for years. In fact, Rain couldn't remember a time when Amma, her mother, had not been ill. For many months, her condition confounded every doctor she saw, until Bapu took his wife to a clinic in Galle where, after all sorts of tests and scans, the doctor pronounced that she had TB, and that whilst her lungs had sustained irreversible damage, given time, she would recover her strength. "Nobody dies of TB these days," the doctor had said.

And although it was true that she had not died, she had not recovered either. To Rain, her mother became a ghost-like presence in the house; skeletal in her cot in the corner of the one room they all shared, coughing and wheezing, then silent in her pain. When she was younger, Rain had felt sorry for her mother and often tried to make her smile. She would put on her Sunday sari and perform little dances for her at the end of her bed, or she would read fairy tales to her from a book she'd borrowed from the school library – Rain was an avid reader even from an early age – but her mother would tell her to stop and wave her away.

Then as she got older, Rain's pity turned to anger; she felt cross that Amma was always grumbling, cross that she had no joy in her life; that she spent her days in that dark room, curtained-off even from her children, never venturing into their sunlit yard to sit under the shade of the papaya, never wanting to read a book, never wanting to listen to the radio.

Why doesn't Amma ever read a book? thought Rain, to whom books meant everything. But Rain did not know that her mother had never learned to read, and that she kept this and many other secrets from her daughter.

Eventually, Rain felt resentment towards her mother, for she had Bapu's sole attention. Bapu who worked day and night as a tuk-tuk driver, taxiing rich tourists to and from their luxurious hotels on the coastal strip between the city of Galle in the north and Lagentle to the south, taking them to visit some of Sri Lanka's many historical monuments or into the forest to see the elephants and leopards; Bapu, who when he did get home, exhausted and dusty from a day on the roads, would immediately attend to his wife who always had many complaints about her own day. Rain thought Amma was being ill on purpose, so that she could have Bapu all to herself. How else is a fifteen year-old girl supposed to make sense of the world, other than to piece together the jigsaw of her life from what she saw before her eyes?

"One thing at a time, Lakmini." Bapu wiped the dust from the windshield of his tuk-tuk as he replied to her question. "First of all, we will get your mother better. Then I will put our affairs in order, including fixing the roof. Now, off you go to St Francis' and light a candle for us. Pray for our safe return, Rain. We will be home the day after tomorrow with good news."

She loved her father for his relentless optimism, she loved everything about him. But he never came home, and nor did her mother.

Rain had watched Amma haul herself into the back of the tuk-tuk, little more than a bag of bones, groaning from the sheer exertion of having to move one foot in front of the other, never thinking it would be the last time she ever saw her. Rain had watched as her father cheerily waved goodbye to his children, and set-off at a pace, knowing that it was a long journey from Lagentle to Colombo and that they would be lucky to get there before nightfall. Not for one moment did Rain think she would never see her father's handsome face again. Why would she think that? Her life had always been uneventful, so much so that often she yearned for an adventure, for something – anything – to happen, but day just followed night, and one quiet week followed another. Nothing much occurred that ever made her consider her own mortality nor that of her family.

The moment dear Bapu's tuk-tuk turned right out of Ingodapokunadi Road, Rain instantly forgot all about going to St Francis of Assisi church to light a candle to St Christopher and to pray for their safe return. Instead, she stood on a rickety white plastic chair and reached up and took from the top of the cupboard above the gas ring, the copy of Daphne Du Maurier's *Rebecca* that she'd recently borrowed from Lagentle library, which now that she had left school, was where she had found a far more exhilarating selection of books. She always kept her library books up there – it was one of the few places where it wouldn't get ruined by the huddle of a family of four in one room – and then she sat in the shade of the papaya tree in their little back yard and continued to read the story that had been enthralling her. The story took her from an exotic hotel in sunny Monte Carlo to the austere confines of a haunted house in cold, wet England – places she found hard to imagine, likewise the feather beds and beaded dresses and banquets, or even romance for that matter, though her heart ached for the heroine who, it seemed, had been duped and whose life was in peril. She read the book from the moment her parents left for Colombo until her brother Anuja got home from school, and she continued to read until it got so dark, she could no longer see. This was her favourite kind of day; immersed in a book, letting her imagination fly. It was as if, through reading, she could escape and lead a completely different life. But more than that, she loved the English language. She excelled at it in school, and she longed to see for herself the places she was reading of.

That night, she had refused to make a meal for Anuja, telling him she was, "taking a holiday." In truth, she was supposed to be working for Aunty-ji, a friend of her mother's who lived near Lagentle Fort and who had a small business sewing tablecloths, sheets, towels, and the like for the local hotel trade. Aunty-ji had loaned Rain an old and treacherous Singer sewing machine that would regularly catch the cotton thread and pull the stitches underneath the sewing foot into a horrible knot.

"Straight lines only, Lakmini," Aunty-ji had said the day she brought the sewing machine over and set it on a wooden crate by the door of their house for, "maximum daylight sewing hours".

Reluctantly – for sewing seemed to Rain a waste of good reading time – she folded a piece of cloth beneath the foot and tried to sew a hem, but the stitches instantly entangled. She tried again and again, to no avail.

"It keeps getting stuck…"

"No straight lines, no funny money."

"But Aunty-ji, it's impossible to sew straight lines on this machine. Haven't you got a better one?"

"Don't take that insolent tone with me, girl!" Aunty-ji had cuffed Rain's ear. "You should be grateful you have a job at all and can help out your poor mother."

Rain looked to her mother pleading with her eyes for moral support, but her mother sighed and turned over in her bed to face the wall.

Despite the dreadful old Singer sewing machine – or perhaps because of it, for she had to be extra vigilant and came to know the exact click of the machine before the needle slipped and pulled the thread – Rain found that she was a very good seamstress. She could easily fulfil her quota of tablecloths in a day, leaving her time to do the things she loved, like writing stories and poems (if she could find a spare scrap of paper to write on) and avidly reading whatever books she could lay her hands on.

To Rain, the day her parents went to Colombo was a rare and precious time of self-indulgence and happiness. She could easily make up her hours the following day, and Aunty-ji would never know she'd taken a time off, because all the hems would be sewn and all the lines would be straight. But tomorrow never came, or at least not the tomorrow Rain had envisaged.

After a blissful day reading *Rebecca*, Rain and Anuja were awoken by a loud noise at what seemed like the middle of the night. And then again, a knock that set her heart racing. Nobody ever came knocking.

Slowly opening the door and peering out, Rain was surprised to see two policemen standing in the darkness, one shining a torch into her face.

"Excuse us for the late hour, but is this the house of Danidu Perera?" one of the policemen asked.

"Yes sir." Rain, shielding her eyes with her forearm,

was instantly aware of the gravity of the situation. Not one but two policemen. Anxiety balled in her stomach and she felt Anuja's hand slip into hers as he too came to see who was at the door.

"Can we come in, young lady?"

"Why...?"

"Let them in, Lakmini," Anuja whispered.

Slowly she opened the door to their home. "Come in, then," and remembering her manners, said, "let me just light a lamp, so you can put out your torches."

As she did so, and the cold white light of the paraffin lamp illuminated their humble home, she became acutely aware of how poor it must appear to two such worldly-wise policemen, but they seemed not to notice the worn rug and stained table, nor the curtained off space where their mother usually lay coughing. The taller policeman pulled out the only two chairs in the house from under the table and signalled for Rain and Anuja to sit in them.

"I am sorry to say we have some bad news, children."

Rain intuitively knew the bad news was connected to her parents and felt her stomach lurch. The policemen looked at each other and the one who had been speaking knelt down so he was at eye-level with Rain and Anuja, a gesture that made Rain feel even more anxious.

"Unfortunately, there has been a terrible road accident this evening, just outside Colombo. We are so sorry to tell you that your mother and father, Mr & Mrs Perera, have been..." the policeman stopped to clear his throat, "your parents have sadly been killed."

"...What happened?" Rain whispered, hardly able to speak.

"It seems their tuk-tuk veered into the path of a lorry.

The driver said he thought your father was trying to avoid hitting a stray dog. There was nothing that could be done to save them. Please accept our condolences."

Anuja kicked the chair from under him and ran out of the open door, into the warm, humid night. The other policeman followed him.

"I am so sorry. What is your name, young lady?"

"Lakmini."

"I am so sorry for your loss, Lakmini. Is there anyone we can call to be with you tonight?"

"No, sir. There is no one."

"How old are you, Lakmini?"

"I'm 15, nearly 16, sir and Anuja is 12."

"Too young to be left on your own on a night like this."

Lakmini thought of Aunty-ji, her mother's friend, but knew she would not thank Rain for calling her out of her bed at this time of night, and in truth, Aunty-ji was the last person Rain wanted to be with right now, as the words the policeman had spoken began to sink into her consciousness and the magnitude of her loss washed over her like a cold ocean wave.

"We will be okay, sir. I have looked after my brother since he was a little boy. My mother is – was – very ill, you see. That's why my father was taking her to Colombo hospital, to see the specialist and I…" Rain gasped, as in that moment she realised that she had forgotten to carry out her father's last wishes.

"Oh no! Oh, please… it is all my fault! It is my fault!" she screamed, her face contorting with anguish. "I forgot to light a candle to St Christopher and say a prayer for their safe journey." She was distraught.

"Hush, hush, Lakmini. I doubt there was anything

even St. Christopher could have done to help your poor parents this night. Please do not distress yourself. It was an accident. Nobody is to blame."

"Did Bapu hit the dog?" Anuja had returned to the house, accompanied by the second policeman.

"There was no dog found at the scene."

"But Bapu hated dogs! Why would he have swerved to miss one? It doesn't make sense..." Anuja was sobbing now, his words coming in fits and starts.

"It is a reflex action, young man. If anything runs out in front of your vehicle, you automatically try to avoid it, no matter what it is. Do not distress yourself with details of what has happened but try to accept that this is God's will." The policeman then gestured to the other officer, and they stepped outside the house.

Anuja stared at Lakmini, who held her head in her hands, great wails of grief escaping through her fingers.

"It's MY fault, Nuji! I forgot to do as Bapu asked and pray to St Christopher; I was in Manderley..."

Anuja didn't have the faintest idea where his sister had been but instinctively went to her and put his arms around her, trying to calm her sobs.

"Don't cry, Lakmini, please. We will be alright."

Holding hands, the two children huddled together, crouching against the cold single block wall as if for dear life, their tears soaking into their clothes. After a short while, the policemen returned, having made a plan.

The kindly policeman with the moustache said, "You can come with me to my home tonight. My wife will make you some food, and you can sleep on the veranda. It is comfortable. Just until you feel better."

"That is very kind of you sir, but no thank you all the

same," said Lakmini. "We would prefer to stay here, at home. As I said, because of Amma's illness and Bapu's job, I have looked after the two of us for many years. We will be alright, I assure you. I will speak to Aunty-ji in the morning. She will know what to do."

The good-hearted policeman looked visibly relieved. Perhaps his wife had looked after one too many waifs and strays of late.

"If you are sure, then. We will call on you tomorrow and let you know what arrangements have been made for your parents' burial. Again, please do accept our sincere condolences."

The police officers shut the door quietly behind them and left the children to take in the enormity of what had happened. They were now orphans with not a soul in the world to call family except each other. They knew nothing of their mother's family, and on the few occasions Rain had asked about them, she was told that it was none of her concern. Similarly, asking about Bapu's family was frowned upon, as if it were some kind of taboo subject. Rain knew that Bapu's father had disinherited him when he had married their mother, but she did not really know what 'disinherited' meant and when she had asked her father about her grandparents or her aunts and uncles, she was told that she had none, that she was better off without them – which had seemed like a contradictory statement to Rain. In any case, they had never met another person they called family outside of the tiny tin and block shack they called home. And Aunty-ji was not a real aunt at all, but her mother's only friend, and a harridan at that, Rain had since discovered.

It was a dark night of the soul for Rain. Her mind

went over and over the events of the day and she chastised herself mercilessly for being a terrible daughter, and for not obeying her father's wishes. She offered her own life to God, if he could arrange the safe return of her parents, knowing of course that her plea would be in vain. She was racked by guilt and remorse and couldn't bear the sound of Anuja's grief, each sob a dagger in her heart. Before first light, she slipped out of the door and walked through the awakening town, lost in her trance of tears.

Without knowing how she had got there, she found herself on the harbour wall as the sun rose and cast long shadows over the water. Usually a place of hustle and bustle, at this hour it was deserted and eerily quiet, the only sounds coming from the jostle of fishing boats which were tied to wooden pilings along the harbour wall.

She wanted to jump in. She wanted to obliterate her pain and be in heaven with Bapu and Amma, but what about Anuja? Who would look after her little brother? At that moment, Rain was past caring; all she wanted to do was wash away her sins.

The water was deep and green and inviting. She could see tiny fish swimming in shoals just below the surface, flitting to and fro in unison, flashing gold in the sunlight. *They look happy,* she thought. *Look at them, all together, one big happy family...*

And then she remembered something Mrs Danvers had said in *Rebecca*: 'We are not meant for happiness, you and I...' and those words seared her soul, for she was certain that she could never be happy again because her parents were dead, and it was all her fault.

And so, she allowed herself to fall – it was easy, she just surrendered – and as she did so, it felt as if time itself slowed. It took her forever to hit the water, so long in fact that she had time to change her mind; time to remember her love for Anuja, her love of life, her dreams of someday marrying and having children of her own, and of visiting England to see for herself what Manderley looked like.

But she could not swim, and the water was deep. Her sari weighed her down, wrapped itself around her legs and restricted her movement. She came up for air but gasped too soon and the warm salty ocean found its way into her lungs; she floundered, unable to move her arms as her sari began to completely unravel. Panic-stricken, she tried to unwind the yards of material that had begun to bind her like rope, but she was tired, and she needed to breathe; she had to breathe… She opened her mouth and the ocean entered again.

One little fish came towards her, almost touching her nose with its own, and as it looked her in the eye, Rain became still, entranced.

Not yet, the fish said with its eyes. *Not yet*.

At that moment she felt strong arms encircle her and roughly yank her out of the water, but she did not take a breath. Then, the two fishermen dropped her roughly onto the stone pier, and as she hit the ground, the jolt of the impact on her body forced her lungs to contract and Rain opened her mouth. Sea water spewed out. She was sick and sick, and between heaves she began to breathe.

"Mōda kella – stupid girl!" one of them said, whilst the other looked at her dispassionately, like she was a pathetic rabbitfish he was considering throwing back in.

Under the gaze of these two men, Rain had the sense of mind to gather her sari about her, aware that her legs were bare, her choli clinging to her convulsing chest.

"Stupid bloody girl," the fisherman repeated and then after kicking her thigh for good measure, he stalked off, annoyed to have had to leave his nets to fish her out. The other fisherman nudged her a little more gently with his bare foot and, seemingly confident that she was alive, he too left her alone and dripping on the pier.

Slowly, life returned to Rain. Her breathing became less scratchy and more regular and the sun warmed her body and began to dry her hair. Eventually, she sat up. There was not a soul to be seen – even the two fishermen had disappeared – it was a miracle they saw her fall into the water. But then, memories of what the policemen had said when they called at her house last night slammed into her brain making her retch once again.

And what of Anuja? Dear Anuja. Would he have got himself off to school, she wondered, or would he, like her, be falling apart? He was a stoic little boy and seemed somehow to take everything in his stride, but perhaps not this earthquake of events. He was used to Rain not being at home in the mornings and would most likely think she'd gone to Aunty-ji's to pick up the day's tablecloths for sewing. He would not be worried about her. No one would be worried about her.

Eventually, she mustered her energy and somewhat shakily she stood up, cold rivulets of seawater running down her legs and pooling around her feet. Slowly, she turned for home. On the way, she would stop by Aunty-ji's and tell her what had happened. It was not something she wanted to do, but she had made a promise to the policemen that she would, and from now on, she intended to keep every single promise she ever made, lest some other terrible disaster should befall her.

She was still dripping a trail of sea water when she arrived at Aunty-ji's house, which was not much different from theirs, though a little bigger. It had two rooms: a tiny kitchen/washroom, and a living room that doubled as a bedroom, and a makeshift lean-to corrugated iron shed where Aunty-ji ran her sewing business. She was a widow with three teenage boys to feed, and each one had a sly look about him, or so Rain thought. They were the kind of boys who liked to pull your hair, or trip you up as you walked past. She didn't trust them one little bit, like she didn't trust their mother.

"There you are – you're late!" Aunty-ji snapped as she opened the door to Rain. And then, "What in God's name has happened to you? Why are you so wet?"

"I had an accident." Feeling exhausted, Rain sat on the wooden bench beside the formica table on which Aunty-ji's sewing machine stood, her tatty notebooks and wads of cash locked away in the drawer beneath, the key tied around her scrawny neck on a filthy piece of twine.

"Get off there! What is wrong with you, coming here making everything wet?" The old woman pushed Rain off the bench.

"Sorry, Aunty-ji..."

"Never mind sorry, girl – where's your linen from yesterday? Don't tell me you forgot to bring it with you. Were you born completely useless?"

"Aunty-ji... something has happened."

"I'm not interested in your accidents, Lakmini. I'm far too busy."

"It's not my accident, it's Bapu and Amma..."

"What about them?" Aunty-ji turned towards Rain, her face quizzical, her bony hands on her hips.

"They, they..." A tear spilled from Rain's eye.

"They what? Spit it out, girl."

"They're dead! Bapu's tuk-tuk went under a lorry..." Rain sat back on the bench, great heaving sobs racking her body.

"No, no, no!" Aunty-ji wailed, leaning on the table for support, as if all the blood had drained from her legs. Then she turned to Rain and shook her by the shoulders. "No I say, this cannot be. Your mother owes me money." Aunty-ji caught Rain's chin in her hand and twisted her face upwards so that she had to look the old woman in the eye. "You will have to repay your mother's debt."

"What debt? I don't know anything about a debt."

"Don't you dare question me, Lakmini. If I say your mother owes me money, then she owes me money and you will have to repay it."

"But how much money?" Rain sniffed.

"Such insolence! Have you no respect for your elders, young lady?" Aunty-ji slapped Rain hard across the face. It didn't hurt. Nothing could hurt through the pain she was already feeling, the aching hole in her heart, the heaviness of stone in her belly, the dizzying sickness.

"But I need to know Aunty-ji, otherwise how will I be sure when I've paid you back?" Rain persisted.

"Because I will tell you. I am sorry about your parents, Lakmini. Your father was... well, his life was hard, but so is mine. I have my own troubles. You and your brother will have to fend for yourself. I can't help you. I have too many of my own cares, so don't come running to me with your worries, do you hear me?" Aunty-ji sniffed and wiped her nose with the back of her hand.

"Don't worry, I won't." Rain hated this old woman

standing before her, without a kind bone in her body.

"Look, you're a clever girl, Lakmini, you're nearly a grown woman in fact — you'll just have to find a way to survive, like we all have to." She shoved a pile of material in Rain's lap. 'Now take your linen and bring it back by six o'clock, sharp. Make sure the lines are straight. And don't get it wet!"

Stunned, Rain rose from the chair, struggling to hold on to the heavy pile of raw cloth already cut into rectangles. Still feeling weak but resolving not to show it, she walked out the door without another word, unable to believe how the old woman could be so callous, her only thoughts of money and debt; no interest at all in how the accident happened or how Rain was feeling. No thought at all for Amma, her supposed friend.

What a vile old woman, thought Rain, and her heart weighed heavy as she recalled her words: 'You will have to find a way to survive...'

That was over six months ago and since then, things had gone from bad to worse. Anuja had become withdrawn and silent, taking himself off to school in the mornings, but not returning home until it was dark. When Rain asked him where he went after school, he said he liked to sit by the main road and watch the tuk-tuks go past; that it reminded him of Bapu.

"But Nuji, doesn't it make you feel sad?" she asked.

"Yes, but feeling sad means he is still in my heart."

She knew exactly what he meant.

Neither child spoke of their mother very much. She'd

been absent from their lives for so long that her death seemed almost insignificant. Rain wondered if perhaps they'd lost her to the TB years ago. And although Rain's grief was palpable, like a heaviness that slowed her whole body and mind, it was the least of her problems, for Aunty-ji had become more cantankerous and demanding as each day passed.

At first, Rain thought little of it, just putting it down to her ill temper: "This seam is not straight Lakmini. I will be docking your money today." Or, "I've added the price of the cotton thread and the rental of the sewing machine to your mother's debt. I don't see why I should bankroll you." But gradually, Rain began to see a pattern emerging. Aunty-ji was laundering in more ways than one and Rain was paying the price. In fact, it was Rain who was bankrolling Aunty-ji.

It was on a Friday evening, as Rain returned the last of the week's sewing that things came to a head.

Tired and hungry, Rain was staring out of the small window in Aunty-ji's shed, waiting for her work to be inspected and to be handed her week's wages from the little drawer beneath the sewing machine. She was keen to get to the market, which by now would be all but sold-out and shut up. She was hoping to get a small snapper and some vegetables to make a stew for their evening meal.

"What is this?"

Rain looked at the neatly sewn cloth that had been shoved in her face.

"What? It looks fine to me."

"Well, it certainly doesn't look fine to me. I shall be docking your wages."

"But why? What's wrong with it?"

"It's obvious, Lakmini. Thread on the top is different colour to thread on bottom. Not compatible, I tell you. Not acceptable."

Rain was incredulous. "But they're both white! And anyway, you gave me that thread to use, or rather, you sold it to me."

"Insolence!" Aunty-ji leaned forward to strike Rain, but the younger woman ducked out of the way. "It is different shade of white! It will not do. Compatible only."

Rain felt anger rise in her belly. She had held her tongue week in, week out, as this mean old woman found fault with her work and swindled her out of her hard-earned wages.

"But Aunty-ji, I can only work with the materials you provide. If you give me the wrong shade of white thread, it is not my fault. You can't keep docking my money and making Amma's debt bigger – it's not fair!"

Aunty-ji rounded on Rain.

"Fair? I'll tell you about 'fair' young lady. Fair is me bailing your family out with my own money when you had not even a grain of rice in the cupboard. Cupboard is always bare in your house, hah? Fair is me getting your *haraka* of a father a job at the taxi rank when no-one else would give him work because he was too unreliable."

Rain winced at Aunty-ji's cuss. "Please don't speak of him like that."

"You know me, speak as I find – and anyway, he was unreliable, he was a daydreamer just like you, always great plans that came to nothing. Useless, all of you." Aunty-ji was now in her stride. "And, whilst we're on subject, who do you think bailed your mother out when she had no money left in her purse? Hah? Me, always me. She kept pestering me for help: 'Just a few rupees Beesha, until next week' – always next week she would pay, but she never did. Who do you think paid for your brother's new exercise books? Hmmm? Me, that's who. Those shoes you have on – I paid for them. Me."

Rain looked at her cheap shoes of black canvas with rubber soles. They were already wearing thin. She would need another pair before too long.

"Your precious Bapu was a soft touch, Lakmini. He was such a fool. For years he tried to make amends with his stubborn old father and what an unpleasant man he was, believe me. But Danidu refused to see wood for trees isn't it – wasting time, wasting money trying to get back in his Papa's good books. I told Danidu, pointless to expect forgiveness, but he would not listen."

"Forgiveness for what?" Rain had absolutely no idea what the old woman was talking about.

"For being an idiot, that's what! For always making bad decisions. Always, the wrong decision." And then, "You don't know do you? Of course, you don't know…" Aunty-ji looked at Rain, with a twisted grin on her face. "Your mean old grandfather disowned your father on the day he married your idle Hindu Amma. Never spoke to him again. Cut him off without a penny. So, don't talk to me about what is fair, young lady, because thing is, you know nothing on the subject. Nothing!" Aunti-ji pulled Rain's ear hard as she spoke, waggling it about and pinching it spitefully. "They don't teach 'fair' in school, do they? Hah?" She spat on the floor as if the words she spoke were rancid in her mouth. "You, with all your clever English words – what do you know about fair?"

Rain's jaw had dropped. What did she mean, Hindu?

And why was she talking about forgiveness? Nothing made sense to Rain, but Aunty-ji had not quite finished.

"And to top it all, I had to pay for their funeral, because there was not a single rupee in your house. Not one. So, do not speak to me of fair, girl, because you will be forever in my debt Lakmini. You will never be able to repay all that I have done for you. Never!"

Rain was stunned. The words 'you will be forever in my debt' ringing in her head like a tolling bell.

"I... I didn't know my father was in touch with his family... Where...? Aunty-ji, where do they live?"

"There is so much you don't know, girl; so much your parents did not tell you, and so why should I tell you, now they are gone? Why?"

"Please, Aunty-ji, tell me! They are the only family we have left."

"They disowned you all, Lakmini, years ago. They think they are too good for the likes of you. They would not speak with you even if you begged them. To them, you are unclean, because you are only half Catholic; half of you will always be Hindu, and for that – for your father marrying your mother – your grandparents turned their backs on you. You didn't know your mother was a Hindu, huh? Well, she converted to Catholicism to please your father, but she was born in Tamil Nadu and her own faith never left her. That is why she did not accompany you to church at Christmas and Easter. That is why she insisted on having a statue of Lord Ganesha on that pathetic altar by her bed. Anyway, they are all long gone now. Your grandfather died – good riddance to his bitter soul – and your grandmother and Aunty Priya moved to Colombo just after Anuja was born, and guess what? They didn't leave a forwarding address."

Lakmini turned and fled, not waiting for her wages. She couldn't bear to hear such hateful words being spoken about her parents. She did not for one moment believe that her father was unreliable or soft-headed. No, Bapu was kind and thoughtful. He would help those in need without asking for anything in return. He was compassionate and caring, but Aunty-ji only saw what was in her own heart, and that was an envious and ugly greed.

Not for the first time, Rain and Anuja went hungry that night. The following morning, she sold her mother's decrepit cot bed to their neighbour for 10 rupees, which gave her enough money to buy a small piece of fish, some rice, a coconut and a mango, and to replace the little gas bottle for their single ring-burner. Beyond that, she did not know what she would do, for there was very little else in the house she could sell. She had no intention of ever sewing another stitch for that miserly old woman, and so she guessed that she had to get a job.

As she walked back from the market, Rain decided to sit under the shady trees that lined the ramparts of the old Fort and eat some of the mango. She was desperately hungry and the fruit was deliciously ripe, though she was careful to save half of it for Anuja. As she ate, a small insect must have been attracted by the juicy aroma and it fluttered onto the mango. It was exquisite with a red carapace fading to yellow and black dots on each wing. Something about it reminded her of the shoulder flash that the friendly policeman wore on his uniform that fateful night when her parents were killed. Just the sight of the little creature broke Rain's heart.

"Bapu…" she whispered into the wind, tears spilling

from her eyes. "Oh Bapu… What shall I do?"

But there was no answer from Bapu.

Picking up her shopping, Rain made her way back through the bustling centre of the town with its colourful shops selling anything from sarongs and flip-flops for the tourists to pink plastic Christmas trees, even though it was the middle of June.

And then she saw it.

On the front of one of the shops, hanging above a huge tinted-glass window covered in dirt and road dust, was a sign that read, 'Set Your Affairs In Order.'

Wasn't that exactly what Bapu had said he would do, when he came back from Colombo? This must be a sign from him, surely…?

Tentatively, she opened the door of the office. A fat, dishevelled man with oily hair and his feet propped on the desk in front of him, was talking on the telephone. He looked at her and waved her away, like she was one of the flies that had been defecating on his shop window. Rain stood her ground. She wanted to speak to this man.

Eventually, he put the phone down.

"Yess?" The man made a strange fat sound when he pronounced the 's'. It made Rain want to giggle.

"Umm, I would like to put my affairs in order please," she said.

Now it was the greasy man's turn to laugh.

"You? I doubt you can afford my services," he said, looking her up and down. His disdain was evident, and it knocked her confidence.

"What are your fees, sir?" she asked politely.

"Like I said, more than you can afford. Now get the hell out of my office and shut the door behind you."

Disappointed, she turned and shut the door so firmly behind her, it rattled in its hinges. The greasy man shook his fist at her from behind the window and swivelled his chair so he was no longer looking at her.

Her route home took her perilously near the harbour, a place she'd avoided since the morning the ocean almost took her, and so she cut through a side street and past the police station. It was then that she remembered the little insect and the kindly policeman, and a fleeting idea came to her. If it had formed more fully into a thought, she might've decided it was a stupid one.

She approached the front desk of the station behind which was a uniformed officer wearing the standard red and yellow shoulder flash. He looked at her and raised an eyebrow.

"Umm, could I speak to one of your officers, please?" she asked politely.

"And which officer would that be?"

"Umm, I'm sorry – I don't know his name."

The policeman sighed. "Look, miss, I don't know if you're aware of this, but the police force in Sri Lanka is on high alert right now, after the massacres, and there's no way we have time to indulge the fancies of a young woman who doesn't even know who it is she wants to speak to. So, if you'll just run along, please. We have real work to do." Again, she was waved away.

"It's okay, Dulaj. I know this young lady," said a voice behind her. "I'll deal with this."

Rain turned around, and standing there was the kindly policeman who had come to see her the night her parents had died. She wanted to cry with relief.

"Lakmini, isn't it? I have a good memory for names,"

he smiled. "My name is Sergeant Gomes. Come with me to my office. Let's see what you have to say."

Rain followed the officer into a tiny room, crammed with filing cabinets and overflowing trays of paper. He motioned for her to sit in the chair facing his desk.

"Now, how can I be of service?" he asked.

Lakmini was momentarily dumbstruck. What was it that had brought her to this place, other than a pretty insect that reminded her of his shoulder flash? Her mind had gone completely blank. But then she remembered the greasy man's shop and her resolve returned.

"Sir, I need to put my affairs in order." The policeman nodded but did not scorn her and so Rain's confidence returned. "You see, after Bapu and Amma died, I found out that my mother owed money to a woman who I have been working for, but this woman will not tell me the extent of the debt, and every time I collect my wages, she deducts money for things that are not my fault, or she adds items to the debt so that instead of growing smaller, it is growing ever larger."

The policeman frowned and rocked back and forth in his chair, fiddling with his impressive moustache.

"Well, I think this should be easy enough to remedy, Lakmini. Just ask her for the total sum and arrange for a monthly repayment until the debt is cleared. She may not want to give you the exact details, but I can assure you, she will give them to me."

Rain's face brightened. "Really, sir? You can help me to put my affairs in order?"

The policeman chuckled. "Why don't we pay this woman a visit. What is her name?"

"Aunty-ji."

And with that, Rain led the way to Aunty-ji's house. The policeman knocked on her dilapidated door, and when she answered, she looked most surprised to see the pair of them standing there.

"And to what do I owe this pleasure?" Her lip curled curtly with the question.

"Let us come in and I will explain," Sergeant Gomes replied. "You don't want the whole world to know your business, surely?"

Reluctantly, she opened the door to her work room and nodded for them to go inside, scowling with ill-concealed contempt at Rain and looking all about to see if any of her neighbours had noticed her visitors.

"I gather Lakmini's late mother borrowed a sum of money from you, Mrs…?"

"Chandran. Yes, she most certainly did and on a regular basis I might add, Sergeant. Whenever I visited her, she always asked to borrow money from me. She and her husband could not run their household properly and if it were not for me, they would all have gone hungry on many occasions."

"You are a good friend, Mrs Chandran."

Aunty-ji straightened her back. "I am indeed," she replied. "Nobody knows how good."

"Now, look here, Mrs Chandran. Miss Perera has asked me to help her set her affairs in order. She needs to know the total sum that is owed to you, and she would like to agree a fair amount to repay each month until the debt is cleared."

"Would she now? And tell me, how is she going to repay a debt if she has no work? You should know that she is an insolent girl. I can no longer have her in my employ."

"Well, I wouldn't work for you again for all the tea in Ceylon!" Lakmini blurted out, angry that Aunty-ji was painting herself as the injured party.

The policeman intervened. "That is as may be, Mrs Chandran, but it is no business of yours how Lakmini will repay the debt, merely what the debt is."

Aunty-ji huffed and puffed to herself. She was used to having the final say in things; she was used to calling all the shots and she did not like being told what to do, not least by this jumped-up policeman with his silly caterpillar moustache.

"Well, I will have to work it out. I cannot say at this exact moment."

"That is fine. We will wait for you to work it out."

Aunty-ji cursed Lakmini under her breath. She found a piece of paper and a pencil which she put in her mouth to moisten, and then she began to write some figures in a column. "600 rupees for annual tuk-tuk rental, for two years running I might add," she said, looking up and eyeing the policeman, daring him to question her. "300 rupees for rent arrears... Now, let me see, 50 rupees for school uniforms and books... 150 rupees for last batch of medicine... and the same again for the previous one, 100 rupees for food last month, oh and the month before that, 150 rupees for..."

The blood drained from Lakmini's face. The figure was going up and up, and Aunti-ji kept thinking of more things to add – and worse still, Rain had no way at all of proving whether any of it was genuine.

Sergeant Gomes quietly twiddled his moustache.

After several minutes of calculations and recalculations Aunty-ji sighed and said, "Well, I think this just about covers it," and handed the policeman the paper.

"3,220 rupees?"

"That's not the half of it, to be sure, but it is all I can remember," Aunty-ji said.

"3,220 rupees?" Rain whispered. "But I shall never be able to pay that off…"

"Then you should have been careful what you asked for, my girl," Aunty-ji hissed at her. "You should have been grateful for small mercies – my small mercies – but no, Lakmini Perera knows best. This is what you wanted, isn't it? Well, isn't it?"

Again, Lakmini was dumbstruck.

"This is what you owe me, and I expect it to be paid off at 25 rupees a week. No slacking."

"But that's more than you paid me for all the sewing each week. There will be nothing left for us to eat."

"Not my problem. I will come to you in the morning to collect my sewing machine and I will expect the first payment on Friday. And mark my words, if you default on any of the payments, I will add 10% interest on top."

"Now then, Mrs Chandran," said Sergeant Gomes, "I think you will find that charging interest is usury, and that usury is illegal in Sri Lanka, unless you are a registered money lender, which I believe you are not?"

Now it was Aunty-ji's turn to pale.

"So, there will be no charging of interest on this debt. We will now go to the Notary's Office and instruct him to draw up this agreement. I will sign it as a witness and send a copy to you. The second copy will go to Lakmini, who will pay the weekly sum into an account set up by the Notary. You will be able to collect the payments at the end of each month from the Notary, and he will make a note of any payment default and amend the balance each quarter. Is that clear?"

"Well... I suppose it is, though I think she has treated me most unfairly. Why do I have to wait a whole month for each payment? All I have ever done is try to help her God-forsaken family out, and what thanks do I get?"

"Mrs Chandran, thank you for helping out the Perera family in their hour of need. You are a good woman and a true friend. Lakmini, please thank Mrs Chandran for all her help to you and your family."

The words stuck in Lakmini's throat. "Than... hhrrr, Thank you, Aunty-ji, for all your help."

"I should jolly well think so too."

The policeman steered a rather dazed and confused Rain out of Mrs Chandran's house, chuckling to himself.

"What is so funny, sir, if I may ask?" Rain sighed.

"That bit about 'usury'! I have no idea if that is the law or not, but it sounded good. You see, Lakmini, the fact is, this uniform I wear gives me authority. People do not challenge me; they accept my word as law."

"But sir, how am I to pay the 25 rupees a week, when I don't have a job?"

"Lakmini, you are quite obviously an intelligent girl with a bit of gumption about you. So, I don't think it is beyond your abilities to get yourself a job."

Gumption, thought Rain. *What does that mean?*

They walked back into town, Lakmini's shopping bag beginning to get heavy, and to stink as the fish wrapped in newspaper reacted with the heat of the day. She was tired from lack of food and worried about what her rash decision had set in motion.

She was surprised when they rounded the corner and

stopped at the shop with the dirty window. What was it the policeman called this place – the Notary's Office?

"Here we are, then" said Sergeant Gomes, opening the door and ushering her in.

"You!" said greasy man, eyeing Rain with disdain.

"Mr Pigera, I am here with Lakmini Perera to have a contract drawn up. Can you facilitate this?"

"Certainly, Sergeant Gomes, but who is going to pay for my services?"

"I will be paying," said the policeman.

Rain's knees felt like they would buckle. Apart from dear Bapu, he was the kindest person she had ever met.

Sergeant Gomes explained the details of the contract he wanted drawn up, and the Notary duly began proceedings, huffing and puffing as he did so.

"Take a seat," he said, the fat 's' sound again making Rain want to giggle. "This will take a while."

"I am going back to the police station," said Sergeant Gomes. "I will return in half an hour or so to witness and sign the contract. Lakmini, I suggest you wait here until our arrangement has been concluded."

And so it was that Rain watched the greasy man – aptly called Mr Pigera, she thought – painstakingly type out the contract between herself and Aunty-ji using his two index fingers and plenty of Wipe-Out, the white liquid paper that covered up myriad mistakes. Mr Pigera stuck his tongue out of the right side of his mouth as he slowly punched out figures on the ancient Olivetti typewriter.

Rain watched with increasing frustration. *How can it take him so long to type a column of figures and a couple of names and addresses?* she wondered, edging towards his desk.

"Would it help if I read the figures out, sir?"

"Don't be so silly, girl – you could knock a couple of zeros off for all I know."

"I wouldn't do that!" Rain was shocked. Did he think she had no integrity?

"Go on then. Let us see if it makes life easier."

Rain began to read out the figures. "200 rupees. Next line, 55 rupees. Next line, 120 rupees..."

Slowly and with far less Wipe-Out, the debt was documented and verified.

"Well, I think that did help a tiny bit," Mr Pigera begrudged.

"I could've typed it faster myself. We learned how to touch-type at school. Not on typewriters, though. We had to draw out the Qwerty keyboard on a blank piece of paper, and then our teacher would stand at the front of the class and shout, 'ASDF, space, colon, LKJ, space' – and we had to touch the corresponding keys on our drawings. I loved it!"

"But you might not be any good at typing if you've only ever done it on paper."

"I suppose so..."

"Here, sit down, and type out what I dictate. Let's see if you can type faster than me."

Rain, not for the first time that day, wished she'd kept her mouth shut. She would probably make a fool of herself and Mr Pigera would charge Sergeant Gomes double for the trouble.

"'Dear Mr Kumar comma new line. It has come to my attention that you have moved the fence that divides our property two feet further into my yard comma gaining for yourself the land that was previously mine full stop.' Let me see how you are doing girl."

He stood behind Lakmini, his hands on the back of her chair, his bad breath turning her stomach.

"Ha ha, stupid girl! If I say comma, I mean type a comma not type the word! But not bad, not bad. You kept up with me and spelt the words correctly. What else can you do? Can you answer the telephone?"

"I have never used a telephone, sir."

"Heavens above! What shanty town have you crawled out from?"

"I live on Ingodapokunadi Road, sir," she said indignantly. "It is a quiet neighbourhood."

"And you went to school, you say?"

"Yes, sir. I went to Handunugoda school – you know the one that was originally set up by the tea plantation estate, but is now a girls' school?"

"Yes, I know of it."

"That is where I learned to speak and write English – my favourite subject. I left just over a year ago, and since then I have been sewing tablecloths for a living."

"Have you now. And how much do you make a week sewing tablecloths?"

"35 rupees, sir." Rain looked to the floor and blushed slightly. She had inflated her earnings, for this conversation was beginning to sound a little like an interview.

"I will pay you 40 rupees a week if you work for me as my assistant, filing documents, typing letters, answering the phone, and so on and so forth."

"45 rupees, sir and we will have a deal." She couldn't believe the words that were coming out of her mouth.

"Miss Perera, I will pay you 40 rupees a week and you will be grateful for it, or not at all."

"But Mr Pigera, you know that I will have to pay 25 of those rupees straight to Mrs Chandran. I cannot pay rent and feed my brother and I on 15 rupees a week!"

"I am sure we can find another way for you to earn a little extra."

She disliked the leer that had hardened onto his face. It made her feel uneasy, but what choice did she have? 15 rupees would just about keep a roof over their heads and a bag of rice and some cooking oil in the cupboard. It would have to do, for now.

"Thank you, Mr Pigera. I accept."

"You will start at 8am on Monday morning and we will see how we get on. If after the first month you turn out to be more of a help than a hindrance, I will pay you 45 rupees a week.

"Thank you, sir." A wave of relief swept over Rain. She hadn't realised how much weight she'd been carrying and not from just the stinking bag of fish.

Whilst the votive candle on the altar had flickered out, her thoughts had not. Sleep simply would not come to her, and the monsoon rains seemed to intensify her loneliness. *How does Anuja sleep through this cacophony?* Rain thought. Her tears had at last subsided, but her sorrows remained. She missed her father so much that at times she felt she could no longer bear the pain of her grief. *Can they fix a broken heart in hospital?* she wondered.

When she'd began working with Mr Pigera, at the Notary's Office, she'd dared to hope that life had taken a turn for the better – at least she no longer had to put up with Aunty-ji's bullying – but this was not to be the case. She found her work easy, in fact she liked typing letters and answering the phone, but her boss was unbearable, and even more of a bully than Aunty-ji had been. He had an annoying habit of reading the letters she was typing over her shoulder, leaning too close to her so that she could smell his acrid breath and feel the moist heat and heaviness of his belly, and it made her feel physically sick, his looming presence forcing mistakes from her fingertips which he would then berate her for. Often, he would put his hands on her shoulders as he leaned over her, and sometimes, he would move his hands over her breasts and then down between her thighs, making her rigid with fear.

One day, whilst she was in the stock room, filing the foolscap papers and contracts into alphabetical order of client surnames, Mr Pigera came into the room, shutting the door behind him. Her heart quickened. At first, he busied himself with some papers, but she could see it was a pretence, because they were all upside down. Then he deftly moved towards her and pinned her to the wall, his fat, oily body pressed hard against hers.

"Please don't, sir…" she pleaded, but he seemed not to hear. He caught her wrist with his hand and held her still, his face bearing down on hers, his breath making her nauseous. He began to stroke her arm and then put his hand beneath her choli and touched her breasts, callously pinching her nipples. Rain's legs weakened and she thought she was going to be sick, but at that moment, the bell in the shop rang and someone shouted out his name. It seemed to bring him back to his senses.

"Hurry up with the damn paperwork, Lakmini," he

scolded, adjusting his trousers as he left the room.

Rain's heart was beating so fast it felt like it would burst through her chest. *Abominable man!*

The same thing happened a few days later, but as he pushed her towards the wall, she managed to duck under his arms and fled back into the shop. She was grateful for the big fly-blown glass window that looked out onto the busy marketplace, as she doubted that even Pigera would try any funny business in full view of the townspeople as they bustled past.

"You can kiss goodbye to that pay rise, Lakmini," he muttered as he returned to the office some time later, doing up the belt to his trousers. "You're too hot-headed, and you have ideas above your station. You must learn to do as you're told by your betters."

In that moment, something inside Rain hardened. She was tired of being treated like a second-class citizen. Aunty-ji had berated and belittled her when she had always tried her best and worked diligently, and here was this despicable man doing the same – both of them blaming her for their own shortcomings. Well she'd had enough of it. She would not be this man's scapegoat.

"Mr Pigera, sir. I know that I am doing a good job here. I know that I am saving you money, keeping your diary up to date, amending your grammar and placating your clients," (she loved using long words that she knew he wouldn't understand), "but if you so much as touch me again, then I will report you to Sergeant Gomes, and we will see what *he* has to say about it."

Pigera's eyes bore into hers. "Lakmini Perera, you are living in cloud cuckoo land if you think that Gomes gives two hoots about the likes of you. You are nothing but a guttersnipe and he just wanted to get you out of his hair, once and for all. Now jump to it and get me the Bandara case file and get a bit of respect for your elders and betters whilst you're about it."

It hurt Rain's feelings to think that Sergeant Gomes might not care about her, for if the truth be told, she had begun to think of him as something of a father figure, daydreaming about his nice wife and his nice house and whether she and Anuja could actually live on his veranda. But since her ultimatum, at least Pigera had not laid a hand on her. Not yet. Nonetheless, he was making her pay for her audacity. Nothing she did was good enough or fast enough; he wanted her to start work earlier in the mornings and stay later in the evenings, but he never paid her any extra money. He had her running errands all over town and never once thought of giving her a break for lunch.

She was absolutely exhausted by it all; by the constant fear of his advances and by his maliciousness. He made Aunty-ji pale into insignificance. She was frightened of Mr Pigera and what he was capable of. And the meagre 15 rupees she had at the end of the week for food and rent were simply not enough to live on. Anuja helped as much as a thirteen-year old boy could. On Saturdays, he would go down to the fish market and together with the caretaker, clean and sweep up after the day's proceedings. He didn't get any payment, but he was allowed to take home the heads and tails of the gutted fish that hadn't already been taken by stray dogs and other hungry people. They would make a good broth.

Anuja was a sweet-natured boy with sorrowful brown eyes, and sometimes the other stallholders would take

pity on him and give him a half-rotten head of cauli-
flower or an unripe mango. Most people who frequented
Lagentle market knew about the fate of his parents, and
some were compassionate enough to share their meagre
rations with him. Yet it galled Rain that they had fallen
so low. Since the contract with Aunty-ji had been drawn
up, she had not missed a single payment, but she was
aware that it would take almost three years to clear the
debt. How would they survive on her earnings? She had
to find another way.

Thursday was the best day of the working week for
Rain, as Mr Pigera would shut the office at 4pm promptly
in order to visit his elderly mother who lived on the other
side of town. He would walk to the taxi rank where Bapu
once worked and take a tuk-tuk to see her. Why it had to
be the same time every Thursday, Rain didn't know nor
care, for she was free to do as she pleased for a couple of
hours. And what she did was visit the library, which was
like a sanctuary to her. It was always so quiet and cool,
its giant ceiling fans whirring gently and stirring the air,
and always, the faint smell of musty books pervaded the
building. It was a smell she loved as it reminded her of
happier times before her parents had died, when she was
able to spend more time in the library than she could
now. The Librarian was always friendly towards her, and
had come to know Rain's likes and dislikes, and so would
often recommend new books for her.

The library had also recently acquired a fascinating
magazine section and she was absolutely smitten by the
glossy colour images of lands and lifestyles so unimagi-
nably different to hers. She thumbed the pages of each
magazine on the stand, gazing at the photos and reading

the articles, absolutely absorbed in the incredible stories that emerged from the pages. She was transported to different worlds and she loved it. She pored over every magazine from cover to cover, adverts and all, and eagerly awaited their next instalments.

The Library also held copies of all the Sri Lankan telephone directories, which were updated every two years. There were eight of them in all and Rain spent hours poring over the letter 'P' looking for evidence of her father's family. She started in Colombo and couldn't believe her eyes. There were countless Pereras – well, she did count them: 74 Perera telephone numbers listed in Colombo. Were any of them her grandmother's number, or her Aunty Priya's she wondered, although she didn't have enough money to ring a number and ask. But she loved reading the addresses and imagining the places where these people lived; the names conjuring her aunt and grandmother alive in her imagination. Perhaps they lived together in Isipathana Road, Colombo? Or maybe they lived in Malabe Compound? But perhaps her aunt had moved from Colombo to Negombo and she was the Perera who lived in Katunayake, or even further afield at No 321 Anniewatta Circular Road? She looked these places up in the Atlas, and in her imagination, she would walk along these roads until she found the right number and would knock on the door and be welcomed into the arms of her father's family like a prodigal child, a beloved long-lost relative in a happy reunion.

The Library was her only joy in life. Well, that and occasionally seeing the young man from PerfectPrint who dropped off the papers from the Courts that had to be witnessed, stamped and dated by Mr Pigera before

Rain filed them away. She didn't know his name, but his shy smile lit up her heart. The library and Mr PerfectPrint were the only lights in her otherwise dark world.

Just before dawn, the monsoon rains ceased briefly, and Rain drifted off to sleep. A deep silence fell upon the Perera household, such as it was: Lakmini and Anuja, orphaned and alone, struggling to keep body and soul together in a world where kindness was a rare thing.

The One Thousand Pounds Cheque

"Nora, I'm expecting a cheque for one thousand pounds," Jay Silversmith said, peering around the arched wooden door of the office. "Have you seen it?"

Nora admired his choice of hat, a navy woollen beret with an embroidered red and green band around the base, his cropped silver hair protruding just beneath, and matched by a cropped silver beard. Jay had good taste in hats, as with most things.

"It's not come in this morning's post," she replied. "I put everything in your in-tray earlier."

"Okay – not to worry, just keep an eye out for it in tomorrow's post, please. I'd like to get it paid in at the bank on Thursday, if possible."

Those were the days before email and the internet, when opening the post was the first thing to be done at *Awaken* magazine and could often take an hour or more to sort into piles for the various writers and editors who worked in the old stone barn that had been converted into two offices; a large open-plan room for all the staff which overlooked a beautiful sunny courtyard, and a smaller space for Jay with views over the back garden of his adjoining house. Nora loved opening the post – it was one of her favourite jobs because although she knew the majority of the letters and parcels were not addressed to her, it still felt a little like it was her birthday, every day. With a cheerful smile, the postman would deliver a huge, wobbling pile of letters and packages onto her desk, and it was Nora's job to open them all.

There would be interesting pre-publication copies of books, and numerous cassettes and CDs of New Age music, all for review. There were heavy piles of slides and sheets of contact prints from Magnum Photos or Getty Images, some of which would be chosen for inclusion in the next issue of the magazine; lots of cheques for a year's subscription, occasional 'Letters to the Editor' or the odd complaint, innumerable requests for Jay Silversmith to give a lecture at some conference or other, and dozens of general queries and other correspondence – and every day the pile of post just seemed to get bigger.

As *Awaken* magazine was 'green' – a word that had recently been coined to cover anything relating to the environment – Jay thought it was important to practice what they preached, and to recycle all the envelopes and junk mail that was received in the post each morning. Nora's system was to chuck everything into a big wicker box under her desk, which when full would be taken to the wooden hut near the fire station in the village for collection by the local council – but mostly, it was used to light the woodburning stove that heated the offices, another of Nora's early morning tasks in autumn and winter months.

After Jay had looked through his teetering stack of correspondence, Nora would go to his office at the far end of the barn conversion, armed with her notepad and pen, and take down in shorthand, his replies to all the letters. She liked it when Jay looked approvingly at her for keeping up to speed with his thoughts. This process and then transcribing the dictation took up the bulk of her working day, and she loved it. She took great pride in being quick, efficient and in pre-empting Jay's every need, answering those queries that he didn't need to be bothered with and finding requested information before he had to ask for it. After all, Jay was a busy man and Nora was ambitious and intended to 'work her way up the ladder'. She wanted to be part of the editorial team herself one day and knew that starting off as Jay's PA was a great first step in her career.

Nora hadn't realised when she'd first started working at *Awaken* that Jay was a bit of an enigma and quite famous in certain circles. Originally from The Bronx in New York, he'd made his fortune writing pop songs for bands in the 1950s and '60s, several of his compositions becoming top ten hits. Jay was part of the counterculture in sixties America and dropped-out of society for many years, living with various indigenous communities in the US, Mexico and later in Brazil. It was during this time, and whilst participating in a vision quest that entailed imbibing the infamous and potent ayahuasca – a psycho-active spiritual medicine – that he received 'a message'. From that moment on, he knew that his life's work must be to raise awareness of the rights of Mother Earth. And then, through a series of synchronicities that could only be described as fate, Jay and his family came to live in a small, archetypally English village in Devon, where he set out to change the world.

Jay was now busy raising funds for his new project – The Seed School – and this one thousand pounds cheque would enable the next phase of his plans to go ahead. He was clearly eager to get it cashed in at the bank. Every Thursday, Nora would walk up the hill into the village with all the cheques neatly listed in the paying-in book, and wait for Barclays Bank to open its doors, as it did for just one morning a week. The bank was situated in the front room of someone's house, aptly called Bank House, and Nora would wait her turn to be served, sitting on one of the many wooden chairs that had been placed around the periphery of the room. Even in the depths of summer, there would be a coal fire burning in the grate of Bank House, and an elderly gentleman – the occupant, Nora presumed – would usher each one in turn up to the cashier, who was seated behind a wooden desk near the fire. It was all rather quaint.

"Are you alright, maid?" Cassandra asked, as she breezed into the office, letting in a waft of warm summer air perfumed by the roses that Jay's wife, Mary, grew in abundance in the courtyard outside. Cassandra was ten years older than Nora, petite and with long dark hair. She always wore high heels to give herself extra stature, but she needn't have bothered because like the tiny wren, Cassandra made her presence felt wherever she went. Cassandra was also her own boss. Not for her a 9am start. She came to work when she was ready, and she left when she felt like it, and nobody questioned her timekeeping, not even Jay. Cassie was a law unto herself.

"Yeah, fine," Nora replied. "Just a bit knackered. I had another late one last night."

"Have you been burning the candle at both ends again, Nora-Noo?"

"Not really, I just got talking to Louisa and didn't notice the time."

"How is she?"

"Oh, you know. Brave."

"Do you want a coffee? I'm gasping."

"Yes, please. Black." Nora had recently started taking her coffee black, in solidarity with Louisa who had given up all dairy products.

"Yuck, I don't know how you can drink coffee without milk." Cassandra hooked her bag over one of the wooden coat pegs by the door. "I was thinking," she said keeping her voice low so as not to disturb the rest of the staff who were in the midst of an editorial meeting, "it would make sense if I sorted out the post on the days I come in, don't you think?" She switched on her computer, knowing she'd have time to make the coffee before it had finished booting up. "It would give you more time to get your dictation transcribed. You're always having to work late to finish it all and the workload is only going to increase, what with this new school Jay's determined to open." Cassandra didn't really approve of these 'extra-curricular' projects of Jay's. She thought he should just focus on the magazine, but that wasn't his style.

"I'm not sure – you know it's my favourite job…" Nora thought she sounded a bit petulant, a bit ungrateful, so added, "Thanks for the offer, though. I'll think about it."

And so the day began. Nora noticed how activity in the office always came in waves. First Jay and then his assistant editor, Marcus, would come bustling in – and eventually silence would return. Then, after some time, the advertising manager or perhaps the designer would arrive, exchanging niceties as they settled at their desks, and later, Cassandra would appear – and then silence again. Later there would be another wave of activity; the talkative cleaner would come in carrying the hoover and news of her unruly family, or a delivery of magazines would result in a flurry of activity as everyone helped unload the fifty or so boxes and stack them in the stock room… and then it would go quiet again. It was like the slow turning of the waves at the harbour down the road, and there was a certain quality to the silence Nora liked; it was a bit like the silence in a library, which has an air of attentiveness woven into it.

In the silence, and even though she was busy with her work, transcribing the last of Jay's dictated letters from yesterday, there was still space in Nora's head to think about Louisa and their conversation the previous night; about how she felt irritated with her younger sister, then guilty at feeling irritated, and about the injustice of it all. Even as her eyes read the spidery squiggles of shorthand on the pages of her notebook, and even as her fingers turned them into words on the keyboard of her new word-processor, her mind was able to contemplate other things. In fact, it was fair to say that over the last few weeks, her mind had not been entirely on the job.

Later that morning, as she made a second brew of coffee, Cassandra returned to the subject of the post.

"What do you reckon then, Nora – about me doing the post? It'll take some of the pressure off you."

"It's probably a good idea," Nora conceded.

"I think it will help with your workload, and you'll still have to do it on the mornings I'm not in the office."

"Yeah, that's true. Let's give it a go. Thanks Cass – I could certainly do with more hours in the day."

"Are you sure you're okay?"

"Yes, why?"

"You've been weirdly quiet all morning, which is not like you at all."

"Oh, it's just something Louisa said last night."

"And...?"

Nora sighed and moved her chair nearer to Cassie's desk. "Oh, it's nothing really..." she whispered. "It was just something she said about her sister-in-law, Amanda – Terry's sister. I didn't know this, but Louisa told me she used to be very jealous of Amanda, who was always ill with one thing or another, and who seemed to get all the attention from Terry's parents. Anyway, because of this Louisa, said that she'd often wished she could have an illness too – you know, so that she could get some attention from his family. And then she got breast cancer. Now Louisa thinks she's brought it upon herself and she's beating herself up about it."

"Well, you know what they say: 'Be careful what you wish for'."

"Yeah, but it doesn't work like that, does it? If it did, I'd have a flash car and new boots."

They both laughed.

"Actually Noo, I think it does work a bit like that sometimes." Cassandra pulled her hair into a bun and secured it at the nape of her neck with a clasp. She was a striking-looking woman, her dark hair framing equally dark brown eyes. Nora had once read about a race of people from the northern lands, called The Picts, who were apparently small, lithe, dark and fierce. Nora thought Cassie must've descended from the Picts. "When you wish for something to happen, when you really put a lot of time and energy into thinking about something, it creates a kind of energetic impulse that enables the molecules to align so it's more likely to happen – like it said in that book we reviewed in the last issue."

"What book? I don't remember reading about that." Nora frowned at her friend.

"The one by Fritjof Capra, I think... or was it Rupert Sheldrake? Oh, I don't know – I read so much stuff in this place, I can't remember who said what or where I read it. Don't worry though, Nora. Louisa's over the worst now. She's just got to think positive and keep well. You're not your sister's keeper, you know."

"I know, you're right. I just wish she wouldn't insist on showing me her lumpectomy scars – she's always saying, 'Do you want to see how my scars are healing?' and I really don't! It turns my stomach."

"Christ on a bike – it would me, too."

"She still shows me though."

Nora knew why Louisa wanted to show off her scars. They were like a badge of honour, a symbol of her bravery. "Look at what I have endured," they declared, but Nora didn't want to think about that.

The next morning, Cassandra opened the mail and Jay popped in to see if the one thousand-pounds cheque had arrived. It hadn't.

"I hope it hasn't got lost in the post. That would be a nuisance. Nora, can you ring ERC and ask them when it was sent to us, please? We may have to ask them to issue another one." Jay seemed rather irritated that the cheque had still not appeared.

"Sure. I'll let you know what they say."

Nora flipped through her Rollerdex to find ERC's telephone number, and was disconcerted to find that it wasn't listed. She recalled that she'd jotted it down on a slip of paper when that nice woman from their office had phoned. But she couldn't find the slip of paper, either.

"Is it in your special filing cabinet?" Cass smirked. She had noticed how Nora quite often found what she was looking for in the wicker recycling box that was shoved under her desk, and she'd named it accordingly.

Nora shrugged her shoulders, pulled out the 'special filing cabinet' and rummaged through the top layers of opened envelopes and A5 fliers requesting money for the victims of the terrible Bhopal disaster in India, or for Survival International. But it was not there. She rootled deeper into the layers of envelopes that had come in at the end of the previous week, and there it was – to her consternation, the missing one thousand pounds cheque lay amongst the discarded papers for recycling.

"Shit for brains..." Nora muttered, disappointed that she was not as efficient as she thought. "Look, Cass, you were right! Here's the cheque," she whispered, waving it covertly at her friend.

"Never mind, babe," Cass chortled. "I'm just glad it wasn't me who chucked it away! Don't tell Jay – just wait until tomorrow and put it in his tray then. Tell him the ERC lady said it should be with us any day."

"Really? Don't you think I should 'fess up?"

"Nah... what's the point? It's Thursday tomorrow, so it'll still get paid in on time. No point in Jay knowing what a numpty you are!"

Nora was about to shove the wicker basket back under her desk when something else caught her eye. It was an unopened airmail letter. She looked over to see if Cass was watching as Nora didn't want her to think she was completely incompetent, chucking away unopened post too. She picked the thin blue envelope out of her special filing cabinet and sliced it open using the small brass paperknife she kept in a jar of pens, pencils and paperclips, on her desk.

Written in unfamiliar handwriting was a letter.

To Whom It May Concern

My name is Lakmini Perera and I live in Lagentle, Sri Lanka. I am sixteen years old. My younger brother and I have fallen upon hard times after the death of our parents in a road accident. Although I have a job, my salary is very small, and I need to find a way to earn some more money. I am a skilled seamstress, but I no longer have a sewing machine as the one I rented was taken back after the death of my parents.

I recently read a copy of 'Awaken' magazine in our town Library. I loved the photos especially. I humbly request that you kindly consider placing an advert in your esteemed magazine on my behalf, to ask if any of your readers would sponsor a small sum to enable me to buy a sewing machine and thereby earn some extra money in my spare time. In return, I would be happy to make each person who has contributed towards the sewing machine, an item of clothing of their choice, by way of thanks.

If you are able to help me in this way, I would be most grateful.

May God bless you and keep you safe.

Yours sincerely,

Lakmini Perera

Nora frowned and sat back in her chair, chastising herself for discarding not one, but two items of post – and this second one from a young girl in Sri Lanka really touched her heart. She read the letter again. Her English was very good and her handwriting so neat, but Nora couldn't comprehend what it must've been like for her to lose both parents in a road accident. Nora's parents were her bedrock – how do you possibly survive when your very foundations are taken from under you?

Nora's Dad was an entrepreneur who could turn his hand to anything, and it was he who helped her to believe that she could achieve her wildest dreams if she put her mind to it; it was her Dad who had once told her that she must be prepared to start at the bottom of the ladder and work her way up, but to never lose sight of the top rung. And it was her Mum, who was 'green' before anybody even knew what green was, who'd phoned her excitedly on the very day Nora finished her secretarial training to say that she'd just seen an advert in *Awaken* magazine for a PA to the Editor. And the incredible thing was that *Awaken* magazine's offices were based in a village only thirty minutes drive from where Nora lived. The timing of the job seemed too synchronistic to be mere coincidence. No, it seemed like fate to Nora who attended the interview for the post of PA to Jay Silversmith, taking all her hopes for the future with her, as well as the brand-new Brother word-processor she'd just bought, as big and heavy as a celebrity's suitcase. Years later, Jay told her, "When I saw you walking down the garden path Nora, I knew you were the girl for the job!" Cassie had inferred that it was because she came as a package, with her very own computer.

"Look at this Cass," Nora said, taking the letter over to her friend's desk. "I just found it in my special filing cabinet, along with the cheque." 'Fessing up' seemed to be the order of the day.

"Oh my God, that's absolutely tragic," Cassandra said after reading it, "but fair play to her – the girl's got some initiative, that's for sure."

"I know, it's so sad. That she should suffer so much at such a young age – losing both her parents at once must have been a terrible shock. How awful..."

Cass nodded. "I've always thought that suffering was one of God's major design faults," then added, "that, and making chocolate fattening."

As one of Nora's work responsibilities was to compile

the classified adverts for each issue of the magazine, it was no problem for her include the request from Lakmini Perera under the Miscellaneous section.

SPONSORS WANTED

DONATIONS ARE SOUGHT FOR A YOUNG SRI LANKAN *AWAKEN* READER TO ENABLE HER TO BUY A SEWING MACHINE AND START A SMALL BUSINESS TO SUPPORT HER FAMILY. ALL SPONSORS WILL BE GIFTED A HANDMADE ITEM OF CLOTHING OF THEIR CHOICE, BY WAY OF THANKS. PLEASE SEND YOUR CHEQUE, HOWEVER SMALL, MADE PAYABLE TO 'AWAKEN' TO THE ADDRESS AT THE TOP OF THIS PAGE, REF: PERERA. THANK YOU.

Nora felt good about being able to help this girl in Sri Lanka, whose circumstances seemed so precarious, but as the magazine was bi-monthly, the advert would not be published until the September/October issue which was over eight weeks away, and so she forgot all about the letter and the advert, for her life was taking some tortuous paths of its own.

Nora lay in bed going over the events of the evening in her head. She was sick of this. Sick of lying awake in a state of anxiety wondering what mood he'd be in when he got home; sick of being treated as if her needs counted for nothing. No, actually, she was sick of not being loved enough; of not being cared about enough. She had come to the end of her tether.

It was a Wednesday night and on Wednesday nights Nora's boyfriend Michael always went to the pub. It was pool night where plenty of pints were sunk during the course of the evening, and Michael had got into the habit of inviting 'the lads' back to their house after closing time to continue carousing. Half a dozen men with the occasional girlfriend in tow would pile back to Nora and Mikey's house at 11.30 or so, loud and boisterous with drink, careless of the fact that Nora was upstairs in bed, trying to sleep; that she had to get up early for work the next day and that she felt responsible for not disturbing their longsuffering and rather elderly neighbours.

For a while, she'd joined Mikey at the pub when there was a home match at least, but she found pool so utterly boring that she'd much rather stay at home and read a book, or make curtains, or continue rubbing down fifty years of congealed and yellowing gloss paint from the stair banister, than sit for hours watching endless games of pool where the skills needed to play well deteriorated in direct relationship to how many pints were drunk. She was witness to the 'law of diminishing returns' as it played out in front of her, and to which the lads seem oblivious. So, in the end, she stayed at home.

On this particular night, she'd asked Michael not to invite anyone back after the pub closed.

"Why not?" he glared at her. He was always defensive, always ready for a fight. "This is my house too, in case you've forgotten. Why shouldn't I ask my mates back if I want to?"

"Well, because I've just asked you not to," Nora replied. "Because you smoke too much weed, and turn the music up way too loud – and when I ask you to turn it down, you turn it up even louder."

Michael chuckled at that.

"And you pee in the garden where the neighbours can

see you, and last week one of you fell down the steps into the road when a car was coming – and it's a Wednesday night, for God's sake, Mikey. You know I've got to get up early for work in the morning."

"Listen to yourself, Nora. All you ever do is moan. Moan, moan, moan."

"I'm not moaning, I'm just asking you to see things from my perspective for once. It's okay at the weekends Mikey, but during the week, I need to sleep."

"Christ almighty, you're such a misery, Nora. You're no fun. Lighten up, can't you? You're just a fucking secretary, for God's sake – what's so important about your job? Why do you have to take it all so seriously?"

"I love my job, Mike, you know that."

"Why don't you come with me and let your hair down for once? You never know, Nora, you might actually enjoy yourself."

"Sorry, Mikey, but I just don't find hanging about in pubs for hours on end watching you play pool that much fun. Maybe if we did something together…"

"Like what? Go to one of your boss's boring lectures? Or the bloody Green Party conference? No way. It might surprise you to know I don't find that much fun, either."

"Well, I'm not asking you to do that, am I? I'm just saying…"

"Well, don't just say. Don't just moan. Get off my back, will you Nora, for Christ's sake. I can't stand the way you constantly *police* me." He rounded on her, his eyes blazing. "I'll do what the hell I like, and don't you dare question me about it. Do you hear me?"

Nora felt the familiar cascade of stress in her body, felt the spike of adrenalin that had once made her throw a hot steam iron at him. Thank God it was still plugged in and the flex was short. It just missed him.

"Not in this house you won't. I pay half the rent, half the bills. Actually, I pay more than half, not that you'll have noticed. I have a say in what goes on here, Mike, and I need you to respect that."

He pushed her aside curtly, and she pitched towards the table. "Oh, please just fuck off, will you!" he hissed.

At that moment, she hated him. At that moment she felt the all too familiar adrenalin spike shoot down her arm and it rose into the air as if it had a life of its own, and then the adrenaline shot through her fingers which flexed – and slapped him hard across the face. Really hard. He lost his balance and stumbled, and she shrank back against the wall, knowing that her actions would light a touchpaper within him.

Time slowed as Nora watched Michael cave in; the inner cogs of his life experience began to whirr and the role-model he grew up with, his abusive father, egged him on. He turned to slap her in retaliation, but instead, his crooked fingers that had not been set properly after they'd broken in a terrible motorbike accident locked around her neck. He pushed her roughly through the kitchen door and then out into the cold hall. She lost her footing and landed awkwardly on the staircase feeling a sharp jolt of pain in her back, and then he shoved himself on top of her and began to squeeze her neck more tightly.

This is it, Nora thought. *He's going to kill me. How strange… I thought I'd have more time than this. I thought I might do something with my life…*

She was aware of how calm her thought processes were, of how time seemed suspended somehow. It wasn't that she'd given in to him, more that she couldn't struggle because the adrenalin had left her as quickly as it had come and she just didn't have the strength to fend him off. She looked at this man in a rage above her, his hands around her neck, his arms rigid, his breathing heavy. She did love him, even though she hated him. He had such a bright spirit, but he was broken in so many ways, and she knew in that moment that she could never fix him. She looked into his eyes, his intensely blue eyes, so deep-set that they made his brow seem almost Neanderthal, and at that moment, he looked into her eyes.

He dropped his hands from her neck and stared at them as if they didn't belong to him. Then he stormed into the kitchen and picked his van keys off the table, slammed the kitchen door shut, slammed the front door shut as he walked out, revved his van up to an alarming extent and sped off up the road to the pub.

It was now almost two o'clock in the morning and to give him his due, he hadn't come home with the lads, he just hadn't come home at all. And the irony of it was that Nora couldn't sleep when he didn't come home, like she couldn't sleep when he did.

She wondered where he was. Had he driven his van into a ditch somewhere and stranded himself? He'd only recently got his licence back from the time he was caught drink-driving. He'd stopped at the pub for a beer or two on his way home from the building site where he worked, and he'd stayed there until closing time, as was his wont. Apparently, he'd staggered out of the pub after having had a skinful and got into his van to drive the short distance home, a distance he could have easily walked, not noticing that a police car was parked with its lights off at the far end of the pub car park. Someone must have tipped them off. As Mikey drove erratically away, the police car followed, and so, panicking, he sped through the village, then did something that Starsky or Hutch could have gotten away with, but which he couldn't: he abandoned his van in a layby and jumped over a hedge to hide in someone's back garden. The police saw his van, stopped their car and started to look for Mikey, flashing their torches around the dark and quiet village streets. Of course, the torchlight picked him out as he crouched behind a hedge, because he was still wearing his hi-viz vest from work. It could only happen to Michael.

So yes, he could well be stoved into a ditch somewhere, and she was appalled to realise that part of her hoped he was – part of her actually hoped that he'd killed himself in a car accident so that she could be free. *Christ, this is not good,* she told herself. *I can't wish him dead just because I don't have the courage to leave…* Or maybe he'd met a pretty girl in whatever small town they'd been playing pool that night, and had gone home with her – she wouldn't put it past him, the temper he was in when he left – and he would do it to spite Nora, because Mikey believed in revenge. Or he could be having a knees-up at someone else's house. But wherever he was, he wasn't with her, and he hadn't been with Nora in any meaningful way for a long time now. For months – no, for years if truth be told.

She rubbed her neck absentmindedly, where a raw, red circle of inflamed skin had appeared. It was sore, but that was all. Her ears were pricked for the sound of a vehicle driving down the deserted street, but none came. Only recently, Nora had realised that waiting for people to come home was a pattern in her life. She'd waited as a small girl for her parents to return home from whatever catering job they'd been on – someone's wedding or 50th birthday party, perhaps. At that time, her parents had their own outside catering business and often worked until the early hours of the morning, and whilst her brother and sister and even the babysitter would all be fast asleep, Nora simply couldn't sleep until her Mum and Dad were safely home. And so she'd sit anxiously at the end of her bed, listening for the sound of their car, watching out for headlights as they turned into the drive. The moment she saw the car's headlights, sleep would take her, and so her parents never knew of her anxiety. Then a few years later, once her brother was old enough to ride a motorbike and go out courting, the same thing happened, and she'd lay awake sometimes until dawn, listening out for the drone of his moped signalling his safe return from an evening of romance. She'd worked out that she could hear the exact moment he dropped a couple of gears and turned off the main road towards home, over three miles distant. And here she was, still listening, still waiting.

Her heartbeat reverberated in her ears, and she felt sick to her stomach. This was not good. She knew it was not good.

The following morning when she awoke, she was alone in bed. He hadn't come home. She got up and had a shower, readying herself for work, then went downstairs into the kitchen to make coffee.

As the kettle boiled, she heard the front door open, and saw him creep in, trying not to be heard.

"Oh, there you are. Did you have a good night?" she

enquired, stopping him in his tracks. He looked and smelt terrible. His long thinning hair was matted as if he'd been pulled through a hedge backwards, and she could smell the sour, acid-drops stench of booze on his breath.

"Yep."

"Are you going to tell me where you've been?"

"Nope."

She picked up her car keys from the table and slammed the kitchen door, then slammed the front door on the way out, and on getting in her car she revved it to an alarming level before pulling off at speed – echoing his actions of the night before.

Our poor neighbours, she thought.

How Nora drove to work she'll never know, as she couldn't remember a single moment of the 30-minute journey, so wrapped up was she in the events of the previous night. It had to be the end, didn't it? It had to be. It felt so final. How does a relationship ever recover from something like that, from strangulation? The irony was not lost on her that it was a metaphor for their entire nine-year relationship. Nine years of tying each other up in emotional knots; of strangling each other with their incompatibility. And yet she loved him, and in his way, she knew he loved her too.

When she got to work, Jay asked her to go straight over to his office for dictation as he was leaving for a trip to the US later that day and he wanted to clear his desk. It really was the last thing in the world she felt capable of doing; she was so racked with emotion and exhaustion that she just wanted to curl up under her desk and sleep. But Jay set to work and somehow, Nora switched into concentration mode, though she'd never been any good at hiding her emotions. She wore her heart on her sleeve and after twenty minutes or so, Jay looked up from his desk.

"Are you alright, Nora?" he asked. He had a good emotional radar.

"…Not really," she sighed, and a tear trickled down her cheek.

"Oh dear – whatever's the matter?"

There was no way Nora would share the gory details of the previous night with her boss. She didn't want him to know how low they had sunk.

"I'm having some doubts about my relationship, Jay. I don't know what to do. I think it's over but a part of me is still invested in trying to make it work."

"Ah, I see – matters of the heart, eh? Never easy at the best of times. Why don't you consult the *I Ching*?"

"Really?" It was the last thing Nora expected to hear. "Do you think that would help?"

"Well, it is an Oracle, you know. Now then, the next letter is to David Attenborough. I'm hoping he will be Patron of The Seed School."

Back at her own desk, Nora started transcribing her shorthand, but she couldn't stop thinking about what Jay had said. *'It is an Oracle you know.'* That's exactly what she needed – some guidance, an answer…

When Cassandra eventually came into work, Nora wasted no time.

"Hey, Cassie, you do *I Ching* readings, don't you?"

"Sometimes. Why?" Cass raised a querying eyebrow.

"Will you do one for me?"

"Well, yes, of course I will, but you have to be certain you want to know the outcome."

"I do, I'm certain."

"Are you absolutely sure?"

"Yes. Absolutely. I have a specific question in my head, and I want – no Cass, I need an answer to it."

"Okay, fair enough. I can do a reading for you. When do you want to do it?"

"Tonight? After work."

"It's urgent, then?"

The day dragged on interminably. Nora couldn't concentrate and couldn't decipher her shorthand either. She had no energy and kept sighing and staring out of the window, until at 3.30 in the afternoon, Cassandra said, "Come on, Noo, let's go. Jay's not here, and the others have already left, so nobody will know if we shut up shop early. I can tell you're good for nothing right now. Let's go back to my place and do the reading – maybe then you'll be able to relax. I can feel your tension right over here on the other side of the office, for God's sake."

Nora smiled wanly. Cassie's antennae were picking up her signals too.

They drove in convoy through the village and out onto the old lighthouse road, then up a steep hill to a farmstead where Cass rented a cottage. Inside, the rooms were dark because the windows were small and the cob walls were two-feet thick, but it was cosy and warm and the red velvet drapes and twinkling fairy lights made her living room feel inviting, welcoming.

Cass lit some incense and some candles, and closed the curtains, then rummaged in her bureau and pulled out a book and a small bag with three coins in it. It was the *I Ching, The Book of Changes*.

Apt, thought Nora.

Cassandra instructed Nora to breathe deeply and to

focus on what it was she wanted to ask the Oracle.

"Do you want me to tell you what my question is?" Nora asked her friend.

"Only if you want to."

"I do want to. My question is, 'Is it time for me and Michael to go our separate ways?'"

Cassandra looked at her friend. She could've told her the answer to that one months ago without consulting the *I Ching*, but she also knew Nora would have to find out for herself, and probably the hard way.

"Okay, Nora. So, pick up the coins and cast them on the table."

Nora concentrated and did as she was asked, and Cassie wrote something down in her notepad.

"Now do it again Noo, keeping your question in the forefront of your mind."

They repeated this process until the hexagram was revealed: No. 40 – Liberation.

"Here's what it says in the book," Cassandra said, putting on her reading glasses. "A feeling of clarity and fresh opportunity follows a thunderstorm, or any time of extreme tension or obstacles. The storm has had the twofold effect of clearing the air and reducing tension. In the realm of human relationships, the rain of forgiveness can wash the human landscape clean after a period of intense conflict. This creates deliverance and freedom from hardship. Old relationship wounds are healed, and you are set free. Within each person liberation must be sought, for each of us makes our own prison.'" Cassie looked pointedly at her friend over the top of her glasses. "'The action to be taken is Untanglement.'"

"Wow..." Nora breathed out a huge sigh, one that

seemed to start in her feet and swirl its way through her entire body. "Wow. That's pretty clear, isn't it?"

"What does it say to you?"

"Well, that I need to untangle myself from this mess I've got into, from this prison I'm in – don't you think? That I need to set myself free. That I can forgive him and liberate myself and create the opportunities for change I've been longing for."

"How do you feel about that?"

"I've known it for a long time Cass, if I'm completely honest with you. I suppose I just needed to hear the truth of it. This reading really confirms things for me – that it's time to let go, it's time to move on." Nora looked at her friend who was nodding in agreement. "I thought I could help him, y'know? I thought I could make him happy – but I can't. I thought that if I was kind enough and loving enough, that he would heal, but it's not enough – because he has to *want* to heal, and he has to want to change, and he doesn't. He doesn't want to change – but I do." These words were painful for Nora to utter, and tears stung in her eyes. "For a while now I've realised that I can't fix him, Cassie. I can't fix him, I can only fix me. That's all I can do. And weirdly, I feel such clarity about it all now. Like I've made a decision that has been asking to be made for a long, long time – thanks to you." Nora reached over and hugged her friend.

"My pleasure, Noo. Sometimes all we need is permission to act. That's what the *I Ching* gives us."

When Nora got home, Michael was sitting at the kitchen table, waiting for her.

"I'm sorry," he said.

"I'm sorry, too," she replied, and she meant it.

He reached for her hands. "It's over, isn't it?" The look in his eyes was unbearably sad, but she was glad he knew.

"Yes, it's over."

He rose from the chair and wrapped his arms around her, and they stood in their kitchen and embraced, tears of love and loss mingling on their cheeks. Nine years of togetherness had come to an end and the pain of that was overwhelming; but there was no going back. Unlike all the other times they had called it a day, this time they knew it was over.

They held each other for a long time.

Then they let go.

Ice-cream in Galle

Rain awoke with a start to find Anuja bustling about getting his schoolbooks ready, eating the remainder of a mango that she'd left out for his breakfast.

"Why didn't you wake me, Nuji? I'll be late for work and you know what Panni's like about punctuality." Rain occasionally called her boss 'panni' – meaning pig – especially when he'd been particularly abusive or cruel, but in fact she thought it rather demeaning to pigs who, in her experience, were rather docile creatures.

"Sorry Rainy. I just thought you might need to rest a bit longer because you didn't sleep much last night."

"How do you know that?"

"Well, I heard you crying and then you were tossing and turning and sighing… Sometimes you wake me up with all your sighing."

"Oh. I'm sorry Nuji. I didn't mean to wake you. It's just – well, you know… I miss him so much. The sorrow, it's just so hard to bear, isn't it?"

"It is. But we will be alright. We will pull together,

like we always have done. Rainy and Nuji – the superhero Ninja Turtles!"

Anuja was obsessed with Ninja Turtles since the previous Christmas when he'd seen a *Ninja Turtle* annual for sale in that funny little tourist shop on the corner of the street by the market. He would creep in and pick it up and flick through its pages until the assistant behind the counter saw him and shooed him away. Rain desperately wanted to buy it for him, but it was extortionately priced at 20 rupees. She could feed them for a week on that and buy a candle to light at St Francis' church, a penance she'd carried out every week since her parents had died, to try and atone for her sins.

"Yeah, Nuji the Ninja!" Rain said giving him a hug. She loved this boy with all her heart, though secretly she thought he was a bit old for Ninja Turtles.

She dressed quickly, drank a glass of cold tea, grabbed the office key from where she'd hung it on a nail by the door and ran out of the house. It usually took her ten minutes to get to work, but on this morning, she did it in double-quick time, not wanting to start the day on a bad footing with her boss. But when she got there, he was nowhere to be seen. What luck.

She knew the PerfectPrint man would be coming in with the papers from the Court to be authorised by Mr Pigera. She'd begun to look forward to Wednesdays for that very reason. The PerfectPrint man had started saying hello to her, and she'd heard Mr Pigera called him Geethan, so now she knew his name. But where was Panni?

Under the counter in front of which their customers would stand to be served, on a wide shelf there was a large metal tray in which Mr Pigera placed all the papers he wanted Rain to file away, once he'd signed and witnessed them. On top of the pile she saw a scribbled note: 'Lakmini – mother ill. Am taking her to hospital today. Hold fort – Pigera.'

It was like the clouds parted and the sun came out. Her boss had taken a day off work. Praise be to God.

Rain breathed a huge sigh of relief. In that breath she released all the anxiety she usually held within her as she went about her day at the Notary's Office: worry that he might pick fault with her work and dock her wages, or worse, ask her to leave; worry that he might try and touch her again, or pin her against the wall in the store room like he'd done once before, his lips livid and specked with saliva; worry that she would have to default on her payments to Aunty-ji. But today was going to be a good day, because Panni was not there.

As she started to sort all the papers into alphabetical order, the grumpy man from the Department of Posts kicked the bottom of the office door open with his foot – a habit he had that drove Mr Pigera to distraction.

'Please do not kick my door,' he would say to the grumpy man, who would shrug, drop the allotted letters onto the counter and walk out without saying a word, and then slam the door behind him contemptuously.

'That man is son of a dog! I will speak to Department of Posts and get him fired!' She could see the postman made Pigera irate and so she approved of his grumpiness.

As usual, this morning the postman dropped a pile of letters on the counter, and turned and left as abruptly as he came in.

"Thank you," Rain shouted after him. "Thank you!"

She picked up the letters and shuffled them into a neat pile to put on Mr Pigera's desk, but one envelope in particular caught her attention. It was of a thicker paper than the rest and a different size, and it had a label on the front that was not hand-written but had been printed somehow. And it had her name on it.

How strange, thought Rain. Nobody knows I work here. How can it be for me? And then it dawned on her and she tore the letter open.

Dear Lakmini

It was lovely to receive your letter and to know that we have a reader of our magazine in Sri Lanka. I was so sorry to learn about your parents and your difficult circumstances, so as you requested, I put an advert in the last issue of 'Awaken' to ask for sponsors to help you buy a sewing machine. I am delighted to say that we had quite a good response. I enclose a list of the names and addresses of all the people who sent in a donation to us, as you will need to contact them to arrange for the item of clothing to be made.

The total sum raised for your sewing machine was £100 which at the current exchange rate works out at just over 5,600 rupees. I hope this will be enough for you to purchase a good quality sewing machine. I have arranged with the Galle branch of Western Union for you to collect the money at your earliest convenience. All you need to do is take a form of identification with you and quote the following code: QX77346

I do hope that once you have your sewing machine, you will be able to earn enough money to be comfortable. I have also arranged for a complementary subscription of the magazine to be sent to this address for one year, as our gift to you.

Thank you for reading our magazine.

Yours sincerely, Nora Harris

Lakmini dropped to her knees, unable to take in the words written upon the paper. 5,600 rupees… FIVE THOUSAND SIX HUNDRED RUPEES! She looked at the list of names.

William Cadman	£25
Karen Allen	£15
George Baker	£20
Mary Boyd	£25
Nora Harris	£15

She re-read the letter and she re-read the list. Such strange sounding names, but these people were now her friends; they always would be. *William Cadman* she said to herself. *He must be a man because William Wordsworth, the poet, was a man.* Karen Allen she wasn't so sure about. George Baker – yes, she was sure George was a man's name because wasn't that Maxim's real name in *Rebecca*? Mary was definitely a woman because she knew all about Mary, mother of Jesus. And Nora Harris… Nora was the one who had written to her; Nora was the one who had arranged the advert. Nora was a kind person. She was sure Nora was a woman's name. She'd be making clothes for men and women.

Then a wave of anxiety hit her. How was she going to get to Galle to collect the money? There was no way on earth she had enough money to get a tuk-tuk, unless she defaulted on Aunty-ji's payment this week... She could do that. Because she had made a decision. Once she had collected the money, the first thing she was going to do, even before she looked for a sewing machine to buy, was to settle the debt with Aunty-ji, once and for all.

She picked up the note that her boss had written on and turned it over, talking to herself as she worked out her sums.

"Let me see. I have been working here for 15 weeks and I have not defaulted a payment. That means I have paid off... 375 rupees from the debt."

She scribbled 375 on the paper.

"The original debt which I don't believe could possibly be so much but is what I have to pay Aunty-ji was 3,220 rupees. For heaven's sake, how can it be that much?"

She scribbled 3,220 on the paper.

"3,220 minus 375..."

She did the calculations.

"So, that's 2845 rupees owed to that miserable old woman. That leaves me with... 2755 rupees for a sewing machine. I should be able to get a good one for that."

But then another thought hit her. How long would 2755 rupees last for her and Anuja to live on? She worked out that she was earning about 2,000 rupees a year but after paying her debts, she was making ends meet on less than 700 rupees – it was not really enough to live on, but 2,755 would be. She could buy herself a new cot bed and the *Ninja Turtles* annual for Nuji and still have money left over. They could live well for two years maybe longer and she could leave Panni's employ for ever.

But I would be letting Nora down, she thought. *I said I would buy a sewing machine and I have to make everyone some clothes... I have to keep my word.*

She was lost in her thoughts, in particular of never having to work for Panni again. It was so tempting, so very tempting for Rain.

Suddenly the door flew open and she looked up, but nobody was there. As the draught and smells from the outside world engulfed her, momentarily she thought she heard a voice.

Your word is your bond, Rain.

"Bapu? Bapu!"

But another voice replied. The man from PerfectPrint was easing his way through the door, a huge cardboard box in his arms, so big he could barely see over it.

"Good morning," he said shyly. "Where is Mr Pigera, please?"

"He is away on family business today," Rain replied, still reeling from Nora's letter. "Can I help?"

"I see. Geethan Cooray, at your service." He extended a hand, still gripping the box, and the sight of it made her laugh.

"Here, please let me help you with that," she said, and grabbing the cardboard flaps on top of the box, together they heaved it onto the counter.

"I'm Lakmini Perera," she said, holding out her hand shyly, though a formal handshake seemed strange to Rain, as in her mind, they were already friends.

"Pleased to make your acquaintance, "Geethan said,

shaking her hand. He didn't seem quite so shy now Mr Pigera was out of the office.

"Did you walk all the way over here carrying that heavy box, or did you get a tuk-tuk?"

Geethan looked over his shoulder conspiratorially then leaned towards her.

"Sshh – don't tell a soul. The court administrator gives me 5 rupees to get a tuk-tuk, but I walked here carrying it, and will keep the 5 rupees. I'm saving up for a new motorbike."

"A new one? Have you got one already?"

"Oh yes, but it is very old and only 50cc. Always breaking down. I want a 100cc scooter so I can go faster and further!"

"But where do you want to go faster and further?"

"I like to go to Yala with my camera. I like taking photos of wildlife."

"You have a motorbike and a camera?" Rain was very impressed.

Geethan looked to the floor. "We are not wealthy, but now I am an only child, my parents spoil me when they can."

"Oh, I'm so sorry. What happened? Don't tell me if you don't want to."

"My sister passed away two years ago. She was born with lots of problems but in the end her heart failed."

He looked at Rain and saw the tears in her eyes. He didn't realise they were for her own pain.

"I'm sorry, Miss Lakmini. I should not have told you. I do not mean to upset you."

Rain sniffed and wiped a tear from her cheek with the back of her hand. "It is alright Geethan, really. It just made me think about my parents who died in a traffic accident nine months ago."

"Oh no! I am so sorry to hear that. How very sad." He looked into her eyes, his own full of compassion. It seemed like the first time someone other than Anuja had genuinely acknowledged her pain since the night of the accident when Sergeant Gomes knelt down to give her the terrible news.

"Look at us!" Geethan smiled, trying to lighten the atmosphere. "We hardly know one another and here we are sharing stories of our tragedies. What good things can we focus on instead?"

Rain looked at this man – well, hardly more than a boy, really; probably only a year or so older than her – and felt intuitively that he had a good heart and that he was trustworthy. She'd learned to read the signs of those who were sad, angry, greedy, mean or lecherous, and Geethan showed none of them.

"Well, we can celebrate the fact that my boss is not here today – but sshh! Don't tell anyone I said that."

Somehow, in echoing his own furtive confession with hers, they were beginning to form a friendship.

"Now we are thick as thieves," he said. "Can I help you unload the box?"

"I can manage, thank you," she said, but a plan had been forming in Rain's mind since the moment Geethan uttered the word 'motorbike'. "Geethan-ji, what time do you finish work today?" She hoped that using the honorific 'ji' version of his name would endear her to him.

He looked at her, questioningly. "Well, as it happens, today is a half-day as they are coming to fumigate the print works. They do it once every six weeks to keep mosquitos, cockroaches and other bugs at bay, so we have to vacate the building and today's the day. Why do you ask?"

"Well, the thing is, I need to get to the Western Union in Galle, and I was wondering if you could take me there on your motorbike?"

She knew she was being bold, reckless even, but she had to sort this money out and today the stars seemed to be aligned in her favour. And she trusted this young man in front of her, though she had no reason to.

Geethan hesitated. "Miss Lakmini, my motorbike is a heap of rust. We might not make it. Why not get a tuk-tuk instead?"

"I don't have… I can't afford it. But never mind. I will find another way."

"I have money. I have the 5 rupees from the last few weeks saved in a purse – here…" and he drew out a small drawstring bag from the pocket of his black trousers, part of his work uniform that gave him an air of authority when most men in Lagentle were bare-chested and wore sarongs.

He jiggled the bag so she could hear that there was plenty of money in it.

"Oh no, I couldn't ask you to do that, Geethan-ji. It's your savings for your new motorbike." Then a thought struck her. "But, actually, once I have been to the Western Union, I can pay you back in full."

"Well, let us do it then."

"So, you'll come with me? I've never been to Galle."

"Yes, I will come with you, and neither have I. Let's have an adventure!"

"Thank you so much Geethan-ji. I really am grateful.

Can you meet me back here at lunch time?"

"But what about Mr Pigera? He is bound to hear that you have closed the shop."

"Yes, I know. But it is a risk I have to take. I will tell him I was sick and had to go home. I don't like telling white lies, but he tells me them all the time, so I don't feel so bad!"

It was true. Panni was always lying to her. "I'm going out to see a client," he would say, then ten minutes later, she would catch sight of him standing in the market, smoking and chatting with the stall holders; or he would tell her he needed to do some reading and was not to be disturbed, and she would notice that in fact he wasn't reading the court notes or the affidavits, but was staring lasciviously at a glossy magazine with photos of half-naked white women in it. It revolted her. He revolted her.

The plan was hatched.

At the appointed time, Geethan arrived at the Notary's Office and Rain slipped out and closed the door, locking the padlock and putting the key in her purse. Then she placed the purse carefully in a plastic bag she had found under the counter, into which she had also placed Nora's letter containing the Western Union code. She felt such a great weight of responsibility, carrying these items. Never before had she been entrusted with anything so important.

"We will have to call in at my house first so I can get my ID card," she told Geethan. "I am afraid of losing it, so I don't carry it with me, although I suppose I should."

"I've never been asked to produce mine," he said, but

I have it in my wallet. From his other trouser pocket, he produced a thin folded leather case with a plastic window in one side, so that the ID card could be read without having to be removed. Rain was impressed. *A wallet and a purse!* she marvelled.

As they walked to the taxi-rank, Rain became quiet. It was the first time she'd been there since her father had died. Geethan seemed not to notice.

They walked up to the first tuk-tuk in the line.

"How much for a tuk-tuk to Galle, please?" she asked the taxi driver.

"20 rupees one way; 35 return," growled the tuk-tuk driver, taking a long drag on his beedi cigarette.

"How long will it take?"

The tuk-tuk driver turned and looked at Rain inquisitively, as if he was wondering why on earth a girl like her wanted to go to Galle. "Two hours each way if it is not too busy. You want tuk-tuk or not?"

"Oh, yes. Return please," said Rain, "but we have to call in at my house first. It's on Ingodapokunadi Road. How much extra will it be?"

"Ingodapokunadi Road, ha? Did you know a man called Danidu Perera?"

Rain bowed her head. "Yes. He was my father."

"Just as I thought. You look like him and he was my friend. No extra charge. Hop in."

Rain turned and beamed at Geethan and they jumped into the back of the tuk-tuk which pulled away in a cloud of dense blue smoke. The tuk-tuk driver didn't say much, but then they could hardly have heard him over the racket of the engine.

As they arrived outside her house, Rain was acutely

aware of how down-at-heel it must seem to someone like Geethan, who had his own motorbike and camera, but he smiled at her, nonetheless. She felt ashamed of her home, of its pock-holed and rusting tin roof, the peeling paint on the door and the curtainless windows. She ran in to get her ID card whilst the tuk-tuk driver turned the vehicle around so it was pointing back towards the main road to Galle, all the time revving the engine as if there was no time to spare – which was the case for tuk-tuk drivers. Time was money and he'd made a deal with them; he didn't want to hang about.

They set off at a pace, the tuk-tuk engine straining as the driver opened up the throttle. Instinctively, Rain grabbed Geethan's arm as they rounded a corner and she lost her balance.

"Do they all drive as fast as this?" she shouted.

"Yes! Mad men, all of them," Geethan grinned. He was obviously enjoying the ride.

The road to Galle took them north-west, parallel to the coastline, sometimes within view of the vast and sparkling Indian Ocean and sometimes running between villages lined with the same kind of house that Rain lived in. Occasionally, she could see train tracks that also ran alongside the road then veered off inland. She began to relax. How stunning the scenery was. She had never thought this way about the country she lived in before, perhaps because she had never seen much of it, but now she realised it was breathtakingly beautiful; dense forests fringed with coconut palms and fields of crops – rice she thought – and was that maybe a papaya plantation they just passed?

She smiled at Geethan, who was also gazing at the

scenery passing them by in a blur of vibrant colour.

"Lovely, isn't it?" she said.

"A day to remember," he replied, which wasn't what Rain was expecting at all. Everything this young man said seemed to please her in some way. He had a lightness about him, a jauntiness. He didn't seem weighed down by life's sorrows as she felt she was. No, he seemed... What was it? He seemed eager for life's adventures. She liked that about him.

Fortunately, there were hardly any hold-ups, just the odd cow wandering in the middle of the road, and busier traffic in the villages, and although it did take two hours to get to Galle, they enjoyed every moment of it. Neither one spoke of it but what they enjoyed most was being in such close proximity to each other. It felt illicit almost, it felt exciting.

Eventually the tuk-tuk driver slowed down as they neared the central bus station in Galle.

"Do you know where the Western Union is?" Rain asked him.

"Of course – we tuk-tuk drivers know where everything is. People's Bank. Not far. Near the Fort." And off they zoomed, through the traffic and animals, Rain not daring to look in case a collision ensued. But the tuk-tuk driver was skilled and before long, they were parked outside the People's Bank.

"Half money now, please," the driver said, turning around and holding his hand out.

Geethan produced his drawstring purse and counted out 20 rupees, giving the money to the driver.

"You go. I wait here. Don't be long."

They hopped out of the tuk-tuk and into the throng.

Galle was much bigger and busier than Lagentle with more tourists, more shops, more traffic – more of everything. Rain looked about her at the women wearing western-style clothing; skirts above their knees and shoes with heels so high she felt that surely they would topple over. She felt drab in comparison to them; dowdy in her old and worn sari, torn at the hem and not entirely clean, her hair scraped back from her face and tied with an elastic band rather than falling in the bouncing curls that adorned these women. She wondered what Geethan thought of them and whether he too had compared them with her.

As she took in the hustle and bustle of the scenes all around her, Rain suddenly became overwhelmed by the strangest feeling. What was it? Panic? Claustrophobia? Foreboding? It was as if the people in the streets were being propelled by an unseen force; as if a powerful whirlwind had picked them up and was whisking them along, jostling them together, bunching them up and causing them to push and shove and fight for space. Her mind reeled, the busyness and hectic speed of life in Galle made her feel unsteady on her feet. She felt as if she might drown in the chaos of it all.

As if he could read her mind, Geethan reached out and took her hand. He looked at her, his eyebrow slightly raised, questioning if it was alright to do so, and she smiled her approval. It felt good to hold his hand.

"This way Lakmini, follow me," he said, and together they dodged the traffic and mayhem and found the door of the People's Bank.

Suddenly, Rain felt nervous. What if they refused to give her the money? What if they doubted that someone like her could possibly deserve five thousand rupees? But Geethan squeezed her hand and it gave her strength.

"Ready?" he asked.

"Ready!" she said, and together, still hand in hand, they went into the bank. Rain realised that Geethan had not even asked what business she had there.

"Good afternoon sir, good afternoon madam," smiled the pretty woman behind the glass panel. "How may I help you today?"

And it was as easy as that. Rain produced her ID, and the letter showing the code number, and the receptionist checked her records, counted out the money and handed it over to Rain.

"Thank you, madam, sir. Have a good day," she said, already looking behind them to the next customer in the queue. Rain all but skipped out of the bank, a wide smile illuminating her face.

"I think the cashier lady thought we were married!" Geethan chuckled, once again catching hold of her hand to guide her through the busy streets.

Rain looked at this handsome young man standing next to her, a stranger really, and yet she felt a bond of friendship growing between them. In that moment she wondered what it would be like to be married to someone like him. To have his level of optimism and certainty in her life, every day. To feel safe – for that was how she felt this afternoon. She felt safe, for the first time since her father had died.

"Thank you so much Geethan-ji," she smiled at him. "I could not have done this without you. And she counted out the 20 rupees and handed them back to him.

"No, thank you, Lakimini. Please keep the money. I

have had fun today, and I'd like to have a little more fun before we go home. Did you see that ice-cream parlour on the corner, near where the tuk-tuk is parked? Shall we go there and eat ice-cream?"

"I would like ice-cream, but only if you will take the money for the tuk-tuk."

Geethan looked at her and saw the pleasure she would take in being able to pay him back. "Okay, it's a deal, but only if you let me buy the ice-cream!"

Rain had never eaten ice-cream before and didn't really know what it was, but she certainly wanted to have more fun. She knew she wanted more of this.

They dodged the watchful eyes of the tuk-tuk driver and Geethan bought two ice-creams in little plastic tubs with plastic spoons. Rain could not believe how much they cost – but the ice-cream tasted so exquisite she nearly swooned with pleasure. She had never dreamed that something could taste like this: so sweet yet sharp with mango, so creamy and delicious. She savoured every spoonful, slowly, purposefully. She didn't want to forget this day in case she never had another like it.

"Geethan-ji? Would you please call me Rain," she ventured, as she scraped every last molecule of ice-cream from the sides of the tub.

"Rain? How lovely! But why?"

"All my friends and family call me Rain, because I was born in a terrible rainstorm. I like it when people call me Rain."

It was true, except for the bit about the friends. Geethan was her only friend.

"Well then, Rain, I think perhaps we had better hurry back or our tuk-tuk driver will have gone home, and we will be stranded here in Galle forever."

"I wouldn't mind!" she said a little flirtatiously and ran ahead of him through the crowds.

That night Rain lay on her damp cardboard mattress, again unable to sleep, but for once it was not due to grief or anxiety, but to the excitement of the day – a day that she could not have imagined in her wildest dreams. For suddenly, there was hope. Hope that she might be able to work her way out of the grinding poverty she'd known for most of her life. Hope that she'd made a new friend, someone whom she could turn to for help and guidance. But most of all, she hoped that the worst was behind her because the underlying, faint yet insistent feeling she had was that somehow, she had turned a corner. And mixed with the hope was another feeling – that she need not be a victim to fate; because hadn't she gone to see Sergeant Gomes, and got a contract drawn up to repay Aunty-ji? And hadn't she written to *Awaken* magazine and asked for sponsorship to buy a sewing machine; and now here she was, with more than five thousand rupees, an unbelievable sum of money that would help her to change everything for the better. Slowly but surely, she had begun to build a new life for herself and Anuja.

She recalled the conversation she'd had with Geethan on their return journey to Lagentle, the two of them huddled closely together so they could hear one another speak over the din of the tuk-tuk engine. Geethan had asked her what made her happy, and she had been unable to answer him at first.

"But Rain," he nudged her arm gently with his, "there must be something that gives you joy?"

"Since my Bapu and Amma died, I have not felt joy," she said and then added, "at least, not until this day. I think ice-cream gives me joy."

"There you have it, Rain. Ice-cream. It is truly a most joyous thing."

"So, what gives you joy, Geethan-ji?"

"Oh! So much. I love photography most. I have a camera which my father gave me for my 18th birthday last year." (*Oh, so he is a little older than me,* Rain thought.) "I think it is the act of being observant that I enjoy most: of seeing things where others might see nothing. Of capturing a moment that may have been lost forever had I not been there. And I love waiting for my film to be developed – it takes such a long time as it has to go by post to Colombo and it is very expensive so I have to save up for ages before I can send it off – but when my photos come back, it is so exciting. Some are not so good, but one or two, I am proud of and my Amma says, 'Give me that, I want to put it in a frame.' She has so many of my photos on the wall!"

Whilst he was talking, she had become mesmerised by his eyes, the way they glinted and widened as he spoke about his passion for photography, then softened when he looked at her. She looked away quickly, a sudden shyness overwhelming her.

"Actually, there is something that gives me joy," she said, then suddenly wished she hadn't.

"What is it?"

She'd never before told anyone of her secret, in case they thought her foolish, but somehow she felt that

Geethan might approve – or at least that he wouldn't tease her about it.

"Please don't laugh at me, but I like to write stories and sometimes poems too."

"Well, I think that's wonderful," he beamed at her. "I wouldn't laugh at you for writing poems, Lakmini, I mean, Rain – you see, I do want to be your friend! So, what do you write about?"

"I… I write about what the birds sometimes say to me; or of how a fish once saved my life. I write about the big green toad with red eyes who lives under the front step of our house, who always croaks before a thunderstorm ."

"That is so interesting, Rain. A green toad with red eyes? I'd like to photograph him one day, and I would like to read some of your stories and poems one day, too, if you'd let me."

"Would you?" She was genuinely surprised.

"Of course!"

"Well, that might be difficult because they are mostly written on scraps of paper that get lost or blown away on the wind or burnt with the rubbish by mistake. But it doesn't matter – they are not very good."

"But I might think they are good."

"Like I might think your photos are good?"

"Exactly!"

"So, perhaps I could see your photos one day, then?"

"Only if you will read me one of your stories."

"Well, yes – if I can find one." She enjoyed the playfulness of their conversation. The little bargains they were striking.

At that moment, the two of them were thrown together courtesy of a monumental pothole in the road.

Geethan instinctively reached out to steady Rain but held on to her a moment longer than was necessary and Rain felt a thrill of excitement course through her body. The tuk-tuk driver looked around to apologise and raised an eyebrow at the sight of these two young people in an embrace.

"Baadu – road bad," he said.

The Thought
Counts

Nora was awoken by weak sunlight filtering through the thin curtains of a small, single-glazed window. Despite the January sunshine, it was bitterly cold inside the caravan and she could see her breath condensing in the air above her head. She'd stoked the woodburner before going to bed, but it was old and inefficient and only half-burned the damp logs before it gave up and went out. When this happened and it was almost as cold inside as it was outside, her breath would hit the ceiling above her bed, condense and then turn into droplets of water, and drip back down onto her duvet. Many a morning since she'd moved into this old and uninsulated caravan, she'd woken up damp and chilled to the bone. She missed the warmth of another body in her bed on nights like these.

She had tried sleeping in the separate bedroom at the far end of the caravan for a few nights, but it was even colder there, the frigid temperatures driving her back into the living room. So, she had made up the sofa-bed and now she slept there, any lingering heat from the woodburner feeling like a blessing for as long as it lasted. Going to the bathroom, which was next to the bedroom, took a leap of courage. It was, as Cass so aptly put it, "Baltic in there."

She got out of bed, still wrapped in her dressing gown because it was too cold to take it off the night before, and padded across to the kitchen area, on the other side of the living room to fill the kettle. She turned the tap on, and it chugged and vibrated but no water came out. The pipes had frozen. She had some orange juice in the fridge but when she tried to pick her glass out of the washing-up bowl, she found that it had frozen in the inch or so of water in the bottom. It literally was freezing in her new home.

When Nora left Mikey, she'd done so in a hurry and had only taken one of everything: one pillow, one cup, one glass, one plate, filling her boot with the strangest of things that she didn't really need, like a spider plant, which instantly went a sickly yellow colour in the cold of the caravan. She had taken the iron but not the ironing board; she took her raincoat but forgot her wellies. She really did need to go back to Mikey's place – once her own home – and pick up some more of her stuff, but she couldn't face it. She couldn't face him, not yet anyway.

Now that she'd left Mikey, Nora had come to realise how much of herself had been subsumed by the relationship, how compliant she had become in order that she didn't constantly feel that churning anxiety in the pit of her stomach. Against all her feminist principles, she had been obedient, bending to his whim, doing as she was told. Mostly. And as the reality of being single settled upon her, a sense of outrage grew ever stronger. At first she was outraged by her own complicity in what was to all intents and purposes an abusive relationship, but then she felt incredible anger towards Mikey. All the slights and cruelties, all his careless hurtful words haunted her now. "You're just a fucking secretary Nora... You're a pathetic wage slave... Don't ever question me... I'll do as I please... You're acting like a child... You're so stupid..." How had she put up with that for nine years? And why? There were occasional redeeming factors, like the night Mikey had opened up to her and in floods of tears had told Nora how much he loved her parents; how he knew his own parents were dysfunctional and motivated by their addictions and how that had made him who he was. But in order for him to say that he'd had to drink himself almost into oblivion, and he didn't want to hear Nora tell him that he could change. Oh, no – that would be a step too far. Nevertheless, Mikey opening up like that gave her faith that things could get better; it was a crumb of hope, a morsel that kept her going, but it wasn't really enough. It was never quite enough.

Nora knew that the real reason she couldn't go back home and get another glass and an extra sweater was because she was afraid of venting nine years of anger, and making matters between her and Mikey even worse. After all, they were still joint owners of the house, so she had to keep some degree of civility between them. But God knows, she wanted to confront him – she wanted to make him see how he'd ground her down with his indifference, how he'd suppressed her vitality and exuberance with his cold-heartedness. Of late, she'd started having dreams about that night when they'd fought on the stairs, only this time it was Nora who kept on squeezing, who wouldn't let go...

She slumped dejectedly on her bed, hugging herself with her arms to keep the warmth from escaping out of her dressing gown. In truth, she was finding being single both wonderfully exhilarating and desperately lonely. She loved only having to answer to herself, having peace and quiet when she needed it, eating what she liked when she liked and not spending long nights wondering where Mikey was, or what mood he would be in when he came home. But at times, sadness overwhelmed her and despite everything, she missed Mikey. Her heart ached, not so much for him, but for what might have been, for what could have been...

She sighed and began to get ready for work, consoling herself that she could at least have her breakfast there. It wasn't possible to have a shower what with everything being frozen – she just hoped the pipes would be thawed when she returned in the evening, so she could at least cook a meal and wash-up.

She opened the caravan door and gasped as breathing in the cold air felt like swallowing knives. She saw that a thick layer of blue-green ice like old glass had slumped across the windscreen and welded the handles of her car firmly shut, and annoyingly, she couldn't even get any water to try and free-up the wipers and the locks because all her taps were frozen solid.

She stood there looking at her car wondering what to do when Andy appeared. Andy was her landlord, a friend of Mikey's from way back, when they'd been in a band together and had set out for the bright lights of London to make their name, only to end up a few months later living in a tawdry squat in Rotherhithe, playing to half-empty pubs and disinterested punters. Their band was called Riotous. The irony was not lost on Nora.

"Alright Nora?"

"Morning Andy. Have you got running water? I'm all frozen up in there." She gestured towards the caravan.

"Bloody hell! Do you want a cuppa?"

"Nah – it's alright. I'll get one at work, but I need to start my car first."

"Hold on a tick," he said, "I'll get some hot water from the house." Andy disappeared back into the pretty cob farmhouse where he lived with his wife and three beautiful little girls – all under six years of age – leaving Nora out in the cold, stamping her feet and wringing her gloved hands, trying to keep warm. He reappeared with a steaming bucket of hot water and some de-icer spray, and before long, they had the door open and the engine running, the remaining ice on the windscreen slowly melting as the heaters belched out warm air.

"Cheers Andy, you're a life-saver," she said, handing the empty bucket back to him.

"No worries. Actually Nora, I wanted to catch you before work this morning. Umm..." he looked down at his feet, as if he didn't quite know how to say what he wanted to say. "Well, to cut a long story short, me and Charlotte decided to put the house on the market. We want to move to Scotland to be near Charlie's family. I thought you should be the first to know, but obviously it means you'll have to find somewhere else to rent."

Don't worry, it's already on my radar, Nora thought. *I can't stand it much longer in this icebox.*

"Oh, wow! Big changes coming up for you guys then. Okay, Andy. Thanks for letting me know. Any idea when this is going to happen?"

"Well, that's the thing, Nora. We put the house on the market on Monday, then we got a viewing yesterday, and they want to buy it. The estate agent hasn't even put the For Sale sign up yet and it looks like we've already sold."

"Shit! Ooops, sorry Andy. That's great news for you and Charlie, obviously. It's just a bit... unexpected, that's all. But I'm not surprised you've sold it so quickly – this is such a lovely place."

"Look, you know how these things go. It'll probably be six weeks or so before all the contracts go through. That should give you plenty of time to find somewhere else to rent."

"Yeah, plenty of time," Nora agreed, but felt a sudden pang of anxiety. Winter lets were easy enough to find in this tourist hotspot, but in the summer all those cottages were rented out to holidaymakers meaning long-term lets were few and far between, and expensive too. And that's what she felt she needed; something long-term, a bit of stability in her life.

She drove to work slowly and not just because of the treacherous conditions, but because her mind was now in turmoil. Suddenly, she needed to find somewhere to live, and quickly. She knew she could ask her parents if she could move back with them, and that would be fine, it really would, but she felt it would be such a backward step. She was young and independent and wanted to find her own way in the world. She didn't want to go running back to Mum and Dad as soon as times got tough. She knew she could also stay with her sister Louisa for a bit, but she had her own family and troubles: two kids, a husband who Nora felt was often absent, even when he was there in the room, and she was recovering from surgery and radiotherapy. No, Louisa had enough on her plate already. She could stay with her brother Dan, who had a dairy farm about 30 miles inland, and that would be okay too, because she got on well with her brother who was kind and funny – one of life's good guys – but that would be one hell of a commute to work every day... Nora would just have to keep an eye on the local papers and put word out amongst her friends that she needed somewhere to rent. Something would turn up. Hopefully.

When she finally got to work, she was the first one there as usual. The office woodburner had almost gone out, but it was still much warmer there than her caravan. She put the kettle on and made a cup of strong black coffee, then raked the embers and blew on them until an orange glow appeared. She added shreds of paper and thin sticks of dried kindling, all the time blowing and caressing the orange glow into a flame. The paper caught, the kindling smoked, and warmth returned to her world.

As the morning progressed, the other members of staff turned up for work in dribs and drabs, all with their tales of woe over the weather. The postman was late, his nose so cold it was as red as his jacket. He now delivered their ever expanding pile of post in a hessian sack which Nora began to sort through, because although Cassie was due in later, her fingers were still too cold to begin typing. She needed to ease herself into the day and opening letters and parcels for half an hour was as good a start as any. At the bottom of the pile, she was surprised to see a parcel neatly bound with string, addressed to her. As soon as she saw the Sri Lankan postmark, she knew it was from Lakmini. Nora snipped open the string and peeled off the tape, and saw that on top of a tissue-paper parcel was a letter.

```
Dear Nora

I pray this letter finds you well
and in good health. As promised, I
have now bought myself a good
quality sewing machine - USHA Royal
Emerald for Rs.2,350 - I have
enclosed a photograph of myself and
the sewing machine which I thought
you might like to see. The photo was
taken by my good friend, Geethan
Cooray Jnr.
```

Nora gazed at the photograph of a beautiful young Sri Lankan woman, probably around 16 or 17 years of age, standing in front of a dark green sewing machine fixed to a table, with a treadle foot. The girl – Lakmini – was wearing a pretty sari of white material with orange floral prints on it, and a border of red embroidery. Her face looked so serene, a gentle smile playing on her lips, and she was holding in her hand, a sign, which read, 'With my sincere thanks to *Awaken* magazine and all the kind sponsors for helping with the purchase of the USHA Royal Emerald.' Nora was so touched and had no doubt that Lakmini would send a copy of this photo to all the people who had sponsored her.

```
Since I bought the machine, I have
been able to earn around Rs.5/day
extra, sewing sheets, tablecloths,
```

napkins etc., for the tourism industry in this area, but I am also going to make items of clothing for the tourists who often want to take home saris, kurtas, sarongs etc. I have spoken to Mr de Silva who runs the tourist shop and he wants me to make some stock for him. He says Sri Lankan clothes do not fit visitors from overseas, so they need be made-to-measure. I am excited to be starting my new business. Thanks to you, dear sister Nora for helping me with the sewing machine. It is a kindness I will never forget.

I have something I need to tell you and I pray you will agree, dear sister, but the balance of the money I have used to pay off a debt accrued by my parents. This way, I can start afresh without owing money to anyone and it means myself and my brother will have a much more secure future.

Also, in this parcel, I have enclosed the blouse I have made for you by way of thanks for your support. As you said size Medium, I hope it is not too big, but please, if it is, send it back to me and I

```
will make alterations, no charge.
With my sincere thanks and love,

Your sister,

Lakmini 'Rain' Perera
```

Nora loved the way that Lakmini addressed her as 'sister' and noticed how the letter, which this time was typewritten, did not have a single mistake in it and was laid out professionally with dates, addresses, paragraphs and perfect punctuation. The paper it was typed on was so thin that the full stop and comma keys on the typewriter perforated it with little holes. Lakmini obviously had many talents and though life had been hard for one so young, Nora had a feeling that she would do well for herself.

Gently, Nora opened the tissue paper parcel to reveal a neatly folded white blouse with exquisite turquoise-blue embroidery on the collar and sleeves and around the three buttonholes at the top of the garment. She shook it out and held it up against herself. There was no doubt it was beautifully made, but it was so small, Nora wondered if it would even fit her ten-year old niece.

"What have you got there, then?" Cass asked as she blew into the office like a whirl of autumn leaves and stamped her feet on the mat to shake the snow off her boots, that had now begun to fall outside.

"My blouse from Lakmini." Nora held it up for Cass to admire.

"Oh wow! It's so beautiful... look at all the work on the collar and sleeves. I think she must have sewn all that by hand, but it's too small for you, Noo..."

"I know! When she asked for my measurements, I just said to make it medium-sized, but obviously women in Sri Lanka must be way more petite than us Westerners."

"You're not kidding! I couldn't even get into it. What a shame you won't be able to wear it, though."

"Yeah, but I can give it to Louisa's eldest, Rosie – I think it'll fit her, and she'll love it. It's the thought that counts, isn't it?"

"Yeah, that's a nice idea." Cass hooked her coat onto the peg by the door but kept her woolly hat and gloves on for a while longer.

"I'm last in again, I see," she grinned.

"Not by much. Everyone's had a bit of an adventure getting to work today."

"Hey, guess what? You know we went for that walk on Boxing Day to Stipeberry, and you were looking at that little cottage and saying how much you'd like to live there?"

"Yeah – Queenie's Cottage it was called." Nora had at once fallen in love with the place – it was perched on the edge of a sheer cliff, its front windows looking out across the bay towards the pretty little village of Shute and on the other side of the front garden, the stream that had cascaded all the way down the steep sided valley turned into a thundering waterfall. The atmosphere of the bay in which Stipeberry lay – probably twenty miles wide from northernmost tip to southernmost – was tangible; calm yet brooding, peaceful and yet with the constant undertow of rocks and pebbles that were shuffled by the restless tide, the air faintly perfumed with the piquant aroma of damp woodland floor that emanated from the dense swathes of oak and ash that clothed the steep cliffs, and which she could smell even down on the foreshore.

And it was a quaint little cottage, to be sure, white-washed on the outside walls, with dark blue window frames and the same colour for the front door. Nora had cautiously peered in through the windows. 'It's empty, Cass! God, I'd love to live here, I really would...' In that moment, in that utterance, her longing was palpable, as if it emerged from her body like a plume of smoke and enveloped the cottage in her desire. She wondered how such a beautiful place could stand empty and unloved. 'I'd give anything to live here, instead of that battered old caravan. Wouldn't it be wonderful?'

Cassandra had looked at her, askance. 'Not really. It's north-facing, Nora. It'd be bloody freezing in the winter because you wouldn't get any sunshine from November to March, and then for the rest of the year, you'd be inundated with tourists looking in through the windows just like you are now.'

'I wonder who Queenie was?'

'I don't know – probably some old hedge witch with delusions of grandeur,' but Cassie's sarcasm was lost on Nora who wasn't listening; she was envisaging living in Queenie's Cottage, all cosy in the sitting room with its huge bay window overlooking the sea.

"Well, it's being advertised for rent. I read it in the paper this morning. It's owned by the National Trust."

Nora's head went into a spin as Cassie's words roused her from her reverie. "You've got to be kidding me?"

"I'm not, look – I brought the paper in to show you."

"No, no, you don't get it, Cass. Andy gave me notice to quit the caravan, this morning. And then you see Queenie's

Cottage for rent. The place I've longed to live in ever since we saw it... What a coincidence, don't you think?"

"I think it's more than coincidence, it's synchronicity. It's meant to be, Nora. Give them a ring, quick. There's bound to be loads of people after it."

The blood rushed from Nora's head and she felt a bit dizzy. In that brief moment, she'd set her heart on living at Queenie's Cottage; it was already hers and she couldn't bear the thought of someone else living there. She took the paper from Cassandra, who'd circled the advert in red pen, and dialled the number.

"Bloody hell... there's no answer, Cass."

"Don't worry - just try again later. Their staff probably haven't got into the office yet – look at it out there! It's snowing hard now. I'll make coffee."

Nora looked at the fat flakes of snow as they swirled around the courtyard garden outside the office window, settling on the path and the windowsills, softening harsh outlines, making everywhere beautiful. There was a gentle hum in the office as people settled about their day and before long, Jay buzzed her phone extension and asked her to bring the post over and take down some dictation.

"Cass, I have to go to Jay's office now," Nora whispered to her friend, so as not to disturb the others. "Can you ring the number again for me? Pretend to be me and ask what the procedure is to apply for the rental of Queenie's Cottage. `Keep trying, will you – please?"

"Sure. Leave it with me."

Nora struggled to focus on the dictation. Her mind was already furnishing the cottage, though she could only guess at what it might look like inside. Nor did she know what the rent was going to be, and she was worried that it might be way outside her price range, which was lower than low. Undoubtedly, hers was a great job, and although Jay recently promoted her to Editorial Assistant (which in reality, she had come to realise, meant doing all his PA work *and* supporting the editorial team too) it wasn't exactly well paid – and being single meant there was nobody else to share the bills with. But she would find a way. She set her jaw in determination and thought of her Sri Lankan friend, an orphan in dire circumstances, who had begun to make something of her life. *If Lakmini can do it, I can do it,* thought Nora. *I'll do whatever it takes.* She so desperately wanted to live in Queenie's Cottage. There was something about the place that appealed to her romantic soul – but more than that, the synchronicity of her longing to live there, getting notice to quit her caravan and then Cass seeing the National Trust advert seemed almost magical, as if she had been spun around like an arrow on a compass and had ended up pointing in one direction: her north node, to Stipeberry.

Somehow, Nora's ears and fingers managed to take down the dictation without her brain being involved and before long, Jay had been through the pile of letters and was ready for his lunch. Nora dashed back to her office, aware that the snow was getting thicker as there was a satisfying crunchy feel to the icy crystals underfoot.

"Tomorrow at 3pm."

"What?"

"Your interview for Queenie's Cottage. Tomorrow at three o'clock, at Pepperbridge Estate Office – you know it don't you? On the way to Tawford."

"Really? That's amazing – so soon..."

"Well, let's hope it stops snowing soon maid,

otherwise you might not be able to get to the interview."

"I know! I'm already starting to worry about getting back to the caravan tonight – it was treacherous driving to work – but even if I do get back, the pipes will still be frozen. Do you know, it was actually freezing *inside* the caravan this morning, Cass."

"Oh, poor you! Been there and done that when I was living in Wales. What a drag. Why don't you stay with me tonight, Nora? Then at least you'll be able to get to Pepperbridge more easily tomorrow. It's just out onto the main road from here, and you haven't got all those dodgy lanes to negotiate from the caravan."

"Are you sure?"

"Yeah, why not? It'll be fun. We can get the wood-burner roaring, make some supper and open a bottle of wine. The kids are at their dad's tonight and tomorrow, so I'm home alone anyway."

"Brilliant, Cass! Thank you so much. You're a star. I wasn't looking forward to going back to that ice box of a caravan tonight."

By 3.30pm everyone in the office had decided that if they didn't leave for home there and then, they probably wouldn't get home at all, and so with Jay's blessing they closed the office early and headed out in various directions in the deepening snow.

Nora followed Cass home, and both vehicles struggled to get up the steep hill to her cottage. Alarmingly, the back end of Nora's car swung out to the right on some ice as she rounded a sharp left-hand bend. She stalled and started slowly slipping back down the hill as the snow filled the ridges in her tyres leaving her with no grip. She manoeuvred back down to where the road flattened out at the bottom of the hill, then keeping the car in first gear, she made another attempt to drive round the sharp bend. Luckily, she made it and crept the rest of the way up the hill in Cassie's tyre tracks, the engine straining against the low gear.

"Sorry car! Just a bit further, you can do it!"

When they finally got to Cassie's cottage, they were both on a high; it felt like they had been on some great adventure rather than just driving a mile home in snow.

"Phew! I need a glass of wine right now," Cass said, reaching for a bottle and two glasses. They went into her living room which was warm as toast, and Cass riddled the fire, added a mossy log and opened the grate so the flames started to lick and dance.

"Ah... That's better. Cheers Nora! Here's to you and Queenie's Cottage." They clinked glasses.

"I really want it, Cass, so much..." A thrill of excitement coursed through Nora's body as she said this. "I want to live there more than I've wanted anything else for as long as I can remember."

"Well, apart from Joe Drake."

"Ah, yes... the gorgeous Joe Drake." Nora blushed slightly. She'd known Joe for years and had always had a soft spot in her heart for him. In fact, they'd had a brief and passionate affair about four years previously. They both felt terrible about betraying their 'other halves' but it just happened one night, unexpectedly and spontaneously. And then it happened again, and then again. For a few weeks one winter, Joe was all she could think of, but eventually, guilt got the better of them both and they realised that they did not want to be the kind of people who were devious and lied about where they'd been, and what they'd been doing.

They'd secretly meet each other in the grounds of a stately home call Beechland House, that was owned by the Caravan Club, half-way between where Joe lived and Nora and Mikey's house. In those days, the gates were never locked and locals walked their dogs and exercised their horses there – and it had a reputation as the perfect meeting place for clandestine lovers. Nora would drive to Beechlands when Mikey was out drinking or supposedly working late, and Joe would meet her as soon as he could get away from work. She always knew it was him coming around the corner as one of his car headlights was always dimmer than the other. She'd jump into his car and fall into his arms. But there was one night that stuck in her memory more than any of the others. On this particular night, they knew these would be their final snatched moments together.

"I'd leave Mike tomorrow if I thought you were ready to leave Chloe," Nora sighed, "but I know you're not – are you, Joe?"

"You know I can't… She's so…" Joe paused, trying to find the right words to explain how he was feeling. "She's so vulnerable Nora – if I left her now, I honestly dread to think what she might do."

"What about what I might do?"

Joe smiled and kissed her. "You'll be alright Nora, you're strong."

"I'm not."

"You are. You know I love you, don't you? But the timing is all wrong. I can't leave Chloe, not now."

"But one day?"

"One day," he said, holding her tight.

"Do you promise me, Joe?"

"I promise. And let's hope that you'll have left Mikey by then and we'll both be free." Joe kissed her tenderly. "Goodbye Noo. I do love you."

It was the most bitter-sweet moment of Nora's life. To be loved and left; and yet she knew it was the right thing to do, because as Joe said, the timing was terrible, and not only that, she knew he really cared about Chloe, who was grieving deeply from the unexpected death of her father. And anyway, Nora had just bought a house with Mikey which they were renovating, and Joe's family were about to move to Cornwall to start a new business there. It would be utter madness to throw a spanner in the works – and so they chose not to. But they did love each other, of that she was certain.

Joe's final words reverberated in Nora's mind as she watched him reverse his car over the wet grass and slowly drive away, 'Then we'll both be free... we'll both be free...' Tears were streaming down her face, the pain almost exquisite. But her sense of relief was immense too. She hated lying to Mikey and she knew she was an unconvincing liar. Not that Mikey ever seemed to notice when she was late getting home: and just like he forbade her from asking where he'd been, Mikey never asked where she'd been. Even so, the affair felt wrong, as if she had sullied herself. She was ready to accuse Mikey of all sorts of misdemeanours, but perhaps hers – betrayal – was the worst of all. No, it didn't feel good to cheat on him, and yet Nora felt sure that whatever was happening with Joe, it wasn't the end; that really, it had only just begun – but where could it go from here? She had no idea.

She started her own car and put it into reverse, but

the wheels just span around and dug into the mud. She put it in first gear and the car hefted to the right and the wheels span again.

"Oh, for God's sake – I'm stuck!" She put the car back into reverse and slowly inched out of the rut, but again, the car slumped back to where it had been and seemed to sink deeper into the mire. Heavy as it already was, her heart sank, and a feeling of absolute despair overwhelmed Nora. She knew she was stuck in a rut in more ways than one; she knew that she'd just let the man she loved walk out of her life.

"Fuck, fuck, fuckity FUCK!" she screamed into the darkness. It was pitch black outside and sleety rain was beginning to fall. Nora was cold and had no torch with her – and the nearest pay-phone was miles away.

What the hell am I going to do? she thought, anxiety gnawing in the pit of her stomach. She got out of the car and felt the mud ooze around the soles of her boots. The desperation of her situation suddenly scared her. She was miles from anywhere, stuck in a field in the middle of the night with no way of contacting anyone and nobody knowing where she was.

Slowly her eyes began to accustom to the darkness, and she started walking towards where she thought the entrance to the estate might be, her arms outstretched, putting one foot tentatively in front of the other as if she were blind. An owl hooted in the distance and made her jump, but there was something in its call that calmed her nerves – another being was out on a night like this. She wasn't alone.

She knew that if she could find the entrance to the estate and then turn right, she would be on the road that eventually joined with the main road. She'd have to walk another mile or so, but she could then take a shortcut through the churchyard and cross over the main road to the pub which had a pay phone. She'd ring Joe's parents' place to see if he was home and he'd have to come back and tow her car out of the mud. In all, it was probably about two miles to walk in the pitch dark with no moon and no stars to guide her, but if Joe could come back and rescue her, she could get home without Mikey finding out what had happened. She paled at the thought of all the deceit it would take to get away with this one.

As she turned onto the tarmac road, Nora began to gain a bit of confidence. She could just make out the hedges on either side and she walked in the grassy bit in the middle of the road so that she wouldn't veer into a ditch. Eventually, as she came to the junction and saw the pub lights ahead of her through the churchyard, she began to think she'd get away with it. She opened the lychgate and made a beeline for the gate at the opposite entrance – or so she thought – but she must've veered off track and in the next moment, what she thought was solid ground gave away under her foot and she stumbled into a shallow pit – a half-dug grave, covered with a tarpaulin. As she stumbled into the hole she grumbled loudly, "Ouch!! What the hell...?" and then mumbling to herself, "I've got one foot in the grave, literally. Can this evening get any worse?"

"Hello?" A familiar voice reverberated amongst the grave stones.

Oh God, no...

"Hello? Who's there?"

Nora had instantly recognised his voice, and knew that

indeed, her evening was about to get a whole lot worse.

"Mikey, it's me."

"Nora? What the…? Where are you?" A torch flashed in her face. "What are you doing down there?"

"I… I fell in."

"But why are you here? Where's your car?"

She wasn't going to get away with it.

"It's up at Beechland House. I got stuck in the mud. I walked all the way here to get help, took a shortcut across the churchyard and fell into this half-dug grave." She didn't think to ask why he was in the churchyard, though she'd often wondered since.

"But, what were you doing at Beechlands?" There was suspicion in his voice.

"I met… a friend there."

"You met a friend? Was your friend called Joe Drake by any chance?"

"How…?"

"I'm not blind, Nora! I'm not stupid. I've seen the pair of you making eyes at each other in the pub; I've seen the two of you laughing and joking when you think I'm not looking, him putting that bloody awful Doors track on the jukebox."

Love Her Madly it was called.

"Look Mikey, can we have this conversation later? Can you help get me out of here?"

"Fuck you. Get yourself out of your own mess." He stormed off, leaving her with one foot in the grave, and her other leg twisted painfully at the knee in the long, wet grass. She heaved herself out, now plastered in mud, just in time to see Mike fling the pub door open, no doubt intent on drowning his sorrows. She couldn't face

Joe, nor any difficult questions from his mother, so she rang her lovely Dad and asked him to come and rescue her. Ten minutes later he turned up and opened the passenger door for her to get in. He didn't say a word, he just raised an eyebrow and grinned that grin which said, 'I know exactly what you've been doing girl, but your secret's safe with me'. Did everybody know?

Mike and Nora had a terrible row that night, both flinging blame and accusations at each other, but Nora had lost her moral high ground, and she knew it. She had become the person she'd always accused Mikey of being: heartless and selfish. And Mikey relished being the injured party for once, throwing so many of Nora's entreaties back in her face, and threatening to go and 'punch Joe Drake's lights out', though he never did do that because secretly, Mikey was in awe of Joe, who was an accomplished musician, something he aspired to be, a skill he greatly admired.

But for years afterwards, whenever Nora and Mikey had an argument, he'd say, "Oh do piss off back to Joe Drake and leave me be," or words to that effect, and after a while, Nora began to notice that it wasn't a taunt; there was an element of hopefulness in his voice, as if that was what he actually wanted her to do.

"So, tell me Noo, what's the story with Joe, then?" Cassie's voice shook Nora out of her reverie for the second time that day.

"Oh – sorry, I was miles away there. It's crazy, but Joe and Chloe called it a day about the same time as me and Mikey, back in November – can you believe it?"

"Yes, I can. It's called fate."

Nora smiled at her friend. "Well, fate or not, me and

Joe had completely lost touch over the years, so I only found out that he'd split with Chloe just after Christmas. Actually, it was the day after you and I went for our walk to Stipeberry. Do you remember, I was going to stay with Alex and Chris for a few days?"

"Yeah, now you come to mention it."

"Well, I drove down to Cornwall to stay with them, and Joe came around to join us for dinner."

Christopher and Alexandra were Joe's brother and sister-in-law, and Nora had been at school with Alex who was one of her dearest friends.

"Do you think they were matchmaking?"

"What? No... Well, maybe, but anyway, all I can say is the old 'frisson' is still there!"

"Is it now?" Cassie chuckled, putting another log on the fire. She knew all about Nora's secret. There wasn't much that Nora and Cass didn't tell one another.

"Most definitely, but we're both feeling a bit tender, you know? We both have broken hearts, and we don't want to just get together on the rebound. If anything is going to happen this time then we want it to be honest and real, not... illicit. We just want to be sure of each other, I suppose."

"Yeah, I get that. Take your time, Nora. There's no rush, is there?"

"None. And I quite like being single, though I do get lonely in the caravan sometimes. And cold! God, I hope I get Queenie's Cottage."

"Well, we could cast a spell to make sure."

"What do you mean, a spell?" Nora looked at her friend. Even before Cass had thrown the *I Ching* for her, she knew the woman was powerful; not just because she had a sharp intellect and a fantastic bullshit radar, but that she had knowledge of things that most people had long since forgotten. She knew about the arcane and the mystical and she was able to draw upon a kind of wisdom that helped Nora to see things in completely new ways.

"So, do you remember backalong when we had that conversation about Louisa and about being careful what you wish for?"

"Yeah…"

" Well, it's a bit like that."

"You mean, if I'm really sure I want Queenie's Cottage, I can wish for it?"

"Yes, exactly, and there are a few things you can do to focus your intention. In quantum physics, I think they'd say that 'intention entrains the molecules', but I'd say it casts a spell."

"Blimey – a spell...? Nora was intrigued. "Shall we have something to eat first?"

Cassandra and Nora went into the kitchen to rustle up their supper.

"I've got a veggie lasagne in the freezer which we can defrost in the microwave. Will that do?"

"Perfect. Have you always been a vegetarian, Cass?"

"Oh yes. Even when I was a little kid, I refused to eat anything that had a face. It drove my mother mad!"

Nora laughed. "Well, I suppose when you put it like that, it does seem a bit grim."

"It is grim, Nora. A lot of the meat sold in supermarkets is from animals that are factory farmed in terrible conditions. Their lives are short and brutal. I just can't get my head around all that suffering, and I don't want any bad karma from eating them."

"I know. That's why my parents bought a smallholding – so at least they could produce meat from animals who'd had a good life, you know, properly cared for and with room to roam."

"Yeah, but they're still killed. They still suffer, even if they are loved in the interim."

"That's life though, isn't it Cass? We all die, and we all suffer... humans as well as animals."

"Well, as I've told you before, I can't see the point of suffering. Suffering sucks." The microwave pinged and their supper was ready. "And anyway, I can't stand the smell of meat. It turns my stomach. I have to cross the street rather than walk past a butcher's shop."

Later that evening after they'd eaten their meal and washed the dishes, Cassandra spread a dark blue velvet cloth with silver edging over the coffee table in the lounge, and then lit a candle, putting it in a pretty gold-coloured glass candlestick which she placed in the centre of the cloth. Carefully, she put four rose quartz crystals at the north, east, south and west points.

"What's your favourite crystal?"

"Ummm, it's aquamarine, my birth stone." Nora said, completely mesmerised by what Cass was doing.

"Okay – two ticks." Cass got up and went to the mantel shelf above the fireplace and from a large wooden box she picked out a beautiful raw aquamarine crystal, the colour of a calm sea on a warm June morning.

"Hold it." Cass handed the crystal to Nora. "Imbue it with all your desires to live in Queenie's Cottage."

Nora had no problem in doing that.

"Okay, now place it here." Cassie pointed to a spot just below the north rose quartz crystal on the grid.

"This represents Queenie's Cottage," she said. Then she took her tarot cards out of their velvet bag.

"This is the Wildwood Tarot. It's one of my favourite packs, and I think it will help us tonight. Shuffle the cards whilst focusing your attention on how you feel about living at Stipeberry. Think of the landscape, the views, what the cottage looks like and imagine yourself opening the front door and stepping into your new home."

She handed the pack of cards to Nora, who again had no problem in doing as she was asked; because it was something she'd been doing for weeks. She imagined a beautiful room with a wooden floor and a lamp on a low table casting a warm glow. A bright fire was burning in the grate and the house seemed to say, 'Welcome Home.'

"Now pick a card and put it face down in front of the candle."

Nora did as she was asked.

"This card represents 'The Issue'."

Pick again.

"This card is 'That Which Must be Avoided'."

Pick again.

"This card represents 'The Outcome'."

A gust of wind rattled down the chimney breast, but Cassie seemed not to notice.

"Turn them over."

Nora turned over the first card, 'The Issue': Eight of Bows – the Hearthfire.

She then turned over the second card, 'That Which Must be Avoided': Seven of Arrows – Insecurity.

'The Outcome' was The Forest Lovers, the final card.

"Wow!" said Cass. "I don't think I've ever seen such a clear spread."

"Really? What does it mean?"

Cassie took some time to look at the images on the cards, then she turned to face Nora. "The Issue is the 'Hearthfire' a place of safety and of warmth, where you can gather with your friends and family for the celebration of life itself. The Hearthfire is a symbol that hope leads to the attainment of your innermost dreams, so never give up hope, Nora. It is also symbolic of fuelling the fires of your self-belief and your values. Then the 'Issue to Avoid' is Insecurity. Look, see here: the Green Woman in the picture is being pierced by arrows. They represent confusion and panic and self-doubt. Insecurity arises when you lose faith in yourself and your abilities, so avoid self-doubt at all costs. These emotions can arise from a feeling of abandonment, but remember, you are not abandoned, you are fulfilling the outcome of your choices. You need to forgive yourself for any feelings of guilt or past failures. If you can understand the motivations behind what you perceive as past mistakes, this will stimulate the process of establishing a secure future."

"Fascinating..." Nora was thinking of her affair with Joe. It had eaten away at her for a long while and she'd berated herself for being weak and feckless and yet, could it have laid the foundations of a future together? She shook her head, unable to process the enormity of that thought.

"And finally, one of my favourites, The Forest Lovers – look at this beautiful image, Nora." Cass passed the card over to her so that she could take a closer look.

Nora saw a man and a woman standing shoulder to shoulder, strong and secure, garlanded with woodland flowers, the Tree of Life growing tall behind them and sheltering them from above. It was indeed beautiful.

"It's me and Joe, isn't it?"

"If you want it to be. It represents a positive spiritual force of creative energy and a quest for harmony. It also represents desire and sacred vows both of friendship and sexual union."

"Wow... amazing! But I'm still not sure how all this relates to Queenie's Cottage?"

"Well, as I see it, once you have secured your tenancy there, you'll be able to start nurturing the relationships that give you a sense of joy and security. It will be a place where that can unfold, a place of safety, and as long as you don't start going down the rabbit-hole of self-doubt and recriminations, by which I mean, sabotaging yourself with 'I don't deserve this, I can't afford this' – then you'll be able to create harmonious relationships, something I know you yearn for. The Forest Lovers tells me they're not just going to be platonic."

"That's incredible..."

"Now, sit for a while, Nora, and focus your attention on the aquamarine crystal that represents Queenie's Cottage. Take the energy into your heart and nurture it. Open yourself to this next phase of your life. Envisage yourself in Stipeberry. Think of Queenie's Cottage as your home. And cast your spell."

Nora fervently did as Cass suggested. With all her heart and soul she wished for Queenie's Cottage, she prayed for Queenie's Cottage, she asked for Queenie's Cottage to be hers. It represented safety, security, her future, her happiness. It was the object of her desire.

After a while, Cass got up and went to the window, opening the curtains to gaze out into the garden.

"You're in luck. The wind's picked up and it's starting

to rain. I reckon it'll all be thawed out by the morning and you'll have no trouble getting to your interview."

It felt like a blessing to be warm and cosy in bed that night. Nora thought about her freezing caravan and literally shivered. She'd definitely had enough of living there. She was staying in the boys' bedroom, though Cass had insisted on putting clean sheets on one of the single beds.

"Well, you know what teenage boys are like," she said raising an eyebrow. "Thank God they're staying at their Dad's tonight, or else you'd have had to bunk in with me."

"Now that would be interesting!" Nora laughed. She realised that for the first time in a long time, she felt relaxed and confident. The tarot reading was so mean-ingful to her that she couldn't countenance any thoughts of not living at Stipeberry. She had a feeling of certainty that it was going to be her home.

And that was not all she wanted. She wanted Joe in her life too; she wanted to be with a man who was warm and funny and who wanted to be with her. She chuckled when she remembered that after she and Mike had split -up, she'd vowed to herself that her next man would be wealthy and have a full head of hair, but although Joe could fulfil neither of those criteria, he was so handsome, so kind and thoughtful… He was the antithesis of Mikey and she felt that, not for the first time, she might be falling in love with him.

That night, Nora had a dream so vivid and intense that she remembered it for the rest of her life. She saw herself asleep in a church, or what seemed like a church – though it was different to any she'd seen before: it had a wooden vaulted ceiling and wood-panelled walls, and a small altar with a candle burning on it, with rows of pews, on one of which she was curled up asleep. All of a sudden, she was awoken by a reverberating thunderous noise. She got up and looked out of the window and saw a huge and cresting wave coming towards her. It crashed ominously against the arched windows of the church and engulfed the building. Then water slowly began to seep in through the gaps in the wooden panels. As she looked out of the window, she saw fishes swimming past and seaweed swaying in the current. As the water rose inside the church, she began to float and then the water reached the ceiling, and she was immersed. She was in the midst of a great flood, but she was alive, and she could breathe under water... She began to swim inside the church diving deep, peering through the windows, but there was no way out. And then, an intense feeling of peace pervaded her.

She woke with a start. What could the dream mean? She had felt the power of the tidal wave, yet she could breathe under water like a mermaid. She thought back to her relationship with Mikey. So often she was beset by wave after wave of emotion; of love and loathing, of anxiety and anger, of sadness and laughter. She had lived amid a roiling ocean of agitation and despair for many years, yet she had survived. She had learned how to breathe and she had surfed the waves. And now she had surfaced once and for all, of that, she was sure.

"Ms Harris? Please, do sit down. I gather you'd like to rent Queenie's Cottage from the Trust?"

"I certainly would."

"And, let me see… you work in publishing?"

"I do. I'm an editorial assistant at *Awaken* magazine. Do you know it at all?"

"Can't say as I do. Where are you based?"

"In Elmsford, about five miles from Stipeberry."

"Oh yes, I do know Elmsford. Nice community there, I've been told. And I assume you will be able to give me references?"

"Yes, here you are. My employer Jay Silversmith has written a reference for me. I've owned my own home for almost five years now, so I don't have a previous landlord reference, I'm afraid."

"Oh, really? So, have you sold your house? Is that why you're looking for somewhere to rent?"

"Umm, no. Actually, my partner and I have… we've ummm…" Cass's voice entered her head: 'don't sabotage yourself with 'I don't deserve this, I can't afford this…' "No, my partner and I recently separated. He's a builder, and the property needs further renovation, so we thought it best that he stays to finish the project and then we'll sell it at a later date."

"That sounds sensible," said the National Trust man. "Now then Ms Harris, what can you afford to pay in rent for Queenie's Cottage?"

Nora was flummoxed. Didn't they usually tell you what rent they wanted? And wasn't it usually too much?

"Well, umm… Okay, here's the thing. I love my job and I want to work my way up the ladder, but at the moment, I'm on a fairly low income, and I'm now single," Nora was channelling her inner diva, "so in all honesty, I can only afford about £250/month in rent. Would that be acceptable?"

"I think that would be acceptable, Ms Harris, and I'm rather inclined to offer you the property. We've had several interviews with prospective tenants today, and you're definitely the most suited to Queenie's Cottage. I will ask my secretary to draw up the contract and I'll get it posted out to you in the next day or so. Shall we start the tenancy on 1st February? We'll need a month's rent in advance as a deposit – will you be able to manage that?"

At first, Nora was speechless. Then a huge smile crept over her face.

"Oh wow! Thank you so much! I'm delighted, and yes, I can cover the deposit."

"Look, I shouldn't really do this, but I feel I can trust you. Here's the key to the cottage. As long as you don't move in before the start date, you can let yourself in, have a look around, measure-up for curtains and the like and start to make it your home."

The words, 'start to make it your home', echoed in Nora's head. *Your home, you're home...* At last she had somewhere to call home. No longer a musty-smelling, freezing old caravan with damp creeping up the walls, but a cottage on the edge of the ocean, all to herself. She could hardly believe her luck, and yet perhaps as Cass said, it wasn't luck, it was fate.

The National Trust man gave Nora a Yale key attached to a big green tag with the words 'Queenie's Cottage' embossed on it in gold. Nora wanted to hug him, though she managed to refrain. She felt elated, as if suddenly, a switch had been flicked and everything was going her way.

After the interview, on her way back to the caravan, she took a detour, turning right off the main road and down the long and steeply winding lane that led into the valley where the little hamlet of Stipeberry nestled at the very edge of the cliff, looking north across the Bristol Channel. It was so picturesque and charming.

She parked her car in Bay No. 1 as she'd been advised. She was delighted to have her own parking space in a place where parking was at a premium, and where often, when they could find nowhere else, tourists in a fit of pique would wedge their cars into people's driveways or garden verges. Parking was a major issue in Stipeberry, and without this space, she would have had to park at the top of the hill and walk half a mile to the cottage, which would not have been convenient on a cold and blustery winter's night.

On a whim, she doubled-back to the phone-box, just beside a narrow set of stone steps that joined the famous south-west coastal footpath from Minehead in Somerset to Poole in Dorset, and put ten pence in the slot.

"Hello, *Awaken* Magazine. How can I help you?"

"Cass! It's me."

"And...?"

"I'm just about to go and have a look around. They've given me the key and told me to make myself at home."

"Oh my God! That's such brilliant news, Noo. I'm so pleased, though I never doubted you'd get the place."

"You didn't?"

"No – not at all. It's meant to be. Sometimes, you just know when something's meant to be."

"I'm so excited Cass. I can hardly contain myself."

"You enjoy every moment, darling. Savour it."

"I will, Cass. I really will..." Nora's voice cracked with emotion. She hadn't realised quite how much was hanging on this outcome.

"This is the start of the next chapter of your life, Nora, when you can do all those things that make you truly happy, the things you've always dreamed of doing."

"I know! Thanks to you, Cass, that's something I do know! I'm so grateful to you – for everything."

"It's my pleasure darling – it's what friends are for."

She put the key in the lock of Queenie's Cottage and turned it, and with a shove, the door opened. It scraped across the concrete floor, having warped somewhat from the damp, but Nora didn't notice this. Nor did she notice the draft that was coming in from the ill-fitting window on the stairwell. She didn't notice the crack in the wall where daylight could be seen between the house and the lean-to kitchen, nor did she notice the dribble of tar that was dripping down the sitting room wall, indicating a leaky chimney. She didn't notice that the back door was rotten and that one of its wooden slats had come loose; nor did she notice that there was only one plug socket in the whole kitchen.

No, that was not Nora's style. She was a glass half-full kind of girl, and what Nora saw was the late afternoon sunlight glinting on the ocean waves, which she could see through the bedroom window. It was so beautiful and so romantic that it brought a tear to her eye. She saw that the bedroom already had pretty little curtains at the window, and that the bathroom was huge and had a bath – oh joy, after the cold showers of the caravan. And best of all, the sitting room had a bay window with a cushioned seat so that she could look out across the waterfall, to the cliffs and the village of Shute beyond, with its harbour wall hooking into the ocean, the beacon at the end of it beginning to twinkle in the early dusk of winter.

All Nora saw was the beauty of the little cottage, the charm of its setting on the cliff edge; all she heard was the roar of waterfall on one side of the cottage and the crash of ocean waves on the other. All she could think about was a future living here with Joe. She knew she loved him with all her heart, and she loved this place too. She was enchanted.

Love in a Hot Climate

Rain yawned and looked at the pile of tablecloths she had sewn that evening. How many tablecloths could the hotels of Sri Lanka possibly need? She felt like she must have sewn them all single-handedly and then, when they were torn or stained, they were sent back to her to be cut into 16 equal rectangles and made into tea towels in a never-ending cycle of linen bundles that were delivered to her door. Not that she was complaining – the choice was entirely hers to continue her work at the Notary's Office and take on this extra work in the evenings and weekends. Rain wanted a better life for herself and Anuja.

After she'd collected the money donated by the *Awaken* readers from the Western Union in Galle, for a brief moment she toyed with the possibility of giving up work and living off the money until it all ran out, but she knew that this would only be a short-term solution; that being gifted the kind of support she'd received only happens rarely – once in a lifetime if you're lucky – and Rain decided she wasn't about to waste the opportunity.

On the morning after her trip to Galle, she plucked up the courage to speak with her boss.

"Sir, I would like to pay off my debt."

"Wouldn't we all like to pay off our debts, Ms Perera." His lisp caused him to spit in her face when he spoke. It was yet another thing about him that she found utterly disgusting.

"Well yes, I suppose so, sir, but the thing is, I am now able to repay Mrs Chandran in full and so I would like to settle my debt to her once and for all."

Mr Pigera turned to look at this young woman who worked for him. He eyed her cheap and worn sari, her tattered shoes, the dark rings under her eyes from lack of sleep and her nails bitten to the quick. He felt nothing but disdain for her and her sort. Had she not been so good at her job, he would've fired her long ago, but she was indeed very good at her job, even though she was, as his mother was so fond of saying, 'Not our type.'

"And how, may I ask, have you managed to find three thousand rupees out of thin air, huh? Have you been out robbing banks?"

Rain bit her lip. *Had he somehow found out about her trip to Galle with Geethan?*

"It's 2845 rupees to be exact."

"Exact, is it? Well, whatever it is *exactly*, how have you come into such a fortune?"

Luckily, at that moment, the door opened and in came Sergeant Gomes followed by Mrs Chandran.

"This had better not be a jolly well joke!" Aunty-ji hissed at Lakmini. "I can't just put everything on hold because you demand it, young lady."

"Don't you want the money, then?" Rain disliked this

woman so much she was utterly exasperated to have to give her half of the precious rupees that had been sent to her from England, and whilst she was sure that Aunty-ji had over-estimated the debt, she couldn't prove it. She did, however, have the good sense to ask Sergeant Gomes to witness the completion of the transaction. She trusted neither Mr Pigera nor Mrs Chandran to conclude the matter fairly, but with a policeman as witness, they could not extort anything further from her.

"Of course I want my money Lakmini, I'm just interested in how you can suddenly find so much of it."

"Me too," said Mr Pigera, worming his way towards Rain, licking his lips as if in anticipation of something juicy – a share in her fortune, perhaps.

Edging away from them, Rain replied, "I have a friend in England, who has helped me out."

"Oooh, she has a friend in England." Aunty-ji's voice was mocking. "An England friend, is it?"

"English."

"What?"

"Who is this friend in England?" Mr Pigera prodded Rain's arm, his face scrunched into a question mark.

"It matters not how Ms Perera comes to be in possession of the funds necessary to repay the debt, Mrs Chandran, Mr Pigera – merely that the funds were legally appropriated, which I can vouch they were. So, let us conclude this matter, as we all have work to do."

Rain beamed at Sergeant Gomes. She had called in at the police station on her way to work, taking the letter from Nora Harris with her, together with 2845 rupees carefully counted out and secured with an elastic band. She had decided to tell Sergeant Gomes all about her correspondence with Nora and the incredible generosity of the *Awaken* readers and had proudly shown him the advert in the magazine. Then she had asked if he could come to witness the debt repayment, which he agreed to do. She also took a smaller bundle of notes out of her purse and handed it to him.

"I'd like you to have this, sir, as my way of thanking you for your time and your help with all my problems ."

Sergeant Gomes looked at the roll of notes Lakmini proffered, probably about 50 rupees in total, and shook his head.

"Lakmini, it really is kind of you to offer this gift to me, but we policemen are not allowed to accept presents or money from the public. It could be seen as a bribe."

"But, I just want to repay your kindness."

"You do not have to repay me. It is my job to help those in need and I get paid for that by the government. You have more need of that money than me, Lakmini. Spend it wisely."

"Thank you, sir. Can you come to the Notary's Office at 11am with Aunty-ji?"

"We'll be there."

As Rain unrolled the bank notes, Aunty-ji's eyes all but popped out of her head and like Pigera before her, she too licked her lips as if she wanted to eat the money.

"This is most acceptable, I must say," she cooed, as she watched Rain count out 2845 rupees. "Most acceptable indeed. You showed a great deal of initiative asking this England friend for help, Lakmini-ji. Do you think your friend might also be able to help me?"

"And me?" Pigera chipped in.

"I would *never* ask such a thing of her. Never! And I

will never ask another thing of you, either Aunty-ji. This money now severs our bond. I owe you nothing more."

"Hold the horse!" Aunty-ji said as she picked up the notes and put them in her purse. "No need to shout."

All that remained was for Mrs Chandran, Mr Pigera and Sergeant Gomes to witness and sign the papers and finally, Lakmini added her own signature.

"We are all done, Mrs Chandran. Your debt is now fully repaid." Sergeant Gomes handed her a copy of the documentation.

"Well, with this little windfall, I think I might wave goodbye to sewing those blasted tablecloths for Jetspan. I don't want to see another tablecloth as long as I live. Now then, if we're all finished here, I need to get home. Food doesn't cook itself, you know. Clothes don't launder themselves." And with that, Aunty-ji flounced out of the door like a leopard who'd made a kill, not a thank you nor a goodbye on her lips.

Lakmini noted the name of the company with whom she might get some sewing work. *It'll be the start of my little empire,* she thought.

And so it was that she now surveyed the teetering pile of items she had sewn during the evenings after work. Once a week, the boy from Jetspan would turn up at her house in the company's tuk-tuk emblazoned with their logo of an aeroplane flying over a teardrop-shaped island, and he'd pick up everything she had made and drop off more bolts of various materials for her to turn into neat rectangles of towels, sheets, tablecloths, face cloths and the like. She would watch him stagger under the weight of all the fabric back to the tuk-tuk that he'd left running outside her house, and which was now wreathed in a haze of blue smoke from the noisy exhaust.

Geethan had rigged-up an electric lightbulb that ran off an old battery from his motorbike, so she could see at night, and even though the bulb was dim and flickered constantly, it gave her enough light to sew for a few hours each evening. Then, when it petered out, Geethan would come and replace it with a different battery and recharge the old one. His parents had electricity at their house.

Now that she'd paid off her debt to Aunty-ji, she had 40 rupees in wages from Mr Pigera and most weeks she earned another 25 or 30 rupees from Jetspan. And she had worked out a deal with the tourist shop man about bespoke sarongs and kurtas for the tourists, who were mostly so huge it took twice as much material to make their clothes as it did for the locals. Every now and then, a sarong would sell, and she would get 30% of the sale price. She was beginning to get back on her feet, to feel a sense of security that had been missing from her life since the moment her parents had died, though little did Rain know when they were alive, how perilously close to destitution their lives were.

Rain glanced around her at the changes she'd made to her home now that she had a little more money in her pocket. Geethan had offered to accompany her to the market where she bought a length of tarpaulin, which, with some effort, they'd managed to lash to the roof, making it watertight once more. This meant she was able to remove all the buckets from inside the house, which gave her and Anuja a lot more room to manoeuvre; and there was no more accidently kicking the bucket in the mornings, either. Then she had bought a narrow cot bed for herself, which she placed in the corner where her mother once slept, and with great pleasure, she'd taken down the rotten curtain fabric which used to give her mother some privacy, so the room became one space again. Removing her damp cardboard bed from the floor gave her the most satisfaction, and she'd bought a woven plastic mat from the market to put in its place.

She even bought a pot of lurid green paint and gave the walls a lick of it. Though it wasn't an especially nice colour, it covered the patches of mould that were creeping up the walls, and made the place feel brighter. Her sewing machine was in the corner by the door, illuminated by the one electric light, and the *Ninja Turtle Annual* was in its usual place on Anuja's pillow. He often fell asleep reading it by the light of the lone bulb, and more than once, he had awoken with a page of coloured print stuck to his cheek.

Rain was pleased with all she surveyed. She'd worked hard for this. It was well over a year now since her parents had died and the pain of her grief was slowly receding. A new normality had settled upon their little home; one without parents but with more stability now that she'd found a way to get rid of Aunty-ji's debt.

She thought about her friend Nora Harris, who lived in a country called England. Rain couldn't imagine it – she'd seen lots of pictures in the magazines stocked by the library, but it was hard to comprehend what snow actually felt like, or what it must be like to drive a car to work or to have a computer – all things that Nora talked about in her letters. Rain opened her 'Precious Drawer', the little compartment underneath the sewing machine that was meant to house cotton reels and spare needles but was in fact was where Rain kept her most treasured items — so few of them: a small metal pendant imprinted with the image of St Francis that Bapu had given to her for her tenth birthday and a plastic flower, possibly an orchid, that she had found blowing along the street and which she thought exquisite in its purple and crimson hues, and now her letters from Nora. She found the most recent one, and under the light of the flickering naked bulb, she re-read it.

Dear Sister

I hope all is well with you and that your new sewing machine is working wonders and helping you to earn enough money to survive and thrive.

I'm writing to you on a cold and snowy March morning as I sit here in my new home by the sea – Queenie's Cottage. I've lived here for a month now and I absolutely love it, although it is quite remote, and I have to drive up a very steep hill to get to the main road. I enclose a photograph of the cottage so that you can see where I live – that's me, standing by the door. My bedroom window looks out across the bay to a little village called Shute, and at night I can see all the lights of the village as they cascade down the hill to the harbour. Living near the sea fills me with deep joy – there is something about the sparkling light on the water and the sound of the tides as they rise and fall that makes me very happy.

Something else that makes me happy is that I am seeing a lovely man called Joe Drake. He lives quite far

away in Cornwall, but he drives up to see me here at
the weekends, and we go for long walks together and
talk endlessly. He is someone who I would trust with
my life. I wonder, do you have a special person in your
life, dear sister?

My work at the magazine is very interesting, and I am
beginning to take on more responsibility for sourcing
the images for each issue and compiling the book
reviews. We have a new computer in the office – it is
so much better than my old word processor which is
just like an electric typewriter that remembers each
line of type, whereas on the computer I can save all
the letters, make changes to them and check for
errors before printing them out and it also has an
in-built filing system. Amazing!

I feel very blessed to live in this beautiful cottage and
to have such interesting work which hopefully makes a
difference in the wider world. I think we do have to
'be the change we want to see in the world', if you
know what I mean? That is a quote from Mahatma
Gandhi which I really like. If we want the world to be a
better place, we have to start with ourselves; being a
better person, being more compassionate. This is how
I am trying to live my life, anyway.

I say this knowing that your own life is full of struggle
and hardship, but also that you are trying to make
things better for yourself and your brother. I really
hope that things are easing for you, dear friend. Please
do write to me again when you have time, and let me

know how you and your brother are getting on. Your letters are a real highlight of my day when I see them in the great pile of post that comes through the office door!.

With love and best wishes,

Nora (Harris)

At first, Rain didn't really understand what Nora meant by 'be the change'. What change? What could possibly change in her life? She could only see work ahead of her. Hard work and struggle. But then, she pondered, things had changed. Yes, they had – now she had a bed, a job, food in her belly and friends: Geethan and Nora. So did that mean that she was being the change? That she was able to create change herself, to make the kind of life she wanted? She wasn't sure. Mostly things seemed to happen to her; things she didn't like or want, like her parents' awful accident and Aunty-ji's debt. But Nora had sown a seed in Rain's mind.

As she had done many times, Rain picked up the photo of Queenie's Cottage and her eyes settled on the figure of her friend Nora as she leaned against the door of the cottage. *She looks so happy,* Rain thought, *a big smile on her face, her eyes as blue as the sea behind her.* That was what stood out most to Rain about Nora – her blue eyes. So rarely do you see blue eyes in Sri Lanka, and always they belonged to tourists.

The cottage looked so pretty compared to her own single-block, single-roomed home. It had big windows and a blue door with some kind of plant growing up and over it. It had another set of windows above the ones on the ground floor and a roof covered in little square tiles, not bound in tarpaulin like hers. It was something from another world, this place; with contours and materials and textures that were unknown to her. What was it like to live in such a place?

And then she thought of Nora's other question. 'Do you have a special person in your life, dear sister?' and Rain's thoughts turned to Geethan as they often seemed to, these days. Geethan, the kind, handsome PerfectPrint man whom she looked forward to seeing as he turned up at the Notary's Office, carrying the enormous boxes of documents that PerfectPrint would produce and collate for the courts, ready for the Notary, Mr Pigera, to sign and hand to Rain for filing. Over the last few months, Geethan had become her friend. Not only had he helped with the trip to Galle, sorted out an electric light and fixed her roof, but he would wait for her after work with a smile, half a mango or some coconut water, and they would walk past the old Fort that had now become a prison, and across the road so that they could sit and look out over the ocean. Geethan loved the sea, though Rain was still wary of it, knowing that it wanted to take her and that, had it not been for that little fish, and then those two surly fishermen, it would have done. And he would make her laugh by recounting all the things that happened at PerfectPrint, which seemed a much more enjoyable place to work than the office she shared with dreary old Panni Pigera.

Geethan Cooray had an air of optimism about him that would often confound her. He saw things so differently to Rain, and anything was possible with Geethan.

Through him, she had begun to hope for a better life for herself, because he believed that was entirely possible. He believed that anything was possible. Yes, Geethan was becoming a special person in her life, a true friend.

Earlier that evening, Geethan had called around on his motorbike to change the lightbulb battery. He always did this before it actually ran out so that Rain could meet her sewing targets.

"I have something for you," Geethan said, handing Rain a large parcel wrapped in coloured paper.

"What is it?"

"A present. Open it and see."

Rain had never been given a present so beautifully-wrapped in coloured paper before. Tentatively, she undid the yellow raffia bow that held the paper in place, and beneath the paper she beheld the most beautiful object she'd ever seen in her life. It was a book, with no title nor words on the cover, just beautiful swirls of colour; greens, golds and yellows, blues and purples in spiralling patterns on what seemed to be a type of silk, and the book was bound at the corners and down the spine by what looked like green leather. She opened the book and was surprised to see that inside it there were hundreds of pages with nothing written upon them, just faint, straight lines.

"Is it for me?"

"Yes, it's for you Rain. To write all your poems and stories in."

"But, Geethan-ji, I couldn't write them in this... it's too beautiful..."

"And so are your poems and stories. Now you can write them all in this book so that they don't get blown away by the wind or burned by mistake. That way, you can keep them forever, and maybe read them aloud to your children one day."

His words suprised her: *your children...* She hadn't thought about having children since that day she was drowning in the harbour and her whole life flashed before her eyes. Instead, she said, "But Geethan, it won't go in my Precious Drawer – it's much too big."

"Then I will make a new Precious Drawer for you to keep it in." He was beaming at her. "Do you like it?"

"Oh, Geethan-ji, I love it. Thank you." She took his hand and held it to her lips, then blushed at the sheer audacity of the gesture. "Sorry..."

"Don't be sorry. I am glad you like it and I hope it brings you great joy when you write your stories. And perhaps one day, you will show some of them to me."

Just hearing him say 'one day...' as if there was no question that they would continue to be friends filled her with happiness and yet immediately she allowed herself to feel happy, a voice in her heart said, *'You were happy the day Bapu and Amma died. Be careful because happiness can easily be taken from you.'*

So she brushed aside her happiness, thanked Geethan again and put the book on top of the food cupboard where she kept her library books.

"I'll see you in the morning," Geethan smiled. She watched as he kicked his motorbike into life and set off down the road, without a care in the world.

Rain yawned and looked at the clock beside Anuja's bed. He guarded the clock with his life, it being one of his own few possessions, given to him by their father for his 10th birthday. It was 9.30pm, and Nuji was fast asleep. Time for bed. Tomorrow was Saturday and Panni was not opening the office, so Rain did not have to work. On hearing about this a few days previously, Geethan had suggested that she join him on his motorbike for a trip to Yala National Park. He had got a new lens for his camera (though Rain was not sure what a lens was), and he wanted to try it out.

Rain had immediately agreed. She'd begun to relax in Geethan's company and always enjoyed the snatched moments of time they spent together. He made her feel special, and because he was so sure that life was wonderful and that people were mostly good-natured, she had begun to believe that perhaps it was actually true. He seemed to have no doubts about anything. Everything was good in Geethan's world, and she liked it when a little bit of that goodness rubbed off on her.

The next morning on their way to Yala National Park, Geethan stopped his motorbike outside the cast iron gates of a house the like of which Rain had never before seen. A perfectly symmetrical building of three stories stood in manicured lawns and flower beds, with a fountain centred right in front of the main entrance it's cascade of water creating rainbows from the sunlight, and behind the house was a forest of coconut palms.

"Isn't it incredible, Rain? Look at all those carved details on the lintels."

Rain had no idea what a lintel was, but she could see ornately carved pale blue and white timbers extending from the entrance creating a pyramid shaped porch over the huge double doors, and that the red tiles of the roof were echoed above each window in the four corners of the house, with similar carved ornamentation. It was a truly exquisite building, and she wondered who could possibly live in such a place.

As he often did, Geethan seemed to pick up on her thoughts.

"Mrs Pigera lives here, mother of your boss."

Rain couldn't quite compute what Geethan had just said; couldn't associate the fat, oily, ill-tempered bully she worked for with this huge and elaborately beautiful building before her.

"Rumour has it that the widow, Mrs Pigera, married a wealthy tea tycoon just before he died, and that she now lives here twice-widowed and alone; and that her son is simply waiting for her to die so that he can sell the place and live with his mistress in Colombo."

"Panni Pigera has a mistress?" Rain wasn't entirely sure she knew what a mistress was. She thought, from her reading of romantic English novels, that a mistress was like a wife, but who, being unmarried, was somehow immoral and scandalous, though Rain could see no reason why the woman should be more immoral than the man in such a situation.

Geethan shrugged. "Yes, rumour has it."

"Well, where does this rumour come from?" Rain was intrigued. Such a big house, such luxury – it seemed a million miles away from the brute she worked with, who pushed her beyond her limits of endurance, who found fault with everything, who never once thanked her for all her hard work.

"There is this man at PerfectPrint – I don't like him very much, to be honest, as he seems to wallow in other people's misery and misfortune – well, he told me that Mr Pigera is up to his eyeballs in debt. Apparently, he is a gambler, and spends money he hasn't got at the casinos in Columbo, where he met his mistress, and who is now his 'kept woman'. Apparently, Mr Pigera owes so much money to so many people in Colombo that even the sale of this beautiful house will not fully repay everyone."

Rain was quiet, recalling all the hushed phone calls, the curses and furrowed brows. It made sense. It would account for why he was often away from the office and why he was always intolerably abusive and bad-tempered when he was there.

"How much is this house worth?"

"They say a half a million rupees. Could be more…"

Rain gasped. She couldn't comprehend a figure that huge. She had felt so rich with the five thousand rupees she'd been gifted by her English friends. Never before had she known what it felt like to be able to afford the best red snapper and a week's worth of rice, nor the security of having paid a month's rent in advance. Half a million rupees was as incomprehensible to Rain as flying in an aeroplane to London. It was a fantasy.

Geethan kicked his motorbike into life, and it roared like a leopard. Rain concentrated on staying perched on the back, her legs hanging 'side-saddle', her feet balancing on the footrest and her sari stuffed between her knees, so it didn't get caught and dirty on the exhaust. Geethan's new motorbike was even more scary, even more exhilarating than the tuk-tuk ride to Galle. In fact, he overtook many tuk-tuks on the road to Yala, whose drivers would beep their horns at him, shaking their fists or occasionally putting their thumbs up. Rain beamed back at them all, a sense of mischief and excitement radiating in her smile, coupled with the thrill of having her arms linked around the waist of the most handsome young man in Lagentle. She laughed, urging Geethan to go faster and faster still, as daily life on the roadside became a blur of colour in her eyes.

And then he stopped, and they were in a clearing of trees by a wide and shallow river flanked with huge flat rocks. She eased herself off the motorbike, slightly stiff, her mind turning momentarily to Anuja, hoping that he was enjoying his day by himself with only his *Ninja Turtle Annual* for company. But she knew he would not begrudge her this; that he would be eager for her tales of adventure when she got home.

Geethan was kneeling beside his rucksack, screwing a large black conical shape to the end of his camera and holding it up to his eyes like a monstrous spyglass.

This must be the new lens, Rain thought.

Then, smiling, he walked towards her and took her photo, and she felt her legs involuntarily weaken. He was so... what was it Daphne Du Maurier called it...? He was so dashing, this man she had struck up a friendship with. Even she could see that. He was tall and slim, with his thick black hair flopping onto his forehead, his dark brown eyes large and lustrous. But it was that smile... she knew of no-one else who smiled like Geethan, just for the sheer pleasure of life.

She smiled back at him, and searching in her own bag, produced two vegetable samosas that she'd bought from the stall at the end of Ingodapokunadi Road earlier that morning. They ate their lunch sitting on the rocks overlooking the river, with a couple of monkeys boldly climbing down the neighbouring tree trunks to search for crumbs that fell from their mouths.

It was a hot and humid day and Rain felt exhausted even before they had set off into the forest, but Geethan seemed not to notice the heat. He was focused and alive to the environment in a way that she had not seen in him before.

"See there," he pointed at a swampy area beside the riverbank that had dried up and become a small muddy pond, with several fallen branches sticking out of the water.

"Yes… what?"

"The water buffalo?"

"Where? … OH!"

The fallen branches were in fact the horns of water buffalos, swept back at acute angles, the beasts almost completely submerged beneath the water to keep cool, with just their nostrils and horns visible. Occasionally, they would hear a release of breath, the only sign that something was alive under the murky water.

"Deeply grumpy creatures," Geethan said. "It's best to give them a wide berth."

A mongoose ran across the road in front of them, momentarily stopping to look them in the eye, a moment Geethan hoped he'd captured on his camera. And then a stork-billed kingfisher glinted in the branches of a tree, its stocky electric-blue body announcing its presence like no call could. *I'm here,* it seemed to say. *Admire my glory.*

Geethan prowled and snapped and grinned as they moved further and further into the forest, bird calls and animal noises drawing him ever deeper into the undergrowth. And Rain felt so dreamy, lost in the moment:

the golden sunlight dappled through the trees and the cool air beneath the forest canopy seemed to drape itself around her, caressing her. She watched as Geethan moved effortlessly, jumping across the flat rocks towards the river to get a certain shot with his new lens. Her eyes devoured him, he was delicious...

Something caught Rain's attention; a strange, rhythmic slapping noise. She stopped and tried to identify where it was coming from. To her right, some distance away, she noticed that the light was different, brighter. There was a greenish-yellow glow emanating from a gap in the trees. She made her way towards the sound and Geethan, noticing her movements, followed.

In a floodplain of the river, long grass was growing in shallow water through which the sunlight reflected, and there in the midst of it was a young elephant, curling her trunk expertly around a hank of grass and ripping it from its roots. Then she slapped the grass several times on her slightly extended left leg to rid it of soil and excess water, after which she popped the morsel into her mouth chewing it noisily whilst her trunk extended out to find more grass.

Geethan looked at Rain and grinned.

"I like the noise she's making," Rain whispered. "Isn't she clever, to clean the grass like that."

"Animals are so intelligent," replied Geethan. "That's why we do not eat animals in my family, we are vegetarians. We do not want to kill or eat creatures as it creates so much pain and suffering."

"Don't you?" Rain was surprised. "Not even fish?"

"Not even fish. We are vegetarians."

"Well then it was a good thing I bought vegetable

samosas for our lunch wasn't it?" she chuckled.

"Yes! When you come to meet my parents, my mother will cook a vegetarian feast for you."

"Oh…" Rain looked away wrapping her arms around her body, visibly shrinking into herself.

"What is wrong?" Geethan looked inquisitively into her eyes.

"I… Well, I have never thought about meeting your parents. What if they don't like me?"

"What if they do?" Geethan laughed. "Why wouldn't they like my friend Rain? You are a very likeable person."

"You're teasing me," she smiled, but the thought of meeting Geethan's parents filled her with dread.

"No, I'm not. I would like you to meet my parents one day…" and then he stopped and gasped. He reached for her hand, pointing upwards.

Rain followed his gaze and at first saw nothing, but then on the uppermost branches of a very tall tree, she saw the outline of two enormous black and white birds. They had huge hook-shaped bills which were echoed by another 'bill' sitting directly on top, making them look as if they were laughing somehow, their beaks agape, their long tails keeping them balanced, stopping them from being top-heavy.

"Goodness me… they're so beautiful. What are they?" Rain was completely mesmerised by their majesty.

"They are Malabar pied hornbills, a male and a female I think," Geethan whispered. "I've always wanted to see one, but here we have two! Hang on whilst I make my picture, hopefully a good one."

Slowly, quietly, he focused his new camera lens and photographed the pair of hornbills as they roosted far above them, high up in the sunlit canopy of the forest.

"They remind me of us," Geethan said, turning back towards her. "A pair of lovebirds."

His words brought Rain back down to earth.

"What? What do you...?"

"Don't tell me you haven't felt it, Rain?"

"Felt what?" She looked at her feet, looked back at the birds. Anywhere except into his eyes, yet she could feel them piercing hers.

"I love you, Lakmini Perera."

Rain's legs gave way and she sank down heavily on the dusty earth.

"You don't know me," she replied, her heart suddenly despondent. "I'm no match for you, Geethan Cooray. What can I offer someone like you?"

"What do you mean, 'someone like me'? I'm nobody! I'm just a kid with a motorbike and a camera. But I know one thing in this life, and that is, I love you. I can't stop thinking about you. I want to be with you all the time and when I'm not with you, it... it hurts. Tell me you feel it too, Rain?."

She looked at him, and it was as if his eagerness itself was too painful for her to bear. All that joy, all that passion he held within him and gave of so generously, and yet it could so suddenly be gone. Taken from her with no warning. Surely it was better not to feel it at all, than to lose it? She didn't know if she could recover from another loss. What if he was killed on his motorbike? What if he found another girl he loved more than her? What if, what if...?

"You don't feel the same." Suddenly he was deflated, the eternal smile left his lips, his shoulders drooped, and she realised that neither could she bear his pain.

"I do feel the same... it's just that..."

"You do? You do!"

"But Geethan-ji, listen to me. I am scared. What if you die...? What if you are taken away from me?" Her words stilled the air around them, caused her to gasp. "When I first saw you Geethan, my heart missed a beat. I'm sure that's what happened. It felt like it, anyway, and I could hardly wait for each Wednesday afternoon when you'd bring the court documents over to our office. And then that day we went to Galle in the tuk-tuk, everything changed, didn't it? I don't know... my life seemed to get bigger and I felt that I had a place in the world after all – you made that place for me..."

Geethan sat down beside her and took her hand in his. A thrill of electricity jolted her body. Just his hand was so precious.

"I am so scared of losing you, Geethan-ji, like I lost Bapu. What if you have an accident? What if you become ill and die? If that happened, I would throw myself in the harbour once and for all."

"But you are living in a world of 'what ifs' Rain. Why don't you say, 'what if we are happy', 'what if we got married'? Why are your 'what ifs' filled with fear?"

"Because I am frightened! I don't want to experience that kind of pain again. Better not to know love than to feel like that, hah?"

Geethan was quiet, all his energy had dissipated. He was turning her words over in his thoughts.

"Perhaps it might help if you remember that when you think of the words 'what if' you are making up a story in your mind that has not actually happened and may never happen. Just because something terrible has happened once before, it does not mean it is going to happen again. What is it they say? 'Lightning doesn't strike twice'. I feel your great sadness Rain, but you need not bear it alone. Let me into your heart, will you? I love you."

Rain slowly turned towards Geethan. She looked at this young man beside her, his beautiful eyes, his kind smile... and something inside her softened. Like a cube of ice left out in the sunshine, the pain she'd felt in her heart since her parents died began to slowly melt.

Shyly, tentatively, she held out her other hand to him and he reached out for it and pulled her gently to him. She put her arms around him, feeling the warmth and solidity of his body, the beat of his heart, and laid her head on his shoulder. He had a slightly musky scent about him, like the smell of the very first monsoon rain after months of searing sunshine, and it reminded her of her father. Perhaps all men smelled like the rain?

"I do love you, Geethan," she whispered. "I have let you into my heart."

It was then that, out of the corner of her eye, she saw in the distance a shadowy creature slink through the dense undergrowth. A creature with a long tail and a golden spotted coat. She gasped, and knew it was the King of the Dusk, the leopard. In that moment the King of the Dusk spoke to Rain of death and rebirth, of love and trust. In that moment her destiny was sealed.

In Sickness and in Health

Louisa had found another lump in her breast. Her family gathered and spoke of how it would be alright, how she would come through it like she had the last time. But Louisa's face told another story. Fear was etched in her eyes, her fingers repeatedly pinching her ear lobe as if to wake herself up from a bad dream. Her children were being mollycoddled downstairs and given their favourite supper by their grandparents, who were placating them in their mother's absence, whilst their mother was in her bedroom, holding court.

Nora sat at the end of Louisa's bed, massaging her feet with lavender oil. Louisa had the strangest feet. Her toes curled in under themselves and had flattened to the side, the nails growing thick in their beds. Nora thought that if a thousand people lined up on a beach in their bare feet, she could pick out her sister without seeing her face, merely by looking for these odd little toes.

"Sorry I'm late, sis. I spent ages looking for the cats when I got home from work. I've not laid eyes on them since yesterday morning, and I'm getting a bit worried."

Nora's friend Geraldine, who lived about a mile along the coastal path, and who regularly hitched a lift into Elmsford with Nora where she worked at the local school – often leaving tell-tale signs of her presence in the car: a teenth of hash, a half-drunk bottle of vodka, and one time, a twenty-pound note – had adopted a feral cat who then promptly had kittens. Almost as a favour to Gerry, Nora had agreed to have one of the kittens, but when it came to taking him home, she couldn't bear to separate him from his brother, the only two remaining kittens in the litter of six. So, she ended up adopting them both; two mackerel-tabby cats, their coats long and grey, their tails thick and expressive. She'd called them Willow and Whisper and they were even more wild and unpredictable than their mother. They would take a swipe at Nora's legs from under the kitchen table, or pounce on her as she walked past the stair, making her jump. She loved them more than they deserved.

Why Nora felt quite so worried by this particular disappearance she couldn't quite fathom, because both cats had a habit of roaming, even though she'd had them neutered. On one occasion, she was lugging driftwood up the beach and something caught her eye. It was old Noel Brimacombe, clapping his hands and calling to something perched high up on the edge of the lime kiln, the derelict stone building where lime that had been exported from the Welsh coast was slaked, and then spread on the fields to sweeten the soil. When she got to the slipway, she could see that her cat Willow was sitting sphinx-like on top of the kiln, about fifty feet above the beach, and a little audience had gathered below, admiring his antics. The cat seemed to be in a rather precarious situation, and Noel was trying to coax him down.

"Oh no! How did he get up there?" Nora wondered, worried that the cat might fall and hurt himself.

"'Reckon 'im'll be alright, maid – e's got isself up there, e'll get isself down. Daft's a brush, cats be."

"I suppose so."

"Strange to see a cat by the beach," said one of the onlookers.

"He was at the water's edge yesterday," Nora replied, "swiping at the waves. I think he sees the sea as a giant plaything and doesn't even mind getting wet."

At then, as if on cue, Willow performed a rather splendid yogic cat pose, yawned, exposing his perfect razor-sharp teeth, and with lithe grace, leapt onto the nearest branch of an adjacent oak tree, as if he were a squirrel. Everyone laughed and clapped, and the crowd dispersed, happy that the cat was safe.

"'Ere, you wan' 'and with that lot maid? Got me zor wi'me." Noel nodded at the canvas kitbag he took everywhere with him.

"Really? Are you sure?"

"Yep."

"Okay then, that would be great. Thanks Noel."

Together they hauled the heavy driftwood Nora had collected up the steep hill and across the village square dumping it in the tumble-down stone barn behind Queenie's Cottage where Nora kept her stash of logs, hoping that they would dry out a bit before she needed to burn them in the old and decrepit Parkray fire in her sitting room, the one that belched out so much smoke before it caught alight that she had to open every door and window in the house, to let the fug out.

Noel took his rusty old saw out of his kitbag, propped one of the branches onto the sawhorse, and began cutting it into smaller lengths whilst Nora stashed the cut logs in a new pile to dry out. After ten minutes or so of sawing and stacking, Noel stopped, stretched and rubbed the small of his back. Then he rolled and lit a cigarette.

"Vunny animals, cats be. Knaws 'xackly what's going on long afore you do. Can't abide the buggers meself."

"Noel, I've been meaning to ask you for ages – why is my place called Queenie's Cottage – do you know? It's a strange name."

"Well, cuz ol' Queenie lived there."

"Did you know her then?"

"Knaw! 'Er was cold een the ground long afore I was borned, but my Grampy told me all about Queenie. Everyone knaw'd about Queenie in these parts. 'Er was what they called in them days, a 'zelkie' – half woman, half seal, an' the village was afeared of 'er, that's the truth. 'Er never wandered var from the beach if 'er could 'elp it, and 'er'd zit for hours just staring into the zea. 'An you wouldn't wan' get on the wrong zide a' Queenie, maid, else 'er'd put a spell on 'e and turn 'e to stone. They say that there standing stone up on Green Cliff used to be ol' Reverend Braund, and Queenie turned 'e to stone one night in a storm. She reckoned he'd poisoned her chickens." Noel puffed on his cigarette as he spoke.

"Well, there's a thing!" Nora was intrigued by the story of Queenie.

"'Er was killed one night by the squire's new automobile. She was out picking mushrooms for 'er pot, up th'ol hill by the chapel they say, and 'er 'ardly ever went that far from 'ome. Squire Vellun just knocked her dead's a hammer. After 'er was gone the house kep her name in remembrance."

"Poor old Queenie," Nora said, "I wonder if her ghost haunts the house? I've never seen her."

"Knaw maid. Don't be zilly, 'er ghost haunts th'ol hill, up by the chapel. 'Er's always there." Noel was one of those people who didn't often say very much, but when he did, his words were never to be forgotten.

Snapping back from her reverie, Nora continued to massage her sister's feet.

"Ah, thanks Noo, that feels so good," said Louisa, who loved having her feet rubbed. "Anyway sis, stop worrying – your moggies will be alright. They've probably legged-it back up to Gerry's house for a change of scene." Like Noel, Louisa didn't like cats very much either.

"Yeah – I hope you're right. It's not like them to be away for so long though. Where's Terry tonight?"

"Oh, he's got to work late again. One of his clients needs a set of audited accounts by Friday, apparently."

"Ah, the joys of running your own business."

"Indeed. Thank God for Mum and Dad, or I don't know how I'd cope, Nora, I really don't. You know I've got to have a mastectomy, don't you? And chemotherapy this time... I'm going to lose all my hair."

Nora looked at her younger sister. She had incredible hair – thick and lustrous, dark and wavy. When they were children, Nora had envied Louisa's hair so much, her own being rather thin and lank in comparison. She remembered the day she'd offered to cut Louisa's fringe, and her sister, who was sweet-natured and longed for Nora's approval, agreed. Nora purposefully cut Louisa's fringe unevenly and much shorter than usual, in the hopes of lessening Louisa's obvious charms, but her plan didn't work. Their mother intervened, gave Nora a stern telling-off and sent her to bed, rectifying Louisa's fringe so that it lay above her eyebrows, making her look even prettier and amplifying her wide, blue eyes.

"Oi, what are you laughing at?" Louisa couldn't think what could possibly be funny about this situation she was facing.

"Sorry, sis, I was just thinking about that time I cut your fringe all wonky – do you remember? I wanted to make you look ugly, because I was so jealous of your lovely hair."

"Oh yes! I remember. You bitch!"

"I'm so sorry Lou, that you've got to face all that treatment. Does chemo always result in hair loss?"

"Usually, yes, but I can wear an ice cap, which sounds like absolute hell. Apparently, it shrinks the hair follicles whilst you're having chemo and stops your hair from falling out so much, but it's also like sticking your head in a freezer for four hours."

"Sounds horrendous."

"It's all horrendous, Nora. I don't even know if I believe that chemo works. I've read that it can actually give you cancer. Can you believe it? What's supposed to be a cure for cancer can give you cancer. What would you do, if you were in my position? Would you have chemo?"

It was a question Nora had asked herself many times. How can blasting your immune system into oblivion be beneficial to your health? How many bits of yourself can you have cut away before there's nothing left to remove? How many times do you subject yourself to a cure that seems as bad as the illness itself, if not worse? She did not know.

"Oh Lou, it all just feels so unfair... Why have you had cancer twice, and yet other people – people who are real bastards and don't give a shit about their lives or how they impact on other people – well, they just seem to live forever." Nora had someone in mind when she said this. Mikey's stepfather Bill, who'd smoked heavily for 50 years, who only ate beige-coloured food with strictly no vegetables, who treated Mike's mother with ill-concealed contempt, and who was basically a bully, a bigot and a racist, and he'd never had a day's ill health in his life. It made her question all the 'psycho-babble' (as Mikey used to call it) about positive thinking, intention-setting and instant karma when someone like Bill never seemed to reap any of the consequences that he sowed. Nora looked at the half-drunk glass of thick green vegetable juice on Louisa's bedside table. It looked disgusting. She really was doing everything possible to care for herself and yet her body refused to co-operate. Why was that?

Louisa looked at her sister. "Noo, do you remember when we were kids and we used to ride the horses every night after school? Do you remember that day we were riding them and talking about the radiation cloud that was drifting across from Chernobyl?"

Nora remembered the moment clearly; two young girls riding feisty horses around the country lanes. She remembered the smell of the horses, and the smell of the hedgerows as if it were yesterday, but mostly she remembered how she and Louisa would bicker. It's easy to become nostalgic when wandering down memory lane, but more often than not, as they hacked the bridleways, the two sisters would be squabbling and competitive, sibling rivalry rearing its ugly head.

"Yes, now you mention it, I do. It said on the news that the radiation was being blown by the wind over the mountains of Wales, and that everyone had to keep all their animals inside for a week, and we were laughing and wondering if a bit of the cloud might have blown across the channel to Devon."

"But do you think it might have? Do you think that might be why I've got cancer? Because of Chernobyl?"

"But if you've got it, why haven't I got it?" This was Nora's perennial question, the one she felt such guilt about; the one that plagued her wakeful nights as she lay, contemplating the injustices of life. Why was it that her beautiful sister – who had two children and a husband, a successful business and everything to live for – had this terrible illness and not Nora?

Nora sighed and rubbed off the remaining oil from Louisa's feet with a clean towel, the massage finished.

"I don't know sis... I wish I did. Do they ever really know what causes cancer? Before I went to college to do my secretarial training, I worked for that electronics company – do you remember? You were at college doing your hairdressing diploma at the time. Well, we used some really dodgy chemicals to clean the circuit boards. I can still remember the name of one of them. It was called 1-1-1 tetrachloroethane. It looked like water, but had a sweet smell to it, and we'd squirt it at each other from the little squeezy bottles we used to clean the printing machines, and before it landed on the other person, it had evaporated, so obviously we were breathing the stuff in. We were told to wash our hands with it too, to get the inks off. Just the other day, I read in an article we're publishing that these types of chemicals are carcinogenic and they get washed into the watercourses and affect the reproductive systems of fish and frogs. So what do they do to us?

"And before that, I worked for a chemical company in Stratcombe – you were still at school, I think. Anyway, part of my job there was to pack and despatch some really toxic chemicals. The boss of that company made me forge the Declaration Forms so that their products could be shipped overseas, because if we'd have said what was actually in the boxes, the shipping companies wouldn't carry them. Good God – that man would stop at nothing. And now I know that those chemicals are called 'forever chemicals' and that they are highly carcinogenic and cannot be eliminated by the body – so I often ask myself, 'Why you and not me?' It seems so unfair, and I don't have any answers. I wish I did…"

"Well, don't speak too soon, Noo – you're still young. You might not be spared either."

Nora looked away. Of course, that thought had often crossed her mind, and she had to banish it quickly otherwise a surge of anxiety would engulf her.

"The most important thing is to take care of yourself now, Lou. You need to rest and have whatever treatment they recommend, and give yourself the best chance of recovery. Look darling, if you lose your hair, it's not the worst thing in the world – you can get some really great wigs now – and we'll all still love you."

"Thanks Nora. I don't know if Terry will. I wish I had your optimism. I just feel pretty crushed by this. I can't face it all again." Louisa's face contorted with anguish and tears spilled from her big blue eyes. When Louisa cried, she just looked all the more beautiful.

Nora crawled up the bed and put her arms around her sister. She couldn't say, 'You'll be alright, we're here for you.' It was just too trite. Who knew whether she would recover from this? Who knew if she would be alright? All Nora could do was the practical stuff – helping with the kids, picking them up from school whenever work allowed, cooking meals and putting the laundry on, and being there for their poor parents who just seemed to imbibe all the stress and emotion, soaking it all up for their children so their burden was a little less traumatic.

"I forgot to tell you, Nora, I've joined the women's choir in town," Louisa said, wiping the tears from her eyes, obviously making an effort to change the subject.

"Really? Good for you!"

"Yeah, it's great. It's lovely – we're just a small group of women, but some of the songs we sing are incredible with complex harmonies and rhythms, and I just love it. I forget all my problems for an hour and a half."

"That's brilliant. Like you say, it'll take your mind off all the other shit that's going on right now." Nora was always amazed by Louisa's ability to compartmentalise her life. Today she was in the pits of despair because of her cancer diagnosis, but tomorrow, she'd be gregarious and vivacious, looking for all the world like the healthiest, most vibrant and dynamic person in the entire room.

"So tell me, how are things going with your lodger from hell?" Louisa asked her sister.

"They're not. I kicked her out."

"You what?!"

"I told her to leave. I just couldn't take any more of

her. It was the last straw on Saturday night. I'd gone out to see a band in Tawford – The Honey Bunches they were called and they were really great, an all-woman ska band. Joe couldn't make it because it was his turn to open up the garage on Sunday morning, so I went with Cassie and we had a really good night. Then, on the way home, I asked Cass if she wanted to come back to mine for a coffee and to sit out on the cliff, because it was a full moon that night and the reflection of the moon over the sea is just wonderful. So that's what we did.

"Anyway, we knew Marcia would be at home because she's always bloody there, so we were creeping around trying to keep the noise down, but we were a bit giggly and I tripped over the cats' water bowl which made a hell of a racket and made us laugh and then, the next thing we knew, Marcia comes storming down the stairs like a woman possessed, and she completely lost the plot with me. 'Do you know what time it is? I've got an early start in the morning and you come back at this hour, waking up the whole neighbourhood. How dare you?' So, that got my back up a bit. I said, 'Give us a break Marcia, it's not even midnight yet. We're going to sit out on the cliff in a minute, so just chill out.' Then she said, 'Well, hurry up about it and don't wake me up again when you come back in, or there'll be trouble.' She actually said that – can you believe it? To be fair, I'd had a bit to drink, because Cass was driving, but I wasn't pissed, just..."

"Merry?"

"Yeah, merry. Anyway, I think I told you that Marica's a recovering alcoholic? She can literally sniff the stuff out like a police dog looking for drugs. When she first moved in to Queenie's, she asked me not to keep any alcohol in the house because she said she couldn't be held responsible for what she might do if she found it! Like she'd actually go looking for it."

"Jesus. That's hardly fair, in your own home."

"I know, but to try and help her, I never did keep any booze in the house. Anyway, it was me who lost the plot then. I'd had enough of her long before this happened, but I just thought it was a bloody cheek to speak to me like that in my own home. She's so weird, Lou, really tricky and disapproving of everything I do. And I never even wanted a lodger in the first place. It really puts the dampers on my weekends with Joe, I can tell you. I was only doing it as a favour to Jay because he'd hired Marcia to help him promote the Seed School and she needed somewhere to live for six months. I think it might even be contravening my contract with the National Trust – you know, sub-letting. Anyway, that was it. I just said, 'Right Marcia, that's it. I've had enough. Nobody EVER speaks to me like that in my own home. I'm going to give you one week to move out. One week, and if you're not gone by next Saturday, I'll move your stuff out myself.' Cass grabbed my arm at that point and said, 'Come on Noo, out we go,' and she dragged me down the garden so that I could cool off a bit. But honestly, I just couldn't stand another day of her in my house, Louisa. Anyway, she's gone. She went the next morning. I think she disliked living with me as much as I disliked living with her!"

"Thank God! Well done for standing up for yourself, Noo. You'll miss the rent money, though?"

"Not really, because on the Friday before I left work, Jay called me into his office and offered me the job as his Assistant Editor. Marcus Jones is leaving to work for a publisher in London, so I've been promoted. The salary's better and will more than cover what Marcia paid me in rent, so it means I won't need to take in another lodger ever again, hopefully."

"Oh! Congratulations Noo – that's brilliant. I know you've always wanted to be on the editorial team. You must be delighted?"

"Thanks sis, I am. I really am! But I'm even more delighted that Joe and I can have the house to ourselves again at weekends. And, I won't have to go and rescue all the fresh flowers that Marcia chucks in the bin every week."

"What do you mean?"

"Didn't I tell you? Every Saturday, without fail, she'd buy herself fresh flowers from that posh florist in Tawford – you know, the one on the quay – and she'd throw away all the old ones, whether they were dead or not. She'd just dump the whole bunch in the bin and replace it with the new ones. Don't you think that's a bit odd? I couldn't bear to see perfectly good flowers being thrown away, so I'd pick them out of the dustbin and put them in my bedroom!"

"Hmmm, that is odd. You're better off without her."

"Yeah, and you know what, I think I've got Mikey to thank for it, because if it wasn't for living with him – who I think is also an alcoholic, though he'd swear blind he's not – and for learning how to stand up for myself and recognise when I'm being bullied, then I might not have had the guts to face Marcia."

"Oh, I don't know about that. You've never been the shy, retiring type! Anyway, at least some good has come out of your time with Mikey. By the way, he called in to see us today." Louisa and her husband Terry had moved into a house in the same village as Mike and Nora three years previously, and were still good friends with Mike.

"Really? How is he?"

"Thin. I don't think he's looking after himself."

"No, he won't be – knowing Mikey, he's probably forgetting to eat. He'll be going to the pub every night after work, and not having proper meals."

"Well, you might be seeing a bit more of him, because Terry's asked him to build a fishpond up in the back garden. You know one of those with glass sides, so you can see the fish swimming around.

"Oh God! You'll have to warn me if he's going to be here. I really don't want to see him or speak to him."

"You'll have to forgive him one day, Nora or it'll eat you up."

Nora was surprised at this remark. "I have forgiven him! Well, my brain has – I can say 'I've forgiven him', but my heart is taking a bit of time to catch up. Anyway, I think I have to forgive myself first, for staying in such a dysfunctional relationship for so bloody long. And it certainly wasn't all his fault, Lou, that I do know. But what do you mean, 'It'll eat me up'?"

Louisa's face fell again. "Oh, don't listen to me. I'm just on high alert for anything that can give you cancer. I read the other day that sustained emotional trauma can affect your cell function and cause cancer; you have to forgive and let go of any emotional residue about difficult relationships, apparently."

"That's easier said than done."

"Actually, I think Mikey might be seeing someone."

"Really? Who?" Nora felt a huge sense of relief that this might be the case. She wanted Mikey to have someone special in his life like she had, someone who could love him, warts and all – and feed him.

"Jenny Deere. You know, the potter who lives opposite the pub, in that little thatched cottage."

"No way! Oh God… she drinks as much as he does. They'll be co-dependent alcoholics before long."

"Maybe not. They might bring out the best in each other? You never know."

"They might, but don't hold your breath. By the way, I got a letter from Lakmini today."

"Did you? How is she?"

"She sends her love and prayers to you – to all of us actually. She always prays for us. I think she's quite devout, especially since her parents died. She lights a candle for them every week at the Catholic church in her town."

"Really? For some reason I thought she'd be Hindu or – what's the other one? – Buddhist…"

"No, she's Catholic. I looked it up. Apparently, the Portuguese brought the religion to Sri Lanka when they invaded in the 1500s, and that's why so many Sri Lankans have the Catholic faith. Anyway, she had some good news."

"Great, I'm glad someone's having good news."

"She's getting married."

"What! Is she old enough?"

"Well, I think she's got to be at least 17, or even 18, and I'm not really sure what the legal age to get married in Sri Lanka is, but she hasn't got any parents to stop her, and she's met this young man called Geethan who has asked her to marry him Isn't that lovely?"

"It is - go Lakmini!"

"But here's the thing Lou, she's asked me to give my consent to the marriage, as her 'sister'."

Nora had told Louisa all about how she and Lakmini

had become friends, and she often read Lakmini's letters aloud to Louisa. She wanted Louisa to feel part of their sisterhood too.

"Shall I read you her letter?"

"Oh, yes please."

"You're not too tired?"

"No, I'm fine. It keeps my mind occupied and stops me thinking about having bloody cancer, again."

"Okay." Nora rummaged in her capacious bag until she found the letter, as usual, typed on thin airmail paper, with the little holes in it from the punctuation marks.

```
Dear Sister

How are you and how is life in your
lovely house by the sea? I pray you
and all your family are well and
happy. Of course, I send especial
love to Louisa and hope that she is
now fully recovered."
```

Nora looked at Louisa. "Sorry, sis – she wrote this before you got your mammogram results back."

Louisa shrugged and sighed, pulling the duvet tightly under her chin. "It's alright. She wasn't to know."

```
Life is treating me well, thanks to
you and your kindness putting the
advert into 'Awaken' magazine. This
was the big turning point for me,
and I can never thank you enough for
```

helping me. I have made some improvements to our house, and I bought my brother Anuja a bicycle last week. It is just an old one, but he has wanted a bicycle since he was a small boy, and I had just enough money in savings to buy it for him. I wish you could see his face as he rides down the road. He does this funny thing where he twists the bike and comes to a halt and the back wheel lifts off the ground. It makes me laugh very much.

When I got home from work yesterday, a representative from Jetspan was waiting at my house. He asked me if I would be prepared to make the towelling bath robes that they provide for the guests in each of the bedrooms in their chain of hotels. I was taken by surprise, but he said that the supervisor who runs their laundry department had recommended me because of the quality of my sewing. Dear sister, they will pay me 25 rupees per bathrobe, which is about the same as I was earning for all the towels and tablecloths I sew each week. This means a big increase in my income. They are hoping I will be able to

```
sew at least four robes a week. The
Jetspan man told me there are three
other sewers making robes too -
quite a little industry we are. It
will mean I have to work every
weekend, as I am still employed at
the Notary's Office, but I am happy
to do this to keep us safe."
```

"Wow! That's great news" said Louisa, suddenly looking very tired. "Just the thought of sewing that many bathrobes makes me feel exhausted. Carry on."

```
"There is other news. I have told
you about my friend, Geethan Cooray,
before. He is a very kind man with a
good heart and a good job. A few
months ago, he took me to Yala
National Park where he wanted to
photograph the wildlife. There, he
told me of his feelings for me, and
I was able to tell him that I felt
the same. Last Sunday, his parents
invited myself and Anuja to their
house for an evening meal. They made
a big fuss of us, especially Anuja.
Geethan's mother, Mrs Cooray, said
she was very pleased to meet me, and
his father asked me about my work
and seemed impressed that I was able
to type letters in English and speak
good English too. They were very
```

hospitable and although I was
nervous meeting them, they made us
feel at our ease, and I know they
are kind people.

Geethan-ji took us home on his
motorbike with Anuja sitting on the
handlebars at the front, which he
loves to do - he is becoming quite
the daredevil, isn't it? - and then,
just before Geethan was leaving to
go home, he got down on one knee and
proposed to me. Dear sister, can you
believe it? He actually said, 'I
would like to ask for your hand
in marriage.'

Well, as you can imagine, I was
completely shocked and did not know
what to say at first, but then I
realised what I needed to do. I told
Geethan that I must first ask
permission of Sister Nora, to accept
his hand in marriage. So, dear
sister, if you think I should do
this and marry Geethan Cooray, then
please give me your blessing, and I
will agree to his request. If you
think I should not rush into things
so soon, or that I should wait until
I am older, please tell me and I
will take your advice. In the

```
absence of my own parents, I ask now
for your guidance regarding this
marriage. I await to hear from you
knowing you will advise me in this
important matter

With my love and prayers -
your sister,

Lakmini 'Rain' Perera
```

"Wowzer… Sister Nora!" Louisa let out a whistle of amusement from between her teeth. "She makes you sound like a nun! But it's so lovely that she should ask for your blessing. It's like you've become family to her since her parents died."

"I think I have, and it feels special, you know – we do have this… connection."

"What are you going to say?"

"I'm going to say that if she truly loves him, and if she trusts him with her life, then, she should marry him. She has my blessing."

"Everybody needs somebody to love."

Louisa had closed her eyes. Nora saw how quickly her energy was depleted these days. Louisa, who'd once sulk if there wasn't a party to go to every weekend was now exhausted before the children were even in bed.

"Night night, darling," Nora whispered, giving her a hug and tucking her feet back under the duvet. "Sweet dreams – I'll see you at the weekend."

It usually took about three-quarters of an hour to drive home to Stipeberry from Louisa's house, but that night there was a thick and swirling fog that made driving difficult. Sometimes it was so dense that she had to slow down to a crawl, keeping her eyes glued on the ditches and hedges either side of the road for guidance, and then the fog would momentarily lift, and it was a clear, starry night again. Nora's brain was also fogged-up, preoccupied with recounting all the conversations and events of the day, so much so that a couple of times she could not work out where she was on the road, nor if she had passed a particular turning or crossroads.

Nora knew that when she got home, Joe would be waiting for her. These days, he often drove the long trek from his home in Cornwall to her home in North Devon on a Wednesday evening, so that they could be together and so it wouldn't seem so long from one weekend to the next, and occasionally, she would reciprocate and go and stay with him. Just the thought of Joe being at home, a warm fire having been lit and a glass of wine to take the edge off the day was enough to alleviate the anxiety about Louisa that constantly assailed her. Why did she always feel so much guilt about Louisa's ill health? It wasn't her fault that Louisa had cancer, and yet Nora felt such self-reproach that she was healthy, and her sister was not.

Eventually, she turned off the main road and onto the narrow lane that led down the steep hill to Queenie's Cottage, still lost in her thoughts, when a white silhouette sprang out of the hedge to her left and landed in the middle of the road ten metres or so in front of her car and turned to look straight at her. Nora jammed on the brake, but the road was wet from rain that had fallen for most of the day, and there were leaves and broken twigs everywhere from recent gales. Her car wheels locked, and she began to skid sideways on the debris. She took her foot off the brake and managed to steer out of the skid, as her Dad had once taught her to do, then she stalled the engine, her heart racing. *What the hell was that?*

Nora squinted ahead unsure of what she'd just seen, looking to see if whatever it was might still be there. The way it jumped out of the hedge was definitely feline, and she recalled a long, cat-like tail, but it was much bigger than any cat she'd ever seen in these parts, and then – Nora put her hand to her mouth as she recalled in her mind's eye how the fleeting image she'd seen suddenly changed shape and sprawled across the road, a woman maybe, in a peculiar white nightdress. That was the moment the car began to skid, as she steered to avoid whatever it was she'd seen lying there in the middle of the road. And then it was gone... as if it was just an apparition. Nora's heart was beating in her chest, fit to burst.

A memory came to her of a conversation she'd had with Noel Brimacombe a few days after she had moved into Queenie's Cottage.

"'Ave 'ee zeed it yet then, maid?"

Nora looked at him quizzically. "Seen what, Noel?"

"Zeed the beast. Could be the beast o' Bodmin Moor, could be the Beast 'o Hexmoor, could be any ol' beast but one of um lives een these 'ere woods."

"Noel! Don't say that, or I'll never sleep at night."

"Speak as I find, maid. I've zeed it wi' me own two eyes is all."

"Where?"

"Opposite th'ol chapel, prowling."

"Noel! Stop it please, you're scaring me."

The old man had chuckled and re-lit the perennial cigarette that dangled from his lips.

That was exactly where she was now... opposite the chapel. Was it an escaped big cat from a zoo or someone's private collection, perhaps? They were a rural myth in these parts, and everyone had a story about somebody who'd seen one, but Nora never really believed it... until now. Of course, she'd told Joe what Noel had said, and Joe often made a joke about it, saying he'd seen a big black cat on the beach or in the garden, egging her on to come and have a look, and when she did, it was only Willow or Whisper, staring off into the horizon.

She caught the lights of a vehicle coming down the hill in her rear-view mirror, so she started her car and pulled into the side of the road to let it pass, but then there was a familiar face waving at her.

"Joe? Joe!" She wound her window down. "What are you doing here? I thought you'd be home by now?"

Joe had jumped out of his car and leaned in Nora's open window. "No... I got called out to an accident just as I was about to leave work." He worked at the family garage on one of the main routes through Cornwall, and they had a breakdown lorry to tow-in vehicles that had been in a collision or broken down on the highway. "It took ages to get everything sorted out. But never mind about that, what's happened to you?"

"I don't know..." said Nora, and she really didn't. She couldn't think straight. "I think, maybe I just misjudged the road in the fog. But... honestly, Joe, I thought I saw a cat – like a lynx or a leopard, a big cat – and then it turned into a person lying in the road dressed in a shroud, a long white shroud… … and so I braked to avoid hitting them, and when I looked again, nothing was there…"

"That's really weird…" said Joe, leaning in the open window to kiss her on the lips. Nora wondered if she would ever get used to the affection Joe always greeted her with. A kiss, a hug, an 'I love you.' For years she'd resigned herself to the lack of it; noticing how Mikey always walked two paces ahead of her, never beside her like Joe did, never with his arm around her. She hoped she'd never take Joe's tenderness for granted.

"Yes… it felt like an omen, a warning… the way the animal looked straight into my eyes, like it was trying to communicate something and then the body just lying there…" Tears came to Nora's eyes. She was often on the edge of tears these days.

Joe caught the emotion in her voice.

"Try not to read too much into it Noo; it was probably just tiredness and this damn fog. Come on, let's go home before the Beast comes back for us both!"

"Oh my God, Joe… it was Queenie… I saw Queenie! I remember Noel telling me she was knocked down here, by the chapel. Do you think it was Queenie?"

"I don't know Nora. Queenie, the Beast of Bodmin, a bloody premonition… Try not to over think it. You're just tired. Come on. Let's go home."

And indeed, Nora was exhausted by the time she'd unloaded her car and finally closed her front door, and grateful beyond measure to Joe who had already lit the fire and poured two glasses of wine. Nora turned the oven on to reheat a cottage pie that was left over from the night before, and as she did so, she noticed that the cats had not been home to eat the bowls of dried food she had left out for them. Once again, a knot of anxiety balled in her stomach.

After supper, Joe and Nora sat pensively in front of the fire, grateful for the heat that, for once, had not been preceded by a houseful of smoke.

"How was Louisa?" Joe asked.

Nora looked at him and shrugged. Where to begin?

"I don't know how she is. I think she's scared out of her wits. I think she's angry and sad and feels like her body has betrayed her. And I feel so guilty, Joe – guilty that I'm happy and that we have each other and this beautiful house. I don't tell her what's really happening in my life; I don't tell her about us, because I don't want to add to the sense of injustice she already feels. It seems like cancer is driving a wedge between us, and I can't be happy because she can't be happy..."

"But it's not your fault," said Joe, twiddling her hair. "You have your own life to live."

"I know that, Joe – but somehow, I can't help feeling it should be me..."

"Ssshhhh! Don't say that Noo. Don't tempt fate."

"It's like, I want to enjoy our life here, just me and you, in this amazing house that came to me like a miracle, when I needed it most. I want to inhabit every inch of it with you because it makes me so happy just to be here, especially now the dreaded Marcia has gone – thank God! – but then as happiness arises in me, it's immediately flattened by this feeling... guilt or sorrow or grief. I can't really tell what it is, but it feels like I can't have it; I can't have happiness."

Joe moved closer to Nora and hugged her. "It'll pass darling – I think we're all living in an emotional time-bomb right now. But it won't always be like this."

Nora sighed and relaxed into his arms. She knew it wouldn't always be like this, but it meant one of two things: Louisa had to get better, or not...

The next morning Nora awoke with a jolt, to a sharp rapping sound on the front door. She nudged Joe.

"Did you hear that?"

"Yes – someone's at the door..."

"At this hour in the morning?" She looked at her clock. It was 6am.

She picked her dressing gown off the bedside chair and threw it over her shoulders, then heaved-up the old sash window and stuck her head out to see who was there. It was most of the village, in fact.

"Nora, you and Joe had better come down and have a look at this," said Martin, the local builder who lived in the house opposite.

"Why? What's going on?"

"Just come down, quickly."

By this time, Joe had got up and begun to dress. He looked at her questioningly as he zipped-up his jeans.

"Come on. Something's up," she said.

When they opened the front door, it was plain to see what was up, or rather down. Their garden, the washing line, the garden shed, her plant pots and vegetable beds had gone, vanished. There had been a huge landslide overnight, which neither she or Joe had heard nor felt, and solid earth and rock that should've been at the end of her garden had completely disappeared, having slipped 100 feet to the beach below.

"Oh no... oh my God!"

"I know," said Martin. "Half of my garden's gone too

– but luckily it didn't take the houses, otherwise we would all be goners."

"Jeeze," whistled Joe through his teeth. "It's strange to see thin air where there used to be solid rock."

"It's a notorious fault line," said Martin, lighting a rollie and inhaling the smoke deeply. Some say it runs from Stipeberry under the sea all the way to Lundy Island, and then on to the south Wales coast. There have been slips before, down towards Shute the last one, but never as big as this. It'll close the beach off for months. That'll please old Mrs Carver – she gets so mithered when people park in her spot – now no bugger'll want to come down here."

Slowly the villagers began to wander back to their own homes, which being further away from the edge of the cliff were relatively safe, and Martin told Joe to call on him if they needed help with anything.

A tear slipped from Nora's eye as she closed her front door. She knew they would have to leave this beloved place. No landlord could rent a property so precariously teetering on the edge of a cliff.

"They knew," she said, turning to Joe. "Willow and Whisper… I think they must've been able to sense that something was wrong and that's why they left."

"Maybe…" Joe sighed. "We'll have to leave too. It's not safe to stay. The sewerage pipes have been severed, and the outfall pipe from the kitchen. And look at this." He pointed to the wall between the main house and the lean-to kitchen which was obviously an extension put on some time ago. "This gap must be an inch wide – you can see the sea through it now. It's bound to have made the kitchen unstable too. I hate to say it, but we're not going to be able to stay here Nora. It's just not safe."

"I know," she sniffed, a sense of intense grief overwhelming her. "I can't bear it Joe… we've only just got the house to ourselves again, and now this…" She turned and buried her head in his shoulder. "I don't want to go – I love it here so much. It's my home. And now we have to leave." She began to cry, tears for herself, tears for Louisa, tears for her lost cats and her lost home.

"It'll be okay. We'll find somewhere else."

"We'll never find anywhere as lovely as this."

"Look, you can come and stay with me in Cornwall whilst we sort things out. Just for a while – and at least we weren't hurt, eh?"

"Do you think it was an omen?"

"What?"

"Seeing Queenie last night?"

"God knows Nora. But we have to count our blessings. It could've been us at the bottom of the cliff, buried in tonnes of rock. We've been so lucky."

"But what if my cats are down there, buried ? None of this feels lucky to me."

"They'll be okay. They're bloody feral, those cats – they'll be curled up somewhere warm, wondering what all the fuss is about. We can put a card in the village shop to ask if anyone's seen them. We'll find them. Don't worry."

Nora sighed. She knew it had all been too good to be true; that somehow she had tempted fate – that she'd been too contented, too happy in her little home by the sea. It felt as if she was not allowed to be happy if her sister could not be happy.

Nora never spent another night at Queenie's Cottage, except that is, in her dreams. For years after they left,

Nora would regularly return to the house when she slept, haunting it perhaps like Queenie did, feeling an umbilical tie to the place. Being wrenched away so abruptly was like a sudden death to her, a huge loss. For many years she grieved for the place that had captured her soul.

The Burning Question

When Rain opened the door to the Notary's Office, she knew something was amiss. She could smell it – arrack – the sweet, fermented liquor that the men in the market would often drink after a day's haggling, passing the bottle from lip to lip, becoming ever more loose-tongued and lecherous as they did so. And now she could smell it in the office.

She looked around for Mr Pigera, but he was nowhere to be seen, and she breathed a sigh of relief. He'd be at his mother's house, tending to her as she lay dying, or so he'd have her believe. But then she heard the stock-room door slam and he shuffled into the office, dishevelled and unshaven, tucking his shirt into his shiny black trousers.

"Good morning, Mr Pigera." Rain took the tray of paperwork and began to sort it into piles for filing.

"Yes it is good morning. Mother is dead!" beamed Mr Pigera, his smile cruel and belligerent.

"Oh… I'm sorry to hear that." At least this explained his inebriated state. He'd obviously been drowning his sorrows.

"Well I'm not! She was horrible woman. Horrible. And now at last I am free!"

Nora looked at this man who had been her boss for nearly two years. In her eyes, he didn't have a single redeeming quality, not one. The fact that he was celebrating the loss of his mother, not mourning her, just confirmed that he was indeed, beyond redemption.

"What do you mean, free?"

"I am off! Getting out of this shithole for good. I am shutting shop and leaving for Colombo."

So, Geethan's work colleague was right.

"And you, Miss Smarty Pants are out of a job."

"What? Have you not got a buyer for the business? I could stay on and help the new owner."

"Buyer? Are you joking? Who would want to buy this fly-by-night operation? Huh? Makes no money, more trouble than it's worth."

Rain knew that was not strictly true. The business did make a profit, but Mr Pigera frittered it away on decrepit second-hand photocopiers and electric typewriters that never worked properly, or the new telephone system that cost an absolute fortune, but which was hardly ever used because none of his clientele had telephones of their own, or on what he called his 'top secret business trips' where he was away for days on end with his associated unaccountable expenses. When Rain – who, of course, had graduated to doing the book-keeping as well as everything else – asked what the expenses were for so that she could list them in the correct columns, he would bark, 'Wouldn't you like to know, Miss Smarty Pants,' (his current favourite term for Rain). 'Just put under Expenses and mind your own business not mine.'

"Anyway, leasehold for premises ends soon and I will sell all the office equipment. Not that I need money now – ha ha. I'm rich man, Lakmini. Rich! I will never have to work again."

Though this statement was contrary to what Rain had heard, she couldn't care less what he was going to do now that he was supposedly rich. Neither would she be sad to see him leave, yet, despite his glowering and unsettling presence in the office, she found she did actually enjoy her job, and although she was able to earn good money sewing bath robes for Jetspan, she didn't want to rely on that as her only source of income. What was that phrase she'd read somewhere...? She didn't want to put all of her eggs in one basket.

"Listen to me carefully, girl. I want you to terminate all customer accounts and wind down business. We close at end of the month."

"But what about the Court documents sir, and all the papers we are holding? We're legally bound to keep them in safe storage for seven years..."

Pigera lunged towards her, shoving his face in front of hers, spitting at her as he spoke. "I don't care about 'legally bound'. Burn them, send them back to the Court House, whatever... Just do as I say, and close down this godforsaken place Lakmini, and look sharp about it."

As he tottered towards the door, he retrieved a small bottle of arrack from his jacket pocket, took a long swig and lurched outside, leaning slightly to the right, in the direction of the market and his fairweather friends.

Rain was stunned. Although Geethan had warned her that Pigera had his sights set on the good life in Colombo, she didn't think it would actually happen, and that her work would be implicated. Now, it seemed that once again, she would be looking for another job to supplement her sewing income.

The post was delivered in the usual surly manner, but there was no letter from Nora amongst it. She was still eagerly waiting to hear whether Nora was in favour of her marriage to Geethan. When she had told Geethan that she wanted Nora's approval of his marriage proposal before she would accept, he took the news solemnly, but made no judgement.

"I will wait," was all he had said, though since then he'd begun to act as if Nora had already said yes; he'd asked Rain to accompany him to St Francis' church to meet the priest and arrange to have the banns read, and then had suggested that they go to Galle to have a look at some wedding outfits. She'd refused.

"We don't know what Nora will say yet."

"How can she say no?" he laughed. "She is your friend. She will want you to be happy. And anyway, I want to see if we can find a beautiful red wedding sari for you."

"I don't want a red sari. It will cost too much money. I am happy to wear my best sari that I keep for church."

"Ah! So, you are seriously considering marrying me?" He nudged her shoulder playfully. "Huh? You're going to say yes, aren't you Lakmini Perera?"

"I'm not saying anything yet!"

Rain was not digging her heels in – she desperately wanted to say yes, there and then – but for her, Nora had become like a guardian angel; someone who'd appeared in her life when she'd hit rock-bottom and didn't know which way to turn, someone who believed in her. Nora had helped her out, had been kind and supportive and had continued to write to her until they'd become friends and then – and Rain genuinely sensed this feeling was reciprocated – sisters. Though they lived thousands of miles apart, had never met one another and had only seen each other in photos, Rain loved Nora. She was family.

Deep in her reverie, she was startled as the office door scraped across the concrete floor and Geethan's head peeped around it.

"Is he here?" he whispered surreptitiously.

"No, he's gone. Coast is clear!" she whispered, and they both fell about giggling. "I presume you've heard the news?" she said, getting up to embrace him. "Come in and close the door will you."

"Yes, of course. It's all around town. Before she is even cold, they are saying, he has appointed an agent to sell his mother's house."

"And he is closing down the Notary's Office."

"Yes, I heard that too. That's what I want to talk to you about, but I can't stay long. I have lots of deliveries to make this morning."

"I just don't know what to do, Geethan. What am I supposed to do with all the Court files we are keeping here? He told me to burn them."

"No! No, don't do that Rain – we will find another way – but first, is there any news from Nora Harris?"

"There was nothing in today's post, but it can take a month or even six weeks for my letter to get to her and then for her reply to get back to me. It's only been three weeks since I wrote to her. We must be patient."

"Well, maybe one day soon there'll be a faster way."

"What do you mean?"

"I have a plan, Rain. A good one. Before too long we

will have enough money to fly to England to see your friend Nora Harris."

"Oh, Geethan-ji, you are a crazy person!"

"Ah, but I am serious, Rain. Listen to me. What if we were to take over the Notary business, you and I? What if we apply for the licence with the relevant authorities, once Pigera has foreclosed? What if we run this business together?"

Rain was astonished. She felt this was an even bigger proposal than getting married.

"It doesn't make that much profit, Geethan."

"I have thought of that too. I have learned a lot in my job at PerfectPrint. I know how to run printing presses, how to repair machinery, how to set text and make the photographic plates. I know how to collate, trim and bind documents. And you know how to run this business. Between us we could easily manage the Notary services and open a small printing office ourselves. Maybe one day we could even buy a computer... What do you say?"

Rain's eyes widened as Geethan was speaking, her mind boggling. Never in her life had she thought about running a business, let alone buying a computer – though it was true that she had single-handedly been running Mr Pigera's business for almost two years. But now she felt a distinct flutter of excitement at the prospect, a shiver of anticipation and of self-doubt too.

"But is it possible Geethan-ji, for people like us to run the Notary service?" Her question hung in the air like smoke, silencing them both for a while. Then Geethan smiled and flicked his fringe out of his eyes in that way that made her heart melt with love for him.

"Well, I would say if it is possible for a person like Mr

Pigera to do so, then what is there to stop us?"

"Money. We need money to start a business, to buy the lease and office equipment."

"Yes, that is true, but I think that if I ask my parents, they will help us out. My father has worked for the railway company all his life, as you know Rain – I heard him telling you all about it when you came to meet my parents, do you remember? And now he is the chief train guard on the line from Beliatta to Colombo. All his life, ever since he started as a ticket collector, he has put a little money aside for 'the day it rains' as he likes to call it. I am sure, if I asked him, he would help us out."

Rain was incredulous. She had never considered the possibility that an ordinary working family such as hers, such as Geethan's, could have any savings, money in the bank for a rainy day. She thought that all of Lagentle's populous lived hand to mouth as she did, as her parents had. She thought everybody went hungry, got behind on their rent, and couldn't buy their children new shoes for the next term at school.

But then she thought of Mrs Pigera's house, of its many windows, each with a little pitched roof above, of its elaborately carved and painted woodwork and the fountain outside the front porch – and of how much Geethan had told her it was worth – and she realised that other people's reality was quite different from hers. She realised that her view of life was really quite small and limited and she saw how Geethan's view was expansive in comparison. In Geethan's mind, absolutely anything was possible. That's what she loved about him.

Still, she couldn't formulate a response, to Geethan's plan. Her mind was reeling with all the possibilities.

"There's only one thing, Rain. For my parents to help us with the money, we would have to get married. I am not trying to pressurise you my darling, but my parents would only help us if we were Mr & Mrs Cooray Junior. And please don't say you'll have to ask Nora's permission."

"I don't know what to say Geethan. I came to work this morning expecting to do the filing and to type an eviction letter to that poor family who live next to the Fort entrance under a ragged tarpaulin – I didn't expect to be buying this business!"

"I understand, my sweet, but it is also exciting, isn't it?" Geethan's head nodded slightly from side to side as he asked the question.

"I don't know…"

"You don't think it's exciting?" His eyes scanned her face, looking for affirmation, something to hold on to, but she couldn't give it to him, not then.

He sighed. "I have to go Rain. I have to deliver a ream of letterheaded paper to that new holiday firm out on the main road to Yala. It'll take me the best part of an hour to get there and back and I've already spent too long here, but I will wait for you after work tonight and we can talk about it some more then, okay?"

"Okay Geethan. See you later."

He walked out of the door, then popped his head back into the office, a deep frown furrowing his brow. "But will you give it some thought? What I've just said – will you at least consider it?"

She just couldn't help smiling at this man she loved, and in that moment she saw his face lift with renewed hope. It scared her, this level of influence she had on him, where one smile could make or break his day. "I will give this some thought, Geethan. I promise you. You are surely the craziest boy in all of Lagentle!"

"Yes, I am!" he shouted as he left the office, "and I am in love with Lakmini Perera!"

Rain laughed and shook her head. Was this what love felt like? Was this how Juliet felt when she was with her beloved Romeo? How Elizabeth Bennet had felt when she first laid eyes on Mr Darcy? And then another thought struck her – was this how her mother had felt about her father? She couldn't imagine Amma having such feelings of excitement, of happiness, and fear too. But she was young once, so perhaps her mother also felt this way...? To Rain, love was an overwhelming sea of emotions, but of late she'd begun to realise that it was also a feeling of safety; that she was no longer alone in this world, and that feeling made anything seem possible, even this curious idea of Geethan's.

She returned to filing the documents in the big metal in-tray under the counter, but she did it automatically, without her brain being engaged in the process, for her brain was mulling and cogitating and considering. Was this idea of Geethan's so pie in the sky that the whole town would laugh at them for even thinking about it? But Rain had been laughed at before. She'd been jeered and bullied and hoodwinked by Aunty-ji – but in the end, she'd found a way to resolve that situation and had freed herself from the tyranny of her mother's only friend. She had been laughed at by Mr Pigera too, but she had kept his business going whilst he slowly fell apart. Though she could not have named her motivations as such, Rain was smart and ambitious. She wanted a better life for herself and her brother Anuja, and as surely as the sun rose each day, Geethan was becoming central to her future too.

There was only one thing for it.

She closed and locked the office door, without a thought as to what Mr Pigera might say, because he was no longer part of the equation, and ran to the police station as fast as her legs could carry her.

"Can I speak to Sergeant Gomes, please?"

The desk sergeant recognised her and nodded curtly. "Take a seat. I will let him know you're here."

Rain walked over to the large plate-glass window and looked out towards the government hospital. It was as if the whole world had become a different place. The fragrant frangipani flowers seemed somehow more vibrant, their creamy waxen petals reflecting the sunlight; she was mesmerised by the swaying branches of the coconut palms as they cast lacey shadows on the buildings, and the yellow feathers of a golden oriole caught her eye as it flitted through the trees. All had somehow come into sharper focus. And she herself felt taller, older... as if the very thought of marrying Geethan Cooray and running a business together had made her into a different person, someone altogether distinct from the ragged orphan from Ingodapokunadi Road.

The red-tiled roof of the hospital opposite the police station shimmered in the heat. If only her mother could have seen a consultant there, instead of having to go to Colombo. Then her parents would still be alive, and she could ask for their advice. 'Bapu, do I have your permission to marry Geethan?' 'Bapu, should we try and buy the Notary business?' 'Bapu, I am so unsure. What should I do?' But there was no reply from Bapu.

She sighed and looked back towards Harbour Road.

There on the low brick wall that surrounded the police compound was a magnificent peacock, his tail feathers extended out like a fan. He was shaking them so each quill swayed and sparkled in the light. No one seemed to notice him as he strutted his stuff, slowly and adeptly turning in a full circle whilst balancing on the parapet of the wall – no one, except Rain that is, who was entranced. Each of the eyes on his tail feathers seemed to be looking at her, piercing into her. It was as if they were all asking her the same question: 'What are you so scared of, Rain? Why are you so afraid?'

"Ms Perera?"

"I'm not afraid of anything!" She turned, confused, and saw Sergeant Gomes' moustache twitching.

"I'm glad you're not afraid. That is a very good place to start!" he said jovially. "How can I help you today?"

"Oh! I'm so sorry, sir – I was… I was in a daydream! I am sorry to bother you but I need to ask your advice, this time about a professional matter."

"Do you now? Well then, you had better come into my office, so that we can have some privacy." He glanced over at the contemptuous desk sergeant and then ushered Rain into his now familiar office.

Two weeks later, Rain and Geethan were sitting at the dining table in Mr & Mrs Cooray's house. It was a rather nice bungalow with spacious rooms full of bamboo and rattan furniture, the big wooden windows opened wide to let the breeze in, and it was set in a large compound with various outbuildings, coconut palms and hibiscus, and six hens raking the dust looking for insects.

"So, tell me what Sergeant Gomes said." Mr Cooray shifted a little in his chair and looked over at his wife, who nodded and straightened her sari.

Geethan started to reply, but Mr Cooray held up his hand. "No Geethan, I would like Lakmini to tell me. It was Lakmini who had foresight to ask for his advice and I want to hear what was said from mouth of horse."

Rain suppressed a smile. Mr Cooray loved his English clichés but he never got them quite right. She composed herself before answering.

"Sergeant Gomes said that in order to run a Notary's Office, an articled clerk has to undertake a public exam, applications for which have to be sent to the Commissioner General of Examinations and then, if successful, they can apply to run the Notary's Office."

"I see. But neither you nor my son are articled clerks, so how can you apply for the public exam?"

"Yes, I admit that is a bit of a setback," Lakmini looked at Geethan, "but then I had an idea. If I study for two years, I can get my certificate as an articled clerk and then I can apply for the public exam to become a Notary. In the meantime, if Mr Pigera were to remain as the Notary in all but name, and we run the business and pay him a small stipend, we can buy him out once I have the relevant qualifications."

"And what makes you think Mr Pigera will consider such an idea?"

Geethan replied. "Papa, I have it on good authority that he is facing bankruptcy, and even after he has sold his mother's house, he will still be up to his eyeballs in debt and he will need an income. But he wants to live in

Colombo, he doesn't want to stay in Lagentle, so this will give him a way out and an income so that he can start his new life." He looked at Rain. Despite his eternal optimism, even he had to admit this was all a bit of a long shot.

"On whose good authority, Geethan, may I ask?"

"A friend at work who knows about these things."

"So many ifs and buts, my son…" said Mrs Cooray, shaking her head.

"There is good news," said Geethan, looking towards Rain for reassurance. "Lakmini has now heard from her friend in England, Sister Nora and she has given her blessings upon our marriage. So, when Lakmini applies for the public exam, she will do so as Mrs Cooray, and the business will be registered in our joint names."

"Well now, congratulations are certainly due to the both of you." Mr Cooray reached out to take the hands of Rain and his son. "Lakmini, you and Anuja are welcomed to our family. My wife and I will be happy to call you our daughter-in-law, and Anuja our foster son. Let us prepare for our meal. We have much to celebrate and much to think about."

Geethan watched his parents go into the kitchen. He knew his father wanted to speak privately with his mother, and Rain was deep in thoughts of her own. She was recalling the letter that Nora had sent to her.

Dear Sister

I am sorry it has taken me so long to reply to you, but things have gone a bit pear-shaped here.

(Rain made a mental note to share the phrase 'pear-shaped' with Mr Cooray Senior at some point.)

Firstly though, in answer to your question, YES! of course you must marry Geethan Cooray, if he makes you happy, if you trust him with your life and if the thought of being without him breaks your heart. If you can answer yes to all of those questions then you have my complete and utter blessings for your wedding. I know in my heart that you can.

A couple of weeks ago Joe and I awoke to find that there had been a massive landslide overnight, and much of the cliff that faces the sea at the bottom of our garden had fallen away, taking our garden fence, our shed and all the drainage system with it. We didn't hear or feel a thing... I am utterly devastated because it meant that we had to leave our beautiful Queenie's Cottage that very day - we just had to pack our bags and go - and I feel a deep sense of grief, as if I have lost a beloved friend. I was really happy there, but it seems we were destined not to have that happiness for long. I just loved lying in bed and looking out to Shute, the village on the opposite side of the bay, and seeing its lights twinkling on the sea - but that is all gone now. We had to move into Joe's house in Cornwall, which means I have to drive over an hour to get to work every day and then back again in the evening. I feel homeless, somehow. Joe's place is nice, but it is so far from the ocean, I feel like a part of me is missing, almost as if I can't breathe.

And my two cats went astray a couple of days before

the landslide. That upset me too. I put an advert in the local newspaper asking if anyone had seen them and one of them turned up in a town called Weston about ten miles away. I went to pick him up, and he spat at me and lashed out and ran into the basket that the kind lady had bought for him, and I knew that he wanted to stay where he was. My other cat, Willow, has never been found. I hope he is safe somewhere and not buried under the rubble.

On the night of the landslide, I had been to see my sister, Louisa. Sadly, she has been diagnosed with cancer again. She told me that just before she felt the lump in her breast, she had an overwhelming feeling of happiness, as if all was well with the world and that her future was bright, and then BAM - out of the blue, she found the lump. She said it felt as if she wasn't allowed to be happy, as if she was being punished for something. And now I know what she means. I feel the same. It feels like my happiness has been taken away from me. I know we will find somewhere else to live, but I loved Queenie's Cottage so much, it hurts to have left in this way.

They feel the same as me, thought Rain. *These women know that happiness is a double-edged sword, which brings with it great joy but can leave in its wake great sorrow. Nora knows it, Louisa knows it and I know it.*

But Geethan didn't know it. "Rain? Rain!"

"Oh… Sorry Geethan, I was miles away…"

"Are you having doubts about this idea? If you are, please tell me. We don't have to do this. I can stay at

PerfectPrint and you can always look for another job or take on sewing more bath robes with Jetspan. They like you there. We do not have to pin all our future hopes on my mad idea to run Lagentle's Notary Office."

Rain was thoughtful, as she had been since she saw the peacock on the wall of the police compound. What was she afraid of? What was her heart saying? She had pondered this question for days on end, and an answer was beginning to form.

"Geethan-ji – I have given this a lot of thought. I have lain awake in my bed going over what it is I am feeling about this idea of yours, of ours. And it is this. I am afraid of being successful, of being happy and then having it all taken away from us. It's what happened with Bapu, and it's what happened to Nora's sister Louisa, and now to Nora too. You make a life and you make plans and you feel happy, and then suddenly, without warning everything is gone. It's gone Geethan, and that scares me. It's too painful."

"But Rain, you can't live your life afraid to feel happy! That's just... oh, what is the word? That is just self-defeating, don't you think, as if you've given up before you have even started? Life has ups and downs, of course it does. We will never be happy all the time, but isn't it better to experience happiness through our own endeavours and hard work, even if in the end we might fail?"

"I don't know Geethan. I am afraid to be happy. I feel happiness welling-up inside me when I am with you and then it turns into panic that something will happen to you, that you will be taken away from me." Tears began to well in Rain's eyes and they softened Geethan's heart.

"I do understand, I really do" he pulled Rain to him

and held her, looking deep into her eyes. "It is what happened to your parents, and yes, it was a terrible experience for you and little Anuja, but my love, you cannot let it ruin your whole life. It doesn't mean it will happen again."

"I know, I know. And actually, I do think it is a great plan of ours to try and buy out old Panni Pigera. I do feel excitement when I think of all the things we could do to improve the business. Really, he has run it into the ground like you would not believe. But there is another thing, Geethan-ji. If we do this, if we get married and run our own business, and if we are able to make a good life for ourselves, then I want to give something back to our community. There are too many families like Anuja and me, where children go hungry and don't know when they will next eat. If ever we have enough money, even just a little bit, I would like to be able to help others in need – we must not do this just for ourselves, Geethan-ji, my love. I would like us to take this risk so that we can assist others who are in need."

"You are thinking of your father aren't you, Rain? You're thinking this will make amends for what you see as your sin of forgetting to pray to St Christopher."

Rain was quiet.

"God has forgiven you, Rain. It was not your fault. You have to forgive yourself. Please tell me that one day you will do that."

A tear slipped down her cheek. She could not reply.

Mr and Mrs Cooray returned into the room carrying the food they had prepared earlier in the day. Rain called Anuja in from outside. He had made a skateboard of sorts from a set of old roller skates and a plank of wood, and he was playing with some other boys out in the road.

He came in for his food rather reluctantly. They all sat together at the table and Mr Cooray said grace, then looked at his wife and spoke.

"Before we eat, Mrs Cooray and I have something to say. As our wedding gift to you both, we will give you the money you have asked for, to secure the lease on the Notary's Office, assuming you can talk Mr Pigera into this grand scheme of yours. No need to repay this money – it is our gift to you. But there is one condition." Again he looked at his wife who nodded back at him. "It must be you, Geethan, my son, who studies to become the articled clerk. It must be you who takes the public exam. People expect the Notary to be a man of good standing and experience. With no disrespect to you Lakmini, but this is not a job for a young woman."

"But Papa! It is Lakmini here who has the head for numbers. It is Lakmini who has run the Notary business for two years now. These are not my skills."

"Geethan, Lakmini, your marriage will bring great joy to this house and to the two of you, but look at it this way. Lakmini is young and healthy. In a year or two, you may wish to have children of your own. What happens to your training then, may I ask? What happens to all your business dreams if Lakmini becomes pregnant as we sincerely hope she will? No. This is our last word on the matter. It must be Geethan who trains to become the Notary. Lakmini will assist him, by all means, but it is a job for the man of the house."

Rain's disappointment felt like a weight in her chest. She had begun to dream of being like those women she'd seen working in the bank in Galle – so smart in their matching saris with their name badges pinned neatly on their cholis. But more than that, she felt it echoed exactly what Nora was experiencing. She was not to be the Notary, because happiness was always just out of her reach.

She remembered her manners, nonetheless.

"Thank you both for your many blessings and for your support of our plans. Geethan and I have much to talk about."

Anuja looked on, confused.

"Before we have any more talking, let us eat," said Mrs Cooray who began removing the lids from the small silver dishes full of thakkali masiyal, string hoppers and roti.

A familiar feeling washed over Rain; one of self-doubt and disillusionment. Of course Geethan should be the Notary – what possessed her to think otherwise? Of course it is a man's job – it is still a man's world, after all, at least that is what she had read in *Time* magazine a few days previously. Even so, she felt crushed by this decision, flattened somehow, as if she had reached for the stars and fallen on her face.

"Lovely food, Mrs Cooray," she said, and smiled.

What You Wish For

The sun was so hot that Nora draped her sarong into the water, waited for the colours to change to darker versions of themselves, then fished it out, squeezed the excess water away and threw the cool material over herself. It created blissful momentary respite from the scorching rays before the material began to dry again. Her fingers trailed in the sparkling water either side of the lilo, upon which she was drifting aimlessly around the pool, listening to Miles Davis's sublime trumpet as it lilted across the water from a pair of speakers that Nora had propped on the windowsill of the kitchen and pointed in the direction of the swimming pool.

It was her new favourite thing – floating, drifting – but today, there was nothing for it but to be in the water. Being on the water was not an option because it was just too hot. She rolled lazily to one side and plopped into the blue, sinking under the water, her hair pulling slightly away from her scalp. She came up for air, smiling as she saw Cassandra seize the opportunity and haul herself, dripping, onto the lilo. It was her turn to sizzle.

Knees to chest, Nora flapped her hands so that she was able to turn in little circles and survey the scene. There were six other women in various stages of undress, either in the swimming pool, or flopped onto sun-loungers and rugs dotted around the garden, making the most of any shade that became available as the sun moved slowly across the sky towards the West. Nora had made them each a large gin and tonic when they arrived, and she grinned as the volume of conversation grew in direct relation to how much gin was imbibed. She just loved the company of women. She loved the company of men too, but there was something joyful about a group of uninhibited girlfriends that inevitably led to gales of laughter, shared secrets and confessions.

Several of the women were naked and Nora worried that their ample bosoms might get sunburned.

"Have you got any sunscreen on those?" she shouted over to Lucy.

"Plenty!" replied Lucy squashing her glorious orbs together then releasing them so they swayed slightly before resuming their original pert positions. Nora loved being naked in the pool – there was just nothing in the world like being immersed in water without any clothes on; it was an utterly different experience to swimming in a costume and felt so freeing and liberating – but she'd always don her sarong once she was out of the water. She didn't have Lucy's body confidence, but more than that, it was a gesture of solidarity with her sister Louisa, who'd recently had a mastectomy and who'd told Nora that one of her many regrets was never to be able to swim or sunbathe topless again.

Some women could 'tough it out' and expose their

scars with pride, but not Louisa, not in public at least. Where once she'd had a breast, Louisa now had an eight-inch scar, puckered and concave where it grazed her ribcage. And, despite protestations, Louisa insisted that Nora should bear witness to it; her shock and distress at seeing the scar seemingly the response Louisa needed.

It wasn't so much the scar – which was healing well – that shocked Nora, but the absence of a nipple. It just looked so... odd. Men are flat-chested, but they have nipples. Some women, post-mastectomy, choose to have a nipple tattooed onto their chests – perhaps an attempt to normalise the aftermath of surgery – but Louisa shuddered at the very thought of this. 'God no! I couldn't bear to have needles so close to the scar, to my ribs... I don't want to endure any more pain,' she'd told Nora.

In fact, Louisa's scar was quite different to how Nora expected it to be. When she was a young girl, probably ten or eleven years old, Nora had inadvertently seen her paternal grandmother's mastectomy scar. Nora had been leaning over the back of her grandma's chair, watching her crochet – an activity which she loved to watch and which always sent Nora into a trancelike state – and her grandma leaned forward to get another ball of wool out of her workbox on the floor. Somehow, the front of her dress gaped open, and the hard plastic prosthesis that she wore fell forward to reveal a star-shaped explosion of scars on her grandmother's chest – not a single neat line like Louisa's but a bunched-up tangle, as if someone had pinched and twisted her breast and then cut it off. Not noticing Nora's shock, her beloved grandma resumed her crocheting, deftly nudging her prosthesis back into place with her elbow.

Nora swam over to the shallow end where Lucy and Gerry were sitting in a semi-circle of glazed aquamarine tiles in about a foot of warm water.

"I was just telling Lucy about my recent trip to Japan with the Scope kids." Gerry hotched over to make room for Nora.

"Oh yes – how was it?" Nora reached for her glass of gin and tonic that she'd left in the shade under a sun-lounger, the remaining piece of ice that hadn't melted popping and pinging in the sun's glare.

"Oh, it was amazing, a wonderful experience in so many ways. Japanese culture is very different to ours, and it did the kids good to see how deferential Japanese teenagers are to their elders!" Gerry sipped her own gin and tonic in which the ice had long-since melted. "But you know, what struck me most was that because our lodgings didn't have baths or showers, we had to use the communal 'sentō' bath-houses, and communal is the way they do everything in the sentō.

"Of course, I went with the female students to the women's sentō, and at first they were really shy about their bodies, you know, insisting on keeping a bikini on or wrapping themselves in a towel, but after a few times of being exposed to every kind of bum, boob and belly shape, or pubic hair arrangement, they began to relax. By the end of the week, those bashful teenagers were stripping off without a second thought so that they could get in for a soak, and nobody took any notice of anybody else. I think it was quite life-affirming for some of them, because they realised that we are all so different that there's really no such thing as a 'normal' or 'average' woman's body."

"Wow – what a brilliant experience for them," said Nora, amazed that somehow, her friends were talking about the very subject she'd been pondering. "Sounds nothing like our field trips when I was a kid. A week camping in East Grinstead under the Gatwick flightpath was the limit for my school! And I'm still bashful about exposing my body, even amongst you lot."

"But you've got a beautiful figure," said Gerry, "you're not a stick insect like me. You're lovely and curvaceous – I'd give anything to be plump like you."

"Gerry!! Don't use the 'P' word on me," laughed Nora, replacing her glass under the sunbed. "Did any of the Japanese women have mastectomy scars?"

"No, not that I noticed, but that's not surprising, is it? The Japanese diet is far healthier than ours. Very little dairy, lots of fish, steamed vegetables with rice, and miso of course. I love miso. I remember reading an article recently that said Japan has one of the lowest incidences of cancer in the developed world."

They heard loud music, then a car pull up in the driveway and a door slam.

"That must be Lily," said Nora, making a mental note to tell Louisa about the benefits of a Japanese diet. "She's due back from Glastonbury festival today. She's been there since Thursday, in this heat!"

Right on cue, Lily came around the corner, hopping on one foot as she tried to undo her sandals.

"Got stuck for two hours on the bloody motorway! I'm burning up," she said and fully clothed, she dived into the pool. She stayed under water for a long time, just soaking up the coolness and the healing powers of the water, even when it's chlorinated. Then she surfaced and took a deep in-breath of air. The water had turned her thick curly hair into long wavy tresses clinging to her shoulders like seaweed. She was beautiful.

"Ah! That's better. All the way along the link road, the only thing that kept me going was the thought of this swimming pool. Oh my God… it was so hot in the car and this is so… blissful." She began to swim languidly up and down the pool and as she did so, the tension visibly left her body. "What an absolute stroke of luck you got this place, Noo!"

But Nora didn't think it was luck at all. She'd yearned for it and longed for it and wished for it so deeply that she made it happen – just as she had done with Queenie's Cottage, and it convinced her forever to be mindful of what you wish for.

On the fateful morning of the landslide at Stipeberry, the day after both of her cats disappeared and she'd seen who she was now certain was Queenie, on the road by the chapel – a visitation that in retrospect seemed to be a warning to her of forthcoming events – she and Joe had reluctantly packed their bags and moved into Joe's house in Cornwall. Nora never spent another night at Queenie's Cottage, yet she was certain that Queenie had laid her body down in front of Nora's car to stop her from going home and potentially being killed in the landslide. Joe argued that it was a bit daft of Queenie because she could have killed Nora in a car accident instead, but Nora was having none of it. Queenie, the infamous Selkie of Stipeberry came to her in a vision and nobody could tell her otherwise.

Having to leave Stipeberry so suddenly was traumatic for Nora, as she loved the place viscerally – she loved beachcombing for driftwood down on the foreshore where she often met her friend Noel, his accent so broad she struggled to understand a word he was saying, but he would always offer to help her haul and saw up the wood. He was a good egg, old Noel, and she missed him. And she loved sitting on the sea wall at high tide, the wind in her face and the sun on her back, just soaking in the roar and pound of the elements, the crash and drag of the waves, the smell of ozone and seaweed; or sitting high up on the cliff-edge, a place that is no more, that no longer exists on this planet, watching the day-blind stars flicker into existence as the sun set on the horizon.

Stipeberry had sunk into her bones, into her being, into her psyche. She had never felt a sense of place so bodily, so wholly, as she had there. It gave her so much joy that to be forced to leave in the way that she had, felt like a part of her had died and she grieved, for months and years. She felt she knew a little of what it must be like to be a refugee, compelled to leave the place you loved whilst every cell in your body yearned to stay. She grieved for her home by the sea and for her cats Willow and Whisper with an intensity of emotion that she had never felt before.

And whilst Joe's home in Cornwall, a one-bedroom annexe to his parent's house, had its own charms (mainly not being damp like Queenie's Cottage), it wasn't exactly ideal either as it was a long drive to work for Nora each day. But it was, at least, somewhere to rest their heads.

For some time, Joe had been wanting to extricate himself from the family business he worked in; it wasn't that he hated his job, so much as he didn't want his parents to also be his bosses nor his siblings to be his workmates. More than that though, he needed to be his own boss, able to make his own decisions for better or worse, not beholden to his parents' approval. Joe and Nora had been making plans to live together at Stipeberry, and Joe was actively looking for work in North Devon when the landslide happened and seemed to set back their hopes and dreams.

Then, one weekend in late spring, when Joe and Nora were staying at Lily and Pete's house in Elmsford, Lily suggested a coastal walk with their two red setter dogs. Pete and Joe declined because they were deep into a jam-session playing music together, their fingers, minds and guitars attuned – so Lily and Nora put the dogs in the car and set off towards the cliffs. They drove up-hill out of Elmsford past an ancient and derelict monastery that stood on the banks of a fast-flowing river, its roof long gone with only the walls remaining, huge arches open to the elements where the windows once were. On the brow of the hill, they came to a small and very pretty hamlet called Tend and on the right-hand side with ornate wrought-iron railings bordering the road was a thatched Devon longhouse called Forest Cottage, with its cob and plaster walls painted white, and its small, many-paned window frames painted black, and the thick straw roof swooping so low you could touch it from the path.

"See that house there," Lily nodded towards Forest Cottage. "I've heard it's got a heated swimming-pool in the back garden."

"No way! God, I'd love to live there."

"So would I!" said Lily. "Wouldn't it be great to live in Tend – you could just walk to the beach every day without having to bung wet dogs in the car."

"It's so beautiful... and look, does that walled garden belong to the cottage too?"

"Yes, I think it does. I think that might be where the swimming pool is."

"Wow!" Nora felt a longing she recognised deep in her heart, and into her mind's eye came the image of a Tarot card she'd once picked: Eight of Bows, the hearthfire. For months she'd been longing to live back by the ocean, nearer her friends and her job. She remembered how in a random conversation with the friendly woman who served at the Post Office, she'd said to Nora, 'I just don't see the point of living inland, maid,' and Nora knew *exactly* what she meant, because she was called to the sea, like iron filings to a magnet and she couldn't resist it, nor did she want to.

Lily braked suddenly as a car came too fast in the opposite direction, the narrow lane unable to contain both vehicles. She reversed back until she was opposite Forest Cottage where there was a small lay-by. The other car sped past them, without even a nod of thanks from the driver.

"Twat!" shouted Lily, as the car hurtled into the distance, but at that moment, Nora felt, almost saw, a tendril of yearning leave her soul and attach itself to the gate of Forest Cottage. *Imagine what it would be like to live here...* she thought wistfully. *Imagine...*

And so that's what she did. She dreamed of Forest Cottage in her sleeping and waking life. She imagined herself making lunch in the kitchen, making love in the bedroom, swimming in the pool in the walled back garden. Even though she hadn't a clue what any of those places actually looked like, she just imagined herself there. In her imagination, she attached herself to the place, like she had done to Queenie's Cottage.

But time passed by and eventually, she forgot about Forest Cottage, as a little house on the High Street in Elmsford became available and Nora and Joe decided to rent it. It was a bit of a dark and poky place, its small front windows being north facing, but it had a sunny back garden and it was convenient for their work, because not long after they moved in, Joe handed in his notice at his family's garage and then apprenticed himself to Pete, making pine furniture in a little workshop that used to be an old forge. Together, they made coffee tables and dressers and aged them with wax so they looked old and worn, and then drove up to London once a month with their haul of furniture in a battered old van, to sell everything very profitably at trendy Portobello Market. Both Joe and Nora could walk to work from their new house on Elmsford High Street, and although it wasn't where they wanted to live long-term, they felt it was a start, a way to rekindle the life they'd dreamed of for themselves when they'd lived at Queenie's Cottage.

One day, on her way home for lunch, Nora called in at The Fat Pear, a fruit and vegetable shop a few doors down from her home.

"Hello Rick." Nora picked up a wire basket from the stack by the door.

"Give me a break – not you again!" Rick replied. He was renowned in the village for his acid humour and his heart of gold.

"Charming – what a way to run a shop! I just need a few bits and bobs – have you got any ripe avocados? I fancy one for lunch."

"Yes, on the shelf behind you, next to the tomatoes. There's a rotten one I've been saving especially for you."

Nora smiled at him and began to feel the avocados to make sure she didn't actually get that one.

"You don't know of anyone looking for somewhere to rent, do you Nora?" Rick began weighing and totalling-up the items in her basket.

"Ummm... No, I can't think of anyone. Why's that?"

"Oh, it's just that a friend of mine who lives in Tend wants to rent out his house double-quick. He's got a job in Dubai and he and his wife are moving out there on a three-year contract, so he doesn't want to sell his place, but he does want to rent it."

As soon as Nora heard Rick say the word 'Tend', her ears pricked up.

"Whereabouts in Tend?"

"The thatched place, at the top of the hill – Forest Cottage. Do you know it?"

"Is that the one with the swimming pool?"

"Yes, that's the one. It's got a self-contained annexe too. Nice place."

"I want it, Rick. I want to rent it."

"But you've only recently moved into No. 14."

"I know, I know – but I've dreamed of living at Forest Cottage for ages. What's the rent?"

"£300 a month."

"What? That's less than we're paying for No. 14."

"Well, he's keeping the rent low, so that he can get a tenant in quickly, without going through an agent."

"Can you ring him now, and tell him you've found someone? And you know me, Rick. You know I've got a good job, and you know Joe, too. We'll be reliable with the rent, and we'll take care of the place. You could put a good word in for us, couldn't you?"

"Leave it with me, maid. Now bugger off and have your lunch. Come back in an hour or so and I'll let you know what he says." Rick looked up to give Nora her change, but she'd already left the shop. She was running as fast as her legs would carry her to the old forge, where Joe was working. She was so puffed-out when she got there that he could hardly work out what she was saying.

"Seriously? The place with the swimming pool?"

"Seriously! Please say yes, Joe."

"Of course, bloody yes! If Rick's friend is up for it. It'd be amazing to live there!"

Nora hugged this man she loved with all her heart. "You're amazing Joe Drake. If it'd been me and Mikey going for the place, he'd have thought of a million and one reasons why it wasn't a good idea. It would be too big, or it would cost too much to heat, or be haunted – something like that! But you, you just get it! You get me. I love you!"

"I love you too. Look, let's try not to get too excited, in case there's a hitch," but Nora wasn't listening.

"I knew there was a reason why we haven't unpacked all our records and books, Joe! Seems like we might be moving again! That'll be the third time this year."

"Yeah – let's hope it's the last."

Much to Nora and Joe's delight, there wasn't a hitch, not one, and by the end of the month, they'd moved to Forest Cottage. And what was more, Lily and Pete had decided to sell their house in Elmsford because they knew a place was coming up for sale at the end of the summer in a nearby village, and they wanted to have the cash ready to buy it. So, they put their stuff into storage and moved into the annexe at Forest Cottage for a couple of months, and their rent helped to ease Joe and Nora's finances for a while. And so it was that both Nora and Lily's wish to live in Forest Cottage came true.

And what a wonderful summer it was – the hottest for years. They spent most of it by the pool, Nora and Joe chuckling at how many friends they suddenly seemed to have now they had a swimming pool. It was a golden, blissful, blessed summer; the only dark cloud being Louisa's pain and Nora's guilt, enfolded in a mantra of 'Why her? Why not me?' Nora did everything she could to support Louisa, inviting her niece and nephew over for long weekends so that Terry and Lou could have some quiet time together. The kids also spent as much time as possible in the pool, their favourite pastime being to climb the slide at the deep end, whizz down it onto the waiting lilo at the bottom and scoot across the pool accompanied by great hilarity all round.

So no, Nora didn't exactly think it was good luck that they lived at Forest Cottage, she felt like she had mani-fested it through sheer willpower and intention. She felt that her desire was so strong it aligned the molecules, as Cass was fond of saying, and everything just fell into place. Like magic. Perhaps it was magic.

She shook her head to clear the reverie and as she did so, shrieks of laughter and a mad dash for towels and clothes ensued as Joe and Pete walked around the corner and got an eyeful of naked ladies.

"It's like we've died and gone to heaven," said Pete.

Eventually, as the sun dipped below the oak trees that hedged the far side of the garden, the naked ladies began to gather their things and dress for home, wandering off in twos and threes, barefooted and bronze skinned.

Nora cleared the glasses and towels away and in the distance, she heard a peacock calling in the Abbey grounds. She loved that sound. It reminded her of when she'd visited Rajasthan in India some years back, and had seen peacocks in their natural habitat, their long, jewelled tails draped from the branches of the trees they were roosting in. And incredibly she'd also seen them strutting confidently through the chaotic traffic of Jaipur, undaunted by the noise and mayhem. The peacocks from the Abbey, which had been built in the grounds of the ruined monastery by the river, were frequent visitors to Tend, holding up the holiday makers on their way to the beach, refusing to be ushered to the side of the road, sauntering with all the time in the world. She'd even seen three of them perched in a row on top of Forest Cottage roof, making friends with the straw owl that the thatcher had made and placed on the ridge, one of his 'trademarks'.

And then her train of thought led her to remember the letter from Rain that had been delivered earlier that morning. She'd not opened it as she wanted to have time to savour every word. So she poured herself another gin and tonic, fetched the letter from where she'd placed it in the letter rack on top of the piano in the hall, and drew a deckchair over to the corner of the garden, setting it in a pool of deep shade skimmed by the low pink rays of the setting sun and serenaded by the liquid song of the blackbird, one of her favourite sounds in all the world.

Dear Sister Nora

It has been seven months since I
received your letter with blessings
for my marriage to Geethan. I humbly
apologise for not writing to you
before now, but life has picked me
up and spun me around like a
whirlwind, and only now has the
dizziness stopped. I am Mrs Lakmini
Cooray! Once we received your
blessing and that of Geethan's
parents, we set a date for our
wedding which was held at St Francis
of Assisi Church in Lagentle. It was
a simple and very special day.
Geethan insisted on buying a red
wedding sari for me, made of pure
silk. I dare not ask him how much it
cost, but you can see from the photo
that it is truly beautiful, the most
precious thing I own.

Nora gazed at the photo of Rain and Geethan, two
young people standing side by side, looking blissfully
happy. Rain's crimson sari sparkled with translucent
beads set in spiralling patterns, and she was wearing a
garland of pretty white flowers, her hair set in a chignon
at the nape of her neck, a shy smile on her face. Nora
could see that Rain was wearing the necklace she'd sent
her as a wedding present along with her letter of consent.
It was a fine gold chain hung with a small, mother of

pearl pendant, the heart-shape made by two interlocking hands. The jeweller had told Nora it was the international symbol of friendship, and it was rather lovely.

Geethan was wearing a cream shalwar kameez with a garland of red flowers around his neck. He was literally beaming into the camera and was very handsome indeed. There was something about him, an openness, a naivety, that made Nora nervous. She hoped that the heart he wore so plainly on his sleeve would never be broken. Flanking the bride and groom were an older man and woman looking solemnly at the camera, who Nora guessed were Geethan's parents, and then standing in front of Geethan and Rain was a teenage boy, obviously Anuja, who just looked bored with the whole thing.

```
Geethan's parents have formally
adopted Anuja, which is such a
blessing to me. They love him like a
son, and I am sure he will grow to
love them too. He likes it when Mrs
Cooray Senior gives him extra
helpings of food, that's for sure.
Anuja has his own bedroom in their
house. It is bigger than the whole
of our place on Ingodapokunadi
Road! As part of their wedding gifts
to us, they offered us some
outbuildings in their compound to
make into our new home. Geethan and
his father spent many weekends
knocking down walls and building
new ones and making the space
```

habitable. Now we have three rooms:
a bedroom, a living space, and a
small kitchen to one side. We have a
bathroom just across the compound
that we all share, even with our
six hens!

It was a wrench for Anuja and I to
leave our childhood home, the one we
shared with our parents, may they
rest in peace, but we are happy
here. I have painted our house dark
pink inside — pink like the tea
roses in Kandy. (I have seen them
only on postcards.) Mrs Cooray gave
us some furniture which she said she
had kept especially for whoever
would be her daughter-in-law (that's
me!) — a bed, a table, a really
lovely chest of drawers with hand-
painted flowers on it, and an
electric lamp for the evenings. We
have electricity here, so I can see
at night to continue my sewing.

I feel so blessed to have met
Geethan-ji, my sweet husband. God
was smiling on me when He showed
Geethan to my door (or should I say,
the door of the Notary's Office,
which is where we met). I count my
blessings every day, though I fear

to be too happy, in case everything is taken from me again.

In other news, we have also taken over management of the Notary's Office from Mr Pigera, who was my boss for two years. We bought the lease of the premises for five years from the owners who live in Galle — that was second part of our wedding gift from Geethan's parents — and we have made an agreement to run the business on behalf of Mr Pigera until Geethan has taken all the public exams necessary to become a Notary himself (about two years of study). After that, we will have to buy Mr Pigera out of the business. He drove a very hard bargain, and I think we are paying him too much for what is, in truth, just the use of his name, but we have our hands tied until such time as Geethan has passed his exams. However, because we now live with Geethan's parents, and I do not have to pay rent on the old house on Ingodapokunadi Road, we can afford to do this.

Finally, I have the most exciting news of all. I am expecting a baby! Yes, it is true. I will be 19 years

old when baby is born, and if I have
my dates right, baby may even be
born on my birthday! This was not in
our plans. We wanted to get settled
with the business first, but it is
meant to be, isn't it? I feel so
happy, but I am scared to be too
happy. I know you understand this
feeling, dear sister. I wish my
parents were here to celebrate the
news with us. Bapu would have been
the world's number one Bapu-ji to
his grandchild, but alas, that is
not meant to be.

Dear sister, that is all the news
from me. I pray you are happy and I
pray for Louisa every single day and
on Sundays I light a candle at
church for her. Please write to me
soon and let me know how she is, and
how you and Joe-ji are. (Do you call
him that?!) I always look forward to
receiving your letters with all your
news. They are big highlight in my
life. I was so delighted with the
necklace that you gave me. I wear it
every day. I will never take it off.

With love and blessings from your
sister, Lakmini Rain Cooray

"Joe! Joe-ji – Rain's having a baby!" said Nora, waving the letter in the air, though Joe was nowhere to be seen. Nora was surprised by how elated she felt at this news. Though kids were definitely not on her own radar – she often joked that she must have had eight children in a past life and so obviously didn't need to repeat the experience – she was so happy for Rain; happy that she seemed to have found true love and a future full of potential.

"God be with you, Rain," Nora whispered, though she didn't know why she said this, because she didn't believe in God.

That evening in bed, Nora told Joe about Rain's news.

"I know we've talked about this before Joe, but are you absolutely sure you don't want kids? I hope you're not just saying you don't because you know I don't? Wouldn't you like a little mini-Joe to love and cherish?"

Joe was thoughtful for a while. Then he replied. "I can honestly say that having kids just isn't on my radar, Noo. Not at all. If it was an overpowering urge, something that filled my every waking thought, then we'd be in trouble, you and I, but it's not. I can't make myself want to have kids. It doesn't feel imperative to my happiness."

"Well, thank God for that. Though it must be really hard for couples where one wants a child and the other one doesn't."

"Yeah...that must be so devastating to a relationship. But what if I flip the same question over to you? Are you really sure you don't want kids? I mean, you are getting on a bit now..."

She swiped at him with her pillow.

"I probably haven't got any viable eggs left, even if I

did change my mind, but I'm sure that's not going to happen. I've told you this before, but I remember seeing a programme on TV when I was a kid, and it showed a shire horse giving birth, and as I watched it I thought, 'There's absolutely no way I'm letting that happen to my body.' I could only have been about nine or ten, but even then, I knew without doubt that birth was not an experience I desired." She paused to gather her thoughts. "But now, I wonder if destiny might have other plans for me."

"What do you mean?"

"Well, there's the tradition of the 'maiden aunt' isn't there – you know, the woman who doesn't have children of her own, so that she can help the women who do. Of course, I'd rather Louisa didn't have cancer and didn't need me, but the fact that she does means I have a really close relationship with her children, and somehow, that feels like a blessing, that something good has come out of the situation. I don't have to actually pass on my genes to have a loving relationship with children."

"I feel the same. I suppose you could say the genetic buck stops with us."

"Yeah. I remember Cassandra once said that you and me are 'selecting ourselves out of the gene pool'. But there's nothing special about us that deserves replicating, is there?"

"Oh, I don't know. I think I have a rather fine jaw-line, and your eyes are quite nice..."

She laughed and hugged him, forever grateful that he felt as she did.

Like Arrows to the Heart

On Mondays and Thursdays, Mrs Cooray Senior worked as a receptionist at the government hospital opposite the police station, and so on those days, Mrs Cooray Junior didn't go to work in the Notary's Office. Instead she stayed at home and looked after her son. She cherished these precious moments with him and spent most of the time just watching as her little boy toddled around the room quietly mumbling to himself, picking up objects and examining them and then putting them carefully back in their place. He was so self-contained and seemed happiest when on his own observing things. Then he would wave the object at his mother and say, 'Amma ādarae' – I like it. Moses liked everything. He was a contented child. His favourite 'toys' were the saucepans that she kept under the table in the kitchen. Rain would half-fill the smallest pan with rice, and Moses would sit under the table and pour the rice into successive pans until, once poured into the biggest pan, he would reverse the process. He would sit under the table for a long time, fascinated as the rice fell like a waterfall before his eyes.

Rain marvelled at him on this day, as she did every day; she could not believe her depth of feelings for him. Now she totally understood why the mother hen flew at her ankles if Rain came anywhere near her chicks; or how a mongoose mother would suddenly become bold and aggressive at any sign of jeopardy, chiding her pups and putting her own body between them and potential danger. Rain felt as fiercely protective as a leopard – there was nothing she would not do to defend her child, this beautiful boy. And yet as deep as her love was, her heart would often become fearful; fear of losing him, of him being taken away from her, as Bapu had been. At these times her love felt like an arrow that pierced her heart.

Many a time, such feelings of insecurity had created a rift between herself and Geethan, who just could not understand why she allowed her happiness to always be tinged with such despair.

"Rain, I tell you, if you think about it too much, it will happen. You have to be positive; you have to think that only the best will befall us – that we will be healthy and happy and have enough food in our bellies. I believe, if you constantly fear death and tragedy in this way, you are drawing it towards yourself."

"But I cannot help it, Geethan! I do not want to feel like this, but it just engulfs me, unbidden. I know you are right, and in my mind, I tell myself to enjoy this moment, and delight in all our blessings and then, before I know it my legs are quaking and I feel sick to my stomach that it will all be taken away again."

Geethan embraced his wife. "Perhaps there will come a day when you regain your trust in God and have true faith that God loves you. Perhaps then you will be able to believe in our family and the life we've built together, rather than continuing to mourn for your father and the love you lost when you were so young."

Rain looked at her husband. Many times she had wondered where his wisdom came from. He was not much older than her but he seemed so worldly wise, and more so now that he was studying to become a Notary. He took his training extremely seriously, staying up late into the night reading textbooks and making copious notes. Rain doubted that Mr Pigera ever did the same, though somehow, he had managed to pass the public exam. Geethan's own exam was scheduled for the end of the month and they were both beginning to feel nervous about it. All their plans rested on Geethan becoming an articled clerk, and then taking the public exam to hold the post of Notary.

Rain's thoughts turned to her parents as they often did, and more especially to her mother, whom she'd felt closer to since becoming a mother herself. When Moses was just over a year old, Rain had become very ill with Hepatitis E and had to spend almost a month in bed. At first, she thought her fatigue, which was intense and overwhelming, was just down to being a new mother, but then the pain in her joints and abdomen became so severe that she had to go and see a doctor at the government hospital. After taking a urine and blood sample, he was able to diagnose her illness, and she was ordered to take bed rest until she felt better. There was no treatment available, but the doctor recommended that she eat oranges every day and avoid kissing her husband and child. He said she would recover in time, which was exactly what they had said about her mother, who never did recover. A shiver of anxiety reverberated through Rain's body.

During that never-ending month of confinement, her kind but rather reticent mother-in-law would come in the morning, just as Geethan left for the Notary's Office, to pick-up Moses and take him over to her house, giving Rain some peace and quiet. At first, Rain baulked at this, insisting that she could care for him herself, but her strength had declined so much that she was unable even to lift her son in her arms, and Moses had crawled off and found his grandmother of his own volition.

Alone in bed, Rain imagined her white blood corpuscles fighting to ward off the virus. She imagined them forming little barriers around the rogue virus cells in her veins and arteries and smothering them. She had learned about this in her school biology class and clearly remembered the diagrams in the big red hardback textbook she shared with six other girls. She remembered the images of how the white blood cells engulfed and killed bacteria and viruses, but now it was as if she could actually feel it happening in her body. The illness seemed to strip her of all other sensations except those that were taking place internally, and as her focus went inward, so she began to understand how her own mother had become steadily cut off from the world. She saw how easily illness could do that to you.

When she was young, Rain had thought her mother was selfish and heartless; now she knew her mother was helpless and heartbroken. And, as if a golden thread of memory had been tugged taut by her contemplation, Rain began to remember times when she was very small when her mother had played with her, brushed her hair and kissed her cheek and held her tightly in her arms; and Rain now realised that Bapu too, remembered his wife like this, remembered her loving ways, and that was why he cared for her ceaselessly to the end of their days. The tears streamed down Rain's cheeks as she began to comprehend the pain her mother must have endured at not being able to care for her own children, nor even caress them. She understood for the first time that her mother's withdrawal from life was as painful to her as the illness itself.

It was then that she recalled something Nora had said in her most recent letter; Nora who was engulfed by the trauma of seeing her sister succumb to the ravages of cancer. Weak as she felt, Rain managed to crawl over to her workbench and retrieve the letter from the Precious Drawer underneath her sewing machine. It was printed out on *Awaken* letterheaded paper. Nora had apologised for not writing by hand, explaining that she'd written this one in her lunchbreak, and it was quicker to type it on the computer and print it out, rather than handwrite it. Rain did not mind one bit. She found the section that had disturbed her so much.

> Last week when I visited Louisa she said something to me that I found unutterably sad. After I had put her children to bed, I went into her bedroom to say goodbye, as it was getting late and I needed to head for home. Louisa held my arm and said, "The worst thing is not the cancer, it's not the pain, it's the thought of not being here to see my children grow up." I knew she had been

thinking about this, but to hear her say it broke my heart. I could not say, 'It will be alright,' or 'we will take care of them,' because that's not what she was saying. She knows they will be loved and cared for, but her pain was because she would not be there to do it herself. She was living their lives in fast-forward, wondering what they would do, who they would marry and what their own children would be like, and the pain of knowing she will not witness it herself is unbearable to her. A mother's love is so utterly unconditional, and Louisa felt she couldn't trust that others would be able to give such love to her children.

"But we love them so much," I said to her. "If you are not here, and Louisa, I still believe you can recover from this, then we will care for them and love them and help them grow into adulthood. All the family will rally round and be there for them." It was then that Louisa made a noise, the like of which I have never heard before. It was a cross between a wail and a scream, a sigh and a sob. It came from her heart and it pierced mine like an arrow. "Nobody will love them like I love them, Nora! Not you, not Mum, not Terry, nobody. I fear for my children. Who will believe in them? Who will be proud of them? Who will love them, no matter what?" I had no answer to reassure her. Dear sister, you who has a child yourself now, will surely understand how her words cut me like a knife. Because she is right. Nobody can replace a mother's fierce love, no matter how hard we try.

Rain put the letter down as Geethan came in from his day's work in the Notary's Office, tears still streaming down her cheeks. Motherhood was proving to be exquisitely and unexpectedly agonising to her.

"I have come to realise that my poor mother must've endured so much pain, Geethan." The tears of grief for her mother, and for Louisa too, would not subside. "She loved me and Anuja just as much as I love Moses. I understand that now I am a mother myself. The pain she felt knowing she might not see us grow up, knowing she may never meet her grandchildren... I think it broke her. It broke her, and I couldn't see it, not then. I just hated her for being so distant, so withdrawn..."

Geethan caught his wife's hands in his and looked into her eyes. "But, there will have been many gifts for her as well, you know."

"What do you mean? How could there have been any gifts in her situation?"

"Well, look at your own illness, my darling wife. Only by experiencing it have you been able to understand what your mother went through, and so you have shed tears of grief for her – something I think you have only done for your Bapu until now? So, your illness has given you a profound gift, has it not? It has restored your love for your mother – and it will have been the same for her. It will not all have been unbearable. Do you remember what the Priest said in church once? 'God never gives us more than we can endure.'"

Rain was thoughtful for some time. She had never considered that her mother's illness might have had any happinesss in it, or any meaning, but perhaps it did. Perhaps in some way, she had found her own peace.

"Thank you Geethan. I wish I could kiss you."

"What for?"

"For helping me, bit by bit, to learn to love again without fear. I bless the day I met you."

"And I you, my beautiful wife. Even when you are ill you look so pretty. I wish I could kiss you too, but the doctor said the virus will be contagious until you show signs of recovery. So, Moses and I will have to be content with hugging each other until that day, though right now he is in the yard with Anuja throwing stones into a tin. Now then, eat your orange and get some rest my love."

That night, Rain dreamed of her mother. She was floating beside the bed Rain shared with Geethan, swaying slightly, her hair swirling about her face as if she was drifting in a current of water. She looked serene and so very beautiful

'Amma...?'

'I wanted to come back to you my Rain, my dear Lakmini, but I couldn't. I saw you in the harbour waters, I felt your pain. We are always connected, you and I. I am with you every day. I am always with you...'

And then she faded away, and Rain awoke knowing that the virus had left her body; she had felt it ebb away with the image of her mother, as if her mother had commanded the virus to leave, like it was her parting gift to Rain.

Geethan woke to hear his wife making breakfast in the adjoining room. He watched her as she came into the bedroom, Moses resting on her hip, a glass of water in her hand for her husband.

"Good morning Geethan. I am going to come with you to work today."

"No Rain, it is too soon."

"It is not, husband. It is time." She told him about her dream and how she felt the virus leave her body. "I feel stronger than ever," she smiled, "because I have my mother's strength with me always, and her blessing. I have been reconciled with her beyond the grave."

"This is a good day indeed!" Geethan swung his legs out of bed and embraced his wife, kissing her and pulling her back under the covers.

"Geethan-ji, no! What about the child?"

But Moses had escaped his mother's clutches and had returned to his favourite place under the kitchen table, filling his pots with rice, oblivious to his parents' passion.

Since that day, the arrows to Rain's heart had begun to miss their target; she had learned how to deflect them, most of the time. Though occasionally they still pierced her heart with fear, slowly she began to rebuild her trust in life, and her guardian angel was her own mother, whom she often saw in her mind's eye, floating like a mermaid at her side.

On the day of Geethan's exam to become an articled clerk, there was an unexpected visitor at the Notary's Office. Panni Pigera himself had deigned to call on them whilst in Lagentle on 'other business.'

"Where is master of the house?" Mr Pigera barked, addressing Rain as he used to when she worked for him, without manners or respect.

"Good afternoon Mr Pigera. My husband is taking his exam today, so he is not here. How can I help?"

"I have decided to put up rent for business tenure. It

has been over two years since we drew up agreement and I have decided to review it. Here is new contract which you must sign."

Rain was aghast. In her opinion they were already paying this obstreperous and malodorous man way over the odds. Standing her ground, she looked him in the eye. "You can't just increase the fees of a contractual agreement without discussing it with us first."

"I think you'll find I can. Sign the damn papers woman, so I can be on my way."

"I will not. The tenure is in Geethan's name anyway and he will not be back for another hour or so."

"Then I will wait." Pigera sat heavily on the chair behind the office counter, where he used to sit picking his nose and farting without a care for who was in the office at the time. Seeing him slouched there made Rain feel sick with anxiety. This detestable man had loomed large over her life for too long, and yet they needed him, or rather, they needed his name as the registered Notary so that they could run the business legally in his stead. She picked up the contract he had put on the counter, and then herself dropped heavily into her chair.

"But this is daylight robbery!" She glared at the man opposite. "You are proposing to increase the monthly fee by over 50%."

"I am not proposing to increase it, I am increasing it. As I see it, you have no choice in the matter. If you want honour of running the Notary's Office, then you must pay for the privilege, isn't it."

"But Mr Pigera, surely you must understand, being a businessman yourself," (she hoped that calling him a businessman rather than a crook would assuage his greed a little), "that no business can withstand a 50% increase in expenses like this overnight. There is no way we can find that kind of money."

"Well, I say either you find the money, or you find another job, Miss Smarty Pants."

Those words lit a fire within Rain. "Mr Pigera, my name is Mrs Cooray, and I think you are calling our bluff here." All the pent-up rage she'd felt over the years for this unkind bully suddenly boiled to the surface. "I think you are so desperate for this money that you will try and twist our arms into paying your debts on your behalf, but we will not, do you hear me? We will not pay another penny to you over and above that which we have already contractually agreed."

Pigera leapt from the chair and grabbed Rain's arm roughly. "I'll give you arm-twisting," he hissed, globules of his spittle specking her face. "How's this, huh?" and he wrenched her arm behind her back, so that he could glower over her. "Don't talk to me about bluffing, you stupid woman," he spat, twisting her arm painfully. "What do you know about bluffing? If I wanted to call your bluff, I could do it in one hundred and one ways. I could bring you and that idiot husband of yours down any time I like. I could make your life a misery just like that." He snapped his fingers in Rain's face, making her jump.

Rain saw red. Nobody called Geethan an idiot, least of all this cowardly invertebrate in front of her.

"How about I call your bluff, Panni? How about I tell you that we resign, here and now." She tried to pull her arm away from him, but he held firm. "Let go of me, you beast!" she screamed. "You can have your business back and you can run it yourself. We quit. Now, do as I say and get your filthy hands off me!" Trembling, she managed to wrench her arm from his grip, glaring at him, anger boiling within her like she'd never felt before.

"What in God's name is going on?" Geethan looked at his wife as he came through the door, concern etched on his face. "The whole town can hear the commotion coming from in here. What is happening?"

"Mr Pigera here is trying to increase our payments by 50%, Geethan, for goodness sake. He is trying to rob us blind, and he thinks we'll just do as we are told, as if we are a couple of children who will do his bidding. So, I've told him he can have his business back. I've told him we won't stand for it."

"How can you let your wife behave in such a way?" Pigera turned his back on Rain and addressed Geethan. "She is an embarrassment. She is a liability. Tell her to keep quiet and let us two gentlemen discuss this new arrangement in peace, without interruption."

"Mr Pigera, there is no new arrangement if it entails a 50% increase in payments. And please do not speak of my wife in such a manner. She is my business partner as well as my wife, and if she says the increase is unacceptable then it is unacceptable. If you insist on pressing ahead with this arrangement, which in my opinion amounts to nothing more than embezzlement, then we will walk away from this business, here and now, and you will receive nothing from us whatsoever. And I can assure you that there is nobody else between here and Galle who is qualified to take over from us, as I've just sat an exam on my own, which proves it."

Rain beamed at Geethan. In that moment he became a man in her eyes. He had always been the boy she loved, the smiling kid with the motorbike who took photographs of elephants and monkeys, but at that moment, he seemed to gain stature both physically and intellectually.

Much to their surprise, Mr Pigera broke down in front of them, his whole body crumpling like a half-empty sack of rice. He raked his greasy hair back from his forehead.

"Look," he pleaded, "let's not be hasty here. Let's talk this through like civilised adults, huh? We can renegotiate, surely? You don't have to walk away. Please don't go – I need you to be here, I need your payments. But it's not enough, God dammit. I need more money, I tell you. What more are you prepared to pay?"

It was as if he had shown all his cards in one go. No wonder he had lost so much money at the poker tables if this was his strategy – he'd played an open-handed game and the odds had suddenly turned against him.

"We are not prepared to pay you any more money, Mr Pigera. This business is not a gold-mine – you of all people should know that. We have made it into a success from sheer hard work and commitment, something you never showed when you ran the place, but we are not prepared to pay you an iota more than we do already. Like I said, if you want to run it yourself, feel free to terminate our contract. But somehow, I doubt you will do that, because you don't have it in you for hard work."

Rain nearly danced a jig. This was her husband and not only was he standing up to Mr Pigera, he was roasting him on the spot. She was enjoying seeing the worm squirm.

"What will you give me then, lump sum, huh? I need to disappear. I need to get out of Sri Lanka for a while. I just need airfare to Bangkok and then I can lay low. Buy me out of business now, I beg you."

"But I am not due to take my public exam for another six months. If we buy you out now, we won't be able to run legally until then."

"I won't tell anybody. Nobody will know. Nothing will change – I am only here in name anyway. You pay me lump sum, I slip off to Bangkok and six months, Bob is uncle and business is yours. Okay? Ten thousand rupees. What do you say?"

"We can't find that kind of money, Pigera! It's out of the question," said Geethan. "And anyway, it would be illegal for us to run the business in your name if you are a fugitive. And, why do you have to run away to Bangkok, for that matter?"

"None of your goddam business! Damn you. Damn you both!" Pigera swiped a box of papers off the counter so they fluttered to the floor. "You will wish you'd never laid eyes on me by the time I'm finished with you," he threatened, and flounced out of the door, slamming it so hard, the glass rattled alarmingly.

Rain looked at her husband, wide-eyed.

"That man is in big trouble." Geethan bent down and began to retrieve the papers that were lying scattered all over the floor.

"It certainly seems so. But where does it leave us, Geethan? Our position here feels quite precarious."

Geethan was quiet, deep in thought for a while, then he said. "Well, yes and no…"

"Oh, my goodness! I forgot to ask you how the exam went today? I'm so sorry. All this nonsense with old Panni Pigera completely side-tracked me. How did it go?"

"That's okay, Rain. It went well. I found it quite easy, and as I said, I really was the only one taking the exam, so it's true that there isn't anyone else who could take over from us right now. And then, I was talking with the Invigilator after the exam and he told me that the public exams are taking place in Colombo at the end of June. That's only six weeks away – something I decided to keep quiet from Pigera. If I pass today, and work hard, I could take the public exam by the end of June, and then we would be in a position to buy Pigera out, once and for all. But now we know that he is desperate, we can call the shots. We won't offer him anywhere near ten thousand rupees for the transfer of the licence. That's just ludicrous. But, we will look at the accounts and set a budget that we can afford and then make the offer to him. We will draw up the papers legally and we will be done with that man once and for all. Then we alone will be the rightful owners of Lagentle's Notary Office."

"Well, that would certainly be a weight off my mind, Geethan. I have always lived in dread of him. He is such a tyrant, and true to form he tried to bully us today, but you wouldn't let him."

"No, my wife – YOU wouldn't let him. It was you who called his bluff; it was you who told him we would quit if he tried to exploit us. I am so proud of you for standing up to him!"

"Oh, my goodness! I can't take this all in," said Rain. "Let me make a pot of tea. As she did so, the fax machine in the corner of the room began to chunter and whirr, making all the preparatory noises to indicate 'Incoming' as they jokingly called it.

Rain went over to see who was contacting them.

"Oh how nice – it's from Nora!" she said. "I was just thinking about her and wondering what she would make of Mr Pigera." Rain waited as the typewritten letter was slowly disgorged from the machine. It was only one page long, which was unusual for Nora.

My dear Rain

Thank you for your recent letter. I think of you often, my sister, and hope that you, Geethan and dear Moses are keeping well and happy. I think of little Moses often and as you know, I was thrilled when you asked me to be his Godmother. To mark his second birthday, I have started a Post Office account here in his name, and I will put a little money in it on each of his birthdays and at Christmas too, so that when he is 18 years old, he will have enough money to do something special, like fly over to the UK to see his aged Godmother, which I will be by that time!

As you know, Louisa is very poorly, and I find I am spending more and more of my spare time by her side. She has almost finished a third round of chemotherapy treatment using a new combination of drugs, but it is making her very ill, so all her family and friends are rallying around to help out with the children and with visits to the hospital. All I know is that we must make the most of every precious day, for we never know what is around the corner. Of all people, you, my dear sister, know that is true.

Forgive the brevity of this letter. I promise I will
make time to write to you properly very soon. I
just wanted you to know that you are in
my thoughts.

All my love, Nora

"Oh Geethan, isn't that sad?" Rain had read the letter
aloud to her husband.

"It is terribly sad," he agreed. "I'm assuming Louisa
can't be very old if she has two small children?"

"She's 30, I think. Too young to suffer so dreadfully.
But then... my own mother was probably not much older
when she died. She had me when she was 18 and I was 15
when she died, so goodness me, she was probably only 33
or 34... Nora is right. We have to make the most of every
day, my dearest husband." Rain went over to Geethan and
gave him a hug, just as the office door opened and Sergeant
Gomes stepped in.

"Good afternoon, my friends."

"Good afternoon, sir," replied Rain with a smile. "To
what do we owe this pleasure?"

"I felt it was my duty to inform you of a turn of events
that affects you indirectly." Rain and Geethan looked at
each other, curious as to what else could possibly happen
on this eventful day. "I thought you should know that
Mr Pigera is in custody. He has been charged with three
counts of burglary, one count of arson and one count of
fraud. The Colombo police have been tracking him and
alerted us when they found out he was travelling to
Lagentle. He has huge gambling debts, and it seems he
is also accused of money laundering. He will be facing

trial in Colombo, and it is unlikely he will get bail. The Colombo detectives seem fairly certain that Pigera is their man."

"Oh my goodness!" said Geethan. "That explains why he wanted us to buy him out of the business with a lump sum so he could flee to Bangkok…"

"Really? I may have to ask you to come to the station to make a statement to that effect, Geethan."

"Of course, sir."

"But where does it leave us, Sergeant Gomes?" asked Rain. "How can the Notary's Office keep running when the Notary is detained in police custody?"

"Exactly." said Sergeant Gomes. "That is why I have come to see you. I think you will have to cease trading until such time as you can legally take office yourselves. I am so sorry to have to tell you this, but I thought you should hear it from me, rather than common gossip."

"Thank you, sir. As always, we appreciate your help." Geethan showed Sergeant Gomes to the door.

"Well, today has gone from the sublime to the ridiculous," said Rain, feeling overwhelmed by what she had just heard. "What shall we do now, Geethan?"

"Don't you see, Rain? God has helped us out. All has worked out in our favour! In six weeks' time I can take the public exam. Between now and then, we do not have to pay Mr Pigera his fee, as he is in police custody. We will save that money and put it toward buying the licence directly from the Department of Justice, without having to buy out Pigera.

"And in the meantime, in the six weeks when we cannot accept any work, shall we give this grotty old office a face-lift and put in that kitchen in the back compound that you have been talking about? Let us paint and decorate, and clean the windows and convert the back room – and do you know what, my darling? I think it is time to lease our first computer. I've heard that emails are better than faxes and we have to keep up with the modern trends in our line of work."

Rain looked at her husband. Was there ever anyone in the entire world more positive than him?

Linda McCartney

Nora shifted in her seat, wishing these old men would just *for God's sake make a decision!* She'd driven 20 miles in a howling gale with horizontal rain to get to the house of *Awaken*'s Art Editor, who lived literally, in the middle of nowhere, and now he and Jay were having one of their interminable design meetings which lasted for hours, but which, in Nora's opinion could've been done and dusted in 40 minutes max.

Be nice, she reminded herself. *This is his job.*

But the Art Editor liked the sound of his own voice, and debated the relative merits of each one of the myriad photographs, paintings and illustrations, *ad nauseum,* only to determine that none of them were quite good enough and could Nora look for something with perhaps a little more 'light' or a little less 'anger'…

Nora smiled. "Of course. No problem." But it was actually a problem. It created a lot more work for her – lots of phone calls and emails to photo agencies, and trips to and from the Post Office to collect and return the heavy parcels of slides and prints that may or may not contain the exact image the Art Editor was looking for

– though one of those agencies, Magnum Photos, had uploaded their entire collection onto something called a website, through which Nora could browse to find the perfect pictures she needed, and then request them to be sent on via the post. *This website malarkey,* Nora thought, *was an idea that might just catch on.*

The Art Editor had enjoyed an illustrious career as an artist and writer, and he obviously knew his stuff, but Nora thought he chose obscure and often ugly images for intellectual or academic reasons, rather than on the merit of the image itself. He didn't like anything too colourful, too romantic, too modern, too pretty, too ordinary, too extraordinary, too suggestive, too objective… He was a hard man to please.

The truth was, Nora wasn't really cross at these two colleagues at all, in fact under normal circumstances, she would've bantered with them, made them smile, helped them to see things from a less patriarchal perspective; no, the truth was that Nora was tired and emotional. She was at breaking point, because for weeks now, she had spent three or four evenings a week with Louisa, helping her in her hours of need. She didn't resent doing it, but she was exhausted and anything either one of these men might say today, could trigger her into a fit of pique, or into tears, and she knew it. She was barely functioning, yet she had a demanding and responsible job to uphold as Assistant Editor. She was Jay's right hand, and she didn't want to let him down. She wanted to be so good at her job that one day, Jay would hand over the editorship to her, and then she could choose any bloody photo she liked!

The meeting eventually came to an end, and Nora

drove back to the office with a hundred and one things to do in her head and the day already half gone. But at least when she got to work, Cass had opened the post and there were only a few letters in her in-tray. All Nora had to do was check her emails and then she could get cracking and find the new images for the magazine, as the Art Editor had requested.

There was only one email in her In-box, but it was the most unexpected email she'd ever received. It was from lakminicooray@notaryservices.lgt.gov.lk

Nora's mind went blank, and then she laughed. Rain had bought a computer!

> Dear Sister Nora
>
> I hope I have surprised you by sending an email! I got your address from the magazine and I wanted you to be the first person we sent an email to, because without your kindness and help with the sewing machine, I truly believe none of my good fortune would ever have happened.

In almost every letter Nora received from Rain, she made mention of the sewing machine. Nora could never have guessed that one small gesture of arranging a free advert would have made such a difference to someone's life. And it nearly didn't happen; if Jay had not been so insistent on finding that one thousands pound cheque (which had become legend between her and Cass), then Rain's letter would've languished in Nora's 'special filing cabinet' – the paper basket – for a few more weeks before being carted off to the recycling centre. But that was not to be the way of things. That was not its destiny.

> I have great news! Geethan passed the public exam and he applied for the Notary licence for Lagentle. The old holder used to be my boss Mr Pigera, but he is in custody awaiting sentencing for several misdemeanours which means he was stripped of his right to be Notary. And as nobody else applied for the Licence, it was granted to us! Praise be to God. Can you believe it, sister?

> I help Geethan three days a week when Mrs Cooray Senior is able to look after my darling Moses. I like this arrangement very much, and between us, Geethan and I have turned the business around and it is now profitable. We have a photocopier which the general public can come in and use for a small fee, and we also offer an email service for those who don't have their own computers. I do most of the administration, and Geethan still holds the contract with his old employers at PerfectPrint to collate, verify and file all court documents. It is wonderful to feel we are giving a good service to our community in this way.

> Talking of which, something I have always wanted to do since I lost my parents and realised how hungry some children can be, was to set up a community kitchen to offer free food to those in need. As it happened, when we bought the lease to the office premises, they offered us the adjoining building as part of the lease – Mr Pigera

did not want it and it was going to ruin. So Geethan and I agreed to rent it, and we have renovated it and made a kitchen area, and it is now a little drop-in centre for the hungry and needy. We open it on Monday, Wednesday, Friday and Sunday evenings from 6pm to 8pm and so far, we have provided nearly 200 meals to children and often their parents. The wonderful thing is that our friend, Sergeant Gomes, from the local police constabulary, has recently been given responsibility for the Police Community Welfare Fund and he kindly made a donation to us which helped us to buy much-needed equipment and food. We are very blessed indeed.

Anuja absolutely loves coming to the kitchen. Mrs Cooray Senior is teaching him to cook – sister, she is a very good cook – and Anuja seems to have a flair for it too. When he finishes school, he runs across town to come to the kitchen to prepare food for our community, or if it is not a cooking night, he works out what he needs to buy for the next day. It is so wonderful to see him enthusiastic like this. He told me he wants to be head chef in a top hotel in Colombo when he grows up, and I believe now that could be possible, because I never thought my life would turn out like this – I thought it was impossible to be happy. But it was not.

My dear sister, it is shocking to see how much need there is in our town. Geethan and I made a

vow to always help those less fortunate than
ourselves if we are in a position to do so.
Because of the love and support of his parents,
we can give a little more than we need to others.
This is another dream come true for me.

Please email me soon! I wait with great
excitement to see your email come to our office.
It is like magic, is it not!

With love, from your sister, Lakmini Rain
Cooray xx

Nora recalled Rain's email as she drove to Louisa's
house that night and made a mental note to send some
money via Western Union for the community kitchen. It
was something she liked to do from time to time, just
little amounts: enough for Rain to buy a new pair of
shoes, or a toy for Moses. Like she would do for Louisa
and her kids at Christmas and birthdays.

Nora arrived at her sister's home around 6pm, and
after a long and tiring day at work, she really did have to
put a brave face on to be cheerful for the kids. It was her
turn to help make supper and put the kids to bed, whilst
Terry worked late, which was something Nora rather
uncharitably noted he'd been doing a lot of lately. Louisa
said they'd landed a new contract and had to pull out all
the stops to keep their customers satisfied; however Nora
felt it was more the case that Terry chose to stay at work
rather than return home and tend to his wife. Nora
thought Terry didn't seem like the tending type.

After feeding the children and helping them with

their homework, getting them in and out of the bath and off to bed having had a snuggle-up with their mother in her enormous divan, Nora at last had time to sit down and relax with her sister. She was exhausted and could see no end to this gruelling routine.

"Linda McCartney's dead."

"What? Oh, yes, I heard it on the news."

"It's terrible, isn't it?"

"Yes, it's very sad."

"No, it's more than that, Nora. Don't you get it? Linda McCartney, one of the richest women in the world, has died from breast cancer. If they couldn't save her, what hope have the rest of us got? She could've paid for any treatment, anywhere in the world. She would've had the best consultants money can buy and still she died. It's hit me like a ton of bricks, Nora. I know I'm not going to survive this." Louisa's sob was full of despair.

"Oh Lou, sweetheart, that's not necessarily the case, is it? Linda's cancer might've been much more aggressive than yours, or she may have had a different prognosis altogether... hers may not have been oestrogen-positive like yours; just because she didn't make it, doesn't mean you won't. Louisa, don't cry sweetie."

"It does! It does mean I won't make it. For God's sake Nora, wake up! Will you please face this; face what's happening to me."

"What do you mean?"

"Well, all the crap you keep spouting about positive thinking and alternative remedies... Linda McCartney will have done all that too, you know, and it didn't save her, did it? She'll have gone to the best homeopaths and ozone therapists and Budwig practitioners; she'll have drunk kombucha and godforsaken beetroot juices until it came out of her ARSE, literally, and she's still dead!"

"Shhhh, shhhh Louisa, the kids will hear. Look, I'm only trying to help... Of course you don't have to try any of those alternatives if you don't want to. I... it's... I feel helpless too Louisa. I don't know what to do... I don't want you to die."

The sisters, unable to reach out to one another, sat quietly, each in their own world of anguish.

"Sometimes I hear myself spouting all that stuff about positive thinking and attracting healing energy and I just want the ground to swallow me up. I hear myself and I think, 'You do it then Nora. If you truly believe it, make her better,' but I can't. I don't know how to make you better Lou. I wish I did."

"You can't make me better, and none of your wishful thinking can either. I'm not going to beat this."

"Oh, please don't say that ...please! I can't bear it."

"Well, *I* have to bear it. I can't speak to Mum and Dad about it – the sadness in Mum's eyes just devastates me. I know how she's feeling – it's how I'm feeling about my kids. You'd do anything for your kids, but you can't die for them. I know Mum would die for me, but it doesn't work like that, does it? And I can't speak to Terry about it because he just clams-up and shuts off. He walks away, Nora. He walks away. He can't cope. You're the only person I can talk to about it. You and Joe. Please, listen to me. I have to tell you this."

"I know, I know." Nora held her sister's hand.

Tears... so many tears. So much snot and sniffing. *How many tears is it possible to cry in one lifetime*, Nora wondered?

"It won't be long now, Noo, that I do know. But I'm going to make the absolute best of the time I have left. I'm not going to have any more treatment. I've decided. If it didn't save Linda, it won't save me."

Momentarily, Nora couldn't think who Linda was – oh, yes, Linda McCartney. It seemed strange that Louisa was referring to her on first name terms, but then Louisa felt a kinship with her. Their paths were following a similar trajectory. Louisa continued.

"So, no more poison, no more chemo. I'm stopping the lot. I'm going to take my chances, sis. I'm going to go to France with the choir at the end of the month – Terry's agreed to come with me – and I'm going to let off steam and have a holiday. I'm going to live to the max for as long as my body – and the steroids – will let me, and then, when the time comes, I am going to face the inescapable. But I'm not doing this anymore. I'm not going to just lie in bed waiting to die. Fuck. That."

Nora knew the steroids were the one prescribed drug that Louisa could tolerate, that seemed to help her. They were like little silver bullets that gave her a shot of life; a pick-me-up that truly did pick her up, spin her around and point her in the direction of life for a brief moment. The dropped her just as quickly, and like a limp rag she lay lifeless and spent until enough time had passed before she could have another pill. Nora knew it was unsustainable. Louisa knew it was unsustainable. But what the hell? What did she have to lose? Linda McCartney was dead.

"Really, Louisa? You're stopping all the treatment? Don't you think you should speak to your specialist first, to see what she thinks?"

"I know what she thinks, Nora. She thinks that death represents a total failure of the health system and it negatively impacts her statistics, so she'll put me on any combination of drugs to see if they work, no matter how they make me feel."

"That's a bit cynical, isn't it? I'm sure she's doing it in your best interests."

"She's not! The system doesn't understand cancer any more than I do. They fight it, and try and destroy it, but I'm in the firing line too – they're destroying me, too. Because the cancer IS me."

"No, it's not... Don't say that, Lou."

"IT IS, NORA! It is me. It's within me and it's part of me. I almost feel sorry for my cancer. It's like... I think some of my cells have forgotten how to function properly. It's like they don't know what they should be doing, so they just keep growing. I feel sorry for them. They just keep getting it wrong. I've tried speaking with them, telling them not to try so hard, to relax, but they don't even know how to do that. So, I'm going to relax, I'm going to chill out and stop worrying and stop taking all that SHIT that makes me feel like SHIT and see if it sets my cells a good example."

"Well, you seem to have your mind set on this course of action, Louisa, and who am I to try and dissuade you? What do I know about what you're going through? You know I'll stand by you, no matter what."

"I know you will. And anyway, I'm going to make my remaining time on this planet count. I'm going to have so much fun, that I'll go out with a bang, rather than a whimper. And talking about 'bang', Mikey called round yesterday and brought me some of this." Louisa reached down the side of the bed and rummaged around in a wicker basket containing her knitting, some magazines, her Sony Walkman and loads of CDs, and goodness knows what else, and retrieved a small plastic bag. "A bit of weed. For relaxation purposes."

"Oh my God, Louisa!" Nora had to laugh. "Mikey's such a bad influence. Does Terry know you've got this?"

"He knows, and he doesn't approve, which makes it all the more appealing," Louisa chuckled. "Do you want some? Shall I roll a spliff?"

"No way – I've got to drive home in a bit."

"Oh, go on. I'm having some."

"But smoking is so bad for your health, Lou."

As soon as Nora said it, she saw Louisa's lips curl, then laughter gurgled from somewhere deep within, and exploded from her like a greyhound out of a trap. "Ahhh ha hahhh! Bad for my health!" she sputtered, "ha ha! Oh my God Nora, did you really just say that?"

And just like when they were kids playing together, the laughter of one sister infected the other, and Nora began to chuckle, and then giggle helplessly too.

"I think I did. I think I might've just said the most ridiculous thing I've ever said to you in our entire lives!"

The laughter took hold, and the tears returned, but they originated from a different source; they felt healing. They were in hysterics, both women clutching themselves beneath the ribs for support against the great heaves and gales of guffawing.

"Oh, stop it, it hurts!" chortled Louisa.

"I can't! You stop it!"

Eventually the laughter subsided, and with it came a feeling of deep calm.

"You're a nutter," said Nora bending over to kiss the pinkened cheeks of her younger sister. "I'm off now. I'll see you at the weekend. Take it easy on the Mary Jane!"

"Don't, or you'll start me off again," smiled her sister, holding Nora's hand that little bit longer than expected; the nanosecond of time that said, 'I love you'.

As usual, after a night with her sister, Nora felt wrung out and exhausted. It wasn't that she didn't love Louisa or enjoy her company, for even in the depths of despair, they would have a laugh, it was that the rollercoaster of emotions she felt just completely wiped her out. They hollowed her out somehow, so she felt empty and fragile. As Nora got in her car to drive home, she realised how utterly spent she was. It was an effort to put her foot on the clutch.

She drove down the hill and followed the road left over the bridge at the bottom of the valley. As usual, and even though it was getting late, she stopped her car in the layby just after the bridge and hopped out to walk back and look over the parapet at the fast-flowing water below. Any bridge, anywhere called to her; the water called to her. It was dusk and the turbulent weather of the morning had blown over. The sun was setting in the west, painting the underbelly of a vast cloudbank a glowing crimson-orange which reflected in the water gurgling over the rocks, making it seem like liquid fire.

Nora's breathing slowed and her mind switched off; time itself seemed to be taking a deep in-breath and the world around her became hazy, gauzy, indistinct. And then, a kingfisher darted onto a branch that was arching out from the riverbank, directly beneath Nora's head. Its sheer beauty made Nora gasp, and the words 'out of the blue' danced through her mind. The bird seemed not to notice Nora, or at least, it did not seem to mind her presence, his own gaze focused on the water below. He was swaying gently on the branch and in that timeless moment, Nora was able to examine his exquisite being in detail. He was not just blue, but electric blue, turquoise blue, blue-green and slate grey, with chestnut orange underparts, as iridescent as the sky. And then in one graceful movement, the bird shot like an arrow from the branch, dove into a pool of still water near the bank and broke the surface with a tiny fish in its beak, alighting back on the branch beneath Nora. The fish wriggled in the kingfisher's grasp, and he flipped it so that it would go head-first down his throat, but he slightly miscalculated and dropped the fish, which fell back into the river.

It had been let off the hook – and that was exactly how Nora felt. She had been let off the hook, because Linda McCartney had died, and Louisa was taking back her life, for however long that would be.

Full Circle

Anuja took the lid off the vast aluminium pan that was perched above the two-ring gas burner in the kitchen at the back of the Notary's Office in Lagentle, and stirred the contents of the bubbling stew within, its aroma telling him that he'd got the combination of spices and coconut milk just right. His sister Rain, with Moses toddling by her side, placed a wicker basket full of rotis on the makeshift counter where they served the meals, together with a pile of paper plates and paper napkins. Mrs Cooray Senior had made the rotis at home that morning and had arranged for them to be delivered via one of the tuk-tuk taxis that plied the rank where their father used to work. All was in order.

"Is it good, Nuji?"

"It's good, though I say it myself. Here, try." Anuja dolloped a spoonful of the hot mixture onto a plate and folded a roti and handed it to his sister, then a smaller version of the same for his nephew Moses, who had clung to his leg like a limpet since spying him. The little boy's face lit up as he was given his supper.

"Blow on it first Mo, like this." Anuja blew on the hot

plate of food, exaggerating the noise and making his cheeks puff out, which made Moses chuckle.

"Hot, Nuji!" said the little boy, his eyes peering up at his uncle, his long dark eyelashes making him even more adorable, if that were possible.

"Yes, it is. Blow on it to make it cool. Good boy!"

Rain watched adoringly as her brother and son effortlessly conversed and bonded. The love between them was palpable and it made Rain so happy; and although the familiar shadow of fear still crept into her heart – that old dread that her happiness would be short-lived – these days, it was merely a momentary thought, because she had begun to believe Geethan's certainty that they could live a contented life.

Already, a few hungry souls were milling about in the yard outside the kitchen, waiting for what might be the only meal that passed their lips that day.

Rain opened the door to the yard.

"Please do come in and get your food now," she said, noting that there were several people who were becoming regulars at their community kitchen.

Rain and Anuja served the food with smiles and a friendly word to all who filed by, noting how tattered their clothes were, how thin their shoes. Rain had already begun to make plans in her head to have a second-hand clothes rack in the corner of the kitchen where the needy might find a clean shalwar, a length of sari material or a decent pair of flip-flops.

Before long, most people had been served their food, but then a familiar figure joined the end of the queue, one whom Rain had not seen for almost four years.

"Aunty-ji? Is it you?"

The old woman glowered at her. "What of it? Do you discriminate amongst the poor now, is it?"

"Of course not! Here, take a plate. Anuja, please can you serve Aunty-ji?"

Anuja was staring at the woman before him, antipathy etched on his face; nonetheless, he dolloped a generous portion of food onto the plate she proffered.

"And a roti?" Rain folded and placed the bread on Aunty-ji's plate.

Without another word, Mrs Chandran took the plate of food and walked back outside.

Rain looked at Anuja. She knew exactly what he was thinking before he said it.

"Horrible woman. What is she doing here?"

"She... must be hungry, I suppose." Though how she could be hungry puzzled Rain. What had she done with all that money?

Taking off her apron, Rain wandered out into the yard, where some of those who had no homes to go to were still squatting in the late evening sunshine picking their teeth with pieces of twig hewn from the sparse bushes in the corner of the compound, and then split into usable toothpicks. Aunty-ji was among them, and having finished her meal, she wiped her plate thoroughly with the roti for any remaining morsels. She looked up and seeing Rain, scowled with ill-concealed contempt.

"I didn't expect to see you here, Aunty-ji."

"We can all fall on hard times, girl. You fell on hard times; now I have."

"But what has happened, may I ask? What about the loan money I repaid you? That was a lot of money, enough to set you up for life, I would have thought."

"Well, as usual, you thought wrong, didn't you."

"But what about your businesses? Can't your sons help you? They must be grown men by now."

"Don't talk to me of sons!" Aunty-ji spat the words at Rain. "I have no sons."

"Whatever has happened?" Rain squatted down in front of Mrs Chandran and looked her in the eye. "Are you okay?"

The older woman let out a long sigh. "Not really. Not at all as it happens. But I don't want to talk about it to strangers."

"Aunty-ji! I am not a stranger, I am your best friend's daughter. And I can see things are hard for you. Is there anything I can do to help?"

"Why would you want to help me? What's in it for you?"

"There doesn't have to be anything in it for me." Rain had forgotten how Aunty-ji always suspected everyone of having a hidden agenda, an ulterior motive, when in fact these were solely her traits.

Mrs Chandran got to her feet, grumbling about her aching back. "There was too much salt in the food," she said, hobbling out of the compound without uttering a word of thanks, but something in Rain had softened towards her old adversary. She was a link to her parents, a reminder of times gone by. Rain hoped that she would see her again.

When she returned to the kitchen, she was pleased to see Geethan there, having just finished work. He was wiping up the remaining curry from the sides of the giant saucepan with the last of the rotis, licking his lips and congratulating Anuja on the quality of the spicing.

"We'll make a top chef out of you yet." He smiled at his brother-in-law – who was now almost as tall as Geethan – and patted him on the shoulder, then hoisted his son onto his own. "Come on little man, shall we help to wash the pots?"

Does it ever diminish? Rain wondered – *this feeling of awe that another human being can be so kind, so loving, so happy, so generous? How blessed I am that I met Geethan Cooray; how blessed I am that he loves me.*

"Oh, I forgot to give you this." Geethan went over to his briefcase, a present from Rain when he passed his public exam. It was a serious-looking brown leather bag with buckles and a sturdy handle, which Geethan was now never seen without. He thought it gave him credibility and made him look like a businessman, which in a way, it did. He fished around until he found some folded paper. "It's an email from Nora – I printed it out so you can read it at home, tonight."

Rain took the email and thanked him, her mind still pondering the reacquaintance with Aunty-ji. Ever since Moses was born, Rain had felt a much stronger connection with her Amma – perhaps being a mother gives you far more compassion for all mothers? – but Rain regretted that she hardly knew her; that her illness had slowly eroded the bond between mother and daughter. On many occasions Rain had recalled the brief conversation where Aunty-ji told her that her mother was a Hindu and came from Tamil Nadu, and that's why they had the little altar in the corner of their house, with the brass statue of Lord Ganesha on it, the one Bapu blamed for all their ills. And just as she had once sought her father's relatives in the telephone directories of Colombo and

Kandy, Rain longed to know more about her mother, even just her name, which she didn't know, or couldn't remember. Mrs Chandran was her only link to the past. Perhaps by offering the old woman some food and some friendship, Rain could find out more about her mother.

Later that evening, Rain remembered the email from Nora, and fished it out of her bag.

Dear Rain

How are you, my friend? I'm sorry I haven't been in touch for so long, but once again, Joe and I have had to move house. The person who owns Forest Cottage decided to return from Dubai six-months earlier than anticipated and he needed his house back. It strikes me that every time this happens, and we have to leave our home, it is not because we want to move, but because circumstances dictate it. We still haven't found our 'forever home' and sometimes I wonder if we ever will. Everywhere we have lived, we have come to love deeply, which makes leaving it so much harder. It is like we put down roots, but they are wrenched out, and each time this happens, it weakens us somehow.

The strangest thing happened on the day that we were leaving Forest Cottage. I was doing some final cleaning up in the kitchen, and I looked out of the window into the garden where the swimming pool is, and a peacock was standing on the other side of the window, looking in at me.

I gazed into its eyes for a brief moment, and it seemed to say to me (though obviously, it didn't speak aloud), 'Don't worry, you'll be back.' It was such a clear message I can't deny it, though I can't see how we'll ever get back to Tend... unless we win the lottery! But I thought, somehow, it was a good omen.

Anyway, I digress. Many years ago, I bought a house with my partner at the time, Mikey. The house was dilapidated and needed a lot of work to make it habitable, but Mikey was a builder and we thought that we could renovate it and make it beautiful. Oh, the best laid plans of mice and men! As it turned out, the house was much easier to fix than the relationship between me and Mikey, and we were unable to bring our dream to fruition, mostly because we found that we just could not live together! And so, I left and found another place to live ~ Queenie's Cottage in Stipeberry ~ do you remember it? That was when we first started corresponding, almost seven years ago. And you know what happened there; a landslide made it uninhabitable, and overnight, we were made homeless.

But circumstances have now brought me full circle, in that I am living back in the house I bought with Mikey, all those years ago, except this time it is my darling Joe who accompanies me, thank goodness. We found out, not long after we were given our notice to quit Forest Cottage, that Mikey is not at all well. I remember now that on several occasions when we lived together, he would have these 'funny turns' – I once found him passed out on the floor, covered in sweat and unable to get up. I just thought he'd had too much to drink, and he refused to talk about it. But as it turns out, he has a congenital heart defect that many of the men on his father's side of the family also have. In effect, his heart is too big and pumps too much blood around his body, making him feel weak and dizzy and also putting a lot of pressure on his major organs. Poor Mikey. He has had to stop work, under doctor's orders, which means he can no longer pay the mortgage on the house. So, he is going to live with his partner in the village, who is a potter, and Joe and I have moved back to the house. We will finish doing it up, and then put it on the market so that Mikey can be reimbursed for all the hard work he has put into the house. He will need the money now that he can't work.

It is very strange being back here. It isn't somewhere I ever thought I would return to, but in the end, I have to take responsibility for decisions I made many years ago when I was a young woman just starting out in life. Thankfully, Joe is totally supportive, and has even used some of his savings to pay off the mortgage debt which Mikey and I had accrued because of our choices and decisions. So here I am, back at square one, but I'm not the same person and it's not the same situation. It reminds me of some lines in T S Eliot's 'Four Quartets':

'We shall not cease from exploration,
And the end of all our exploring,
Will be to arrive where we started,
And know the place for the first time.'

I suppose it is the start of a new adventure for us.
That's how we are looking at it anyway. And one
bonus is that I am back in the village where
Louisa and the kids live, so it's much easier for
me to spend time with her. She has decided to
have a breast reconstruction which is a very big
operation, and it will take her weeks to recover. I
don't really understand why she is putting herself
through this operation, but it seems important to
her, and she is going ahead with it. So at least by
living back in the same village as Louisa, I can
help her out.

Life is so full of twists and turns, isn't it Lakmini? I
wonder what has been happening for you of late?
Please write and let me know. Your emails are
always such a pleasure to receive.

With love, your sister, Nora

Rain gazed at the email for a while, incredulous that
a peacock had also spoken to Nora like the one that had
spoken to her when she went to see Sergeant Gomes
about the Notary's licence. How strange, she thought,
that this creature should appear to both myself and Nora
in times of change, as if to give us hope. To Rain this
reaffirmed the fact that they really were sisters. Though

they had never laid eyes on one another in all these years, their lives seemed to run along parallel lines, with similar emotional experiences, even down to the creatures who spoke to them in their imagination. She recalled the poem she had written shortly after seeing the peacock on the wall at the police station, and so she went to the bookshelf that Geethan had made and fixed above the kitchen table, and took from it her journal, the one he'd given to her before they were married, the one that was too big to go in her Precious Drawer, and into which she had copied all the stories and poems she'd ever written. There were now only a few blank pages left in it, and along with her own words, she had stuck in the book many of Geethan's photographs, mostly of little Moses it has to be said. Rain thought that Moses was the most wonderful story they had ever created, far better than any poem or photo could ever be. Her son was the story of her life now. He was her reason for being and her reason for writing. He was everything, her world, her heartbeat.

She flicked past the story she had written after her first visit to Yala National Park with Geethan, called 'King of the Dusk' about a leopard. It was now Moses' favourite story and he'd asked her to read it to him so many times that he knew the words by heart. And then she found her peacock poem and read it through. She didn't really know if it was good or not, but she thought that she might send it to Nora in her next letter, just to affirm to her dear friend that what she had experienced, that other-than-human connection, Rain knew of too – and had even written about several years previously.

She put down the journal and looked over at Geethan who was sprawled across the bed, fast asleep, with Moses in his arms. Geethan could fall asleep in an instant, whereas it always took Rain hours to drop off. Luckily, Moses took after his father in this respect. She liked to watch Geethan as he slept; she liked to examine the curve of his cheek, the flutter of his eyelashes as he dreamt, the strong line of his jaw, his wide shoulders. But the joy she took in his physical form was tempered by the possibility that he too could become ill, like Mikey; that this man she saw before her, so full of life and energy, could lose his health and vitality. She'd seen it happen to Bapu, saw him fade before her eyes. She had often wondered why it was and thought perhaps it was just the constant worry of her mother's illness that was gnawing away at him.

Suddenly the old familiar shadows of fear seemed to spring from all corners of the room and envelop her. All her courage, all her faith seeped from her like water being squeezed from a cloth.

She began to weep, for her mother, for Louisa, for Nora, for her own sorrows, still close to the surface though it had been many years since her parents died, and even for Aunty-ji, who seemed so forlorn and worn down by life, her own dreams now rags caught in the wind, drifting hither and thither with no direction. Rain knew Aunty-ji was desperate, for nothing else would have driven her to lose face and come to the community kitchen. Rain's grief felt like a lead weight in her heart, as if she were grieving for the whole world.

A couple of days later, as Rain and Anuja were once again feeding some of Langentle's hungry and destitute souls, Mrs Chandran joined the queue. Rain plated up some of the yam stew and folded a roti and took it over to the woman she had once despised.

"Here, Aunty. Come and sit in the kitchen with me and meet my son."

"You have a son?" Mrs Chandran snatched the plate and began mopping up the stew with the roti, smacking her lips, clearly enjoying the fare.

"I do, and his name is Moses. Come and say hello."

"He will break your heart," said the old woman, but when she laid eyes on the little boy her face softened, and she knelt down to address him. "Hello little Moses," she cooed. "Come and say hello to Aunty-ji."

Moses retreated behind his mother's legs, holding on to her sari, yet still curious, a part of him wondering who this person was and how she knew his name.

"He's a bit shy," said Rain, drawing up a white plastic chair for Mrs Chandran. "Sit here and finish your meal. I'll get you a glass of water."

The old woman did as she was bade, looking around her at the outbuilding that the Coorays had converted into a little kitchen and store room, sniffing as the spicy food made her nose run.

"How can you afford to do all this, hah?" she asked, nodding at the room. "What gives you the right to lord-it over the rest of us?"

Rain chuckled. "You haven't changed a bit, Aunty-ji. Still suspicious and grouchy."

"What is this 'grouchy', hah?"

"Oh, never mind. We just wanted to do something to help people who are less fortunate than us, that's all. We are not lording-it over anybody, just trying to give back a little of our good luck." Rain was proud that she and Geethan were able to help their community in this way, but not all of their savings went into the kitchen. Since her wedding day, and with Geethan's blessing, Rain had saved a few rupees each week for the day she hoped she would be able to take her family to England, to meet Nora. She knew in her heart that she would be saving for years, indeed that she may never be able to save enough for such a journey, but it gave her such a thrill every time the rupees dropped into the little money box she had bought for her savings. That sound kept her dream alive. And, she reminded herself regularly, other dreams she hardly dared to dream – like marrying Geethan and running a business, had come true – so why not this one?

Mrs Chandran sniffed again and ate the last mouthful of her food. "No such thing as luck, just fate, just destiny."

Rain ignored her comment, wondering what had happened in this woman's life to make her so cynical, and full of despair. Instead, she ventured to ask a question that had been on her mind for a long time.

"Aunty-ji, I want to speak with you about something important, if you don't mind?"

The old woman looked at Rain, raised an eyebrow and wiped a drip of stew from her chin with the back of her hand, and then nodded her agreement.

"Do you remember what my mother's name was? You once told me that she came from Tamil Nadu, that I do remember, but I do not even know her name."

Aunty-ji was quiet for a while, as if casting about in her mind for a fleeting memory. "Deepti Udayar. That was her name. We called her Dippy, your father and I. She liked that; it made her laugh. Dippy and Danidu. What a pair."

"Dippy... Of course – I remember!" Rain exclaimed. "Yes, I remember Bapu calling her Dippy. It is a long-forgotten memory. Thank you, Aunty." Rain reached out to embrace the old woman, but she shrank away.

"What part of Tamil Nadu did she come from Aunty. Can you remember?"

Mrs Chandran smoothed her sari and leaned back in the chair, letting out a long and satisfying belch.

"She told me she came from a little village just south of Puducherry, but for the life of me, I cannot remember its name."

"So, how did my parents meet?"

"Well now, that I do remember. Dippy often talked about the first time she met your father, and even though I had heard the story a hundred times, she would tell me again. You see," Aunty-ji said, picking at some stew that had congealed on her threadbare sari, "every year, the Catholic diocese of Lagentle sent a group of children from their Sunday School to St Mary's in Puducherry for a holiday, and the children from St Mary's would come to Lagentle. And one year, your father was sent by his very devout mother to help out, as one of the chaperones who cared for the children." It seemed like Aunty-ji had begun to enjoy her storytelling.

"On this particular day, Dippy was on the beach at Puducherry selling trinkets and incense to the French tourists, when she saw your father coming towards her. He had lost several of the children in his care, silly billy, and was running up and down the beach in a state of panic looking for them. Dippy told me how handsome she thought he was, and so she decided to try and help him find them."

Rain was rapt by the story. "That's fascinating. So, what happened next?"

"How should I know?" snapped the old woman. "Your mother just said it was 'Love at first sight', if you believe in such dicky-bird nonsense."

"So, when did Deepti come to Sri Lanka?" It felt strange calling her mother by her proper name, but Mrs Chandran's patience had run out. She was renowned for not having much of it.

"Questions, questions. Too many questions. Leave me be, woman. I have no more to say."

"But will you come back on Sunday, Aunty-ji? I will save a big plateful of food for you. Will you come back and tell me more?"

"I'm a busy woman. I don't know what I'll be doing on Sunday." Without warning, Mrs Chandran had reverted to her old, irascible self. Yet Rain now knew more about her parents than she'd ever known in her life.

A Tapestry of the Unexpected

Nora opened the front door to see Mikey standing there, a smile on his face, a bottle of wine in his hands.

"Mikey! Hello – thanks for coming."

"Hi Nora." He proffered the bottle of wine to her. It was an expensive one.

Nora looked at this man before her, someone she had once shared her bed with, someone she had once told her most intimate secrets to, but she could see he was not the same man now. She had never been able to see auras, but the thought came to her that something of Mikey's aura had diminished.

"Come in, Mikey. Come in. Joe's in the kitchen, and the kettle's on – unless you'd prefer a glass of this wine? I can see it's a good one."

"Tea would be nice, thanks Noo. I stopped drinking alcohol about six months ago."

His use of her nickname felt a bit too familiar, too affectionate somehow, and it unsettled her. Even so, she managed to keep her composure.

"Really? God! Well done Mikey, that's amazing. Go on through to the kitchen – you know where it is..."

Nora shut the front door and followed Mikey as he walked through the hall and into the kitchen, noticing how thin he was looking; how ruddy his face had become, his long hair now shaved off, nothing more than a silver tonsure on the crown of his head. And how small he looked, too. Joe towered over him.

"Alright, mate? Haven't seen you for a while." Joe clapped Mikey on his back in a friendly gesture but just the weight of Joe's hand seemed to buckle him.

Mikey leaned on the back of a kitchen chair to steady himself.

"Yeah, great thanks, Joe. It looks nice in here. Nora always was good at interior design." Mikey pulled out a chair from under the kitchen table and sat down heavily, gazing around the room that was once his domain. They had done quite a bit of titivating since he'd left: they'd painted the teal blue walls a less intense 'Morning Mist' and had sanded back and oiled the old oak floorboards which now looked fabulous, then they'd bought a new kitchen table and put in a trendy light fitting above it, like something from an old steam ship. It did look rather lovely, Nora thought.

"What's all this about then?" Mikey enquired, though Nora was sure he must have guessed.

"Well Mikey, thanks to you and the incredible job you've made of the renovations, we've had an offer on the house!" And Nora meant what she said. Although he had got into arrears with the mortgage repayments, and when they'd moved back in, the place was in a bit of a mess, Mikey had actually crafted some really beautiful elements to the place. All the front windows had wide window-seats beneath them, the mortar intricately pointed so that the shape of each carefully chosen stone stood out clearly; in the guest bedroom he'd installed a wood and glass door with a footbridge across the passageway underneath, linking the bedroom to the steep, wooded garden opposite; there were curious little niches excavated out of the stone walls in each room where candles or trinkets could be displayed, and he'd made a bespoke wardrobe and dressing table in the main bedroom with stained glass panels and clever patterning in the woodwork – to say nothing of plastering throughout and fixing the leaking chimneys.

Nora realised that he was a master of his craft, and really had worked hard, and what he'd created was a work of art, a beautiful home.

"Wow, really? I didn't think it would sell so quickly." Mikey seemed genuinely surprised.

"You don't mind, do you? You're still okay with the plan to sell up?" Joe wanted to be absolutely sure that Mikey was ready to let go of the place he'd lived in and worked on for many years.

"Of course! Yeah, it really is great news – don't get me wrong, I'll be pleased to get everything sorted once and for all. And I have to admit that the money will come in handy now that I can't work anymore."

The phone rang and Joe went into the hall to answer it. Nora placed a cup of tea in front of Mikey, noticing that as he spoke, he became quite breathless.

"How are you doing, Mikey?"

"Yeah, great! But I have to say, you were right, all those years ago, Nora."

"What do you mean?" It was once rare for Mikey to give Nora credit for anything.

"Oh, you know, yoga, meditation, breath work, eating clean… It's all becoming part of my life now. I really should have paid attention to you way back when."

Nora found his words rather perplexing, because if he had listened to her, changed his ways, opened up, would they still be together? She couldn't countenance that, not now that she was with Joe, who she loved deeply, who completed her. *Perhaps everything happens for a reason?* she thought, *though we cannot see it at the time. Perhaps in being who you were Mikey, you released me and I released you to be who you are.* But these were words she couldn't share with him. Instead she said, "You're doing yoga?"

"I am! I love it. It really helps me to relax. And I'm also reading a really good book that's helping me come to terms with what's happening, to live in the moment, you know, without worrying about what might happen in the future. It's called *Comfortable with Uncertainty.*"

"So, what is happening, health-wise, Mikey, if you don't mind me asking?" Once upon a time, she wouldn't have dared to ask this question of him. He would've immediately clammed-up and become secretive, but Mikey had changed, she could see that. He was more open, more communicative. She thought that perhaps Jenny Deere was a good influence after all.

"Well, I'm on medication that really does help. It lowers my blood pressure and stops me getting dizzy, and now that I'm not doing any physical work, I don't seem to get so many symptoms."

"That's good. I'm pleased to hear it."

"Yeah, I feel so much better, and I'm going on a 10-day

transcendental meditation retreat next week."

Nora could hardly believe her ears, "What? Bloody hell Mikey – looks like this illness is good for you!"

They both chortled.

"I know. How ironic is that? It's crazy, but it's like... it's given me a reason to live. I've had to stop all the hedonism and start looking after myself, and in doing that, I've found so much that interests me, so much I want to know about."

"You're still keen on the 'out of body' experiences, I notice. I mean, transcendental meditation isn't for the faint-hearted." And then, realising what she'd said, she added, "Oh, sorry Mikey, I didn't mean to..."

"It's alright Noo – no point beating about the bush. I have got a weak heart, I have to accept that – so did my Uncle George and my Uncle Patrick, and they both died in their 40th year, though it seems my father has got away with it."

"Maybe that's because he hasn't got a heart?" Nora had said it before she'd had time to think about what she was saying, but luckily, Mikey laughed.

"You're right there! But I'm 40 this year Nora and I'm not under any illusions. I might not have long. They want me to have a heart transplant, you know. But I've said no to that."

"You have? Why, Mikey? It might give you years longer to do all the things you love doing."

"With someone else's heart? No... it doesn't feel right, to me. Would I still be me with someone else's heart? Would I still feel the way I feel? I don't think so. That's why I'm interested in the transcendental stuff – I want to connect with my soul purpose, to find out if there really is something out there that's bigger than me, that has a plan for me. I suppose you could say I'm looking for God."

Tears pricked Nora's eyes, but fortunately just at that moment, Joe reappeared with a grin on his face.

"That was the Estate Agent. The buyers want to come back at the weekend to have another look around, and they've instructed their solicitors to go ahead with all the contractual stuff, so it really is happening. We've sold the old place."

"So what are you guys going to do, then? I've got somewhere to live, but what about you?" Mikey sipped his tea with his little finger cocked daintily, which Nora had always found incongruous and amusing.

"We're going to go and stay at Nora's parents' place. You know John's converted the old milking parlour into a little apartment? Well, we're going to rent that from them for a while – and in true John-fashion, he's done a lovely job and it's a really nice pad."

"Yeah, small but beautiful," Nora added. "It'll be a bit weird living next door to Mum and Dad, though. We'll have to be on our best behaviour! But at least we can have a bit of breathing space there, and we'll still be near enough to take care of Louisa."

"How's she doing?"

Nora was quiet for a moment, wondering how best to answer that question. To the outside world, Louisa seemed on good form; since she'd stopped the chemo-therapy over a year ago, her hair had grown back, she'd put on a bit of weight and she'd made lots of friends at the choir. She'd always got someone visiting her, and often Nora could hear them practicing some two-part harmony as she put her key in the back door, to let herself in and get supper on for the children.

And it seemed to Nora that Louisa was always either getting ready to go out, out, or planning to be somewhere else. It was like she couldn't bear to be on her own, didn't want to be at home, couldn't be still for a moment. She had to keep on the go in case her illness caught up with her. It was as if, in always keeping busy, she didn't have time to think about anything else – and it seemed to be working, on the surface at least. But Nora knew better.

About six months previously, Louisa had undergone breast reconstruction surgery but because she'd already had radiotherapy on her chest area she couldn't have a silicone implant, so she had to have a 'trans-flap', a much more invasive operation where they took an area of skin and muscle from her stomach region, and transplanted it to her chest, making a mound that simulated the shape of a breast. They were careful to keep all the veins intact, so that there would be a living blood supply to keep the tissue alive.

Nora thought it was a totally horrendous prospect and had tried to talk Louisa out of having the operation. Given her sister's life expectancy, she couldn't really understand why she would put herself through the trauma – but Louisa was sure she wanted it done. She'd hinted to Nora that she hoped it would improve her sex life. Louisa would stop at nothing to try and recreate the kind of normality she'd once enjoyed.

After the surgery, Louisa had taken much longer than the six-weeks they'd said she'd need to recover. At first, there were signs that her body was going to reject the trans-flap, which the surgeon had made clear was a possibility, but then things seemed to settle, and Louisa got physically better – but mentally, she was on the verge of collapse.

In taking the section for the trans-flap, they'd scored around her belly-button and close to her pubic bone. One of the 'benefits' of the operation, they'd said, was that she'd get a free tummy-tuck at the same time. But to Louisa's horror, a few weeks after the operation, she saw a thin line of pubic hair grow where her cleavage once was. She'd always had a beautiful head of hair, always been quite hirsute, but to have this daily reminder of the pain she'd endured – to see pubic hair growing where once her beautiful breast had been – it was all just too much, and Louisa fell into a deep depression, which she was only just surfacing from. The breast reconstruction was a failure in her mind, and Terry continued to work late into the night.

"Ah, you know, she's up and down, but I think the choir is a real lifeline for her. They're off to France again this year, and Louisa's planning on partying like it's 1999."

"Ah, well – good job it is then!" said Mikey. "She's amazing, your sister. She's a real inspiration to me, you know. When I start to feel sorry for myself, I just think of her courage and, well, it helps. Right then, I must be off. Let me know if there's anything I need to sign, or anything I can do to help with the sale."

"Will do Mikey. Take care of yourself. It's been really good to see you again," said Joe.

"You too." Mikey eased himself up slowly from the chair. As he did so, Nora saw that his ankles were badly swollen and a bruised purple colour. She assumed it was part of his blood pressure problem and she felt a wave of compassion for him. Poor old Mikey.

"Christ, we don't get very long at being young, before we're old, do we?" she said to Joe as she shut the front door.

"That's exactly what I was thinking," Joe replied. "It seems like only yesterday that Mikey was in a band and living life to the full in London, and now... he's like an old man. I suppose we're getting that way too..." He swatted her playfully with the tea towel.

"Speak for yourself! We're not even 40 yet, and they say life begins at 40..."

"Let's hope so, because the first 38 years have been a bloody nightmare at times." Joe gave Nora a hug and cleared the table and began to wash up.

"Actually, Joe, I think Mikey is much worse than he's letting on. Did you notice how breathless he gets when he speaks, and how bruised his ankles are? He told me that two of his uncles with the same condition didn't make it past 40."

"Really? Jeeze... But it's not inevitable that the same thing will happen to him, Noo. He's got his own path in life and he's made of strong stuff, is Michael."

"I'm not so sure about that. He said his consultant recommended that he should have a heart transplant."

Joe paled visibly. "Oh, my God. That's serious. Is he going to go for it, do you think?" Joe leaned on the sink, trying to take in what he'd just heard, shocked to hear that Mikey was so ill.

"No, he's not. He says he doesn't want someone else's heart in his body." Nora was feeling tearful again.

"Well, that's understandable, I suppose. I don't think I would want that either." Joe sighed and then remembered something. "Oh, by the way, there's a letter for you on the hall table. I forgot to tell you – it came in this morning's post. I think it's from Rain."

Nora shook her head, trying to dislodge the thought of Joe getting ill, like Mikey was. *Please God, don't let that happen,* she thought. *Not to my Joe...*

Only that morning, Nora had been pondering how she'd not heard from Rain for a long while, so she was pleased to have a letter from her dear friend in Sri Lanka. She picked it up from the hall table and went into the living room to read it, sitting on their old but comfy sofa and tucking her feet under her. A letter from Rain was something to be savoured, something to linger over, and even though they both had email now, they often preferred to write to each other by hand. It took longer, but it felt so much more personal, more intimate somehow. It seemed to Nora that emails were for updates, and letters were for stories.

Dear Sister

I pray all is well with you and Joe, and that Louisa is also in good health. I have lots of news to tell you, and the first of it relates to why I am writing and not sending an email. You see, I have more time now, as I am not in the office so much at the moment. This is mostly because the morning sickness is keeping me at home! Yes, I am going to have another baby! He or she will be born around the same time as my birthday, which as you know is also the birthday of Moses. Isn't that strange! It was not at all planned, but that is how it is. Geethan is overjoyed at the prospect, but it is easy for men as they do not have to carry the baby in their belly, isn't it! Moses will be four when the baby is born. So, now I have a little more time to write, which is one gift of being pregnant.

The other news is a longer story. As you know from my previous letters, we have started a community kitchen and Anuja is our top chef, cooking wonderful meals for those in need in our town. Well, some time ago, an old friend of my mother's came in called Aunty-ji, and she has fallen on hard times herself, though she wouldn't say why. I asked her some questions about my mother's family and she was able to tell me my mother's maiden name and a little bit about her life in Tamil Nadu, before she met my father and came to Sri Lanka.

It was like a ray of sunshine for me, dear sister, to hear of my mother and to know her name: Deepti. What a beautiful name, isn't it? I told Geethan all about it and he said that one day, perhaps we will be able to take a holiday in Tamil Nadu and see if we can trace any of my mother's family. This made me very happy, although I don't know if we will ever be able to afford to travel to India.

Then one day, just before I found out I was

pregnant, Geethan and I were in the office and a very well-dressed lady came in and asked to speak to Lakmini Perera. Geethan looked at me, and I said that I was Lakmini Cooray, née Perera, and this lady burst into tears, there and then, on the spot. 'Lakmini, Lakmini,' she said, putting her arms around me. I was very surprised and drew back to look at her, and when I did, she reminded me of someone though I couldn't say who right at that moment. 'I am your Aunty Priya. I am Danidu's sister', she said, and that was it, I knew who it was she reminded me of; my Bapu! And so there we were, standing in the middle of the office, both of us in tears and embracing then looking at each other again, unable to believe what was happening.

Geethan made cups of tea and set two chairs in the back kitchen so that we could have a bit of privacy from the customers who were gawping at us, and Priya told me her story. And now I want to tell it to you. My father, Danidu, went to Tamil Nadu in India when he was a young man, to chaperone children on an educational exchange trip organised by their church, and there he met my mother. They fell in love on a beach (how romantic, isn't it, dear sister!). When Bapu returned to Lagentle, he asked his father for permission to marry Deepti, my mother. But my grandfather was a devout Catholic and Deepti was Hindu and he refused to sanction the marriage. But Aunty Priya told me she was on Danidu's side. She said she thought falling in love was a blessing from God, and so she encouraged my father to listen to his heart. Thank goodness she did, or I would not be here to tell this story to you, dear sister.

What I then learned was that my grandfather was good friends with a Mr Jayasinghe, and that he had promised his son Danidu to Mr Jayasinghe's daughter, Abeesha in an arranged marriage of sorts. Priya told me that Danidu and Abeesha had already been introduced to each other and had been meeting each other every Sunday at church for almost a year before Danidu went to India and came back in love with Deepti. Abeesha, was understandably distraught. But the surprises didn't stop there, dear sister, for Aunty Priya told me that I know of this Abeesha, but that I call her Aunty-ji! Yes, Abeesha is Mrs Chandran, a woman who, until recently, I thought was my enemy.

It seems that my father came back from India a changed man in love with another and determined to marry her. Abeesha went to see Priya begging for her help to make Danidu see sense. Of course, Abeesha wanted Priya to persuade my father to agree to the marriage their parents had already sanctioned, and apparently Abeesha was deeply in love with my father, but Bapu's mind was made up. He wanted to marry Deepti, and Priya decided to help her brother instead of Abeesha.

Together, Danidu and Priya saved every penny they could until they had enough money to pay for Deepti to travel by bus from Puducherry, south to Pattukkottai where she got a boat to Jaffna. There my father met her and escorted her back to Lagentle. That must have been a real adventure in those days, as it would still be today. Danidu thought that as soon as my grandparents met Deepti, they would fall in love with her too, and approve their marriage.

Aunty Priya told me that my mother's family were quite poor, and that they saw her marriage to a Catholic Sri Lankan as a 'step up the ladder' and that Deepti would be able to send money back to Tamil Nadu, once she had settled into her new home, and so they had encouraged the liaison. But, when Danidu introduced Deepti to his parents, instead of falling in love with my mother, they banished my father from his home, and forbade Aunty Priya from ever speaking to him again. How sad, isn't it, dear sister, that there is so little understanding of matters of the heart. What would I have done if you had said 'No' to my marriage to Geethan?

For a long time after that, my Aunty Priya was only able to keep in touch with Bapu via Abeesha, because rather than lose Danidu altogether from her life, Abeesha decided to befriend my mother, so that she could keep them both close, although as Priya said and I had witnessed, in the end Abeesha became very unhappy: she was resentful of my mother and bitter towards my father, and yet she always helped them out in times of trouble. Dear sister, this is the same woman who I had to give half of the sewing machine money to, and who I grew to detest as a bully, and yet now I am a little older and wiser in affairs of the heart, I can see that all her life, she loved my father, despite her love being unrequited, and though she got married herself and had three sons, she always did her best to help Danidu and his family. So it seems that somewhere deep inside Abeesha, there is a beating heart, though I am yet to find it!

When my grandfather became ill, Danidu tried in vain to be reconciled with him, but to no avail. My grandfather died without forgiveness in his heart and my grandmother decided to return to Colombo where she had grown up, taking Aunty Priya with her. Being the only daughter in the family, Priya was expected to dedicate her life to caring for her mother, and that is what she did. And her mother, my grandmother, lived a long time. It seems she only passed away a few months ago. I feel sad that I wasn't able to meet her, but Priya told me that she never spoke of Danidu again and sadly, she would not have entertained seeing me and my family.

But, now I know that Aunty Priya had never forgotten us and she said she had even held me when I was a baby, secretly, and that she loved me. Can you believe it, dear sister! She has loved me all this time. I find that such a wonderful thing. Even when I thought I was truly orphaned and alone, I wasn't because I had an Aunty who loved me.

As soon as Grandma Perera was in grave, Priya made contact with Abeesha again. She was too worried to go straight to my father, whom she thought might have come to resent her for leaving and losing touch. At first, Abeesha would have nothing to do with Priya, but then, with the promise of some rupees, Abeesha told her the whole sorry story of my mother and father's death. Poor Aunty Priya! She was hoping to reconcile with her brother only to find him dead. But she found me instead, and Anuja, Geethan, Moses and a baby on the way, and suddenly dear sister, Anuja and I have an Aunty, my father's sister and it feels like such a blessing, after all these years.

So, there is my incredible news, Nora! One day, I hope that I will be able to introduce you, my sister in England who saved my life with a sewing machine, to my Aunty Priya, without whose love and encouragement for my father, I might not have had a life at all! Isn't it all just an incredible tapestry of the unexpected?

I must close now. I have exhausted myself with all the writing and my hand is aching so much!

Please write to me soon. I always love to hear your news.

With all my love, your sister and your friend

Lakmini Rain Cooray

PS: I loved your story about the peacock. I too have a connection to this bird, and many years ago, before I married Geethan, I wrote a poem about it. I am shy about sending it to you, as I am no poet, but I thought you might like to read it and know that a peacock has spoken to us both.

On a separate piece of paper, Nora found the poem which Rain had neatly typed up. And as she read and re-read the poem, again tears came to her eyes. It was a day for tears. In those words, Rain had laid her soul bare and yet her fears were allayed by a bird, a winged creature. That a peacock should give them both hope in dark times seemed incredible to Nora – what was that all about? Why did a peacock communicate to both Rain and Nora so deeply, so reassuringly? It was a mystery, and indeed an amazing tapestry of the unexpected.

When Nora first knew Rain, she was an orphan, all alone in the world except for her young brother whom she cared for as best she could. And now seven short years later, she had made a family and found family. It gave Nora hope. Hope that Mikey might live a long and happy life now that he had cleaned-up his act; hope that Louisa might in fact be cured and that her remission might last for years and years; hope that she and Joe would one day find their own home, the place where they could finally put down roots. Being something of an optimist, hope came easily to Nora, but on this day, when so much of what had been seeded in the past now seemed to be coming to fruition in the present, Nora felt overwhelmed with a sense of deep gratitude.

"Thank you," she whispered to the heavens, as she heard Joe gently strumming his guitar in the kitchen. "Thank you."

IN YOUR EYES

Bird, in your gilt and glory
Mysterious, eyeing me
I wonder what it is you see
In your sightless eyes?

My own vision so blurred by fear
Yet there is something I can't quite hear
Listen... the burning question:
Girl, why are you so afraid?

Countless eyes, and countless reasons
I cannot speak them all
Yet the question burns as fire
And like the sun, it glorifies
In each of your enquiring eyes
An answer forming in the light.
You turn full circle colours bright
And show me how things come aright
With courage, faith and pure delight
In that fleeting moment
Where happiness resides.

I am breathless, overcome
My question answered
All is done.
Be not afraid of happiness
Be not afraid to suffer
They dwell in love
Halves of the whole.
This wisdom your eyes offer.

Y2K

Lakmini Cooray < lakminicooray@hotboxonthego.
co.lk> wrote:

Dearest Nora

Here I am at my Aunty Priya's house near Cinnamon
Gardens in Colombo, using her laptop computer to send
this email! Can you believe it? I was diagnosed in
Lagentle with possible preeclampsia and my doctor
wanted me to go for bed rest in the hospital. But Aunty P
offered to bring me to Colombo where there is an
excellent maternity unit near to where she lives. Geethan
insisted that I should go and arranged for a taxi to bring
me here. Cost a lot of money, so we had to shut
community kitchen for a while.

Aunty P's place is very lovely. Now, I have seen the
specialist and he thinks that I got my dates wrong and
that it is not preeclampsia, but that baby will be born
soon! Now, I don't know what to do. I want to go home
to Geethan and Moses for Christmas, but doctor thinks

taxi journey back home may bring on labour. What a pickle. I am comfortable here, but I miss my family so much it makes me cry. Aunty P has worked all her life as a book-keeper at a big hotel on the sea front – very chic, I think you say – and she inherited Grandma's house. It is an old-style house with a wooden veranda and even a garden, amongst all the modern apartment sky-scrapers.

So, Aunty P is spoiling me, and I must admit that I do feel better for just resting. Today she brought home butter cake from a bakery in Lipton Circus, and I haven't tasted anything so delicious in my life – except for the first time I tasted ice cream, with Geethan in Galle. Colombo is so huge, with lots of traffic and people everywhere, very noisy – makes me feel dizzy. And Aunty has a television, so I am watching lots of films I have always wanted to see. My favourite film is Sound of Music. England looks so green and pretty. So many mountains you have.

What should I do sister? Please tell me if I should go home or stay with Aunty P. I am confused. Love Rain xx

Nora Harris < n.harris@awaken.com> wrote:

Dearest Rain

I am so sorry to hear about your health worries. It is hard to know what to do for the best, as I'm sure you are feeling a little homesick, but under the circumstances, I think you should stay with Aunty Priya and let her care for you, at least until you know more about when the baby might be due. If it is only a week away, then you can't risk it and you are better to be near the hospital.

Would it be possible for Geethan to come and stay with you for a few days in Colombo? Could Mr & Mrs Cooray Senior and Uncle Anuja look after Moses for a while so that Geethan can come and be with you? My advice is to relax in the care of your Aunty Priya and trust that you are in the right place at the right time.

My news is not so good. Unfortunately, Louisa is also in hospital. She has a very severe case of jaundice. Apparently, it is due to the side-effects of all her treatment, which has damaged her liver and kidneys. I went to see her in hospital, and her face and hands were as yellow as a banana. It was terribly shocking, and I wondered how she would ever recover, but after only a few days in hospital, she is feeling a little better and the jaundice is receding. She also wants to come home, but we are insisting that she should stay where she is and rest.

So, I find both of my beloved sisters are in hospital at the same time and my advice to both of you is to trust the doctors, trust that you are being well cared for and just be present in your body and allow the healing process (or the birthing process) to take its natural course.

I send you my love dear Rain. Please let me know how you are, if you can. It's so exciting to think your baby will be born soon.

Biggest hugs – Nora xxx

Lakmini Cooray < lakminicooray@hotboxonthego. co.lk> wrote:

Dearest Sister Nora

I have now been in Colombo for ten days. It is the longest time I have ever been away from Geethan and Moses and it is breaking my heart. I speak to them on the telephone every night which cheers me up, and I tell Moses about the films I am watching. He wants to see Jungle Book, which I have told him all about. He says Papa will take him to the jungle to see a real elephant as soon as I get home. Apparently, baby is fine and healthy. They have done so many tests sister, all those machines. Now they think I have something wrong with proteins in my blood from the baby which makes me feel so ill, but as long as baby is fine that's all that matters. I pray to God to give me strength for the baby and I can cope. They now tell me baby is due on 25th December – Christmas Day – which is two days after my birthday (and Moses' birthday, isn't it!). This was my original calculation, but still they say I must stay in Colombo so they can monitor me. So, I have over a week to go. Geethan-ji says he cannot come now as we cannot afford to shut down business at this busy time – our best time of year – but he will close on my birthday and come to Colombo then, with Moses. Can you believe it! They will be here for Christmas. Oh, sister, the days drag by. Aunty P is so kind to me – she says I am like the daughter she never had, which makes me feel very happy, as now I think of her like a mother and best thing is, she knew my mother and speaks to me of her. I feel closer to my mother now than I ever have. Geethan and I have agreed that Aunty P. should be Godmother of new baby. Oh, but I miss home so much. What is this feeling? I think it is called homesickness and that is a good description. I have never felt it before, but I even long to see Aunty-ji! Must be going mad. Just writing about it all makes me tearful. Oh sister, I am sorry for to moan so much but I am not myself. I don't even have energy for paragraphs and punctuation. My English teacher would rap my knuckles with a ruler to read this letter! Tell me your news dear Nora. How is Louisa. I pray to God she is out of hospital by now. With love – your weary sister, Rain. Xxx PS: What is this Y2K? I do not understand.

Nora Harris < n.harris@awaken.com> wrote:

Dear Rain

Thank you for your emails – I like to think of you at Aunty P's house eating cake and watching films. What good news that Geethan and Moses can join you for Christmas, and no doubt, Aunty P will look after your son whilst you are in hospital delivering the baby. It's very apt at this time of year for you to be giving birth. It's not long now!

My news is not so good. Louisa has been unable to eat for several days now. She cannot swallow and even struggles to drink the protein shakes they give her at the hospital. She had a scan and sadly it has revealed that she has a tumour in her oesophagus. It is secondary and too advanced for an operation to remove it. They have also detected other 'sites of concern' and have told us there is little more they can do to help her. We are all feeling incredibly sad.

Yesterday, Louisa discharged herself from hospital. She wants to spend Christmas at home with the children and to make it as normal as possible. She says she is determined to see in the new Millennium, and that she wants to know what the year 2000 will be like. That is, of course, unless the Millennium Bug (Y2K) is true. I think it is a conspiracy theory by people who want us all to live in fear. They say all the computers in the world have been pre-programmed with a 'bug' and that they will self-destruct on the stroke of midnight on the last day of 1999. If we are unable to communicate by email any more, then you know it will be true, and we will have to return to good old airmail!

I feel great sadness that we may be facing our last

Christmas with Louisa. Part of me still hopes she can get better from all of this. I never give up hope, but I think she has, and I think she is utterly spent. She has nothing more to give, except one last happy Christmas for her children.

I will think of you on Christmas Day, as you await your new arrival, and I will do everything I can to make our family Christmas the best it possibly can be. After that, who knows what will befall us.

With my love always, Nora xx

Lakmini Cooray < lakminicooray@notaryservices.lgt. gov.lk> wrote:

Dearest Sister Nora

How are you, and how is Louisa? Every day, you and your family are in my prayers, and I think of you all often and with much love in my heart.

It is with great pleasure that I tell you of the birth of my beautiful second son, named Danidu Joseph Cooray, who was born at a healthy weight of 8 pounds exactly! Yes, we have named him after my father and that makes me so happy. I think he looks like his namesake, but perhaps it is too early to tell? Anuja says he thinks Danidu has Bapu's ears, which do stick out a little bit like his grandfather's, it is true.

But my new son certainly took his own sweet time coming into this world. Despite several false starts, I did not give birth until 1st January 2000. So, Danidu is a new Millennium baby and he even got his name and a photograph in 'Ceylon Today' newspaper. Can you believe it? First baby in Sri Lanka born in new millennium. We are so thrilled and happy.

We have just returned home to Lagentle after what seems like a lifetime away for me. It is so good to be back – the homesickness I experienced was hard to bear. In the end, I think Aunty Priya was quite happy to see us go. I was with her for over a month all in all, and as someone who is used to living the quiet life on her own, I think our noisy family became too much for her in the end, although she was so kind to us. She made us all feel very welcome and gave us lots of lovely presents at Christmas, which was so kind and unexpected. So many things she gave to Moses – she loves the children and cried when we left. Perhaps, tears of relief! Now I have settled back in to being at home, I feel much happier. Home is a feeling, as much as it is a place, I have realised. I feel so at home here in Lagentle. Colombo is a whirl of noise and chaos in comparison. Today, I decided to pop in to office for ten minutes to send this email to you telling you of our wonderful news, and check up on a few things. Of course, filing has not been done whilst I've been away!

Danidu is a very easy baby, or perhaps it is because I know what to do this time? As I sit here in office, Danidu is asleep in his carry-cot in the back kitchen with Geethan, Moses and Anuja. They are planning on reopening our community kitchen soon as people are still hungry, isn't it? My son Danidu looks into my eyes already and our bond feels so deep, and he kicks his little legs as if he wants to get up and run. Once we got home, after the excitement of the holiday had worn off, my firstborn son had a little sulk and sat in the kitchen playing with his saucepans and refused to come and hold the baby. But now he is 'Mummy's little helper' as we call him and loves to spend time with Danidu, singing to him and holding him close.

I feel so happy, Nora. I feel too happy – is that possible? Can this all be taken away from me just like that, like it was for my Bapu and Amma? These are questions I try not to think about. Even Abeesha (Aunty-ji) came round to see us today, and she brought some sugar mice for the children. Wasn't that kind of her? She seems to be, what is the phrase… mellowing in old age. I find myself very tired but feeling much more like my old self. I have put on some weight since the baby was born and I don't feel faint or sick anymore.

So things are returning to normal for us, but of course, I am thinking of you and Louisa constantly. I hardly dare ask how things are? But at least the world survived, and Y2K was a hoax! We can be thankful about that.

With love, your sister Rain, wife of Geethan, mother of Moses and Danidu xxx

The Departed

It was late February, and Rain was sitting under the shade of a huge old bulu tree in the Cooray's backyard compound, gently rocking her son Danidu in his cradle and watching her other son Moses as he dug a moat for the fortress that he and his father had been building in the sandpit, itself a gift to the children that Geethan had made whilst Rain was in confinement in Colombo. It was hot, but under the shade of the bulu tree it was very pleasant and being between the two monsoon seasons, the air was neither humid nor cloying.

Rain was lost in a reverie, part of her wondering how poor Louisa was getting on, aware that she'd had neither email nor letter from Nora since Danidu was born, and as each day passed, she became more and more convinced that Louisa was no longer of this world – otherwise why had Nora not written for so long? But these were just fleeting thoughts on the periphery of her consciousness, because mostly, she was adrift in love for her children, dreaming the afternoon away in a tranquil state of happiness as one son slept and the other played in the quiet safety of their home.

She heard the latch on the garden gate click open.

"Yoohoo! Lakmini!"

Danidu stirred but did not wake.

It was Abeesha. She had taken to visiting on a regular basis since Rain's return from Colombo. After their tentative reconciliation at the community kitchen, Abeesha had begun to open up to Rain, and now that Priya – who she once saw as her adversary but who was slowly becoming a friend – had returned to the family fold, Abeesha began to relax a little and perhaps even trust that Rain's friendship didn't require anything of her in return. Geethan said that he thought she'd given herself status as honorary Aunty to the boys, and that he could detect a bit of 'competitive Auntying' between Priya and Abeesha, which made Rain chuckle.

"Hello Abeesha-ji! Come and sit down. I am just resting and enjoying the afternoon warmth."

"Resting, is it? I never had a moment to rest when my boys were babies, but they were difficult children, every one of them. Whereas Moses, here," and she tickled the little boy's chin, as he had wandered over to stand by her – in truth to find out if she'd brought him a sugar mouse or other such treat – "you, my little man, are a treasure." She pinched his cheek a little too hard and drew from her worn bag a tiny painted tin soldier. Instantly, Moses was mesmerised. He reached out his little hand and took the present, examining it carefully.

"Bohoma Aunty Beesha," he said and dashed off to his fortress placing his new tin soldier on the parapet. Abeesha could not have endeared herself to him more, and Rain guessed that the toy had once belonged to one of her own sons.

"And what of the little one? How is my Danidu?"

"He is an angel," Rain cooed. "What more can I tell you? He is perfect in every way. Simply perfect. He feeds well, and sleeps for hours. He is everything I could have hoped for and more."

"He will break your heart."

"You've said that to me once before, Abeesha." Rain liked calling this woman by her proper name, rather than Aunty-ji. She felt it put them on an equal footing as two independent women of the world – that, and the fact that she was no longer afraid of her. "Tell me, why do you say that?"

Rain reached over to the low bamboo table and poured Abeesha a glass of water.

"Because it is true. They may not mean to, but your children break your heart into little pieces – boys or girls – though both you and I are cursed with boys."

"I do not see my boys as a curse, Abeesha. So tell me, how have your boys broken your heart?"

At first, Rain thought the older woman was not going to answer. She sat there with her eyes closed for a long time. Then she sighed.

"Ah... I may as well get it off my chest once and for all. Lakmini, do you remember the debt you repaid to me just after your parents died?"

"How could I forget?"

"Well, to you it seemed like a lot of money and it was in a way, but in truth I don't think it did cover all money I gave to your parents over the years." Abeesha grabbed Rain's hands and looked into her eyes whilst she said this, beseeching her to believe what she was saying. "It was not easy for me, Lakmini. I had to keep it quiet from my own husband and I could only give Danidu money that I had earned myself, but my sons found out what I was doing, and they began to threaten me that they would tell their father, may he rot in hell."

"But if it was causing you so much trouble, why did you continue to help us?" Rain looked at Abeesha. Years ago, she was probably quite a striking woman, but time had not been kind to her. She had a few teeth left, but not enough to keep her cheeks from sinking inward, giving her a sullen, mean look. And she had broken her nose somehow and it had not been set straight. But most of all, her eyes had become hooded and her gaze had hardened.

"Priya-ji has told you some of the story, but she can't tell you the whole story. She doesn't know it herself."

"Know what?"

"She doesn't know that Danidu had cancer, Lakmini. He had cancer and that was why he was wasting away. And I was giving him money – all I could manage – because he had to take so much time off work for the treatment. He wasn't just working long hours, he was also having chemotherapy and then radiation at the hospital too. It made him feel so tired, so ill. But believe me Lakmini, the only thing that was important to him was that he could care for Dippy and for you and Anuja. His family meant everything to him, everything, and he kept his illness a secret because he did not want you to worry about him. I was the only one who knew about it. Your mother, God rest her soul in heaven, she did not know either."

Rain was aghast and could hardly take in what she was hearing. And yet, it answered so much...

Abeesha sighed. "I loved him, child. I never stopped loving him from the day I met him at 16 years of age. That is why I helped your father, that is why I gave him everything I could, but it was not enough. He was never able to love me in return. And then when you told me he had been killed in an accident, I just got so angry, like a fire-breathing demon. I was so angry with him, that he had left me on my own, and so I took it out on you. I beg your forgiveness, Lakmini."

Rain was quiet, and then she asked a question that had lurked in her mind since that night Sergeant Gomes said that her father had swerved to avoid a dog on the road, but that no dog had ever been found at the scene.

"Do you think he did it on purpose?"

"Did what?"

"The accident. Do you think he made it happen so that he and Amma could go to heaven together?"

"That is something we will never know, but it has crossed my mind too." Abeesha sighed deeply and wiped away a tear that was dangling from the tip of her nose. "He was going crazy crazy with worry, Lakmini. He couldn't sleep, he didn't know where to turn. I was the only person he could talk to about all his worries. But I do know he truly thought that once your mother had been to see consultant in Colombo, that she would get better, back to her old self. I know he believed that, so why would he make accident happen? No, your father always lived in hope, but he got in such a pickle with money because he couldn't work."

Rain was quiet for a moment, trying to comprehend what she was hearing. If Geethan was terminally ill, would she sacrifice the happiness of her children to be with him? No! Never!! She would never leave Moses and Danidu, and she didn't believe Bapu would purposefully make orphans of her and Anuja either.

"Thank you for helping us, Abeesha-ji. I don't think I have ever thanked your properly for all that you have done for us." She held her friend's hands and squeezed them affectionately. "But that still doesn't explain why you said my sons will break my heart."

"Well, perhaps you will be spared, but if your boys are anything like my sons, they will. As soon as you had given me the repayment money – and in truth I could not believe you managed to even repay a single rupee given the circumstances you were in; you are clever girl Lakmini – my sons began to blackmail me. 'Give me 100 rupees or I will tell Papa what you did.' 'Give me 200 rupees or I will tell Papa you are a *kari kariya* – a whore'. Excuse my language, but the way they spoke to me was terrible. And then their Papa died, and things just went from bad to worse. He was a broken man, their father, troubled and cruel, but they were scared of him and so they never laid a finger on me. But after he died, they were no longer afraid of his wrath, and so they began to hit me if I didn't give them money. In just over a year the money you gave to me was all gone, Lakmini. Can you believe it? They took every penny from me and with the last few hundred rupees, the three of them got a tuk-tuk to Colombo and I have not seen nor heard of them since."

"Oh, my goodness, Abeesha, you did not deserve to be treated like that. Life has not been kind to you."

"I don't care about the money really. I always find a way to survive, but I did care about Danidu, I loved him so much, and even now all these years later, my sorrow is like hole in the heart."

The old woman began to cry, and Rain realised, not for the first time in her adult life, that things were never quite as black and white as they seemed on the surface. What must it have been like for Abeesha to live with unrequited love for all those years, seeing the man she loved making a family with someone else?

She reached out to embrace Abeesha as she rocked back and forth in her chair.

"I'm sorry child. I'm sorry for venting my anger on you. You deserved better – you are his daughter after all, his flesh and blood."

Rain held Abeesha in her arms, and for a long time both women were lost in their world of remembrance.

"You know, Abeesha, perhaps you did me a favour. If you had not asked for your money back, I may never have put an advert for a sewing machine in *Awaken* magazine; I wouldn't know Nora and I would not have got the job at the Notary's Office – and perhaps I would never have met Geethan, which doesn't even bear thinking about. Maybe everything happens for a reason and we just can't see it at the time? Perhaps your sons will come back to you, like you have come back to me? And until then Abeesha, you will always be welcome in my home, and you will always be Aunty Beesha to my boys. You risked everything to help my Bapu, and I want to help you. We've asked Priya to be Godmother to both boys as well as my sister Nora in England, but I would like to ask if you will be too? And Danidu seems to me so much like his namesake that I know you will love him as much as you plainly love Moses."

That set Abeesha off in another round of tears, the kind of tears that sanctify, the kind of tears that heal.

"Aunty Beesha? Please will you tell me the story of King of the Dusk?" Moses had sidled up to the old woman and placed his hand on her arm, perhaps sensing that she needed gentle reassurance.

"My boy, I do not know this story."

"Amma wrote it, didn't you Amma? Will you tell it to Aunty Beesha?"

"Perhaps another day, Moses. I don't think Aunty wants to hear a story now."

"Oh, but I do," said Abeesha. "Especially if little Moses here will sit on my knee whilst you tell it," at which, Moses grabbed a handful of her sari and hauled himself up onto her lap.

Abeesha and Moses looked at Rain expectantly.

"Oh, very well then! In our country, the leopard is known as King of the Dusk, but not many people know why he got that name. This is a little story I wrote after Geethan and I had travelled to Yala one day before we were married. Geethan was busy taking photographs, and I was daydreaming, when out of the corner of my eye I saw a leopard watching us in the undergrowth. I have told the story to Moses so many times that it has become his favourite story. And now I have two little boys to tell this story to. What a miracle!" Rain cleared her throat and began.

> "Once upon a time in a knot of jungle
> spilling onto the shores of an island
> shaped like a teardrop, there lived the
> King of the Dusk. He was a magnificent

leopard. His eyes were like polished amber,
and his coat of burnished gold was dappled
with shadows.

The King of the Dusk had a very special
trick. He was able to disappear like magic,
blending into the shade cast by the trees
and becoming invisible whenever he wished
to. And that's why he was the King –
because he could disappear at will and
nobody could ever find him, no matter how
hard they tried.

Into this knot of jungle on the
tear-drop shaped island, hundreds of
tourists would descend each day, brought by
noisy tuk-tuks belching a haze of blue
smoke as if they were on fire. Off the
tourists would go and 'Snap, Snap, Snap'
with their cameras hoping to take a picture
of the King of the Dusk."

As Rain said the words, 'snap, snap, snap' Moses did
too, and he made a little gesture with his finger as if he
was clicking the shutter of his father's camera. He broke
Rain's heart with love as he did this, and Abeesha too
smiled at him adoringly, encircling him in her arms.

"Snap! A photo of water buffalos
wallowing in mud, deeply grumpy creatures
that they are. And yet the King standing
proudly in the shadows remained unseen.

Snap! A photo of Malabar hornbills,
lovebirds roosting in a tree. Yet there too

was the King himself perched upon a trembling bough, invisible in his speckled robes his amber eyes aglow.

Snap! A photo of mother mongoose chiding her unruly pups whilst the King lurking in the long grass watches, but is not watched.

Snap! A photo of a kingfisher in his coat of dazzling blue, and there too is the King, swimming in the river, his amber eyes twinkling like light upon the water, his magnificence hidden in plain sight.

At the end of the day as dusk fell, the fiery tuk-tuks took the tired and hungry tourists back to their hotels, not one of them with a picture of the King of the Dusk. Because they were not really looking. They were too busy snapping. Snap! Snap! Snap!

One day, a girl and a boy came to the forest, the boy with a new camera to Snap, Snap Snap. But the girl was not looking at the franjipani flowers, nor the bee-eaters fluttering on the shores of the river, she was looking within, trying to understand why she always felt so sad.

As she walked quietly beside her friend, the day grew long and the light began to fade, and out of the corner of her eye she saw a movement in the shadows and two polished amber eyes staring back at her. It was the most wondrous King of the Dusk, his coat of burnished gold aglow.

'So, you are here?' she said to him in
her thoughts.

'I am always here,' replied The King
baring his sharp and sparkling teeth in a
smile. 'But I only appear to those who need
to see me. I have come to tell you
something that you must try to remember,
especially when you are feeling sad. Dear
child, you will always find those who need
to find you.'

And then, The King of the Dusk flicked
his superb tail and disappeared into the
jungle, his coat becoming the light, his
eyes becoming the sparkle of the water on
the river."

"Again Amma! Again, again!" Moses was bouncing
on Abeesha's knee with excitement.

"You wrote that?" said Abeesha to Rain, her eyes
wide with admiration. "Best story I ever heard."

As Rain told her story of The King of the Dusk, not
for the first time, she marvelled at how it was that the
story had come true, for hadn't the fisherman and
Sergeant Gomes found her and come to her aid, and
hadn't Geethan appeared behind a box of files with his
grin and his faith in life; and hadn't Nora been there
with her through thick and thin, and then Priya had
found her and Abeesha had come back to her... and
didn't they all need each other, just like The King of the
Dusk had told her? It was as if it was all meant to be.
As if everything was perfect.

On her return to work after Danidu was born, Rain found that the filing was indeed in a terrible state, and it took many days for her to get all her admin systems in the Notary's Office back to what she deemed orderly, but she was pleased to be at work with Geethan once again, the two of them focussed on building their business and securing their family's future. And, it seemed to Rain, that Mrs Cooray Senior could not wait for her to leave the house on the three mornings a week that Rain worked in the office, so that she could have her grandchildren all to herself. It was, Rain thought, the perfect set up.

On Anuja's instigation, they had also reinstated the community kitchen and begun serving evening meals once again, this time with Abeesha helping to prepare, serve and wash-up the pots afterwards. Aunty Priya had spoken with the Head Chef at the hotel where she worked and asked if he would consider taking Anuja on as an apprentice in his kitchen, and – because the chef adored Priya (everyone at the hotel adored Priya) – he had agreed. So, Rain knew that they only had Anuja's cooking skills for another four months, until he had taken his exams at school, and then he would be off to Columbo to live with his Aunty Priya and begin his training as a chef. In those four months, she had a secret plan to put Abeesha in charge of the community kitchen, to give her a sense of achievement and also, Geethan and Rain had worked out that they could pay her a little money for her help, something they knew she would appreciate.

And still she had not heard from Nora, despite

emailing most weeks with her news. Of course, Rain continued to fear the worst, and then four months after Danidu was born, Rain received an email and the worst was confirmed. Louisa had died.

Nora Harris < n.harris@awaken.com> wrote:

My dear sister, my dear Rain

Forgive me for not writing to you sooner, but I did not have the heart nor the energy to do so. My darling Louisa, my beautiful sister passed away at eleven minutes past midnight on the very first day of this new millennium.

Rain gasped as she read the email. That was exactly the moment Danidu was born. He came into the world as Louisa took her final breath. She remembered reading once about reincarnating souls, and how within the same soul family as one passes, they often choose to be immediately reborn. Could that be the case with Louisa and Danidu? She knew Geethan would find it a fanciful idea, and perhaps Nora too, but to Rain there was so much meaning, so much synchronicity in the timing that surely, this was God's work?

Louisa's passing feels to me as if a bomb has gone off in our family, as if something has exploded and shattered us, and we don't know how to pick up the pieces. I find myself in the shower, howling with the pain of it, wondering when everything will get back to normal, and then I realise that it won't, because she has gone... All we are able to do right now is focus on Louisa's children and take care of them. Being present for them does at least lessen the pain. They have been incredibly resilient, seemingly far more so than the adults. It is they who have comforted us, rather than the other way around. It is they who have brought joy into our lives. Louisa would have been so proud of them.

My dear Rain, I know it has been a long time since I was last in touch with you, and I apologise for that, but please know that you are often in my thoughts – all of you – and I appreciate your emails to me so very much. Please keep sending them and please forgive me if I am slow to reply. But now you know why. I am in a place where I feel too numb to do very much except exist. I trust that things will not always be this way, but for now, they are.

With love from your sister, Nora

By the end of the email, Rain was in floods of tears. She recalled that sadness, that feeling of numbness, how the world seemed to take on a translucent, surreal quality. Nothing felt real, everything seemed brittle, like glass. And yet the world kept turning, and people did normal things like go to work or to the market, and Rain remembered how she could not believe that it was possible for the world to be normal in the wake of her parents' death. Nora said her family were shattered and that is exactly how Rain felt when Bapu and Amma died. And the worst of it was that there was little she could do for Nora in her pain, except perhaps send photos of her children, and stories of her life, hoping that these would take Nora's mind off her loss, if only briefly.

And so that is what she did, for many months. She kept in touch, but Nora's silence grew until such time as Rain doubted that her emails helped at all, nonetheless, she kept sending them.

Then a few days after Danidu's first birthday, a letter came, by airmail.

My Dear Rain

Forgive my long silences and please know that you are always in my heart. As we near the anniversary of Louisa's death and the first birthday of your darling son, Danidu, I wanted to write to you to let you know that at long last, I feel a kind of acceptance of all that has happened. It is a sweet sorrow, tinged as it is with memories of Louisa and the happy times we spent together, and when I look at her children I see her in their faces, so in that respect, she will always be with us. But it is more than that. I have come to understand that a fulfilled life is not necessary a long life. Let me explain.

For quite a while after my sister died, I would see people in our village or in town, old or young, men or women, smoking cigarettes or falling drunkenly out of pub doorways and I would rail at the injustice of it all - why are they alive, killing themselves by degrees, when my sister is dead?! Or I would see an old, old woman coming out of the doctor's surgery, bent double with arthritis, using a frame to walk, and think, how can such a frail body still keep going, when Louisa's young and seemingly strong body succumbed? I was consumed with anger for quite a while; anger at the injustice of it all, and anger at everyone else for still being alive when my sister was not. And I knew the anger was eating me up. I would lash out at Joe, at work colleagues and my friends, knowing they'd forgive me but sometimes I'd say the unforgiveable. I was so lost.

And then my darling mother told me that she had a dream, or maybe she was awake – she couldn't quite tell – and Louisa came to her and spoke to her, and this is what she said. 'Do not grieve for me, mother. I am completely at peace. When I came into this world, I knew I would not make old bones, but my Soul desired to have children who would learn from the lessons of my mortality. My children desired to live life to the full, to fulfil themselves and their destiny knowing that all can be taken at any moment. I knew that what I was giving them, although painful for them and for all my family, was a profound gift. You now know that life is for living in the moment, and that love is for giving in the moment, because tomorrow may never come. That is my gift to them and to you, a gift I chose to give. I knew before I was born that my life would be sacrificed for the greater good. Do not grieve for me, mother. I am completely at peace.'

That is what my Mum told me, Rain, and from that moment on, it was as if Mum was redeemed, as if her grief had transformed and become a poignant reminder of her love for Louisa's, life rather than the fact of her death. At first, I didn't quite understand what Mum said, but now I do. And it has become a kind of gift for me too - because I had put my life on hold since her death, feeling guilty that I was still alive, but now I know that I have to say 'Yes' to everything, to give life my all, to live in the moment, because tomorrow may never come. That truly is a gift, a gift from Louisa.

And so, my dear Rain, I have finally come back to you too. Thank you for your patience with me as I learned this painful lesson. I know you will completely understand this, after experiencing the death of your parents. Perhaps that was their gift to you too? I feel like I have woken up to my life, at last. I feel like I was sleepwalking through life, but now I am awake and aware of my choices.

One choice I have made, and I have spoken with Joe about it, is to come and visit you in Sri Lanka! It may not happen for a while as we have to save up and get the time off work, but perhaps next year, or in 2004 we will be able to meet you at last. Now, that really would be something to celebrate, would it not? Can you imagine the joy of meeting each other at long last?. Until then, let us share our lives by letter and email as we always have done, honouring the love and the losses in equal measure.

Your sister, Nora xxx

Rain was so relieved to get Nora's letter. Yes, reading

between the lines, she knew that Nora was still in the depths of grief, but the fact that she had found some meaning in her sister's death gave Nora something to cling on to, a reason to continue living her own life with purpose. And that is what gave Rain the most comfort. For she knew from bitter experience that there is an invisible thread that binds you to a loved one who has passed, and that thread though gossamer thin, can drag you down. It can wrap you in memory and loss and grief and pull you from this realm into the next. That thread was what had pulled her down into the waters of the harbour, the morning after her parents were killed. It anchored her, weighted her in despair and she clung to it, feeling an undercurrent of death calling her, dragging her down, down into oblivion. And yet, it was that little fish who jolted her back to life and told her that it wasn't her time. In that moment, Rain knew that she had a destiny, a life to live.

Many times she had thanked those fishermen with all her heart for plucking her out of the water, and though in later years, she'd been back to the harbour looking for them, wanting to thank them in person, she'd never laid eyes on either one since. Perhaps they were her guardian angels and not fishermen at all? God works in mysterious ways, of that she was certain.

Lightning Strikes Twice

Nora's work at the magazine had been the one thing that saved her sanity after Louisa died. She was now co-editor, sharing the job with her dear friend and long-time colleague Verity – Verity with her long legs, wild hair and loving heart; Verity who lived up to her name and always spoke the truth, even if nobody wanted to hear it – and together, Nora and Verity were a good foil for Jay who was becoming ever more absent, spending most of his time away from the office, travelling to lectures and conferences all over the world. He was in demand, and rightly so because his message offered hope in a world darkened by fear.

Together, Nora and Verity ran the operations at *Awaken* magazine with aplomb, and had become close friends. Nora's responsibilities were many, but job-sharing with Verity meant her role was also creative and fun, and after Louisa died, she found that diving into her work for eight hours a day or more, helped. It really helped to alleviate the grief, or at least to take her mind off it for a while, so that she could momentarily forget about the gnawing anxiety in the pit of her stomach that just wouldn't go away, or the sadness that veiled her every waking hour.

Cass and Verity between them held Nora gently as her anger, despondency and sadness came in waves. On one day she could be bright, almost back to her old self, laughing with Verity about one of Jay's more obscure ideas, or working creatively with the designer on a specific concept for a layout; then the next day, she could be in floods of tears in the staff cloakroom – Cass coaxing her out with coffee or Verity sitting next to her on the floor, just holding her hand.

At first, the waves of grief came crashing down on Nora, leaving her gasping for air through her tears.

"Will life ever go back to normal, Cass?" she'd asked her friend after collapsing by the photocopier in great heaving sobs of anguish, the monotonous hum of the machine seeming to hit home the pointlessness of life.

"No, darling, it won't. Life will never be the same again. You'll never feel as you once did, but you won't always feel like this. When people give you all those platitudes about 'time being a great healer' you have my permission to punch them on the nose," (this made Nora laugh through her tears), "but perhaps what they mean is that in time, you begin to create a 'new normal' where Louisa's name comes to your lips every day, but it no longer cuts like a knife to speak it. You'll find ways to remember her and honour her that are joyful, not painful. And eventually, you'll be able to let go of that guilt that you still carry about 'why her, why not me?'"

"Do you think so?" Nora wiped her eyes with the cuff

of her sleeve, grateful for her friend's reassurance.

"I know so." And she did, for Cassie's first partner Chico had died and left her with a young son to care for on her own. Cassie's words were like a lifeline to Nora.

Eventually, the waves of grief no longer pounded and threatened to drown her but subsided and lapped at the edge of her consciousness, wearing her down, eroding her sense of self, but also smoothing her edges at the same time, easing away the guilt, little by little.

One afternoon, about six months after Louisa had died, Verity asked if Nora fancied going for a walk. Verity prioritised a walk after lunch every day because she was one of those women whose energy needed to be expended by exercise. It was her meditation, her 'me time' and everyone respected that, but she'd asked Nora to join her, and as it was a beautiful day and Nora was bored rigid with the article she was editing, she agreed. A walk would be a pleasant diversion.

Halfway along the green lane that led to the river, Verity caught Nora's hand in hers. "I'm pregnant, Noo."

"No way!" Verity already had two small boys and it was sometimes a real juggle for her to get to work if her husband was travelling or the childminder was ill, or some other catastrophe had hit, as is often the case with family life: chicken pox, sleepless nights, car trouble, cows escaped (Verity and Charlie had a smallholding to care for too) – so Nora was surprised at her news, thinking she probably wouldn't have any more kids.

"Well, that's wonderful Vee, congratulations." She hugged her friend warmly. She loved this woman deeply and was genuinely pleased for her.

"It's bloody madness, that's what it is. And totally

unplanned. We thought we'd got the rhythm method down to a tee, but obviously not!" They laughed again. Nora often laughed when Vee was around. "But I'm going to have the baby Nora, and then Charlie will get the snip, but he doesn't know that bit yet. The thing is, it'll mean you'll have to take over the reins again whilst I'm on maternity leave."

Nora had already done this once before when Vee's second son was born, and it had been hard work without her, but eventually, Jay had agreed that they should have an assistant to help with the workload, and when Verity returned, the assistant had stayed. Johanna had become their right-hand girl.

"We'll manage, darling. We'll miss you, but Johanna knows the ropes now. Don't worry about a thing."

"Thanks NooNoo."

"Don't thank me Verity. It's the least I can do after everything you've done for me. I don't think I'd have got through the last few months if it wasn't for you and Cass, picking me up time after time. And work is the one thing that really does help me to focus on something other than what happened to Louisa. Anyway, me and Johanna will cope until you're ready to come back. So, do you know if it's a boy or a girl?"

"I do, but I'm not telling!"

It was during Verity's maternity leave that Nora realised sisterhood does not diminish when one sister passes, but in fact, it expands. Louisa had died and her loss was hard to bear, but Cass and Verity, Lily and Gerry and many others had stepped into the void, willingly and lovingly doing everything in their power to support her. And then, seeing Verity's body transform as she embraced her pregnancy linked Nora to Louisa in unexpected ways and remembrances, as she recalled her sister's two pregnancies and the birth of her nephew and niece. And when Verity's baby was born – a girl, a girl! – and Verity asked Nora to be her Godmother, it felt as if life had come full circle. Sisters are not only those bound by blood – Nora knew this from her relationship with Rain – but truly, sisters are all those women motivated by compassion, love and friendship. The sisterhood is boundless, and this alone helped restore Nora's faith in life. For a while at least...

When Nora found the lump in her own breast, she was driving to work. It was her 40th birthday and she'd asked Jay for the day off, but as he was travelling to Canada the following day and could not fit the editorial meeting in at any other time, he'd asked Nora and Verity to attend the meeting in the morning, and then Nora could have the afternoon off. Verity had only just returned to work after her maternity leave and was still finding her way back into her role at the magazine. Nora's plans to go to St Ives with Joe for a few days would have to be put on hold until the weekend. It was no big deal, but she always liked to have the day off work on her birthday if possible.

Living in the cottage next to her parents' house meant that Nora had a half-hour commute to work. She didn't mind, as she found the drive settled her in to the day somehow, giving her time to plan and think and imagine. The seatbelt of her car always irritated her as it felt too tight, and she would often drive with her right hand on the steering wheel and her left hand pulling the seatbelt away from her body. But on this day, the seatbelt seemed particularly tight over her left breast, making it feel sore. Unconsciously, she rubbed her breast where the seatbelt had lain and at once felt it, a lump, hard and the size and shape of an almond. All the blood drained from her extremities and her heart began to pump on overdrive. She pulled into a lay by and sat staring at the road ahead for a few minutes, then tentatively felt her breast again. It was still there.

"For fuck's sake!" she screamed into the rear-view mirror. "I thought life was supposed to begin at 40!"

She didn't say anything to Verity or Cass, though how she got through the meeting, God only knows. She didn't say anything to Joe either and tried to enjoy their long weekend away, but all the time anxiety gnawed within, an anxiety that was all too familiar. On the last day of their holiday, he stood behind her as they gazed out of the balcony window across the bay, the tide high and glistening a deep azure blue, despite it being early March. She moved Joe's hand from around her waist, to her breast.

"Can you feel anything?"

"What do you mean?"

"There. There, can you feel it?" She moved his fingers over the lump.

"Oh please God, no..."

When they got home, Nora made an appointment with her GP, the same man who had looked after Louisa. He was from Iraq and was abrupt and seeming lacking in compassion, and had infuriated Louisa when he'd said, "In many ways, cancer is a kind illness – it gives you plenty of time to say goodbye." That was not something Louisa had wanted to hear. Not then. Although it was true.

When Nora went for her appointment with him at the surgery, he was equally blunt. He felt her breast and said, "I think you know what this is." That was not what Nora wanted to hear either. She wanted him to say it was a cyst, an enlarged lymph node, anything but that.

When she got home, she couldn't speak. She just looked at Joe and nodded. He put his arms around her, told her they'd be okay, that they'd get over this. But Louisa had died, and Linda McCartney had died, so why would Nora be spared?

"Can you phone Vee and ask her to tell Cass and Jay? I just can't face speaking to anyone," Nora said. "I don't know how I'm going to break the news to Mum and Dad..." It was the beginning of Nora's turning inwards, the body's necessary response to healing. She had to look to herself now.

And then the medical establishment kicked into gear. First a mammogram, then a biopsy and the agonising wait for results, and then disbelief, legs giving way, as confirmation came that she had cancer and that, like her sister, she was going to lose her breast. It all happened so fast, and she was in a whirlwind of decision-making and stomach-churning anxiety.

The day of the surgery came, and all Nora could think of was Louisa. Nora never knew just how brave she had to be until now – even more so in Louisa's case because she had to put a brave face on for her children too. They marked her breast with black felt-pen, a cross over it, so the surgeon would remove the correct one. Nora felt so sorry for her breast, like it didn't deserve to be treated like that. She said goodbye to it with such sadness as the anaesthetic took her into oblivion.

When she came to, all she wanted to do was eat nuts. Strangely, that was all she could think of, as if her body knew that there was something in nuts, some trace element or nutrient that she needed, and so she sent Joe down to the hospital shop to see if he could buy some. Dear Joe, dear handsome, beloved, kind and shell-shocked Joe, such a pillar of strength to her and yet she knew it took all the strength he could muster to be her hero. She felt high, she felt like celebrating because she was still alive – wounded but alive.

And then, reality set in. The nurses wanted her to get up and walk and as she moved her body for the first time since the surgery, she felt the tightness of her chest and looked down, to find nothing but plastic drainage tubes sticking out of her body, where her breast once was. She wanted to be sick. These were the days before breast reconstruction was offered as a matter of course at the same time as the mastectomy, and so there she was, lopsided, asymmetrical, flawed, nauseous. She made it to the bathroom but she wasn't sick, nor did she need to pee as they had fitted her with a catheter, she just looked at herself in the mirror in disbelief as she saw her once lovely, curvaceous body had been maimed. Like a tree that has lost one of its limbs, leaving it ungainly and unbalanced, she too felt askew, like she might fall over. So she did. She fell to the floor of the hospital bathroom, but tears would not come. Instead, a voice whispered, 'You can do this, Nora! Get up! Be strong! If I can do it, you can do it.'

"Louisa...?"

And then the tears did come and they would not stop. She cried and cried until her sides ached and her head ached. She cried for every woman who'd lost a precious breast; she cried for her lost innocence and in the knowledge that now and forever more she would be living with the Sword of Damocles hanging over her head: 'When will it get me...?'

The medical establishment left just long enough for recovery from one trauma before another began. Once the drains were removed from her body and her own eight-inch scar was beginning to heal – so similar to the scar Louisa insisted on showing Nora, and which Nora couldn't bear to look at – talk of chemotherapy began. It was a horrendous process but for once in her life, Nora had decided that she would do as she was told; that she had to trust the medical profession and their advice, even if her whole body was screaming 'Nooooo!' She didn't want to be injected with huge syringes full of bright red liquid that smelt like disinfectant, tubes and tubes of it. She didn't want to take the anti-sickness medication that instantly made her feel sick. But they said she would have a 75% chance of living for five years if she did. So, she did.

And despite the disorientation, pain and nausea, a kind of peacefulness descended on Nora. After all those years, the mantra of 'Why Louisa, why not me?' finally ceased, because now it was Nora's turn to experience all that Louisa had gone through and it brought with it an intense feeling of closeness to her sister. At times, Nora felt overwhelmed with love for her and a renewed and intense feeling of respect and admiration for Louisa's bravery. How incredibly brave she had been, and how brave Nora now had to be – for Joe, for her family and most of all for herself, because to brave those syringes, the incessant needles needing to find a vein, the sickness, constipation, waves of pain… it took every single ounce of energy she had and more.

After the first bout of chemotherapy, just like when she came to from the anaesthetic, she craved something, and this time it was cherries. Joe stopped at Sainsbury's on the way home and bought a kilo of cherries, which Nora ate in the car. It took an hour and a half to drive back from the hospital and by the time they arrived home, she'd eaten the lot. That night, she threw-up the contents of her stomach into the kitchen sink. It was like the scene from the film, The Witches of Eastwick, where the woman ate cherries and vomited cherrystones everywhere. Cherry-sick is the colour of blood, and the colour of the chemotherapy liquid itself. Nora's kitchen looked like a murder scene by the time she'd finished being sick. She felt as if her lifeblood was being drained from her.

The next morning, as she got out of bed, she saw her pillow covered in hair. She'd already had it cut short in preparation for the inevitable hair loss, but to see so much of it on her pillow was a shock. Joe got out his clippers and shaved the rest off.

"It suits you," he'd said. "Your head is a nice shape."

Nora thought she looked like an alien without hair, and though she had been given a free wig on the NHS, it was so itchy and hot she could only bear to wear it briefly. After an hour or so, she'd wrench it off her head and fling it across the room. Anger often came to her in those early days of treatment. She felt mutilated and ugly. She knew now why Louisa had the reconstructive surgery, and perhaps why Terry worked late so often. She wondered if Joe might stop loving her…

After the second bout of chemotherapy, Nora's ovaries were destroyed. She felt the process viscerally, doubled-up in pain, wondering how to survive the agony. In desperation, Joe dialled the hospital, but it was one o'clock in the morning and nobody picked up the phone. Nora ate more painkillers than is safe and eventually they knocked her out. She never had a period again.

Then her cravings changed to carbohydrates. If she ate carbs, she felt grounded somehow and the nausea abated for a while. Potatoes, those little round lumps that live in the ground, and which ironically looked like a tumour, were her saviour, in any form. They seemed to soak-up whatever it was that was making her feel sick like a sponge, but she began to put on weight. Again, the irony that she was putting on weight when most people become skeletal during chemotherapy didn't escape Nora. There was something more to this process than merely the physicality of it; something that Nora couldn't comprehend. Not then.

Cassie and Vee and sometimes Lily when she could get time off work, gave Nora all the moral support they could during this time, and together with many of her other girlfriends, they took it in turns to drive Nora to and from the hospital once every three weeks, so that Joe didn't always have to take time off work to do it.

"I was thinking about you this morning Nora. It's weird but don't you think your treatment is rather like pregnancy," Cass observed on another long journey to the hospital, her erratic driving setting Nora's already shattered nerves on edge.

"In what way?"

"Well, because it lasts for nine months, you're putting

on weight, you're getting cravings, and you feel terrible."

"Yeah, but I don't get a baby at the end of it!"

"No, and count your blessings there, maid," said Cass, whose younger son had been getting into trouble with the police of late, "but you do get your life back."

"Hopefully," said Nora who no longer took anything for granted.

After nine months of gruelling chemotherapy, on the day that her hair began to grow back – "Look Joe, I've got a fringe!" she'd said, pointing to the one fine hair that she noticed growing at her hairline – the hospital called to book her in for 25 sessions of radiotherapy. By this time, Nora was able to drive herself to and from the hospital, but a three-hour round trip of driving coupled with the treatment itself, every weekday for five weeks took its toll. Nora was fond of saying that radiotherapy was a walk in the park after chemotherapy, but its effects were far more subtle. She was so focussed on getting through the treatment, she didn't know how exhausted she'd become.

And then, once the radiotherapy was over, they put her on Tamoxifen, a drug so foul it knocked all the other treatment into a cocked hat. Nora felt like death warmed up and she was told she had to stay on this drug for five years. Five years? How the hell could she possibly do that? The thought was too awful to contemplate.

Then, not long after the radiotherapy was complete, her surgeon advised her to have her ovaries removed.

"But they're dead. They've stopped working. I don't have periods anymore…"

"The thing is Ms Harris, it's possible that they could still be producing a small amount of oestrogen. As your cancer is oestrogen-positive, I think it would be wise to have them removed."

Nora doubted her ovaries would have the audacity to produce any oestrogen, but once again she acquiesced to the experts and went under the knife. She felt like the last remnants of her femininity had been taken from her. Who was she now she had only one breast, no ovaries, no oestrogen, and an uneven stubble of hair? Was she still a woman or was she transitioning into someone new, without a clue who that might be…?

Throughout this whole time, Nora continued to write to Rain, not really going into much detail about the treatment she was undergoing, but more because she felt the connection as a lifeline to her old self and her life before cancer; it was a connection to a woman who had also experienced great loss and suffering and who in her humility, gave Nora the strength to carry on. And she chose to write by airmail, relishing the pauses between letters as if it were a deep, cleansing breath.

My dearest Rain

Not much has happened since I last wrote to you and yet everything has happened. I have now finished all my treatment, all of it, except for the course of medication that it is recommended I take for the next five years. But I am not sure I want to take what feels like poison for that long. Every morning I look at the little yellow tablet in my hands, so small yet so powerful, and though I am told it is helping me, it doesn't feel that way. I have done as I've been told by the medical profession for well over a year now, never questioning, just accepting - but I do question this drug. I don't trust it and my intuition feels so strong that I have to force the thing down my throat. I don't know how long I can continue to do this. I often wonder, will I ever trust my body, my innate wisdom again? Sometimes, it feels as if my body has betrayed me. I remember Louisa saying something similar, but I didn't know what she meant until now.

The strange thing is that now it is all over, I feel really vulnerable... I've received so much help and support, so much love over the last year or so, that now there are no more appointments, no more scans or injections or operations I feel lost at sea. It is such a relief that it is all over, and yet I feel like a toddler taking her first steps: wobbly and uncertain. I keep stumbling and I am fearful of what is to come. Cancer has stripped away so much that once gave my life stability - my self-confidence has disappeared, my faith and optimism have taken a battering and I don't know who this 'new me' is. All I know is that step by step I am having to rebuild myself from the ashes of the old Nora, like the proverbial phoenix. It is all I do, each day just putting one foot in front of the other, slowly recovering, slowly opening up to who I am now. I am learning how to be me all over again.

I spoke with my homeopath today about this, about how I feel stripped bare, and she said something that really resonated with me: "It's true - you have been stripped bare, Nora. Suffering is sandpaper for the soul; you have been sandpapered by this experience so that all your rough edges are now smooth, and all your imperfections have been polished away so that now you can sparkle. That is the purpose of suffering: it softens all our hardness and reveals who we really are. We become less judgemental, more compassionate, more humane." Her words brought tears to my eyes, but I think she is right. I think that suffering is sandpaper for the soul...

Sister, I don't know if I can sparkle yet; I'm still overwhelmed by thoughts of death, of how I may not have long to live, of how much I want to do before I die, and yet those words have affected me deeply because they have given a meaning to all that I have experienced. It means there is a point to all this suffering, it is not just enduring pain. I can't grasp it yet, I really can't, but I know there are gifts that I will come to understand as I slowly assimilate all that I have been through. Who knows how long that will take!

I think that is what true healing is. It's not the chemotherapy or the radiotherapy or the surgery – all that just treats the symptoms, the immediate, life-threatening crisis – but healing is asking that I deepen into what it is that makes me who I am, and how this has changed me and the lessons it offers. At this very moment in time, I feel too exhausted to even contemplate all that. I need to give myself time for this to unfold into some kind of coherence. As a toddler does, I have to learn that the first step is just part of the process, that confidence and balance and a sense of adventure only come with practice, and that is what I have to do now - I just have to practice how to walk again.

It gave me such joy to know that Anuja has qualified as a chef and is working in Negombo (a place I hope to visit one day, when Joe and I finally get to travel to Sri Lanka.) The idea of taking a holiday, a trip of a lifetime for three months or so, has been forming in my mind. I realised when I was having my treatment that there is so much of life I want to experience before I die. For years, I have longed to see a wild elephant, a rainforest, a whale, a coral reef but most of all, I want to see you, dear Rain, dear sister. All this time we have been friends, and still we have not held each other in our arms. Now, it is time, and Joe and I have decided that we are going to travel the world! We have a little money saved from the sale of the house I used to own with Mikey, and so we have decided to visit Cambodia, Vietnam, Sri Lanka and then on to India. Can you believe it! It really will be the trip of a lifetime, not just because of all those wonderful places that we can enjoy, but because I will meet you, at last, my dear sister, after all these years.

I will keep you posted with plans, and perhaps it is a little too early to get excited about meeting each other, but it will happen, one day in the not-too-distant future.

Sending you so much love — your sister, Nora xxx

It was the Summer of 2004 – over four years after Louisa's death – before Nora began to feel a glimmer of happiness in her life again, just a slight hint of possibility that she may have a future she could look forward to, and yet she felt so nervous about feeling happy, so nervous in fact that she would banish the feeling, because she knew, at any moment, it could be crushed.

Family Ties

Rain thought the internet was a glorious thing. She had never forgotten the conversation she had with Aunty P that day she came into the Notary's Office and asked to speak with Lakmini Perera – the day that Rain finally found out the truth about her father's family. That was the day she vowed to herself that she would try to find out more about her mother's family too. When business was slack, and Geethan was out making deliveries, Rain would go online and find a map of the world and look at the region of Tamil Nadu that encompassed the coastline around Puducherry. She wondered whether her mother might have lived in the little village of Ariyankuppam or across the Chunnambar river in Thavalakuppam. She daydreamed that her mother's brothers and sisters, her aunts and uncles and their children, would be alive and well, and that one day she could introduce her own family to them.

Then she put the words 'Udayar, Puducherry' into the search engine and got page after page of entries which made her feel despondent because how was she ever going to find her own family amongst so many people?

She spoke to Geethan about it as they were walking home from work one evening, the cool breeze blowing off the Indian Ocean a pleasant relief from the heat of the day. They sat for a while in their favourite spot, at a quiet crossroads between the main town and the beach, where someone had placed a wooden bench giving splendid views of the harbour and sea beyond.

"Maybe it would help if we were to visit Puducherry, and then perhaps we could go to the Registrar's Office ourselves, and see if we could track down your family that way?" Geethan put his arm around his wife and picked a small white feather out of her hair.

"Really, husband? Might that be possible one day?"

"Anything is possible my love, isn't it?"

"It is in your world, Geethan, and I love you for it – you have never ceased to be an optimist. But there is something I want to tell you. Today, I had a letter from Nora, and in it she told me that she and Joe are planning to come and visit us, here in Sri Lanka! Can you imagine what a celebration that will be?" Rain offered a slice of mango to her husband, wiping the juice from her fingers on the bottom edge of her sari.

"I certainly can, but ..." and then he knew why there was a glint in Rain's eye. "Ah... I see. So, if Nora and Joe are coming to Sri Lanka, then the money you have been saving to visit them in England, we could use to go to Tamil Nadu instead."

"Exactly, husband! My dream is to one day look upon Nora's face, but now I know she is coming here, we can perhaps think of visiting Puducherry. It won't cost so much, but do you think we have saved enough?"

"Well, you know the accounts as well as I do, my

beautiful wife. The business is doing well, and we want for nothing – not much, anyway. I think even if we don't have quite enough saved, we can find the money from somewhere. Yes, I think we can do it."

Rain hugged Geethan and kissed his lips, looking deeply into the eyes of this handsome man it still gave her a thrill to call 'husband'.

"It's strange, but for some reason as the years go by, it is becoming more and more important for me to know about my mother's family, my Indian heritage. I think having Priya and Abeesha in my life has opened up the possibility somehow. You know, when we first met after my parents had died, I felt like I was an orphan, like I had nobody in the world to care for me, and now my family just keeps getting bigger and bigger, and still, I don't know half of them!"

Deep in thought, Geethan ate the last of his mango, then wiped his own fingers on the hem of his wife's sari – a gesture they both found amusing as Geethan had once chided her for this habit.

After a while he said, "Look Rain, I don't think we can afford to go for very long – perhaps a week – but if we went during the Christmas holidays, we could take the kids with us, and we wouldn't have to shut the office, because it would be shut anyway."

"Really? Oh, my goodness – how exciting!

"Or perhaps we could stay a little longer, if Binula feels he can cope on his own?" Binula was a young assistant whom Geethan had taken on to help him when Rain was in Colombo waiting to give birth to Danidu Junior, and whom they'd kept on ever since. He worked the printing press and the collating machine and was a dab-hand at mending anything, but he was painfully shy and did not enjoy speaking with the customers, preferring to be out that back amongst the reams of paper and tins of ink.

"I think we could persuade him, with a little bonus perhaps. And Abeesha virtually runs the kitchen single-handedly now, so we have no worries there."

"Shall we make firm plans then, Mrs Cooray?"

"I can't believe it! In a few short months we will be in India – our first holiday together, and we may even find some long-lost relatives too."

"Please don't get your hopes up too high about that, my love. Just keep a little faith in your heart." Geethan smiled at his wife, and she saw the gap where he had recently lost a tooth. It made him even more handsome in her eyes, if that were possible.

The seed of the adventure they had sown that day, sitting on the bench at the crossroads, began to grow. The more Rain thought about it, the more excited she became about going to Puducherry. She was so inquisitive about where her mother grew up, wanting to see which trees Deepti may have climbed, and which roads she may have walked as a child. Rain had a feeling that visiting India would allow her to complete the puzzle of her childhood and her heritage; all those things she'd had to guess at until now. And, even if she didn't meet a single one of her relatives, she knew that just being in Tamil Nadu, and the beaches of the Puducherry region would bring both her parents alive again in her imagination: as they were then, when they were young and in love, happy and healthy.

One evening a week or so later, after the boys were in

bed and they were catching-up on some paperwork –
which they often did in the evenings because the business
had become so busy during the day – Rain raised the
subject of their travels.

"Did you speak with Binula-ji? Can he look after the
business so we can stay a little longer in India?"

"I did, and he will, though I think he rather paled at
the thought of being in charge. But he is old enough to
take such responsibility, and we deserve a rest after all
these years of hard work."

"Then I want to make it an extra-special Christmas
for all of us this year."

"Do you have anything in mind?"

"Yes, in fact I do."

"Ah, no surprise there," chuckled Geethan, using a
sponge to wet the sticky edge of the stack of envelopes he
was sealing. "What are you thinking?"

"Well," Rain edged closer to her husband and caught
both of his hands in hers, "I have seen a 'home stay'
advertised near a place called Paradise Beach can you
believe! The owners live in a flat upstairs, but we can rent
the whole of the downstairs for our family. I think we
could afford it for about ten days. And do you know, we
can fly from Colombo to Puducherry directly – I have
checked – and I was thinking, perhaps we could leave
the day before our flight and stay with Aunty P. So, of
course, I rang her today to ask if we could stay with her,
and she agreed, which is very kind of her. Then she asked
why we were going to Puducherry. I told her about my
wish to see where it was that Danidu and Deepti met,
and to possibly reconnect with some of Amma's family,
and she became very emotional and tearful about it all.

In the end, she had to put the phone down so that she could gather herself together."

"Goodness me. Poor Priya – I know she still misses her brother to this day. They were very close."

"You are right, they were very close." Rain tucked her hair behind her ears. "Anyway, about ten minutes later, Aunty Priya phoned the office – it was when you were helping Binula to pour the ink into the tank of the old roller – and to cut a long story short, she has offered to pay our air fares! Can you believe?"

"Really? Goodness me…" Geethan repeated, rubbing his chin, a habit he had when he was surprised about something. "That is very generous of her, very generous – but can we accept Rain, when she has been so good to us already?"

"That is what I said. 'No, we cannot accept – it is too generous'. But then, she became very insistent about it. She said that she had always felt she abandoned us when Grandpa Perera refused to sanction my parent's marriage. She said she was given a choice: between her brother or her parents and she chose her parents, though in secret she sometimes did manage to visit us, with Abeesha's help. But ever since then, it seems she has regretted the choice. Grandpa and Grandma were mean to her, as we now know, and she lost touch with us completely after Grandpa died and they moved to Colombo. She said it would enable her to make amends and be at peace with herself if she was able to help me find some of my mother's relatives. Can you believe it, Geethan?"

"Somehow I can. I understand why it is important for her to help you Lakmini. You are like a daughter to her. She never married and had her own children, so now we are her family. She wants to help us, and she can afford to because she has worked all her life, and like my father and like we do now, she saves a little money every day." Geethan sealed the last of the envelopes and turned to his wife. "So, it seems we are meant to be in Tamil Nadu this Christmas, Rain. We are going to have a holiday in India with our boys in a place called Paradise Beach. I have a feeling it will be life-changing for all of us, especially you, my beautiful wife, if you find your long lost relatives."

"You're right Geethan-ji. This is meant to be, and I cannot wait. But one thing I will say is we must keep this a secret from the boys until the day we head off for Colombo, otherwise they will speak of nothing else and drive us crazy with their excitement for weeks to come."

"Agreed."

"That's settled then," said Rain. "We will keep it a secret from the boys, we will accept Aunty P's gift and we will start to plan our holiday."

"Wonderful, but what about me?"

"What about you?"

"Well, *I'm* going to be excited for weeks too."

"You'll cope my beloved husband – you're a big boy now." Rain kissed her husband tenderly on his lips and led him off to bed.

About a month later, as Rain was sorting the mail in the office, she saw amongst the pile of letters an airmail envelope from the UK.

"Geethan-ji – see here, there's a letter from Nora. Let me read it aloud." Rain opened the letter with her tortoiseshell paperknife.

Dear Sister

It seems all the more important to call you 'sister' as it is a word I use less often now Louisa is gone. I have some news. After all the trauma of the last few years, Joe and I decided that we needed a fresh start, so we have moved to a beautiful house on the edge of a country estate, close to the place we once lived in that had a swimming pool. I know you will remember that I wrote and told you about a moment of connection with a peacock on our last day at Forest Cottage, because you wrote back about your own connection with a peacock, and you sent me your beautiful poem. Anyway, the peacock was right because he told me – not in words of course, (I don't really know how he told me) that we would be back; that one day we would return to Tend, and now, here we are! It feels like some kind of prophesy has come true.

The house is big and has enough space for Joe to create a music studio – which as you know is his first love – and for me to have a large office, which I will need because I have made a decision. I am going to start my own magazine! If there is one thing that cancer has taught me, it is that life can be short – you know this only too well, dear Rain – and that we have to seize the day. So, I have decided to start a magazine for women who have had breast cancer: it will be full of stories of courage and transformation, and also stories of loss and grief – because I want to tell the whole story, not just the good news. In each issue, there's going to be a column by a nutritionist, giving advice about health and wellbeing, and a column by a psychotherapist to help with the mental health issues that come with cancer. I've also got an advertising agreement with a company who make special clothes and prostheses for women who have had breast cancer and this will help to pay my salary in the early days, along with other advertising – and best of all, the magazine will be free to all those who want it, because I've received a start-up grant from a health charity who recognise a need for this kind of support.

I'm so excited, Rain – I can hardly stop myself jumping for joy. We are back in a village that feels like home, in a house where there is space for us both to be creative, and I am going to be doing work that supports the journey of women who have had a similar health crisis to me – and Louisa. I am doing this in her memory. It feels so right. Somehow, it feels like the whole of my life has led to this point, and that everything had to happen – all those terrible things had to happen – because it has led me here. I keep getting a bolt of fear; fear that I'm too happy and that it can all be taken away from me again. But I know you have this fear this too. We have spoken of it many times. It's something we share.

There is more good news! And this is perhaps the best news of all. Joe and I have booked our tickets for our 'trip of a lifetime'. We are going to travel for three months, before I launch the magazine in May 2005. Our plan is to travel to Cambodia in November, spend Christmas by the beach in Vietnam (Joe's cousin Mark runs a resort there) and then fly on to Sri Lanka, where - of course! - we will come and visit you, Geethan and the boys, and finally on to Rajasthan to finish our travels. After all these years, can you believe that we are finally going to meet one another? And only a few short months away now. We plan to be in Sri Lanka from mid-January for about a month, so we will have plenty of time to be together.

It feels like a dream come true - that we will finally meet, dear sister - you and I. All these years and at long last, we are to see each other with our own eyes. I still cannot believe it. A little nearer the time, we will make firm plans for our long-awaited first moments together. We have read about some lovely villas on a beach just outside Lagentle, so we will book one of them, which means we will be near you and can visit often. We have a whole lifetime of conversations to catch up on.. At last, we can make a start.

With so much love to you and your family, and - I can hardly believe I'm writing this - I will see you soon.

Nora xxx

Geethan hugged his wife after she finished reading the letter. "How pleased are you? Scale of 1-10?"

"Eleven, of course! Isn't it wonderful news Geethan? First, we will be in Tamil Nadu meeting my Indian family, then when we get home, at long last we will meet my English family – my English sister!"

At that, Rain burst into tears.

"What is it?" Geethan held her close absorbing her sobs until they diminished.

"Well," Rain sniffed, wiping her tears with the edge of her sari, "isn't it amazing – that we should even be friends? All these years, just writing letters to each other and being there for each other through thin and thick, and now I have a sister who I have never met yet who is coming to see me. Us. It is like a miracle, isn't it? An absolute miracle."

"Yes – miracles do happen, my beloved."

"I might be tearful, Geethan, but I'm so happy."

"And I can see that happiness shining from you, like starlight."

Rain smiled at her husband. "I might use that line in one of my poems."

"You should," he replied, "because it is true."

All Is Gone

"I just wish Rain would reply to my emails," Nora said, retrieving a pair of flip-flops from her huge and bulging rucksack, one that thankfully had wheels. The only time she had tried to put it on her back whilst in Cambodia, she'd almost toppled over, it was so heavy.

"She will – when has Rain ever not replied to you? They're spending Christmas in Tamil Nadu aren't they? Maybe they haven't got very good internet there."

"It could even be worse than it is here!"

"Surely that's not possible? Don't worry, Noo. She'll be in touch as soon as they get home to Sri Lanka."

"You're right. I'd just like to finalise plans that's all."

"Just relax – we've got loads of time! Let's just enjoy Christmas, yeah? There's going to be a big party on the beach tonight and then a fireworks display on the stroke of midnight to welcome in Christmas Day. Mark has asked me if I can help him cordon off a safe area and put some signs up, so I'll head off and see you later."

"Okay. I'm going to write a few postcards, so I'll wait here until you get back, then we'll have lunch."

Nora busied herself in the pretty wooden hut with

the shady veranda that Mark had reserved for them on the edge of a white sandy beach fringed with palm trees. It really was a slice of paradise, which made her feelings of unease all the more jarring. She wanted everything about this trip to be special, including getting excited with Rain about their imminent meeting. But as Joe had said, the internet in Tamil Nadu was probably intermittent at best, as it was in Vietnam – little better than dial-up really.

Vietnam was the place on their travels that Nora had been least excited about visiting – were it not for Joe's cousin Mark being able to give them a good deal on their accommodation at the resort he managed, they may not have visited the country at all. But Nora was so glad they had. The people were incredibly friendly (given their experience of white Westeners, Nora thought), and the food was sensational, but what amazed Nora most of all was how the landscape seemed to have recovered from the ravages of the terrible war that raged there through the 1960s and 70s. Nora hadn't known what to expect, and in a way was fearing the worst, but everywhere they went, she saw how time, natural processes and human ingenuity had helped to rebuild a countryside that was devastated by chemical weapons. It gave her hope in a way she had least expected: if this landscape could recover from the devastation wrought by agent orange then maybe her body could heal from its own chemical barrage too? Unexpectedly, she felt an intense kinship with the land, a sense of compassion for all it had suffered, and it softened her to the place. She had grown to love it.

For the truth was, Nora was still struggling with the aftermath of the cancer, the mastectomy, chemotherapy, radiotherapy, the oophorectomy and then the dreaded Tamoxifen that left her in a daily chemical haze. And the reality of traveling, the gruelling heat and humidity, the unfamiliar food and inevitable gastroenteritis was taking its toll on her. On many a night, Nora had retired to wherever they happened to be staying, suffering with what she called 'chemo brain', a kind of fogginess that made it hard for her to concentrate or even communicate.

Fortunately, Joe and Nora had decided to pre-book a luxurious hotel in each country they travelled to where they would stay for the first three or four nights, just so they could get their bearings and rest from the journey, and this really helped to steady Nora and get her back on her feet. She liked a bit of luxury. Then after that, they would strike-out on an adventure, with only the *Rough Guide* to hand, trusting that they would find interesting places to stay and have wonderful experiences along the way. Part of Nora had wanted to organise and book everything in advance and have their itinerary planned throughout, but Joe was keen to get off the beaten track, not wanting to be confined to the tourist hotspots or predetermined schedules, but to find the hidden gems of each country. And so that is what they had done.

Cambodia had been a bit of a baptism of fire: they'd been ripped off mercilessly by tuk-tuk drivers who over-charged them, and by the hawkers selling tourist trinkets and street food, but after a couple of weeks they became savvy, and good at not making eye contact; they found their travelling feet. Apart from the hotels they'd booked beforehand, this stay at Aminda Resort in Vietnam, courtesy of Mark, was the only bit so far that had been remotely touristy – and Nora was loving it. From the opulent bed with its satin sheets, to the fluffy towels and the little sweets they put on the pillow when the bed is 'turned down' at night, Nora felt as if, for the first time in over two years, she could truly begin to relax. Everyone had said how brave she'd been, how positive – and it was true that Nora was naturally an optimist and saw the best in everything – even terrible things like chemo-therapy had redeeming qualities, like the fact that you were shown so much love, for example, with nobody expecting anything of you. But in truth, Nora often felt she would never recover; that she'd never be the person she was before bits of her were cut out and burned in the hospital incinerator. As Cass had told her, life was not the same as it had once been. She was older, ravaged, her femininity gone – taken by the scalpel and the pill – and she felt heavier somehow, as if weighed down by life. She'd lost something intrinsic to herself along the way but couldn't quite work out what it was. Her innocence perhaps.

That night, a banquet for the resort guests was served on the beach, with children from the local school coming to enact a rather bizarre version of the nativity, in the heat of a tropical night, under a canopy of gently swaying palm trees, the sound of the ocean lapping against the white crystalline sand, which in the moonlight seemed just like snow. It was a charming if somewhat curious clash of cultures, the plastic Christmas trees and cicadas creating an odd ambience for a rendition of Silent Night. And then the music and dancing started, and a huge bowl of punch was wheeled out on what looked like a sleigh. Mark had been very excited about that find in a local market and had spent hours painting it red and spraying fake snow on it. And to top it off, fireworks cascaded into the night sky and were reflected on the sea. It was romantic and exotic and life-affirming, and Joe and Nora partied with gay abandon until dawn.

In fact, they hadn't realised that Joe's cousin Mark was such a party animal, because after the hangover had worn-off on Christmas Day, thanks to a leisurely dip in the ocean and a barbeque on the beach, another round of partying began. Nora thought at first that she didn't have the stamina for two parties in a row, but soon found that she did. It wasn't really until the day after Boxing Day that Joe and Nora surfaced from the frivolities, and that day was spent sleeping and nursing perhaps the worst hangovers of a lifetime.

And then, Mark wanted to show them the sights, hiring a landrover to take them on a safari to the local national park, that had been spared the worst of Agent Orange and still had an incredible array of wildlife. They saw a sambar deer and a bizarre species of monkey with red furry legs which looked just like it was wearing a pair of corduroy trousers.

As they bounced around in the cab of the landrover on the way back to the resort, Mark said, "Terrible news about the tsunami, isn't it?"

"Tsunami?" Joe looked at Nora quizzically. "We've not seen the news in weeks, mate. What's happened?"

"Oh, a massive earthquake and tsunami has hit a place in Indonesia. Banda something or other. Complete and utter devastation, apparently. So sad."

"Jeeze," Joe whistled through his teeth.

It felt like their stay in Aminda had been one long party, and by the time New Year was over, Joe and Nora were more than ready to move on. They just didn't have the energy to keep up with Mark and Kara, his Swedish girlfriend, who seemed to be able to live on vodka and a couple of hours sleep a night.

Nora's thoughts had returned to Sri Lanka, the next stop on their itinerary, and the most exciting prospect of all: meeting Rain. Yet, despite their flight being booked for the end of the week, she still hadn't been in touch.

"They'll definitely be back home by now," Nora said to Joe, one morning over coffee. "I wonder why she's not contacted me? It's not like her."

"Let's borrow Mark's scooter and go into town, to that little internet café on the corner of the square, near the shrine – you know the one? It seems to have the best internet connection around here. You can check your emails from there, and we can also confirm our flight times."

It was there that Nora found an email in her inbox with an unfamiliar hotmail address. She felt a sudden rush of adrenalin course through her body and opened the email with trepidation.

J. Binula Arul < j.b.arul@hotmail.com > wrote:

Dear Madam Nora

May I introduce myself. I am J. Binula Arul, print press operator at the Notary's Office in Lagentle of your friends Mrs Lakmini and Mr Geethan Cooray. I am extremely sorry I have the bad news.

Your friend Mrs Lakmini is no more. Her husband
Geethan is returning to normal after almost two week in
trauma care and critical surgeries. Their son Moses was
unconscious in coma but is now awake but unable to
speak. Danidu their second son is okay and safe.

On December 26th the family went for a celebration trip
to meet relatives in Cuddalore in Tamil Nadu. Danidu Jr.
had sore throat so he stayed in care of home-stay owner.
As you know Asian countries were washed away on 26th
December. All is gone. Lakmini, Geethan and Moses
were attending church on the beach with also hundreds
of pilgrims who were there celebrating Mass when a
huge wave took everybody into the sea. Hundreds are
dead. Second wave came in and took remaining people
and then third wave. It is all gone. We only got the news
days later on radio as my family also in Lagentle lost our
house and animals, though none dead, thanks be to God.
But I knew my employers were being there for
celebration and such news was terrible indeed.

Local volunteers from Cuddalore found Geethan and
Moses the next day half a mile inland from beach and
took them to hospital but they could not find Mrs Lakmini,
until two days later with three tourists under rafters of
building that had been washed away by the wave. It is
so terrible.

Mrs Lakmini was included in mass burial with prayers,
while Geethan had spinal injuries and punctured lung.
Two days ago he was flown home with son to Colombo
hospital but now still recovering. He may not walk again.

I try and keep Notary open, but it was badly damaged in tsunami. All machines broken and no power or lights. Today I visit Mr Geethan in Colombo hospital who instructed me to email you terrible news.

We pray for Geethan, Moses and Danidu. We pray for our sister Lakmini's soul in heaven.

I am sorry about the bad news this way in email.

Sincerely, in service of Mr Geethan Cooray.

Yours J. Binula Arul

Nora cried out, and Joe peered through the beaded curtain into the dark little room at the back of the café that housed an array of old and dusty computers.

"What's the matter? What the hell…"

Tears cascading from her eyes and unable to speak, Nora shook her head and pointed at the screen.

Joe pushed the curtain aside and stood behind Nora, placed his hands on the back of her chair and leaned towards the computer to read the words on the screen.

"Oh no… oh my God; Jesus… that's terrible…" Joe put his arms around her. "I'm so sorry Nora… how truly awful."

Nora was sobbing uncontrollably. "Oh Joe… I didn't know India and Sri Lanka had been hit too. I thought it was just Indonesia…? Why didn't we check?"

"I don't know… like you, I just didn't realise. We've just been so wrapped up in our own travels, I suppose..."

And then the enormity of what had happened began to dawn on Nora.

"No, no, no... I'm never going to meet her. She's gone, she's gone..."

Pain radiated out from Nora's breastbone into her throat and down her arms all the way to her fingers; it took her breath away and made her feel faint. She recognised that this was how grief took her and surrendered to it. Her sister was gone – like Louisa, just taken from her, leaving her bereft and shocked at the finality of it all. Not one more word would come from the woman she had never met but had grown to love. They would be forever apart.

Joe had put the words 'Tsunami, India' into the search engine, cursing at the slowness of the loading pages. "It seems Tamil Nadu in India was really badly hit, and that's where they were on holiday, weren't they?" Then he began to read news report after report about the impact of the tsunami in the eastern seaboard of India and all the way to Colombo, Galle and Lagentle in Sri Lanka and beyond.

"Please don't Joe – don't read any more, I can't bear it. I didn't know... I just didn't... know... I should've put two and two together. I should've realised this was the reason she hadn't been in touch. We were so wrapped up in our own lives that we forgot about her."

"But Noo, even if we'd realised what had happened, what could we have done?"

Nora was inconsolable. The shock of it was terrible. That doctor was right; with cancer there is time to say goodbye – but a tsunami, a natural disaster? No – your loved ones are ripped from you and there is no warning and that parting, that abrupt and unexpected parting felt like a gaping wound to her. It hurt so much.

After the initial shock had dissipated, Nora phoned the airline to see if they were still able to fly to Colombo. She wanted to meet Geethan, to console him, to care for him. But the airlines were in turmoil. Emails were not answered, phone calls were not picked up. In the end, she phoned their travel agent in the UK to find out what their options were. They could change their destination and fly to Delhi directly from Vietnam, but they couldn't fly to Colombo. All flights had been cancelled except for aid flights. And anyway, tourists were being flown out, not in. How could they possibly be catered for when everything was in ruins?

Nora didn't have the heart for India. She just wanted to go home. Their trip of a lifetime was over, and it had ended in the most devastating way imaginable. They left Vietnam with heavy hearts, not because their holiday was over – they knew they could take another holiday – but because Rain's life had been taken from her, just like that, with no warning. One moment she was here, a beautiful presence on a beautiful planet, and the next moment she was gone, and the world dimmed, noticeably, at least for Nora.

They arrived back in the UK in a snowstorm, a whiteout. It was a metaphor for how Nora felt: blanketed in the cold bleakness of grief, which rekindled the latent sorrow of Louisa's death. Both sisters gone. It was a weight almost too heavy to bear.

On their return to the UK, Nora emailed Geethan every Friday without fail, week in week out, not expecting an answer, not even knowing if he was still alive, but just as a connection, however tenuous to her beloved Rain. At first the emails were brief, just sending her love and concern for his wellbeing and that of his family. And then she began to add some memories of her friendship with Rain, hoping that her words would console him in some way, if that were ever possible. There was never an email in return, and she didn't expect one.

Once more, a focus on work eased Nora through her pain, as she launched her new magazine, *Phoenix*, and began to write about her experiences as a woman who danced with death.

And then, one day, there in her inbox, was an email from Geethan.

> Geethan Cooray <g.cooray@notaryservices.lgt.gov.
> lk> wrote:
>
> Dear Sister
>
> It is with heavy heart that I write to you. Without my Rain I am nothing. I feel unable to function without my beloved wife by my side. But I hear her say, "You are a father, Geethan-ji. Be strong for our boys." So, I am trying to be strong for Moses and Danidu.
>
> I left hospital last week. After four months of rehabilitation, I can now walk with crutches. Pain in my back is constant but nothing compared to pain in my heart.
>
> You know, her whole life she was waiting for that day. She knew that if she was too happy, everything would be

taken away from her, just like that ~ and it was. She told me over and over that we must not be too happy, but I laughed at her; called her silly billy. I told her that it is impossible to be too happy, isn't it; and so we became too happy and God took Lakmini from me and gave her back to her father.

Binula my assistant has kept Notary's Office going, and fortunately the compound we share with my parents suffered only minor damage in the tsunami, though much of Lagentle region was devastated. It is terrible to see the hardship of people who lost everything in the waves and who now live under tarpaulins with only handouts of food to eat. At least we have a home and my parents were spared, and at least I still have a business of sorts, though I have no heart for it. But people need help with rebuilding their lives and that is what I am focussing on ~ trying to help others in their hour of need, because that is what my Rain would have done. So I keep busy with doing what I can to help – which is not much – and of course, looking after our boys who are also lost and bewildered like their father. We miss her so much that life without her seems pointless. But we must carry on in her memory.

Please keep sending the letters, dear sister. Rain loved your letters, and when I read them now, I feel connected to her.

With my sincere thanks for your friendship.

Your brother, Geethan Cooray

Geethan's words pierced Nora's heart and tears came unbidden. *What must he be going through?* she wondered. *That he survived and his wife didn't... How do you live with that?* But she knew that Geethan would indeed be strong for their boys; that he had to live for their boys. She wrote back to him immediately, thanking him for being in touch, telling him how much it meant to her to have this connection with Rain. And she kept writing to him.

She waited eagerly for Geethan to reply. It was four months later that another email from him arrived.

> Geethan Cooray <g.cooray@notaryservices.lgt.gov.lk> wrote:
>
> Dear Sister
>
> We are alive. We eat every day. We go to church on Sunday to pray for Rain's soul, the same church where we got married, but our hearts are dying. Without her, this is not life. Moses will not speak now. He refuses to speak. What he saw on that terrible day has traumatised him so much that words no longer come to him. I know what he saw. I was with him – people's eyes wide with fear as they were washed away from their loved ones, mothers floating lifeless with dead children in their arms, limbs torn from bodies, cows stuck beneath vehicles, bodies drifting upside down, blood and fear... No child should see these things, dear sister. He cannot speak of them. Perhaps it is best that he does not.
>
> For a long while I kept thinking of something Lakmini told me once when we were first married. After her parents

died, she was crazy with grief, feeling all alone in the world and consumed by sorrow, and so she jumped into Lagentle Harbour, wanting to end the pain of it. Did you know she did that, sister Nora? Did she tell you, I wonder? How I know that feeling now.

And so she jumped into the water, and she could not swim because her sari weighed her down, like ropes tied to an anchor. But then a fish, a tiny little fish with big, bulging eyes swam up to her, and she said it looked at her, straight in her eyes. And it said to her, 'Not yet'. It didn't speak in words of course, but into her heart, and she knew it was not her time; and then two fishermen pulled her out of the water and threw her on the ground to live or die. But always she spoke of this fish, of how it saved her life, not the fishermen, but the fish. Now I know that the water wanted to take her, and when it was time, it did, it took her. The ocean took her away from me.

Last week for first time, I looked at her journal, where she wrote down all her poems and stories. I gave the journal to her many years ago and it became precious to her. She would not let me see it, but often she would read her stories and poems to me. She wrote a great deal – did she tell you that? And I found her fish poem, that she'd written about that day she jumped into the harbour after her parents died. I think she was only sixteen years of age when she wrote this poem, so I could hardly believe her words. I thought that perhaps you would like to see the poem too, so here it is:

I WILL COME FOR YOU

This young skin is old
It seeks not the light of another day.
Out of my way, Fish
Let me join my father in a watery grave.

Out of my way Fish, I say!
I will not heed your words
Tell me not of love and hope
How can they now be mine?
For this world I am no more
Fish, let me sink to the ocean floor.

Yet now that I can see some light
I thank you for the gift of life
For keeping your gaze upon mine
And telling me of love and hope
At a time when all seemed gone.
And though I knew not how to cope
My leaving then was wrong.

For life is for living until it is lived
Long or short, it is always a gift
You saved me with that look, those words.
'Not yet, but I will come for you.
Until then, child, live your life'.

Sister, her poem bought floods of tears to my eyes, and
they do again now as I read her words. I wonder if the
little fish came for her when the tsunami struck? I hope
he did. I pray to God Almighty that he found her, because

she would have needed a friend to be with her as she left this world in the hardest way imaginable.

I try not to relive that day in my memories. It is too terrible to remember and yet I do not wish to forget it either, for it is the last day I saw her, the last day I held her, my beloved wife, Lakmini Rain Cooray. Just saying her name is like knife in the heart. Will this pain ever end? Life is full of suffering, is it not, dear sister? You too have suffered more than your fair share of hardship and despair. You have lost both of your sisters and you have suffered pain and loss. We have that in common.

I read your emails to Moses. I know he likes them. Perhaps you can send special emails to him once in a while? Perhaps your kind words will give him hope, like they did to his mother all those years ago, when you helped her with the sewing machine and like the little fish, you too saved her life. You are the one constant in our lives, dear sister Nora. For that, we are grateful.

With brotherly love.

Geethan

That night Nora lay awake, mulling over Geethan's letter. Later, Joe came home from band practice, trying to be as quiet as possible so as not to disturb her.

"It's okay. I'm awake."

"Sorry I'm late. I thought you'd be asleep."

"I can't sleep. I've been thinking about Geethan and Rain. I miss her so much, Joe. I didn't know it was possible to miss someone you've never met."

Joe slipped under the duvet and put his arm around her. "But you did meet her, didn't you? Your hearts met, through your letters and your words. You loved each other through your words, that I do know."

"Yes, we did... Isn't it amazing that those little black squiggly things on a piece of paper can connect two women from different sides of the world more deeply than most friendships ever do?"

"It is incredible when you think about it. And Rain even wrote to you in her second language, not her mother tongue, and yet still love flourished. That is something to honour, I think."

"It is. But I keep thinking of that recurring dream I have, Joe – you know, the one of the great tidal wave that comes towards a church, and I'm lying in a pew, watching as the water level rises above the windows and eventually engulfs the whole place – do you remember me telling you about it?"

"Of course I do. It always unsettles you."

"Every so often, for years on end, I've had that dream but always, when the water gets to the ceiling, I'm still alive and I can breathe underwater, and watch the fish as they swim past, and the seaweed as it ebbs and flows with the current. Why would I have that dream Joe? Why would I dream of a tsunami for years and years and then my friend, my sister, is killed in a tsunami... it's unreal, don't you think?"

Joe found her hand and squeezed it. "It is pretty weird, Noo, but it's you not Rain in the church. Unless it's a premonition... At least this place is well above sea level." He turned over as if to sleep.

But Nora was still beset by her thoughts. "Do you think she was okay, Joe – under water, I mean – like I am in my dreams? Do you think the little fish came to greet her?"

"God only knows…"

It was a few days before Christmas when Nora received the third email from Geethan. It was clear from his words that he'd been dreading the anniversary of Rain's death; obvious that he had been thinking of that terrible day, and why it was that they were on that beach in Tamil Nadu at that fateful moment.

Geethan Cooray <g.cooray@notaryservices.lgt.gov.lk> wrote:

Dear Sister

It is nearly a year, and the pain is still in my heart. Moses now speaks sometimes, and he does love your letters. Thank you for sending them. Danidu is too young to be badly affected by loss of his mother, and my own mother now cares for the boys when I am at work, thanks be to God in his mercy.

Sister, there is something I want to tell you. Rain wanted to go to Tamil Nadu, because she wanted to find members of her mother's family who still lived there. For years after her parents died she felt like an orphan, but when she met her Aunty Priya, she found out that she was not, and that she might even have family in India, and so we planned to go. And then, eventually we had enough money, and so we did go, and we did find some of them. But they were not at all who Rain hoped they would be.

We met her Uncle Kavin, her mother's brother and his wife, but before even one hour had passed, they asked Rain for money. Of course, she gave them what she had in her purse; but when we met them again the next day, and when Rain asked whether there were any other relatives she could meet, Uncle Kavin told her that if she wanted to know, she had to give them 50 rupees for each name. Rain gave them more money, much against my advice, though I understand why she did this. Uncle Kavin told us that his younger brother Ramasamy had a jigar stand on Cuddalore beach and she could find him there. Rain was delighted as we knew that Cuddalore beach was where here parents Deepti and Danidu had met – two birds with one stone, isn't it. Go to beach where her parents fell in love and find her long lost Uncle Rama.

If she had not asked them that one question, perhaps she would be alive today. We would not have gone to the beach that day, we would not have sat in that wooden church with the other pilgrims, saying our prayers, but would have stayed at our apartment in Paradise Beach, (which wasn't a beach at all, but a huge concrete block of flats in a part of the town that was untouched by the wave). Ironic isn't it that she met her death on the same beach where her parents had fallen in love? It must be fate, don't you think? The more I think of it, the more I think it was meant to be. It must have been her fate. Otherwise, why? Why?

Dear sister, the pain is hard to bear, but bear it I must. I cannot see my future now without my beloved Rain. But something she said to me I want to share with you, dear sister who has also suffered. One day, Rain and I were sitting on bench by the harbour after work. Often we would stop there because it is a beauty spot and on our way home. We would sit for a while and speak of our day, share a mango, sometimes just sit in silence. On this day, and I will never forget it for as long as I live, I remember that Rain grabbed my hand and looked deep into my eyes."It is sandpaper for the soul, Geethan-ji," she said. Not having a clue, I replied "What is, wife? What is sandpaper for the soul?" She replied,"Suffering is. Nora told me so in a letter. That suffering smooths off our rough edges and makes us kinder to others who are struggling in life. Geethan, beloved husband, that is a wonderful thing, is it not – that something as painful as suffering has meaning and purpose to it. It perfects us."

Your words helped her so much, dear Nora, to come to terms with the best and the worst of life. And now they are helping me. This suffering I feel at her loss, it tears my heart open, it hurts so much – but perhaps some good will come from it, because Rain believed that goodness always prevails.

I also want to tell you that I recently received a very nice letter from a retired policeman called Sergeant Gomes, who helped Rain out quite a lot after her parents died.

Here is the bit from his letter that I'd like you to see:

'Please accept this letter of condolence as we near the first anniversary of the passing of your wife, Lakmini Cooray. I was extremely sorry to hear that she was one of the souls who lost her life on that terrible day the tsunami struck our shores. When I first met Lakmini she was a young girl, and I was impressed by her courage at a time of great sadness and loss. She always showed such bravery in the face of hardship and injustice, and I admired her very much for that. Despite the odds, she made a good life for herself and her brother, and she was always ready to lend a helping hand to others. Lakmini had the heart of a leopard: she was intelligent and brave, and the world is a better place because of her. I will never forget her. May she rest in eternal peace.'

His words are very special to me, dear sister as I know they will be to you. Rain will never be forgotten because there are so many who love her still. Last week myself and the boys and my parents drove to Yala National Park, where they opened a memorial to all those who lost their lives in the tsunami. It is a metal sculpture of three giant waves representing the three waves that took so many souls back to the ocean. It is near a place where Rain and I first spoke of our love for one another; where we saw a pair of lovebirds, Malabar hornbills, and where Rain saw a leopard, who she called the King of the Dusk. My wife has the heart of a leopard. She is Queen of the Dusk.

With love from Geethan, your brother.

When Nora read those words, it was as if all the threads that had woven the tapestry of her life were pulled taught and created the clearest of pictures. She had dreamed of that wooden church and the great wave that overwhelmed it so many times, she had seen herself diving into the depths able to breathe under water. And yet it was not her fate, but that of the sister she was never destined to meet; the woman whose life wove a eulogy with hers, the woman called Rain.

Breathe Rain, breathe.

Epilogue

It is now nearly twenty years since the Asian tsunami where Rain was lost to the ocean. Nora, who defied the odds and is still alive, continues to write to Geethan just as she once did to Rain – though not quite as regularly and not quite so openly, but they too have become friends through those little black squiggly lines. Yet this story may have remained untold were it not for something that happened which reignited these memories.

Several years after the tsunami, Geethan married again, to Binula's sister Martha, and they had two children, two little girls. The Notary business suffered the highs and lows of the fluctuating economy of Sri Lanka, and Geethan was the first to suggest that it lacked Rain's drive and creative flair, but the family survived and thrived. And then many years later Covid-19 reared its ugly head.

Like his mother, Moses felt a great compassion for the suffering of others, and so he volunteered to help in the government compounds that had been set up to isolate those with the virus from the general public. Despite being young, strong and vaccinated, Moses succumbed to Covid-19 and passed away serving others in his community, when he should have had his whole life ahead of him.

When Nora heard this news, she was incredulous: that one family should lose two members to these global catastrophes, situations which were completely outside of their control – perhaps it was even their destiny? And yet, that one family should suffer so much seemed like such a cruel twist of fate. But, it is not just one family: every family suffers, whether through great historical events that will stand the test of time, or through small cuts that refuse to heal. Suffering is what makes us human and humane, because it sandpapers our souls to perfection.

It was then that Nora decided their story had to be told. And so, this book is for Louisa. And this book is for Rain. And this book is for Moses too.

Books co-authored
by Lorna Howarth

The Soulistic Journey:
A pilgrimage to the source of your being
By Genevieve Boast & Lorna Howarth
Published by Panacea Books, 2020

The Language of Love
By William Blyghton & Lorna Howarth
Published by Panacea Books, 2022

Visit lornahowarth.com for more information.

Printed in Great Britain
by Amazon